# THE ROSWELL LEGACY

# THE ROSWELL LEGACY

Frances Patton Statham

Fawcett Columbine · New York

A Fawcett Columbine Book
Published by Ballantine Books
Copyright © 1988 by Frances Patton Statham

Library of Congress Catalog Card Number:
87-91867

ISBN: 0-449-90250-1

Cover design by James R. Harris
Illustration by Oliviero Berni
Manufactured in the United States of America
First Edition: September 1988
10  9  8  7  6  5  4  3  2  1

# THE ROSWELL LEGACY

# CHAPTER
## I

"Fool! Do you realize what you've done, Charles? Thrown over everything I've worked so hard for these last twenty years. And made *bastards* of our children, too."

Araminta's voice was harsh, stabbing. He *had* been a fool. But it was not because he'd accepted the Washington appointment, nor even because he'd chosen to leave England. It had happened long ago, when he'd married Araminta, his wife's sister-in-law. He'd never meant to go near her again. The Bermuda high winds were responsible—they had damaged the British frigate, *Haddington*, forcing the captain to put into the Savannah harbor for repairs and spewing the passengers, including Charles, onto dry land.

The storm had proved as disastrous to Charles as to the ship, and the damage to Charles had been more far reaching.

Dr. Charles Coin Forsyte tried to conceal his pain at Araminta's accusation, even as he had taken great care earlier to conceal his true identity from the world, changing the spelling of his last name and choosing to be called Charles, rather than Coin, to protect Allison from any chance of future scandal.

He tried to sound clinical and dispassionate, for Araminta had an uncanny knack of ferreting out any sign of emotional attachment and ripping it to shreds.

"My turning up alive, after all these years, is bound to be a shock to Allison. But I'm sure she'll see what's at stake and not say anything to jeopardize our children's happiness."

Araminta suddenly pressed her lips into what, for her, passed for a smile. "Or her position as Senator Meadors's wife. It would be rather difficult, don't you agree, for her to explain to him that she's a bigamist."

Charles's careful facade cracked. "When she married him, Araminta, she thought I was dead. And remember," he warned, "if the truth gets out, you have just as much to lose as Allison."

Araminta's smile turned into a pout. She picked up another chocolate-covered cherry and popped it into her plump mouth. The juice squirted through the gap made by the newly pulled tooth and she quickly wiped her chin with a lace handkerchief retrieved from the bosom of her pale blue afternoon gown.

"You should stop eating so many chocolates, Araminta. The excess weight isn't good for your heart."

She ignored her husband's warning.

"I'll always rue the day when, behind our backs, Ginna

was introduced to that Meadors boy. It seems almost incestuous, having them—"

"For God's sake, Araminta. They're not related at all. Now if Morrow and Nathan had become interested in each other, then that would have been another matter entirely."

"That's silly. Nathan is only eleven."

"I was merely making a point."

"Well, I still don't like it."

"Neither do I. But it's too late now."

Charles stood up, walked to the window, and peered out at the quiet Washington street. Congress was in recess until August and most of the lawmakers were back home courting their constituents. Only a few of the more dedicated men were left to deal with the upcoming special session.

The summer sun was still high in the sky, but the giant elm trees lining the avenue shaded the front sitting room of the brownstone he had recently leased. Finally, in the distance, Charles could see the familiar carriage from the White House approaching. It looked no different from any ordinary carriage, for secrecy was of the utmost importance.

"I have to go now, Araminta." Charles picked up his medical kit and forced himself to walk over to the chair to kiss his wife good-bye. "You won't be able to reach me for the next several days. But if you need anything, just get in touch with Hadley at the clinic."

"I think it's inexcusable of you, Charles, to leave me just at this particular time and not even tell me where you're going."

"You'll survive, Araminta. You always do."

There was a discreet tap on the door. "The driver's waiting, Dr. Forsyte."

"Thank you, Barge. Did you put my suitcase in the carriage?"

"Yes, sir." The white-coated manservant followed the surgeon and held open the front door. He knew better than to offer to carry the medical kit. Dr. Forsyte was peculiar about that, as Barge well knew.

From the window at the upstairs landing, a worried Ginna Forsyte watched her father's progress down the walkway. As he opened the gate to the street, she called out, "Good-bye, Papa."

Surprised, he turned and looked up at the open window. What was his daughter doing at home in the middle of the afternoon rather than at the art institute? Oh, God, he hoped she hadn't overheard his heated conversation with Araminta.

He waved. "Good-bye, Ginna."

Charles settled into the carriage and prepared himself for the long drive to the yacht basin. By the next day, he would be in New York, where the best team of surgeons in the nation was being assembled. Once the operating room had been set up on Benedict's private yacht, which was waiting on the banks of the East River, then the doctors and nurses would be prepared to receive their clandestine patient: President Grover Cleveland.

With the life of the president in jeopardy, Dr. Charles Coin Forsyte pushed aside his own family problems. He would have to deal with them later.

For Allison Forsyth Meadors, the month of July was an old wound that she tried to forget every year. She was now in her forties—past time for all vestiges of the earlier trauma to have disappeared entirely. But like a scar that forms a distinctively patterned ridge and begs for occasional remembrance even as it fades, the calendar prompted her to remember the war and the tragic events that had made her a widow and then a wife again.

The light tap on the open door elicited no response. Finally, Jonathan, her son, spoke. "If you're going to call on Ginna's mother this afternoon, don't you think you should finish getting ready instead of staring into the looking glass?"

Jonathan's amused eyes met hers, and she smiled. "Yes, of course."

Allison quickly picked up the jaunty silk hat and placed it on her head. With no sense of self-consciousness, she stood and waited for Jonathan's inspection. The years had been kind to her, and today Allison was glad, especially for her son's sake. She had no wish to embarrass him before the family of the young woman he wanted to marry.

"Well?"

He nodded, taking in the smart green silk dress with pleats that fell to the floor and the matching hat with a black veil that barely masked the brightness of his mother's amethyst eyes.

Six months ago, he'd thought he would never find another human being half as beautiful. That is, until he met Ginna.

He tried to sound nonchalant. "You'll do. Especially for an old lady." Then he grinned and reached out to give her a hug.

She pushed him away and straightened her hat. "Such extravagant compliments. I don't know how you manage them."

Allison retrieved her purse from the dressing table, opened it to make sure she had her engraved calling cards, and then, seeing them, snapped the purse shut.

"Has Browne brought the carriage around front?"

"Yes, Mother. He's been waiting for the past ten minutes."

They walked down the winding stairs to the front entrance. The oval-glass-paneled door opened onto a carefully painted porch, where feathery green ferns sat on top of twin balustrades standing guard at the steps.

Allison paused on the walkway and turned to her son. "If your father gets home before I do, tell him I haven't forgotten the dinner party tonight." At his nod, Allison resumed walking toward the carriage.

Jonathan Meadors stood by the hitching post and watched until the carriage pulled out of the circular driveway. Usually cool and self-assured, he felt perspiration trickling down his collar. He was actually nervous about this duty meeting between the two mothers—the same feeling he had when awaiting the outcome of a close horse race. He laughed at himself as he took out a clean linen handkerchief and wiped his brow. Better to keep his mind on the thoroughbreds. Let his charming mother take care of the social amenities.

"Oh, Maudie, I've changed my mind," Ginna said. "Hand me the pink dress instead. Papa always says I look best in pink. And I *do* want to look my best when I meet Jonathan's mother this afternoon."

"Won't matter much what you wear, Miss Ginna. I don't think you'll be seeing Mrs. Meadors today, after all."

"She isn't coming?"

"Oh, she's coming, all right. Only I just heard your mama tell Barge to bring the carriage around back for you and Mr. Nathan. That you'd both be leaving in a few minutes for your sister's house."

A crestfallen Ginna looked at the maid, who was hanging

up the yellow silk organza. "But I came home early from the art institute to supervise Clara in the kitchen. To make sure everything would be perfect: the silver trays polished, the tea biscuits exactly right. I'll just die if I'm sent away without meeting her. Mummy can't do this to me, Maudie."

"Not much you can do to stop her, Miss Ginna, if she makes up her mind. She's done it to you before."

Maudie was right. And the few times she had tried to rebel or cross her mother had resulted in an even worse situation. No, she had too much to lose, this time. Her mother might find some way of keeping her from marrying Jonathan.

"Then I suppose I'll wear the yellow dress after all, Maudie."

Later, a dispirited Ginna slowly walked down the stairs to the parlor. A fidgety Nathan was already waiting.

He was small for his age, and slender, with unruly blond hair that took only a few minutes to escape from the brush's attempt at control. Below his dark cotton knickers, his left sock was already three inches below his right one. He was busy cupping his hands to make the funny squeak his new friend, Pinky, had shown him.

"Stop that awful noise, Nathan," Araminta admonished her son just as Ginna walked into the parlor. At her daughter's appearance, she forgot about Nathan.

"Well, you certainly took long enough to get dressed. Mr. Meador's mother is due any moment."

"I'm sorry, Mummy."

"I've told you, Ginna, to stop calling me Mummy. We're not in England anymore. People around here might think you're talking to some ancient Egyptian relic on display at the Smithsonian."

When Ginna looked as if she might sit down, Araminta

9

chided her again. "The carriage is waiting, Ginna. I've decided you and Nathan will be better off over at Cassie's house this afternoon. First meetings between mothers are always awkward."

"Please, won't you let me stay, even for a little while?"

"No, Ginna. The marriage isn't certain. Your father may not like the Meadors family. And it will be much better this way, for you not to become involved with them before matters are settled one way or the other."

Ginna's face turned white. Not to marry Jonathan? He was her life, her future. It had been so unbelievable that he had chosen her—a nobody—from all of the others. Senator Meadors had an impeccable reputation in Washington, as well as in his home state of Kentucky. He had money, position, and integrity, and his son was exactly like him. So how could her mother even *speak* of his family in that way?

"Go with your sister, Nathan. No, not out the front door. The carriage is in the alleyway. I don't want you to bump into Mrs. Meadors coming down the street."

A few moments later, as a disheartened Ginna climbed into the waiting carriage, Nathan said, "Don't cry, Ginna. Here, you can hold Green Boy if you want." Nathan reached into his pocket and pulled out a frog.

Ginna laughed as she brushed away a tear. "What are you going to do with him when we get to Cassie's house?"

"I thought you might hide him in your purse for me. Then I can take him out when Cassie isn't looking."

"It's going to be a long, dreadful afternoon, Nathan."

"That's why I brought Green Boy along. You'll help me, won't you, Ginna?"

"Yes. But I don't think I want to hold him just now, thank you."

When the Forsyte family carriage began to wheel out of the alleyway, Ginna peered down the street. She watched as a smart open carriage, pulled by two matching black horses, approached their house and came to a halt.

"Barge, stop the carriage, please."

"You forgot something, Miss Ginna?"

"No. I just want to see the woman getting out of the other carriage. Then we can go on."

From her carriage, which was partially hidden from view by the elm trees, Ginna saw the woman alight from the other carriage and walk toward the front door. She was dressed in cool green silk, and even from a distance, Ginna could tell that Jonathan's mother was slender and beautiful.

When the woman disappeared down the walkway, Ginna said, "You may drive on, Barge."

# CHAPTER
## 2

"Hello, Allison."

Araminta opened the door and waited for Allison, coming in from the brilliant sunlight, to adjust her eyes to the dimness of the Forsyte hallway. Her smile was smug, for she was in a superior position, having planned her surprise carefully.

It was but a brief moment from Araminta's greeting in a disturbingly familiar voice to Allison's realization that she was standing before a caricature of her former sister-in-law, her brother Jonathan's widow. Araminta's once attractive face was now marred by a double chin, her bloated body encased in a rigid corset that did nothing to hide her indulgences. Only her reddish-brown hair with its lustrous sheen had remained the same.

"Araminta?"

"Yes." Araminta's brown eyes showed her satisfaction at the incredulous expression on Allison's face.

"I don't believe it. *You're* Ginna's mother?"

"Right again, Allison. But don't let me keep you standing in the hall. Come into the parlor. We have a lot of catching up to do."

Like a sleepwalker trying to awake, Allison followed her former sister-in-law and took her seat in the chair Araminta indicated.

The heavy draperies at the windows, combined with the dark furniture, gave the parlor an oppressive atmosphere. A varnished English landscape in a heavy gilt frame, which hung over the mantel, added to the somberness of the room.

"Charles and I have been back only a month. We're still unpacking boxes. Such a lot to do when one moves, don't you think? Especially after spending the last twenty years in England."

"So that's why my letters never reached you," Allison commented, still dumbfounded to be sitting opposite a woman she hadn't seen for a number of years.

Araminta picked up the small silver bell on the table and rang it vigorously. "I sent all the servants away, Allison, except poor Clara in the kitchen. Once she brings us some refreshments, we can settle down to talking. And we needn't worry about her overhearing anything. She's too stupid to understand. But servants' gossip can be so harmful, especially in Washington where your . . . where Senator Meadors has such a sensitive position."

Shortly after Clara had appeared with the large silver tray

that Ginna had helped to polish, Araminta poured tea into a bone china teacup and handed it to Allison. "I hope you don't mind having *hot* tea, Allison, instead of iced. It's a custom both Charles and I have gotten used to every afternoon." Without waiting for Allison to comment, Araminta said, "Now we can talk. Tell me, how did you ever wind up being married to a Yankee?"

"Rad is a fine man, Araminta. And he came into my life when I *needed* someone." Allison's eyes clouded with tears as she remembered the family tragedies she'd shared with her sister-in-law. "Oh, Araminta, the war brought so much sadness to both of us, with Jonathan and Coin being killed. I named my son for our Jonathan, Araminta—yours and mine. But then you must have realized that.

"Right after Coin's memorial service, I wrote to you, but you evidently didn't receive that letter, either. I was desperate, with no money and a baby to support."

"So you married one of Sherman's Yankee officers. I'll hate Sherman and his entire army till the day I die, Allison, because of what he did to Savannah."

"Rad wasn't in Sherman's army, Araminta. But I dislike Sherman as much as you do. Roswell suffered under him even more than Savannah. Do you remember my servant, Rebecca?"

"Yes. I never really liked her, though. Too sassy for her own good."

Allison ignored Araminta's comment. "She died several years ago, Araminta. But she was a true friend, and I wouldn't have survived without her." Allison took a sip of tea and then continued talking. "When I didn't hear from you, I decided the only way I could get back to Cypress Manor was to earn enough money to hire a wagon or a carriage for the trip home. So Rebecca and I swallowed our pride and asked for jobs as weavers in the Roswell mill. But on the second day Sherman's troops came and burned the mill. All of the women were arrested and shipped north. Rebecca and I were in that group. And my baby, Morrow, too."

Allison's eyes showed her sadness. She had no wish to relive this part of her life or to parade all of her hardships before Araminta. So she quickly glossed over the months that she and the three others had spent working on a tobacco farm in Kentucky until the owner, Major Rad Meadors of the Union army, returned from the war.

"I met Major Meadors a year later. We were married, and a year after that our son Jonathan was born. Which brings us to Ginna. So, now tell me about this Dr. Forsyte and where you met him."

"You mean you don't know who he is, Allison?"

"I know only what Jonathan told me. That he's an eminent surgeon who's just been appointed to the staff of the medical center here. But, of course, I wondered if he might be some English relative of Coin's, with a slightly different spelling of his name."

"Allison, he *is* Coin."

"I beg your pardon?"

"You heard me, Allison. Coin didn't die in the Battle of the Wilderness. He was merely hurt and out of his head for a long time. Then he went back to the fighting. And after the war, when he returned to Roswell, you had completely disappeared. When we got married, we both thought you were dead.

"Do you want some laudanum, Allison? Charles might have some in his cabinet."

"No, I'll be all right, Araminta. It's just the shock of being told that Coin is still alive. . . ."

"And the shock of realizing that you're a bigamist, Allison, with a son who wants to marry *my* daughter. For the good of everyone concerned, we've got to keep them apart. They mustn't be allowed to marry each other."

Halfway across town, Cassie narrowed her eyes as she looked at her half sister Ginna, who was seven years younger than she. The girl's skin was perfect, and her large eyes were a breathtaking azure. And she had inherited their mother's brown hair without the red that Cassie was plagued with.

Seeing Ginna looking so beautiful, Cassie felt all the old animosity returning. She even remembered the very day it had started, a small happening that caused a steady, aching, devouring anger to erupt suddenly. She had been eleven, the same age that Nathan was now. She had been tending to the four-year-old Ginna that day in the park, when the boy she liked finally came up to talk with her. But he had accused her of telling a fib when she told him Ginna was her sister.

"You two can't be sisters," he'd said, looking from one to the other. "You're as different as freckled cheese and clotted cream."

Recalling his words, Cassie fanned harder to cool her flushed face. She was beginning to feel like freckled cheese all over again, what with her pregnancy and the awful July heat. But then she remembered who she was: a married woman with a husband who had a promising future. Of course, Stanley wasn't the handsomest man in the world, but he had provided her with a nice house and furniture. And when her mother had advised her to have a baby as soon as possible, before he lost interest in her, as all men do with their wives sooner or later, she had complied. Only her mother hadn't warned her how uncomfortable she would be.

"Cassie, it's hot as blazes in here," Nathan complained. "Can't we sit out on the porch instead?"

"No, Nathan. Mama told me to keep a sharp eye on you two this afternoon, and you know I don't like the sun in the middle of the afternoon. We'll stay inside."

At Nathan's groan, Cassie said, "But I'll get Harriet to bring us some iced lemonade. You'd like that, wouldn't you, Nathan?"

"If you've got a scone to go along with it."

"Can I help, Cassie?" Ginna offered.

"No. Just stay in the parlor with Nathan to make sure he doesn't break anything." Cassie put down her fan and left the room.

"She still treats me like a two-year-old, Ginna," Nathan complained. "How much longer will we have to stay? I want to go home."

"So do I, Nathan. But we just got here."

A croaking sound came from the nearby purse. "Cat's pants! I almost forgot Green Boy," Nathan whispered, opening Ginna's purse and standing up to slip the frog into his pocket just as Cassie reappeared.

She saw the conspiratorial look on their faces, but she said nothing. Let them have their little games. They'd be separated soon enough. Nathan was to be sent away to boarding school in September, although he didn't know it yet. And Ginna's marriage to that Mr. Jonathan Meadors wasn't a certainty. If her mother had anything to do with it, Ginna would remain at home to oversee the smooth running of the Forsyte household, instead of establishing one of her own at her age.

"Harriet will be here in a few minutes with the lemon-

17

ade," Cassie announced. "And do sit down, Nathan. You're too close to the flower vase Stanley gave me for my birthday."

"I haven't touched a thing, Cassie."

"Well, see that you don't."

A large tray with a pitcher filled with iced lemonade, three crystal glasses, and a plate of scones was brought into the parlor.

Nathan returned to his seat beside Ginna while Cassie carefully poured the glasses half full and meted them out as if they contained a rare nectar.

"What did you say, Nathan?"

"I didn't say anything, Cassie." The boy shifted position, trying to make the frog in his pocket more comfortable.

Quickly, Ginna prompted, "I think Cassie is waiting for a thank-you for the lemonade, Nathan."

"Oh. Well, thank you, Cassie. For the scone, too," he added. But just as he leaned over to select a pastry from the plate, Green Boy escaped from Nathan's pocket. As the frog hopped onto the tray, Cassie screamed. With a second hop, the frog landed with a splash in the pitcher of lemonade.

Nathan's glass overturned on the carpet as he struggled to retrieve the frog. And through it all Cassie continued to scream.

"It's all right, Cassie," Ginna said soothingly. "It's only a harmless frog. I'll help you to clean up."

"No. I want you both out of my parlor. Mama had no right to fend you off on me when I'm in such a delicate condition. Because of you two, my baby may be marked for life."

"You know that's poppycock, Cassie. You heard Papa say so more than a dozen times. . . ."

18

But Cassie was in no mood to listen to Ginna. "Just take your damned frog, Nathan, and both of you get out of here. You can tell Barge to drive you around until four o'clock. That's when Mama said I could send you back to the house. But you, my little brat of a brother, you're going to be sent away permanently in September."

Cassie disappeared upstairs while Ginna took her handkerchief and mopped up the spilled lemonade.

"What did she mean by that, Ginna?"

"Oh, you know how Cassie exaggerates. She probably overheard Papa and Mummy discussing where you're to go to school. That's all."

"But I don't want to go off again. I want to stay where you are, Ginna."

"But after I marry Jonathan, we'll live in Kentucky. So, you see, I'll be going away, too."

Seeing the stricken look on his face, she added, "You can come to visit us during the summers. And Jonathan will let you choose your own horse to ride. You'd like that, wouldn't you, Nathan?"

"I guess so."

Harriet appeared because of all the commotion, and Ginna said to her, "Nathan and I will be leaving now, Harriet. Will you please tell Barge to bring the carriage to the front?"

"Yes, Miss Ginna. And I'll finish cleaning up the spill."

"My sister's rather nervous these days, so I would appreciate it if nothing is said about this afternoon."

"I understand, Miss Ginna. And I'll have this room good as new before Mr. Stanley returns."

"Thank you, Harriet."

Later, two carriages wandered aimlessly through the streets

of Washington. One contained Ginna and Nathan Forsyte, watching the time carefully until they could go home. The other held Allison Meadors, who had no knowledge of time, no desire to return home. That afternoon her world had toppled around her, threatening the happiness of her entire family.

# CHAPTER
## 3

When Rad Meadors left his Senate office, he took out his watch and looked at the time. Six o'clock—so much later than he had intended to stay, especially with the dinner party at Senator Drake's home that evening. The meeting with the other committee members had been a worrisome one, with serious disagreements about the way to proceed with the pending investigation.

"You're going to alienate half the attorneys in Washington," Edwards had warned.

"If it's the half dipping into government funds illegally, then I don't care," Rad had responded.

He had voted against much of the legislation enacted in those four years between Cleveland's two terms, but this last veterans' thing was the worst of all. It had bestowed a government-approved license to steal on any unscrupulous man with an unscrupulous lawyer. He wasn't happy at being appointed to chair the committee to investigate the matter. But there was nothing he could about it since it came by Cleveland's request.

Although the president had finally gotten a telephone put into the White House, it had done no good that afternoon. Cleveland had suddenly left town and couldn't be reached. Rad had demurred from calling the vice president, for the two were on opposite ends of the political pole, especially with the upcoming session to repeal the Silver Purchase Act.

As the carriages waiting in the shaded park across the street began pulling up to receive their passengers, Rad waved to his friend, Miles Johnson, and began the trek down Pennsylvania Avenue to the livery stable where his black horse, Sumi, was waiting for the gallop home.

God, how he missed Bluegrass Meadors, his estate outside of Lexington. Although he had turned over the running of the stables almost entirely to his son Jonathan, the horses and the races were still in his blood. And it was on days like this, in the middle of summer, when he had to deal with graft in the government, that he missed his life in Kentucky with Allison.

He hadn't thought about Bourbon Red in a long time, but as he approached the livery stable, Rad began to think about his old war-horse, who had lived out his last days in peace on those hazy blue acres far from the noise of battle.

Lately, he'd begun to think he might do the same: leave the Senate after this session and retire to the country. Wendall, one of the congressmen from Kentucky, knew the ropes well, and with just a little push, he might run for the seat vacated by Rad.

"Good evening, sir."

"Good evening, Dorty."

"You're a little late. Thought maybe you'd decided not to come. Won't take but a minute, though, to get Sumi saddled up."

"I hope he's in the mood for a gallop. I need to clear my head after sitting in a hot, smoke-filled room all afternoon."

"He's every bit as anxious for a gallop as you are, sir."

The livery man was right. A small twister of dust took shape as the two—man and beast—galloped down the road toward the turreted house that had been a second home for Rad during his past seventeen years in Congress.

With a slight rising of the wind, the heat of the day was now beginning to dissipate. Straight ahead, a few dark clouds forecast a late-afternoon thunderstorm. Rad wanted to get home before the rains began, so he urged the animal on even faster.

When he reached the house, Rad saw his son waiting on the front steps. Jonathan was a younger version of himself: tall, broad-shouldered, with a muscular physique that spoke of his outdoor life. But now, underneath the sweep of dark hair, his brow was wrinkled in a frown, an unusual thing since his gentle temperament had been the one trait inherited from his mother.

"Did you see the family carriage along the way?" Jonathan called as he walked down the steps toward Rad.

"No. Is your mother still out?"

"Yes. She's been gone far too long, and I'm worried about her."

"Isn't this the afternoon she was to call on Mrs. Forsyte?"

"Yes."

Rad laughed as he swung down from his horse. "You already sound like an impatient bridegroom, son. Your mother is all right, I assure you. But if something's gone wrong with the carriage—a loose wheel, perhaps—then remember, Browne is with her. He'll take care of the problem."

"Well, if she isn't back in a few more minutes, I'm going out to look for her."

Rad called Higgin from the carriage house by ringing the bell at the hitching post. "Sumi has had a hard run, Higgin. Walk him a bit and then give him a good rubdown."

"Yes, Mr. Rad."

Rad had merely pretended to be unconcerned to Jonathan. He was worried, too. It wasn't like Allison to be out so long, especially because of their important dinner engagement. Even though they were friends, Senator Drake was a stickler for protocol and he didn't brook his guests being late, unless they'd gone to their own funerals.

As Rad began to remove his dusty clothes, he listened to every small sound, straining to hear the familiar crunch of carriage wheels along the driveway. A leafy branch rubbed against the second-story bedroom window and a sudden gust of wind swept one of the giant ferns from its balustrade, sending the greenery tumbling down the steps.

Rad put on his robe and walked downstairs. "Jonathan," he called out. "I think you're right. You'd better go look for your mother before the storm breaks."

The water in the park bubbled over the gray rocks, polished smooth from the constant bombardment of the stream. Occasionally, a twig from a nearby tree floated on the surface, became prisoner for a time between the rocks, and then steered its way downstream.

Allison watched the trickling of water as if her life depended on its steady flow. And she stared at the small twig that had not budged from its prison between the rocks as the others had done.

Strange how something as insignificant as a twig caught between rocks could affect her—it was as if it were an omen for her own life.

She had been so happy these past years, putting all the old heartaches behind her. Now, in one afternoon, her world had crashed around her. And she was no more certain of what to do about it than she'd been two hours previously.

"Miss Allison, a storm's brewing. Are you ready to start home now?"

Allison looked up to see her servant standing on the bank. "What time is it, Browne?"

"Almost six o'clock, ma'am."

Allison quickly stood and brushed the debris from her skirt. "I didn't intend to stay here so long." Her voice was apologetic. "Yes, let's start for home immediately. Everyone will be wondering where I am."

She took one last look at the water lapping against the rocks and then hurried to the carriage. As the wheels picked up speed, Allison came to only one conclusion. For the next several days, she must keep this heartbreaking revelation to herself. Neither Rad nor Jonathan must learn the truth until she'd had a chance to meet Coin face-to-face.

Jonathan had ridden only several blocks when he saw the family carriage. The horses were at a steady trot, as if trying to make up for lost time. He brought his horse alongside the carriage. "I was just coming to look for you, Mother. Are you all right?"

"Yes. I'm sorry if I gave you cause for alarm."

Jonathan smiled. "You and Mrs. Forsyte must have gotten along remarkably well to have spent the entire afternoon together. What were you doing? Planning every detail of the wedding and the honeymoon, too?"

Allison forced herself to smile. "It didn't get quite that far, Jonathan."

"Well, how did you like her?"

"Mrs. Forsyte?"

"No, I mean Ginna. She's beautiful, isn't she, Mother?"

"I'm sure she is. But I didn't see her this time. She wasn't at home. I only met Mrs. Forsyte. Ride on, Jonathan," Allison urged, "so Browne can get me home. We'll talk at length later."

A disappointed Jonathan looked at his mother closely. Her bright smile almost achieved the illusion that everything was as it should be. But he knew his mother too well. Something had gone wrong and she was doing her best to hide it from him.

"Oh, Lord, I have to do better than this," Allison said to herself as she watched Jonathan's horse break into a gallop. Her son was too perceptive. It would be much harder to deceive him than Rad, preoccupied as he was with the upcoming legislative session. Now, if she could only get through the dinner that night without having Peggy Drake suspect that something was drastically wrong with her best friend.

The fact that she was late in arriving home worked in her favor. Allison dashed up the stairs and into the bedroom, where Rad was struggling with the studs of his shirt.

"Hello, darling," she said, turning her face upward for a quick kiss. "I'm sorry I let the afternoon get away from me."

"We were beginning to get worried about you."

"So Jonathan told me."

"Well, no harm's done. Unless you take an hour to get dressed for dinner," Rad teased. "I just got home a few minutes ago myself."

Allison walked toward the bath, but as she reached the door, she had a desperate need to stop and look back into the bedroom, to watch Rad as he casually ran the silver brush through his dark hair. He was gray at the temples now, and only slightly heavier than on that day he'd ridden home from the war.

As he turned around, their eyes met. "What's this? Something wrong with my evening suit?"

"Have I told you lately, Major Meadors, what a fine-looking man you are?"

He grinned as she disappeared into the bath. But once she was out of the room, the mirror reflected a sober, thoughtful Rad. He was much more perceptive than he let on. Only this time, he didn't guess the new disaster that had shattered Allison that day. It was July again. For him, that was reason enough.

By the time Allison came out of the bath, Rad had gone downstairs, and Maggie, a young Irish girl, was waiting to help her dress.

"It's raining so hard, ma'am," Maggie said, "would ye be wantin' to wear your rainy daisy instead of your longer skirt?"

Allison had hardly noticed the rain until the girl mentioned it. "No, Maggie. I'll wear whatever you've already laid out for me."

Allison was like a doll being dressed. She held her arms up so that the gown slid over her head. She was only vaguely aware of its color—pale yellow lace, with satin ribbons tied at the cinched waist and the fluffy jupons falling in graceful folds at the back. Still wooden, she sat at the dressing table while Maggie repaired her hairstyle, finishing it by clipping on an evening ornament of jewels and small feathers.

When the carriage appeared in the porte cochere, Allison's dress was covered by a light cape to ward off the rain, which showed no signs of abating. With Rad at her elbow, she stepped gingerly over the small puddles and climbed into the carriage. She felt the chain of the small yellow lace evening bag on her arm. Maggie had seen to that, too.

Allison didn't know when she'd paid less attention to the way she looked. If it hadn't been for Maggie that night, she more than likely would have been an embarrassment both to herself and to Rad.

"I'm glad you're here in Washington with me, Allison. Official dinners can be so boring, even at the Drakes's."

Rad's words sounded as if they were coming from far away, through some tunnel.

"I don't relish this night, Allison," he confided. "All of the vultures will be there, looking at me and wondering how much of the carcass they'll get to keep once the committee has finished with it."

"Surely it won't be as serious as that."

"Not during dinner. But once you ladies retire and the cigars and brandy are handed out, all hell will break loose. A pity you're not in a delicate condition, Allison. That way I'd have an excuse to leave early."

"Well, actually, I *am* beginning to have a headache. Would that be a suitable excuse?"

He squeezed her hand. "Not for Peggy, or Tripp, either. We'll just have to stick it out, Allison, however unpleasant it gets."

Allison turned her face away. The fear and despair that had come upon her that afternoon began to weigh even more heavily. But for Rad's sake, she would have to maintain a semblance of composure. She could not come apart in front of his colleagues. And because of that, Allison knew that the evening would be one of the worst she would ever have to live through.

# CHAPTER
## 4

Charles Forsyte had long ago ceased to think of himself as Coin. That part of his life had been put aside, a gate locked—with no desire on his part to look beyond it.

But the legacy of the past had finally caught up with him, forcing him to tear down the decades-old barrier he'd set up. Now he would have to deal with the old hurts, the sense of anger he'd felt on that day when he'd finally found Allison. From a distance, he'd watched her, standing in the winner's circle at the Saratoga racetrack with another man.

He'd wanted to call out to her from the crowd, to tell her what he had been through for two whole years. That it wasn't fair for her to make a new life for herself, even if he *had* been reported dead. He was alive, and now that he'd finally found them, he wanted his wife and daughter back. They were a part of the dream that had sustained him.

Then he'd seen her servant, Rebecca, on the green, tending to Allison's new son, Jonathan. And he knew then that the dream was gone. He had found Allison too late.

With Rebecca sworn to secrecy, he'd left for Canada, never intending to return from that wilderness. For Allison's sake, he would remain dead, a victim of the carnage between North and South.

Now his past was finally reaching out to snare another victim: his daughter Ginna.

Through the years, the child had helped to ease the pain of his unhappy marriage to Araminta, as well as the pain of losing Morrow, his daughter by Allison.

He had seen Morrow only once—with Rebecca, that same day at Saratoga. The war had kept him from being present at her birth. And in the end, it was the war that had parted them for a lifetime.

Yes, Ginna had received not only her own share of a father's love but the portion that Morrow would have received, too. Until Araminta had guessed her vulnerability and begun to use Ginna as a means of striking back at Charles. Fortunately, Nathan had fared better.

But now Ginna was more vulnerable than ever, and there was little Charles could do to protect her. Out of all the people in the world, how had Ginna managed to meet the one young man who could bring such discord into their lives? He blamed himself for sending her to Washington a full three months before he and Araminta had left England.

For the past half hour Charles had ridden along in the carriage with little thought of the other doctor, Bennett Jamison, seated opposite him.

Finally, the man cleared his throat and spoke. "I suppose the others are already in New York."

"More than likely."

"I have an uneasy feeling, Charles. I realize the need for secrecy, but the president should be operated on in a decent hospital, not on a yacht sailing the East River."

For the first time, Charles took a hard look at his colleague. "What, precisely, bothers you, Bennett?"

"The instability of water, for one thing. What if the boat hits something or the water suddenly swells just as the scalpel is—"

"Do you usually get motion sickness?"

Bennett gave a start. "How did you know?"

Charles smiled. "You're beginning to turn a little green around the gills."

"I don't believe anything escapes you, Charles."

"You're quite wrong, Bennett. Sometimes I even think the more apparent things are to other people, the more obscure they seem to me."

Bennett laughed despite his discomfort.

"The yacht will have a lot less motion than this carriage, I assure you," Charles went on.

"Then perhaps I'll survive," Bennett answered.

The two looked at each other but said nothing more. The last word used by Bennett prompted Charles to think of the president's chances of survival. Cancer was a dreadful disease in any part of the body. But cancer of the mouth was particularly dangerous, with the chance of gross disfigurement even if the patient survived.

It was merely intuition on Charles's part, yet he couldn't help but feel that Cleveland's love of cigars had played a role in the disease. He had seen it in England with men who smoked excessively—whether cigars, pipe, or opium. The clinics had been filled with them.

The carriage wheeled its way through the countryside, slowing down for a stray cow or pig in the road and then regaining its speed. As the wind began to rise, Charles watched the boats, tiny specks upon the watery horizon, trim their sails and head for home. But by the time the carriage arrived at the basin, few had reached the safety of the boat slips.

All around him, the air was alive with the vibration of halyards, thumping like some out-of-control bass fiddle. And from the sound Charles knew that their trip on the water would not be a placid one. For himself, he did not mind. But like Araminta, Bennett would not be the best of passengers.

Because of the rough trip from England, Araminta had not been interested in getting on the water again, however hot it was on land. And so the previous week he had taken only Ginna and Nathan on the excursion down the Potomac to Mount Vernon, to give them a history lesson of their own country, which they'd never before seen.

That day had been so perfect, with Araminta unable to spoil their enjoyment. Now, as Charles and Bennett arrived at the marina, he was once again glad to leave Araminta behind, even for a few days.

In the low, sloped curve of the basin, a special white yacht, its polished brass catching an occasional glint of sun, sat unobtrusively in the water. It was a replica of the others usually berthed at the marina. Only the flag was different— green and yellow, with a small white crescent in the upper left quadrant. Standing guard were two burly-looking characters in deckhand clothing, a suitable disguise, Charles thought, for the president's men.

The carriage did not go directly to the waiting boat. Instead, it drew up behind a tackle shop, where the two doctors were quickly ushered into a small room with its single window obscured by layers of dust.

"You will please change clothes in here."

Outside, a dog barked, while the odor of bait, trapped in the afternoon heat, permeated the dingy backroom. An old gray tarpaulin had been spread on the floor, and hanging on two hooks were two suits: cleanly pressed white duck trousers, shirts, and navy coats with gold buttons. Each suit was carefully labeled with the initials of one of the doctors.

When Charles saw the costumes, he laughed. "If the aides wanted anonymity, they should have provided simpler clothes. I'll feel like a riverboat captain on the Mississippi in this outfit."

"It's really a good disguise, Charles. This is the official dress of the Georgetown yacht club. We're right in style. But, of course, you wouldn't know that, being from England."

Charles started to say something but changed his mind.

Within a few minutes, the two men had stripped themselves of their street clothes and put on the others provided for them. By the time they emerged from the tackle shop, carrying fishing gear, also provided for them, the carriage they had ridden in was gone. In its place was a second carriage.

"Damn!"

"What is it, Charles?" Bennett whispered.

"Our bags, my medical kit . . . They're in the other carriage."

There was nothing to do but go to the boat and tell the president's men they couldn't leave until they chased down the bags. And so, with Bennett, a chagrined Charles, blaming himself for letting his medical kit out of his sight, climbed into the second carriage for the short ride the rest of the way.

As the carriage pulled alongside the boat slip, one of the men stepped forward to open the carriage door. "Dr. Forsyte?"

"Yes."

"And Dr. Jamison?"

"Yes."

"You will please come aboard quickly."

"We can't leave yet," Charles responded. "Our suitcases were left in the other carriage—"

"They're already in your quarters."

"The medical kit, too?"

"Everything. Now I'll take your fishing gear for you, if you'd like."

As soon as they set foot on deck, a third man was waiting for them. He was another burly, mustached fellow, tanned from his life on the sea. "I'll show you to your quarters. I'm afraid you'll have to remain belowdecks until we're safely out of the harbor. We hadn't counted on all the boats returning so soon. But once we're on the waterway, you may come up on deck at any time."

"I daresay you won't be seeing me until we reach our destination," Bennett said. "I plan to spend the entire journey on my back."

When Charles reached his quarters, he saw his medical kit with his suitcase. But he would not be satisfied until he opened it and made sure all of his equipment was safe.

His medical instruments were made of the finest English steel, a sacrifice on his part when he'd purchased them. But now they were an extension of him, fitting his hands perfectly, never disappointing him in what he required, however intricate and delicate.

They were all there, none the worse for his brief lapse of stewardship. Satisfied, he closed the case and set it beside his luggage.

Charles's image was reflected in the opposite mirror, the same round shape as the small, open porthole, where the stiff breeze was beginning to penetrate the cabin. Except for the lines marking his forehead and the slight, almost imperceptible slackening of his jawline—both natural signs of getting older—his face was still that of the young man who'd fought on the losing side in the war. He parted his sandy hair on the left, not in the middle. His shoulders were still straight, his body still of medium height and weight. But nevertheless he was a totally different man. Too much had happened in the after years for him to remain the same.

The metamorphosis had begun in Canada in the logging camp. With such hurt knotted in his gut, Charles had welcomed the physical labor that allowed him to strike out at the trees.

With the starting up of the yacht's engine, there was nothing for Charles to do but wait until the boat was out of the marina. He took off the navy-blue coat with its gold buttons and hung it up. Then he lay down on the bunk, and with the steady, soothing hum of the engines, the movement of the boat slicing through the water, Charles closed his eyes.

Long-ago images flashed through his mind: the great Canadian wilderness, with trees that reached toward the sky; logs floating in steady convoy downriver; logs jammed, the walking-across floats, the path cleared, and the small boy, struggling in the water while ten tons of wood rushed down-stream toward him . . .

"Hey, Reb, clear out fast," a voice shouted. "The sluice gate's open."

That was the warning that struck fear in every logger's heart, especially the troubleshooters who rode the floats. But for Charles, it was an everyday occurrence, just a part of the new job he'd taken on. He was the man with nerves of steel. For him, the extra money meant little. Rather, it was a game, challenging fate since he had nothing more to lose but his life.

Barely in time, he crossed one section of logs, balancing himself with the logger's pole. Directly behind him, the telltale roar of water announced the approach of virgin tim-ber felled from the high country. It was a massive migration to the sawmills, like salmon rushing relentlessly to their spawning grounds.

Just as he was ready to jump clear, he heard a man's cry. "My boy! My boy! Somebody save him!"

Downstream, directly in the path of the logs, a child's head, encased in a red toboggan cap, bobbed up and down in the water. The anguish in the man's voice was the same deep anguish Charles had felt on the day at Saratoga when he'd given up his own wife and child as if they were dead.

The boy had one slim chance of survival. And it de-pended on the man riding the logs.

Charles remained on the float, balancing himself with the pole. A sudden jolt knocked his feet out from under him and wrenched the pole from his hands, sending it into the water like a swift harpoon. The new timber had taken its place behind him.

The current was running swift because of the melting

lakes of snow in the spring. Charles struggled to his knees on the slippery logs.

"Save him! Save my boy!" the voice cried again.

With the second cry, the wooded banks along the water began to fill with loggers, who put down their axes to watch the tragedy unfold. Out of the corner of his eye, Charles saw only blurs of red woolen plaid dotted among the trees, for his attention was aimed at the small blob of red almost directly in front of him.

With one, and only one, try allotted him, a wet and cold Charles poised to scoop the child from the water.

In a rapid movement, Charles grabbed the child and rolled backward immediately to keep them both from disappearing underwater as the first logs divided.

For a moment, Charles panted hard to get his breath back, while the child in his arms coughed up water. The easy part had been accomplished.

They were now in the middle of the flotilla heading mercilessly downstream, the logs ramming and annihilating everything in their path.

Charles had never ridden the logs this far downstream before. The river was much wider now, presenting an acute logistics problem in his getting to shore. As Charles debated how much longer to ride the logs before attempting it, the distant roar of a waterfall ahead decided it for him.

"Climb on my back, son," he ordered, "and whatever you do, don't let go."

The child was too scared to do anything else but obey. His arms went around Charles's neck in a near stranglehold.

Charles's first attempt at standing was not successful. He went to his knees again as the logs shifted. Then, on the second try, he came up quickly and took a balancing step.

The step was followed by another and still another, as Charles carefully wove his way across the logs to the bank.

But the bank had changed drastically in the past several hundred yards. No longer on a level with the water, it formed a ragged bluff, with the stream cutting deeper into the wilderness. A rainbow of mist caught in the filtered sunlight, announcing the peril of the falls beyond.

The few remaining logs separating Charles from the bluff gave way, and man and child plunged into the icy water. A parting blow from a log struck Charles in the side, but it was not severe enough to pry the child from his back.

They were swept along toward the falls. Charles reached out for a limb, a bush, anything that would slow their progress to certain disaster. A sharp pain cut across his palm as he grabbed for a limb and found thorns instead. A stone in place of bread. Separation instead of reunion. He belonged to no one, had nothing except his own tormented anguish. But in that instant of pain, a miracle occurred. All his anger and hostility toward God for taking away his dream was washed clean. And he knew he didn't want to die. He wanted to live.

With that realization, a quietness, a strength came to him. He no longer reached out for every small limb and twig. He flowed with the water and the logs until he saw the chance for his and the boy's survival. It was a giant, weathered tree, its fallen trunk hanging directly over the precipice.

"We're going over the falls!" the child screamed.

"No. Hang on, son."

Charles's arms wrapped around the tree trunk; his feet came out of the water, while directly beneath him the logs surged and plunged downward into the rainbow-colored mists.

Surrounded by the roar of water, the battle of logs, Charles held tight to the tree trunk. Then, after a few moments of rest, he began the tedious climb along the trunk, edging little by little, toward safety.

When Charles finally reached the top of the deserted bluff and gently pried loose the small boy's arms from around his neck, he lay on the ground, exhausted. "We'll rest for now," Charles said.

The child began to shiver. "I'm cold."

"I know. So am I." Charles drew the boy closer to him for warmth.

Later, when the trembling of his arms and legs had subsided somewhat, Charles stood. "It's time to go," he said.

But Charles did not return to the sluice. They were now on the same side of the river as the logging camp, and he knew it was more important to get the child into dry clothes than to waste valuable time looking for the father.

As Charles stepped into camp with the boy in his arms, one of the cooks, presiding over the fire, looked up from his cooking pot. "*Mon Dieu*," he said, crossing himself. "I am seeing a ghost."

"Not a ghost, Tony. Just two bedraggled river rats needing something hot to drink."

With Hudson Bay blankets wrapped around them, Charles and the boy were sitting before the fire when three men returned to the camp.

The boy stood and ran toward one of the men. "Papa!"

"Edward! You're alive. Someone told me, but I didn't believe it."

"We rode the logs, Papa. And almost went over the waterfall. But this man saved me."

The child's father walked slowly toward Charles. And

in a voice filled with emotion, he said, "If you had one wish in all the world, monsieur, what would you wish for?"

Charles's smile was ironic, for no one could grant him that. But as the image of the Wilderness battle flashed through his mind, the cries of the wounded surrounding him, he said, "I would become a doctor."

On the yacht, Charles opened his eyes and glanced at the surgical kit within arm's reach. On the day he'd saved the child, his second wish had seemed as impossible as the first. But then he had not known that the child, Edward, was the heir to the Bernet logging empire.

It was Alphonse Bernet, himself, who had arranged the London surgical training that was responsible today for Charles's summons to the bedside of the president of the United States.

# CHAPTER
## 5

On a tree-shaded knoll overlooking the long vista to the Washington Monument, a Georgian redbrick house sat majestically behind an iron fretwork fence. The matching iron gates were open, revealing a cobblestoned drive that pointed the way to the well-lit house.

The Meadors's carriage followed the familiar drive and then, at the circular island closer to the house, swept its way in a wide curve, finally ending its journey directly before the house steps. White-coated servants, who had been standing on the porch, raced down the steps with umbrellas to shield the arriving guests from the rain. And just beyond the porch, Peggy and Tripp Drake waited by the door to greet their last guests.

With coats relegated to the maid's arms and the senator steering Rad away for a private word or two before they joined the other guests, a relieved Peggy Drake gave Allison a perfunctory peck on the check. "I'm so glad you're finally here, Allison."

Allison looked at her friend of seventeen years. "Are we late, Peggy?"

"Oh, no. You're right on the dot. But you can't believe how edgy I've been after all that's happened today. I'm counting on you, Allison, to keep this party tonight from turning into a complete fiasco."

"I'm sure it will be every bit as enjoyable as the last one you gave, Peggy."

Her assurance was greeted with a shake of the head. "You wouldn't say that if you knew who Tripp made me invite at the last minute."

For a moment, Allison felt a sense of terror. Please don't let it be Araminta and Coin, she prayed. After so many years, she couldn't bear to face her former husband in a room filled with Rad's colleagues. Then she remembered. Coin was out of town.

"Who?"

Peggy looked around her to make sure that no one else was within ear's reach. "That Maddie creature. You know, the barmaid that Senator Birmbaugh of Nevada married. Tripp said the senator is much too powerful to snub, especially with the session coming up, so I was to invite her. I told him I wasn't about to speak to that woman, much less ask her to this house. And if he made me, then I just might pack up and go home tomorrow. But no amount of tears on my part could dissuade Tripp. She's sitting in the parlor with the others right now."

The distress in Peggy's eyes prompted Allison's compassion. "I'll do whatever I can to help, Peggy." And she added, "But things could be much worse. At least Frances and the president aren't here."

"I guess that's my only salvation. Heaven knows, this is one dinner party I hope Lottie misses writing about for the society column."

"I hear she's out of town, too. So let's go in and face the dragon."

Peggy gave a slight, nervous laugh. "Well, she's not really a dragon. In fact, she's quite pretty—in a rather common way."

The large entrance hall where the two women stood was a square, high-ceilinged room with black and white marble tiles on the floor. The oversized, circular velvet ottomans had been covered with chintz for the summer months, and huge pots of ferns and greenery in every available space gave the room the look of a conservatory.

Brushing past one of the fronds, Allison followed Peggy into the formal parlor, where the female guests were being entertained with discreet, soft music that was coming from the adjoining music room. The instrumentalists were barely visible beyond another display of palms and ferns. One of the maids was also busy offering crystal goblets filled with golden sherry to the guests. Most of the women took the offered refreshment, for they were not a part of the Prohibition movement.

"Now the party can begin," Peggy announced, as she entered the room. "Allison and Senator Meadors have arrived."

With her hand on Allison's arm, Peggy guided her around the parlor. "I believe you know almost everyone here. . . ."

"Allison, how nice to see you again."

"Hello, Rosetta. I'm so happy to see you, Mrs. Forbes. Letty . . ."

Allison made the complete journey, going almost full circle with her hostess, acknowledging old friends and acquaintances. The routine was ingrained by rote, requiring nothing more than a smile, a nod, and an appropriate few words here and there. And then Peggy stopped before a woman Allison had never seen before.

"May I present Mrs. Birmbaugh, the senator's wife. Mrs. Birmbaugh, Mrs. Meadors."

"How do you do?"

The woman smiled at Allison, and at that moment, Allison was reminded of Madrigal, the young mill worker who had been shipped north on the same train as Allison, Flood, and Rebecca and had wound up on Rad's plantation in Kentucky for a time. But Madrigal had ridden away from Bluegrass Meadors years before, with Rad's brother Glenn, and neither one had been heard from since.

Catching herself staring at the woman before her, Allison knew that she had to pull herself together. It was the red hair, of course. But the experience that afternoon with Araminta had done something to her emotions, causing her to conjure other faces from the past, even in this stranger before her.

"I already know a lot about you, Mrs. Meadors."

Peggy quickly intervened. "Then why don't you take this chair next to her, Allison? That way, you can get to know Mrs. Birmbaugh while I see how much longer it will be before dinner is served."

There was nothing left for Allison to do but take the offered chair. She was aware of the interested glances and the undisguised feelings of sympathy directed her way for having been selected to keep the stranger in their midst from total ostracism.

But she also saw the grateful look on Maddie Birmbaugh's face. And she felt a kinship with the woman, so alone in a room filled with people.

"I didn't really want to come tonight," Maddie whispered. "But the senator made me."

"It's always difficult, isn't it, to walk into a room where you don't know a soul."

"That's the Lord's truth. I thought I was gonna be beside Tug—I mean, the senator—all evening, but we got separated the minute we stepped inside the door."

"Well, it won't be long before we're all together again at the dining table."

"That's what's bothering me the most. I wouldn't say this to another living soul in this room except you, because I've already heard how nice and kind you are. But I'm scared to death of embarrassing Tug at dinner. What if I use the wrong fork or spoon?"

What a small worry, Allison thought, in comparison to the one she carried in her own heart that night. Yet, to Maddie, it was a major crisis.

"I understand we'll be seated near each other," Allison said. "So if you're not certain, just watch me to see which one I pick up."

"Oh, what a load off my mind. I can't tell you how grateful I am."

For Maddie, each bit of struggled conversation that Allison managed was welcomed. Caught up in her own self-consciousness, she didn't seem to realize that Allison Meadors was sadly lacking that night in vivacity and wit, that she was merely going through the formality of casual conversation while her mind was elsewhere.

Peggy returned to the room at the same time that Tripp and the other men appeared from the library. "Dinner is ready," she announced. Then she turned to her husband. "Tripp, take Allison into the dining room. And Rad, will you please escort Mrs. Birmbaugh? Senator Birmbaugh will be my dinner partner tonight." In quick succession, she paired off the other men and women, separating the wives from their spouses.

The long table in the oversized dining room was covered in the finest white Irish linen, with Capo di Monte candelabra spaced at intervals. And midway on the table stood an extravagant centerpiece made of fresh-cut flowers to resemble a peacock with its tail feathers spread wide. The porcelain china was white with bands of cobalt blue and gold. As usual, Peggy Drake had managed to blend the decorations with her own costume, a blue silk dress with a small band of peacock feathers in her hair. And at each place, a small porcelain peacock held a snow-white place card with the name of a guest carefully penned in flowing script.

Like a child, Maddie Birmbaugh clapped her hands in delight. "Oh, how beautiful," she said, surveying the table.

Rad smiled at his host as he seated her. "Mrs. Birmbaugh is right. Peggy has outdone herself tonight, Tripp."

"In more ways than one," Senator Drake responded in a dry manner.

With his wife and Maddie's husband at one end of the table, it was up to Tripp, as host, to guide the conversation at the other end. And as the servants walked around with silver trays and porcelain platters filled with food, Tripp turned to Maddie. "I understand you arrived from Nevada just a few days ago, Mrs. Birmbaugh."

"Yes, I did." Maddie laughed. "I was so dirty that Tug

didn't even recognize me at the station. Thought I was one of the servants until I called out to him, 'Hey, Tug, aren't you gonna give your wife a kiss?' It's taken me the past three days just to scrub off the train soot. I'm plumb raw, I can tell you that."

Seeing the horrified look in Rosetta Morgan's eyes, Maddie turned to Allison. "Did I say something wrong, Mrs. Meadors?"

"Long journeys are always difficult," Allison countered without answering her question. "Particularly on trains."

"I much prefer going by boat," Rosetta said with relish. "Don't you, Allison?"

"Much."

Like two skilled players, Allison and Rosetta rescued the conversation each time Maddie made a gaffe. By the time the dessert appeared, Senator Birmbaugh's wife had successfully spoken on every topic that was taboo at the table: religion, politics, money, and one's personal cleanliness. But at least she had watched Allison for her cue for the correct flatware. And only the more understanding people at one end of the table had overheard her comments, for Peggy was busy holding court at the other end.

As the candles burned low and the silver finger bowls were dispensed with, Peggy stood. "Ladies, if you will join me, we'll leave the gentlemen to their cigars and brandy."

The announcement brought the men to their feet. Amid the shuffling of chairs, Rosetta leaned over to Allison. "I don't know when I've had such fun. This dinner party has given me enough to talk about for the rest of the summer."

"Are you staying for the entire special session?" Allison inquired quickly.

"No. The last two weeks in August, the children and I will go to the shore. And you?"

"I'm not sure. I may go home for a while. And you, Mrs. Birmbaugh. Will you be staying in Washington?"

"I guess so. Not much to do in Nevada, since Tug bought out my . . ." Maddie caught herself. "Seeing I just got here, I might as well stay."

The women went up the stairs and dispersed in various directions, and a few moments later, Allison sat down before the dressing table in one of the bedrooms and began to go through the motions of repairing her hair. Peggy sat in a nearby slipper chair and watched.

"A half hour longer and then I can collapse," Peggy announced.

Allison turned from the mirror. "I don't know why you were so worried, Peggy. You managed quite well tonight."

"The others took their cue from you. You realize that, don't you, Allison? *You're* the one who kept the party from certain disaster."

Before Allison could dissent, Peggy continued, "I've been so busy that I haven't even asked about your visit with the Forsytes this afternoon."

At that moment, Letty appeared in the hallway, followed by Rosetta and Maddie. "Maddie and I were just admiring the new painting in the guest bedroom, Peggy," Rosetta commented. "Where did you find such an attractive piece?"

"It came from my aunt's estate," Peggy replied. Allison, grateful for the diversion, stood and joined the others in their walk down the stairs. She had no wish to discuss the afternoon fiasco with Peggy.

Now assured that her role as Washington's premier hostess had not been damaged despite her unwanted guest, Peggy held court for the rest of the evening with her usual verve. But for Allison, the last half hour sagged dreadfully.

The tinkling of laughter, the small talk were grating on

her nerves. Like someone who had held her breath far too long and yearned to drink in great draughts of fresh air, so Allison yearned to leave the restricted atmosphere of the parlor, where the sickening sweet scent of tuberoses had combined with the summer heat to overwhelm her. The headache that had threatened earlier now came in full force.

Oblivious to the sudden streak of lightning outside the window, Allison could stand it no longer. "Peggy, I really must go. . . ."

Once again the other women followed Allison's move. "Yes. We'd better get home before the storm breaks."

Within a few moments, Allison and Rad, along with the Birmbaughs, stood together on the porch and waited for their carriages to pull up to the steps.

"Remember, Mrs. Birmbaugh, tea on Tuesday, at my house," Rosetta Martin called out as she rushed past them.

Maddie nodded and then turned to Allison. "I won't ever forget your kindness tonight, Mrs. Meadors," she said, holding tight to Tug's arm.

In turn, the senator confided to Rad, "I've been thinking it over, Meadors. Just want you to know you can count on my fairness in the vote."

With a shaking of hands and good-byes, Rad and Allison rushed to their carriage. Once the carriage started down the driveway, Rad laughed. "In one short evening, Allison, you did more than all my aides have done in a month—caused a hostile senator to rethink his position. It's a pity that wives aren't paid for their work. But maybe I can find some way of remedying that." He leaned over to kiss her and she gave a start. "What's wrong?"

"I really do have a dreadful headache, Rad."

"Then close your eyes and rest your head against my shoulder."

The man seated beside her had been a rock of strength

through so many years. But now she had no right to draw on that strength.

To take her mind from her own problems, she began to think of Maddie Birmbaugh. There was something not quite right about her. But she couldn't put her finger on it.

"Rad, how long have the Birmbaughs been married?"

"Nearly . . ." He stopped abruptly, and Allison could feel the muscles in his arm tense. "I'm not sure. Why?"

"Oh, it's not important. I was just wondering."

They rode the rest of the way in silence. But Rad remained wary. Sometimes he thought that Allison had a sixth sense about things. He was probably the only one, besides Tripp, who knew for a fact that Maddie couldn't possibly be married to Tug, since his wife still lived in Ohio. But if Tug wanted to pass this woman off as his wife, it was his choice. Only heaven help him if Peggy Drake and the other wives ever found out what he'd done.

Late that night, the lights were still on in a three-story redbrick row house on First Street. In the bedroom, Maddie smiled at Tug and said, "Well, how did I do?"

His hands curved around her waist as he drew her to him. "You did real well. I don't think a single one of those uppity women had an inkling." He laughed as he tightened his hold on her. "I promised you, didn't I, that I'd show you Washington society? And you saw it tonight."

"You sure do keep your bets, Tug."

"And now it's time for you to show a little gratefulness. Sashay out of that new dress, gal. I like you better without a corset on."

She turned her back to him. "Then unbutton me, Tug. Or you want me to wake that Irish maid you hired?"

"We'll probably wake the maid, anyway," he said. "I never knew an old man could get so excited over a woman."

"You might have a few years on you," she admitted, shimmying out of the dress the senator had bought for her. "But you've got the staying power of a rutting buck I once watched at mating season in the canyon."

She stood poised against the gossamer curtains of the bed and waited for Tug to remove the last vestige of her clothing—the silk chemise that barely covered her well-formed body. As he cupped one breast in his large, rough hand, she whispered, "What'll it be this time, Tug?"

He reached under the bed pillow and took out the long, thin rope that he had hidden early that evening. "Spread-eagle me to the bed, Maddie, the Indian way. I want to be love-tortured tonight."

Maddie giggled as she complied. From the drawer in the nightstand, she pulled out the feathered Indian headband. After setting it on her red curls, she crept up to the side of the bed, slid over the sheet, inch by inch, until she reached him, and began the slow, sensual torture with her mouth.

A half hour later, the maid in the attic bumped her head as a bloodcurdling sound caused her to sit up straight. The two in the bedroom below her were evidently at it again.

Young Meara McClellan pulled the pillow over her head and began to recite a psalm. Tomorrow, she would give notice and start looking for another job. She couldn't take this another night.

At the same time of the evening, in the Meadors's white clapboard house, the air stirred by the ceiling fan brought little relief to Rad. In the darkness, he could see Allison's outline and hear her steady breathing. If it had not been for her headache, he would have found comfort long ago in her sweet body. Instead, he got up, drenched his face with cool water, and then went back to bed, unassuaged.

# CHAPTER
## 6

The rains had ceased. The slight motion of Benedict's pristine white yacht, *Oneida*, anchored in the East River, lulled its passengers with a gentle, soothing roll, unlike the bombarding fury of the earlier storm.

All of the doctors were now assembled: the plastic surgeons, the anesthesiologist, the dentist, and the nurses. Only the patient was missing.

That afternoon, for the first time, Charles had met with the other members of the operating-room team. The sterilizers, the auxiliary generator, and the medical equipment, dressings, and drugs had all been checked over. The entire ship had been disinfected from top to bottom, and one of the staterooms converted into an operating theater.

As Charles sat in his cabin and listened to the night sounds across the water, he rehearsed every step of the operation. The trial run that afternoon had gone quite smoothly. But he knew that the real test would come the next morning when the president was actually under the scalpel. Cleveland was a huge man—he weighed two hundred and fifty pounds. That in itself was a surgical danger.

Charles recalled his internship under the eminent Harley Street surgeon, Gaylord Runyard. He remembered the man's words, spoken so long ago. "Mr. Forsyte, your operation was a success." His pride was struck down in an instant by the indicting words that followed. "Unfortunately, your patient died."

That had been a severe blow to his ego, for nothing could be more heartrending to a young surgeon than to lose his first patient. Unless it was his present one—the president of the United States.

Charles glanced at his watch and then got up to wash his face and hands. The president should be coming aboard at any moment with his personal physician, Dr. Bryant, who was traveling with him. Keeping a man who loved food, especially Polish sausages, as much as Cleveland did on a strict diet was not an easy job. But the president had been made to realize the harm of overeating prior to an operation.

Wiping his hands on a towel, Charles heard the creak of the yacht and footsteps on the deck. And a few minutes later, someone knocked at his door.

When he opened it, Bennett Jamison said, "Our patient has just come aboard with Lamont, the secretary of war. He's asking for you. Are you ready?"

"Yes, as soon as I get my coat and stethoscope."

The two walked to the stateroom, where the president

sat in an oversized chair that was suitable for his oversized figure. He was surrounded by the other doctors in their white coats, and Charles, seeing the scene, was reminded of the ancient medical painting of patient and consulting physicians that hung in his private office.

"Good evening, Dr. Forsyte."

"Good evening, Mr. President."

Charles had already done his homework, going far beyond the president's case history. He knew he was a beer-drinking, cigar-smoking man, fond of outdoor sports. But Charles was more interested in the man's spirit, in his determination. He knew that it was the strong desire to overcome adversity that sometimes decided whether a man would live or die.

Grover Cleveland had more than his share of determination. Charles hadn't been in Washington more than a week before he'd heard people calling him "His Obstinacy" behind his back.

Charles listened to the man's heart through his stethoscope. The steady, strong, pulsing beat was a good sign. Then, using the blood pressure cusp, he took Cleveland's blood pressure. It was slightly elevated, but of course that was to be expected because of his excess weight.

"What did you eat for dinner, Mr. President?"

"Mighty little, Forsyte. A small fowl, potatoes, beans, and bread."

"Any alcoholic beverages?"

"No. A glass of buttermilk instead."

Charles nodded. "You may have water to drink until midnight. After that, nothing by mouth."

"I understand."

"I'm sure Dr. Bryant has explained the general procedure to you. Tomorrow morning at seven, the nurse will come in to shave off your mustache. Then you'll be given a slight sedative and taken to the operating area by eight o'clock."

"How long will the operation last?"

Charles hesitated. "Several hours. Longer, if needed. But you're in relatively good health, so I don't foresee any complications. Do you have any other questions?"

"How soon can I get back to work?"

Charles smiled. "If there're no complications, as soon as your mustache grows back to its former glory."

The president's hearty laugh filled the stateroom. But then he became more serious. "There's so much to do, with the upcoming special session. I've already been castigated by some of my detractors about taking a pleasure cruise at this time."

"I wouldn't worry about that if I were you, Mr. President. Your main concern now is to get a good night's sleep. Affairs of state can wait."

After bidding the president good night, Charles left the stateroom with Jamison. "Are you up to a stroll on deck before turning in?" Charles inquired.

"Yes. I'd like some fresh air."

The two stood at the railing and gazed into the distance toward the flickering lights. Their voices were deliberately muted to avoid the amplification of sound over the water.

"I hate to think what would happen to this country if Grover Cleveland didn't make it, Forsyte," Jamison commented. "You might not be aware of it, coming from England, but he's one of the few totally honest men in government today. We can't afford to lose him, especially now when we're on the very edge of bankruptcy."

Charles nodded. "I was aware of some of the problems before I sailed. A political cartoon in one of the London magazines portrayed Cleveland as an angry man driving the money changers out of the temple of government."

"Well, his action lost him the election to Harrison, but the people finally came to their senses once the treasury door was left ajar."

"Whatever the eventual outcome of the cancer, he'll probably be in the White House for most of his second term. That should give him time to set a lot of things straight."

"Unfortunately, the Senate is still a closed club of special interests. But I hear he's got a good man in Meadors from Kentucky."

At the mention of the name, Charles became abrupt. "I'd better turn in, Jamison. Today's been a strenuous day. Are you coming?"

"I think I'll stay out a little longer. See you in the morning."

"Good night."

Charles turned from the railing and rushed belowdecks, as if some hound were nipping at his heels. The scheduled operation had managed to push Allison out of his mind for a brief time. But with the mention of her husband's name, Bennett had spilled ancient blood and revived his nightmare.

That night, as the Benedict yacht rode at anchor, with the accompanying sounds of boards and halyards, Charles dreamed that he was adrift with no sight of land. From the time he'd first seen Allison with the other man, he had roamed a mythical sea, constantly searching for a faithful woman yet never finding her, and never reaching land.

During the past years, he had put the nightmare to rest with only an occasional recurrence. But with Jamison's unwitting words, he once again became the restless wanderer, doomed to a troubled night.

The odor of cigar smoke drifted through the air as the president and his friend, Commodore Benedict, stayed on deck well past midnight. Then they, too, went to bed.

Early the next morning, the steward's knock on Charles's door came far too early. But through the porthole, Charles could see the glittering sun. It was time to get up.

He went to the door, opened it, and, after seeing his breakfast tray, stepped aside while the steward entered. The man put the tray on the table and then was gone.

Charles had never considered himself a prima donna. Yet from the moment he'd set foot on this particular yacht, he had been treated as one, with his every physical wish fulfilled. And this morning was no different.

His appreciative eyes took note of the eggs, done to a turn, the bread warm and sweet, two kippers in cream, orange marmalade, and a pot of steaming hot tea. With Araminta as mistress of his house, he had never really enjoyed his breakfasts, for they had been prepared by an indifferent cook and served to him by an indifferent servant—until Ginna had taken over.

As he stared at the breakfast tray, he felt a sense of puritanical guilt. Here he was, getting ready to enjoy a bountiful breakfast while the president went hungry. But then he dismissed the guilt. The morning would be a wearing one and he needed all the sustenance he could get, whereas it was imperative for his patient to have no food at all in his stomach lest he aspirate during the operation.

One hour later, Charles was ready. As he walked toward the operating room, the *Oneida* crew hoisted anchor and set sail for Buzzards Bay. And along the shoreline, the citizens, eating their own breakfasts, going to work, or enjoying a lazy summer holiday, were unaware of the drama unfolding on the sleek luxury vessel passing by.

Dressed with sterile mask and gown, Charles joined the team of doctors and nurses. They waited while the first procedure was undertaken by the dentist: the extraction of molars from the affected upper jaw. And when that was over, the removal of the cancerous growth could begin. As the dentist worked, Charles could see that the nitrous oxide was not adequate as a sedative for a man as large as Cleveland. So before the more serious procedure began, he gave the anesthesiologist the signal to administer ether.

"Count to ten, Mr. President," the voice urged.

The president complied. "One. Two. Three . . . Four . . . Five . . . Si . . ."

His breathing became heavy; his pulse rate lowered. All signs indicated that it was time for the operation to begin.

The blue steel of the scalpel glinted as it caught the light from the bright electric beam overhead. For a brief moment, the scalpel remained poised in the air, an instrument of life or death fitted into the palm of the surgeon's hand.

With razor-sharp action, the first incision was made. As the work began everything but the operation was swept from the doctors' minds. With each incision, blood vessels were tied to keep the president's life blood from escaping. The sponge was ready at any time to absorb the seepage, as all members of the team worked rapidly. Each one was secure in his place. The procedure advanced, with the malignant growth attacked by the scalpel. The sound of deep sleep combined with the subtle, almost imperceptible noise of cutting and scraping against bone, sinew, and flesh. Curettage was done, the surgical instruments digging into the hidden recesses of cancerous cells, a fact attested to by the biopsy sent earlier to the Army Medical Museum for examination.

Carefully, dexterously, each centimeter of diseased tissue

was removed with an ever-widening circle of surrounding tissue.

The president's vital signs were carefully monitored, and the needs of both patient and surgeon were attended to. Beaded sweat formed on Charles's forehead. But it was quickly removed with sterile gauze, which was disposed of by one of the nurses before it could contaminate the patient's open wound.

One hour passed, then two. As one surgeon rested, another took his place, following the careful, expert path that had been set forth.

During all this time, Dr. Jamison watched, waiting and mentally measuring. His job would come later, for, as suspected, the cancer had spread into the entire upper jaw. It would be a tedious task to return the president's face to some degree of normalcy. But he was used to matching a vulcanized rubber prosthesis to the hearty, robust look of a man's face.

Charles quickly glanced at Jamison. Their eyes met in mutual understanding. He was glad that Jamison was part of the surgical team, for he was one of the best. Too many men, injured in the war, had lived out their miserable lives in back rooms, hiding from the public because of their hideous injuries. Only their families had known that they were still alive. Yet they, too, could have been helped, if there had been more men trained in Jamison's technique.

Once the operation was finally over, the president's collapsed cheek was packed with gauze to await the fitting of the prosthesis.

As the second team remained in the operating room to monitor the president's recovery, Charles and Bennett Jamison retired. They removed their surgical masks and gowns in the anteroom, scrubbed up, and then sought fresh air.

"Looks like Lamont is going to have his job cut out for him explaining the president's condition," Bennett said. "I hear the reporters are already waiting at Gray Gables for him."

"I see no reason why President Cleveland won't be able to walk under his own power by then. With the dentist at his side, there's a good chance that Lamont will get away with it, saying he merely had his teeth attended to."

Then Charles changed the subject. "Are you ready for a belated lunch, Bennett, or are you still seasick?"

He smiled. "This yacht is a lot smoother than the carriage ride, Charles. In fact, I think I could grow rather fond of sailing. I might even buy a small boat some time in the future. But for now I guess I'll just settle for a small bowl of soup. What about you?"

"I need something a little more substantial," Charles admitted.

The sun was now high overhead, priming the water with a glittering coat of gold while the darker hues of green and gray gradually crept and spilled over the rocky coastline.

For a moment, Charles watched the gulls flying, their impatient cries to each other filling the air. He was impatient, too, now that he knew the president would be all right. The operation had taken precedence over his personal life. But it was time for him to get back to Washington—and to his confrontation with Allison.

# CHAPTER
## 7

Allison was early.

She stood before the tall, enclosed fence and watched a pink flamingo stretch its neck and preen itself while balancing on one long, spindly leg. To the left, just beyond the water sanctuary, a tall giraffe gazed curiously at her and then returned to stripping the succulent green leaves from the upper branches of the acacia tree.

The park zoo was almost devoid of people. A young mother paused near Allison for a moment, gazing at the flock of pink birds. Then, as the child in the large-wheeled buggy grew impatient, she moved on, talking to him in crooning, soft tones that finally faded into the cacophony of animal sounds.

It had been five days since Allison's meeting with Araminta—five of the most nerve-racking days in her life. She had merely gone through the motions of living while she waited for Coin to get in touch with her.

Luckily, Jonathan had left Washington for Kentucky the morning after the party at Peggy Drake's house. Their early-morning conversation had been brief. Otherwise, Allison would have found it difficult not to break down and tell him the truth. But the slight reprieve had given her little respite from the churning in her stomach, the feeling of impending disaster that had even marred her few hours spent alone with Rad since then.

From the moment in the carriage when he'd leaned over to kiss her, she had felt as if she were a scarlet woman, living in sin. And because of it, she had been as skittish with him as one of the mares at brooding time. Yet, in the days that had passed, he'd been too busy to notice—or too polite to comment on her withdrawal from him.

Today, because she had not wanted a witness to her clandestine meeting with Coin, she had ridden to the park on Marquessa, the chestnut beauty that Rad had given her on their last wedding anniversary, rather than coming in the family carriage. The horse was now tied to a hitching post near the entrance.

Unknown to Allison, Charles approached, stood beyond the evergreen hedge, and watched her for a time. She was still beautiful and slender, as somehow he'd known she would be. With the old, familiar stirring at the sight of her, he straightened his shoulders and forced himself to walk slowly in her direction.

"Allison?"

She thought she would be prepared for the sound of his

voice, but she wasn't. A constricting band cut short her breath as she uttered his name. "Coin?"

"I prefer to be called Charles now."

"Of course."

The urge was strong for her to look at him fully, directly, to see what time had done to the face she'd loved so long ago. But he was standing against the blinding rays of the hot summer sun.

Quickly, he said, "We need to talk, Allison—not only about Ginna and Jonathan but about us, too. Would you like to sit on a bench, or would you rather go for a walk?"

"Let's walk for a while," Allison said. And they began to stroll away from the animals toward the stream where Allison had fled the afternoon of her visit with Araminta. She was aware of his presence beside her, the cool, antiseptic aura of a stranger so different from the warm, ardent young soldier who had fathered her firstborn.

"I—"

"Did you—"

"I'm sorry," Allison said. "What were you going to say?"

"Just that I know what a great shock it was to you, finding out after all these years that I'm still alive."

"I suppose it was just as shocking to you, too, to discover that I survived the war also."

For the first time they stopped and faced each other directly. Allison searched his face, looking for the familiar blue eyes, the shape of chin and jaw that had haunted her for so long. And as she met his gaze, she cried out the indicting words that she'd sworn never to utter. "Oh, Coin, how *could* you marry Araminta? You never even liked her. . . ."

Her words hung in the air, heavy and accusing, while

she waited for the man to defend himself. But she knew that any reason, despite its logic, would never satisfy her.

"When I came home to Roswell after the war, you had completely disappeared."

"And you didn't think enough of your own wife and baby to try to find us?"

Her questions, spoken in anguish, were almost more than he could bear. He couldn't tell her that he *had* looked for her continuously for two whole years, only to discover that she had already married someone else and had a son by that man. He must never let her know that he had found her—too late. As much as it hurt him to be thought an uncaring husband and father, Charles knew he must allow Allison to feel that *she* was the injured one.

"I thought you might have gone home to Savannah, if you and Morrow had survived. But Araminta hadn't heard from you, either."

"I took a job in the woolen mill to earn enough money to get back to Cypress Manor. But Rebecca and I were treated like criminals—arrested with the other mill workers and shipped northward."

"And Morrow?"

"She survived, too."

"Where is she now?"

"Living in Chicago with her husband, Andrew. You're a grandfather, Charles. A little blond-haired boy that you can never claim. He calls Rad Grandpapa."

Charles averted his face and tightened his jaw.

"I'm sorry," Allison said. "I didn't mean to sound so bitter. Whatever happened between us is in the past. Jonathan and Ginna are the important ones now. What are we going to do, Co—Charles? Araminta said we must not allow the marriage to take place. But that will break Jonathan's heart."

"Ginna's, too."

"Then what is the answer?"

"I think we should give our consent for the wedding, Allison. No one need know that you and I were once husband and wife. That's something that we shall always have to keep secret, no matter how hard it is."

"But what about Araminta? She was never able to keep a secret. And I doubt that I would have the strength to hide this from Rad. Jonathan, perhaps. But never Rad."

"Then you must tell him, Allison. As for Araminta, leave her to me."

"And you think it will work? That we'd be able to go through with it, knowing that you and I are still legally . . ." Allison couldn't bring herself to finish the sentence.

"Many families were separated during the war. What happened to us was not that unusual, Allison. We both had to make new lives for ourselves. Others did the same thing."

Charles longed to reach out, to smooth the troubled lines that marred Allison's brow. "Do you want me to talk with your . . . husband?"

"No," she said, much too fast, much too loud. Looking in the direction of children playing near the hedge, she lowered her voice. "Not until I talk with him first. It wouldn't be fair for him to hear it from anyone else."

"I understand. When will you do it?"

"I don't know. If I were brave, I would stay up and talk with him tonight after his committee meeting."

"The longer you put it off, the harder it will be."

"Don't you think I know that? I've hardly slept at all for these past five days, waiting for you to come back to town and get in touch with me."

She made a move to go, but Charles reached out to stop her. "Don't leave yet, Allison. Please. Let's sit down by the stream and talk. There're still so many things I want to know about you and Morrow."

And so, under the shade of a gnarled oak, Allison sat down. She removed her riding hat and smoothed her hair. But then she picked up her riding crop and twisted it in her hands as she stared in silence at the rippling stream.

"Is . . . Rebecca in Washington with you?"

"No. She died several years ago. But she has a daughter, Allie, who's almost her carbon copy. Allie works for Morrow now."

Charles took his handkerchief and mopped his brow. He didn't realize he had been holding his breath for her answer. He relaxed somewhat. "I suppose Rebecca named her for you."

"Yes."

"Tell me about Morrow. Is she as beautiful as her mother?"

"She's far lovelier than I ever was," Allison answered quickly. "Although she has my coloring—blond hair and the violet eyes—she also has some of your mannerisms. The same smile. And sometimes the way she holds her head to the side, waiting for an answer, reminds me—" Allison suddenly stopped. "You're doing it now."

"What?"

"Leaning to one side, as if to catch every syllable I'm saying."

Charles straightened immediately. "I wasn't aware."

"And Ginna? Who does she resemble?"

"That's right. You didn't see her the other day, did you?"

"No. Araminta had sent her away."

"She has Araminta's hair. But that's the only feature she inherited from her. In every other respect, she resembles my sister Anna Rose. You remember when we were first married we used to go together to put flowers on her grave."

Allison suddenly stood. It was not good to remember too much of the past. Especially now. "I have to go."

He was still loath to lose her. "But we've settled so little."

"That's true. But we can do nothing for our children's happiness until I tell Rad about the terrible nightmare that has encompassed us all. After that he'll want to talk with you, I'm sure."

"Allison, I wish it hadn't happened this way. Oh, God, I wish that—"

"No, Charles. Don't say any more. The past can't be undone."

For the first time, Charles Coin Forsyte looked old. The bleakness in his eyes spoke of unfulfilled dreams that had shattered in the uncompromising wake of reality. He watched as Allison turned her back and began to walk toward the entrance.

Then he rushed to catch up with her. "I presume you came by horseback?"

"Yes, I rode Marquessa. I thought it would be better if I didn't come in the family carriage."

The sounds of the animals in the zoo reverberated through the air—the shrieks of mynah birds and the trumpet of an elephant combining with the roar of a lion. Allison and Charles, walking together toward the exit, passed a bench where the young mother Allison had seen earlier was sitting with her sleeping child in the buggy beside her.

She followed their progress, as she had watched them the entire time. What a fortunate decision she had made to spend the afternoon in the park. Stanley Quail would be extremely interested in the news that his enemy, Senator Meadors, had a wife dallying with another man in a public park for all the world to see.

# CHAPTER
## 8

At the Female Art Institute, Ginna and her friend, Martha Gregory, sat near one of the studio windows and dipped their brushes into the same pot of gold leaf. Their dresses were protected by large white aprons, already smudged with various pastel hues from the paint pots.

"Do you think you'll finish your entire set of china before the wedding, Ginna?"

Ginna carefully traced the delicate swirl design on the teapot dome and then laid down her brush. "From the way things are going at home, I'll have enough time to finish *ten* sets."

"Why? What's wrong?"

Again Ginna hesitated. "Martha, sometimes I think that Mummy doesn't want me to get married at all."

"But if she's anything like my mama, she surely won't want you to be an old maid. According to Mr. Rouchard's *Book on Culture*, any lady who remains unmarried has few options. Teach school, if you have the intelligence for it, or take in boarders, if you have the house for it." Martha suddenly giggled. "My mother is doing everything to make sure I soak up plenty of culture. She thinks that's the only way to attract a husband. But she would *die* if she found out what I'm actually doing on Tuesdays."

"Aren't you going to music class?"

Martha shook her head. "Can you keep a secret, Ginna?"

"Of course. That's what friends are for."

"I'm learning how to use the typewriter. I'm going to become a secretary in a Washington office."

"Martha, you aren't!"

"I am so. Typing's a whole lot more fun than sitting here painting china."

"But what will your mother say when she finds out?"

"We might be genteel, but we're poor, Ginna. We've been poor ever since Papa left us and went west. But Mama has always been too proud to admit it out loud, even to me, until two months ago when I asked about going to college. You should have seen her face. It was the hardest thing she's ever had to do—telling me I couldn't go."

"But I thought you said your mother had her heart set on your marrying one of her boarders—that bachelor congressman."

"That's all she talked about from the time Mr. Cleveland got married to that young Miss Folsom. She tried everything to get Mr. Wells interested in me, but then she finally realized it wasn't doing a bit of good. Mr. Wells is a bachelor and every sign indicates he's going to stay a bachelor. All the china painting and music lessons are merely a waste of time and money."

"But how will you ever go about finding a job?"

"That's one good thing about Mr. Wells. I know he'll help me when the proper time comes. That is, when I get my certificate for the course."

"Ladies, it's time for cleanup now," a woman's voice said from the other end of the long, barnlike cavern. "Just leave your china on the tables. It will be safe until tomorrow."

The teacher began to circulate around the room, speaking to one and then another pupil. When she reached the space shared by Ginna and Martha, she beamed when she saw the teapot Ginna had been working on. "What a lovely work of art. I'm sure some young man will be most appreciative to have his morning tea poured from such an exquisitely painted teapot."

"Thank you, Miss Radnick."

In the same manner, she scrutinized the other pot beside it. But her smile became a little more fixed as her eyes turned from the china to Martha herself. "If I were you, my dear, I would work on some brilliant, scintillating breakfast conversation. Perhaps then your future husband will not be so disappointed in your lack of artistry."

"Thank you, Miss Radnick," Martha parroted, pretending not to notice the gentle insult.

As they walked out of the redbrick building, Ginna saw the family carriage. But instead of Barge, her father was waiting. "Oh, Papa has come for me," Ginna said, pleased. "Can we give you a ride home, Martha?"

"No, thank you. I'll just run along. And promise me, you won't tell a soul what I told you in confidence, about the typewriter."

"You have my word, Martha."

The two parted company, with Martha hurrying up the street while Ginna rushed to the carriage.

"I thought you were still out of town, Papa."

"I got home around noon," Charles commented. "So I decided to take off the rest of the day." He held out his hand to help Ginna up. And once she'd found her place beside him, he signaled the horses and began the leisurely drive toward home.

They had gone only a few hundred yards when Ginna, her parasol shading her face from the sun, said, "I'm glad you came for me, Papa. There're so many things I need to talk about. And it's much easier here than at home."

"What things, Ginna?"

Her eyes became sad. "To start with . . . Why does Mummy hate me so much?"

"Ginna, darling, what makes you ask such a thing? We both love you very much."

She reached over and touched her father's hand. "I've never questioned your love—for either Nathan or me. Or even for Cassie. But while you were gone, Mummy sent me away when Jonathan's mother came to call. And she won't tell me anything at all about their visit. She doesn't want me to marry Jonathan." Her eyes pierced Charles. "You *do* like him, don't you, Papa? If you didn't . . . if something happened to keep me from marrying the man I love, I think I would die."

Charles had wrestled with his own feelings all the way from the park. He was no stranger to the emotion his daughter was now confessing. But he knew that even though people might talk of a broken heart, the malady was seldom fatal. It was something one learned to live with, like a hair shirt, constantly chafing and reminding one of the hurt.

"Don't worry, pet. Your mother just has to get used to

the idea of losing you. And once the weather is cooler, she will more than likely be herself again."

"The weather won't help."

"Why do you say that?"

"Oh, Papa, you've pretended for so long that things would get better with Mummy, with each change of season. And I've always loved you for it. But I'm an adult now. There's no need for us to pretend anymore. She'll never change. Mummy is Mummy. And that's that."

"But—"

"Several days ago, Nathan told me about Rudy."

"Oh, Ginna, I'd hoped that you'd never find out."

"I guess Nathan couldn't keep the secret any longer. He wasn't supposed to know, either. Poor little Rudy. He was such a sweet and gentle dog. He didn't deserve to be chloroformed, Papa. I knew I couldn't bring him with me to America. But I'd found such a wonderful home for him. Why did Mummy have him put to sleep instead?"

"Sometimes, Ginna, I think your mother wants to hurt people because she's been hurt. She lost Cassie's father in the war, for one thing. . . ."

"If she loved him so much, then why did she tell him that she hoped he'd get killed by the Yankees rather than come home after the war?"

"Who told you that?"

"Cassie. A long time ago."

"Ginna, Cassie was terribly young when her father left. If she happened to overhear the two of them fussing, she must realize now that adults sometimes say things in anger, things they don't really mean."

Ginna sighed and tucked her hand under Charles's arm. "Papa, I hope you'll champion me just as strongly as you do Mummy."

73

"Wouldn't you rather have Jonathan Meadors wearing your colors instead of your tired old father?"

"You mean . . ."

"He's a fine young man from an excellent family, and I see no reason why the marriage shouldn't take place as planned."

She laughed with delight. "I knew once you came home you could make things right again."

Her confidence in him was too encompassing. Although he could wield a scalpel with unusual dexterity to help others, he was powerless to heal his own wound. As for his daughter Ginna, he might be able to persuade Araminta to behave herself for a short time. But he couldn't guarantee that it would last.

"Don't expect miracles of me, Ginna. I'll do my best. That's all I can promise."

"Thank you, Papa."

In the turreted white house where the ceiling fan on the side porch lazily turned with the slight evening breeze, Allison glanced over the freshly set table.

For the past hour she had been rehearsing her lines, as if she were an actress ready to walk onstage at Ford's Theatre. "Rad, I have something to confess." No, that sounded too much like an intentional sin. She started again. "Rad, you remember my telling you that Coin was killed in Virginia?"

No matter how she tried to frame them, the words still sounded foreign, like a monologue chosen for her by an unsympathetic playwright. But if she felt sorry for herself in being forced to say them, she felt equal sympathy for Rad, so unsuspecting of what the evening would bring.

She adjusted the bowl of musk roses, gathered from the garden. A small dark ant fell from the nectared sepal of a full-blown rose and landed on the white tablecloth. Like an Indian apologizing to a deer before drawing his bow, Allison murmured an apology even as she quickly removed the ant from the table.

And then she heard the small creak of the staircase, an indication that Rad was coming downstairs after his wash.

"We're going to have supper on the porch, Rad," she called out, walking toward the threshold of the large dining room.

She stopped in the doorway, smiled, and waited for her husband to appear. A lingering ray of sun pierced the shadows gathering around her, framing her into a snow-white frieze of stone until the breeze tugged at the sleeve of her delicate white lawn blouse.

He loved the way she looked: the pure, uncluttered simplicity of her dress with its single brooch, so different from the other Washington wives who decorated their bosoms as lavishly as they did their parlor mantelpieces.

"Go on and have a seat, Rad. I'll bring the food out."

"Isn't Browne here?"

"No. I let him go early. You remember he and Crete have a revival at their church tonight."

Rad didn't remember, but he nodded, anyway.

As Allison brought the food to the table—cold chicken, fruits, vegetables, bread, and cheese—Rad voiced his appreciation. "I'm so glad, Allison, that you recognize how hungry a man can get even in this hot weather."

Allison smiled. "I thought of giving you a presidential supper instead. . . ."

Rad laughed. "Crackers and buttermilk, my pet, and you would be sent home in absolute disgrace."

Allison's smile faltered for a moment. But quickly she remarked, "That must have been quite a blow to the hostesses in Chicago to have the president end the day at the

75

exposition with such a snack, when they'd gone to such trouble preparing a feast for him."

"Well, I can understand how tired he was after such a long day. And who knows? If this investigation drags out as long as most of us think it will, *I'll* probably be too old for solid food."

"Well, then, enjoy your chicken while you still have your teeth, Mr. Meadors."

A comfortable silence wrapped around them, the product of years spent together when words were not a prerequisite to a feeling of oneness. And if Rad did not sense the deliberate attempt by Allison to maintain this state of being, perhaps it was because of his own troubled conversation with Stanley Quail before his committee meeting that afternoon.

The twilight lingered; there was a lazy hum of bees in the garden. Gradually, the sun sank beyond the terraced lawn that disappeared into the darker shadowed row of trees.

Rad finished the fruit and cream dessert but made no effort to leave the table. Instead, he moved his chair and reached over to take Allison's hand.

"I didn't want to bring this up while we were still eating, Allison, but we have to face some unpleasant news."

"Oh? What news?"

"It concerns the Forsytes. I'm afraid it might put Jonathan's engagement in peril."

No. Those were *her* words—the lines she'd rehearsed to say to Rad. They shouldn't be coming from her husband's throat, but from her own.

At the alarm registered on Allison's face, Rad continued. "Just hear me out, Allison. Because the two of us need to decide what to do about the situation before Jonathan comes back to Washington next week."

# CHAPTER
## 9

"Stanley Quail is one of the attorneys who will be censured by the committee for fraud in the government pension windfall."

His remark made no sense to her. "Am I supposed to know this Mr. Quail?"

"Perhaps not by name. His wife is Ginna Forsyte's older sister. So you see how embarrassing it is for everyone concerned." Rad didn't wait for Allison to respond. "I don't think the man started out to do it deliberately. I fully believe he was reasonably honest. But the temptation became too great when he saw all the boodling going on around him."

"I'm so sorry to hear that. For Jonathan's sake—" Allison stopped short. She had almost given herself away, speaking of her late brother. For with Rad's mention of Ginna's married sister, she realized it had to be Cassie, her brother Jonathan's child by Araminta, who was married to Stanley Quail.

Unaware of the slip, Rad said, "Yes. It won't be too comfortable for Jonathan, especially with the enmity between Quail and me. We had a regular shouting match today."

"You have proof of his guilt?"

"Undoubtably."

The legislation passed in a previous session to give away hundreds of thousands of dollars to veterans from a war that had been over for more than twenty years had now resulted in a scurrilous scheme. For the legitimate claims of veterans had given way to fraud, with clients and certain attorneys banding together to share in the retroactive disability windfall that neither deserved.

"One of Quail's clients broke down today, under oath, and confessed that he'd never fought in the war, much less been injured. He'd gotten drunk ten years ago and hurt himself when he fell from his wagon."

"Perhaps Mr. Quail didn't know that, Rad."

"The man also testified that Quail had agreed to represent him and file all the necessary papers, including a bogus army discharge, in exchange for half of the windfall.

"But if it gives you any comfort, there are a dozen more lawyers guilty of the same thing. Only none of their actions has a direct bearing on our personal lives."

"Surely Jonathan and Ginna can weather this unpleasantness if they're forced to, Rad. But I am sorry that you're the one having to deal with it."

Rad searched Allison's face. Puzzled at her reaction, he said, "I thought this news would devastate you, Allison."

"Perhaps I have even more devastating news to share with you, Rad, than the actions of Mr. Quail."

It was now Rad's turn to become alarmed.

Allison continued. "Heaven knows I've spent these last several hours rehearsing what I was going to say to you tonight. But all of the finely turned phrases have left my brain. So I suppose I'll have to start somewhere, if I'm to tell you."

"Allison, wait. Before you say anything, let me tell you this. I know you've been unhappy here in Washington this past month. I've sensed it, yet I could do so little about it because of the meetings. But I don't want you to go back to Bluegrass. I want you with me for the rest of the summer."

"Do you, Rad?"

"Of course, even though I haven't stood on a soapbox to tell you. I suppose no man shows his true feelings every day, especially after twenty-five years of marriage."

"What would you say, Rad, if I told you that we weren't really married?"

"I'd say you have a mighty poor memory, my dear."

Allison reached out and touched a pink petal that had fallen from the bouquet. As she brushed her finger across its velvet texture, she said, "I've just learned that Coin Forsyth is still alive."

Without taking her eyes from the tablecloth, she waited for the full impact of her words to take effect.

The overwhelming silence was finally broken by a sudden chattering of squirrels in angry protest at the neighbor's cat, which had crept into the yard.

"How long have you known?"

Rad's voice sounded different, impersonal, with all the caution of a man holding a government inquiry.

Allison finally looked up and met his eyes. She longed to reach out to touch him, to feel his strong hand on her own, but he had withdrawn, much too far away for her to reach.

"How long?" she repeated. "Ever since I called on Ginna's mother the other day."

Her sense of outrage erupted. "He married my own sister-in-law, Araminta. And Ginna is *their* child."

Rad should have been more shocked at her confession. Yet he only felt relief. If Coin Forsyth had married again, then he was not free to take Allison from him.

"He changed his name to Forsyte. I have no idea why, unless it was easier for him in England. He was just as shocked as I was to learn that we had both survived the war."

"Then you've seen him?"

"Yes. This afternoon in the park."

"What does he want to do about this . . ." Rad hesitated. ". . . this turn of events?"

"He wants to meet with you to decide what's to be done about Jonathan and Ginna."

"How many people already know the truth?"

"Only the four of us—Araminta and Coin, or rather, Charles, and you and me."

"Ginna doesn't know? Or Stanley Quail's wife?"

"No. And Charles thinks we should keep it that way, for the protection of all concerned. I'm sorry that this has put you in such an awkward position. If you think there's even the remotest chance of scandal, then I'll leave Washington immediately."

"And what would that solve?"

"Well, with the pension investigation and the special session, it's imperative for your reputation to remain unblemished."

"You act as if everyone else around here is lily-white, with no skeletons in the legislative broom closet. That's not true. But do you think I care about my own position here, Allison? Lately, I've been thinking of retiring from Congress. But I'll leave when I'm ready. This matter won't precipitate it even if the whole world finds out."

"But it's such an awkward mess. And I'll be uneasy until you and Charles have talked and come to some conclusion." Allison hesitated. "He'll be at the medical clinic at Trask by nine o'clock tomorrow morning, but won't go into surgery until half past ten. Is there a possibility you could meet with him tomorrow morning?"

"Of course, Allison. I'll make the time. I suppose I should confirm the appointment?"

"It won't be necessary. He said he would leave the morning open."

"Allison, before I see him, I have only one question to ask you."

"Yes, Rad?"

"Do you still love him?"

"I love *you*, Rad. The man I saw in the park today is a stranger."

Rad nodded. He tried to disguise the relief that swept through him with her forthright answer. He pushed himself back from the table and stood. "I'll be in the library," he said, and left the summer porch.

But afterward, as Allison slowly gathered the dishes to take to the kitchen, she realized that she had not been entirely truthful. Of course she loved Rad. And the Charles Forsyte she'd met in the park *had* been a stranger to her. But for a woman, a first love was always a powerful force, finding a place in the heart that no later love could ever dislodge. Coin Forsyth had been Allison's first love, a fact that she had never been able to forget.

That night, when Allison and Rad retired for the night, he made particularly intense love to her. Allison knew that it was Rad's way of proclaiming that he alone had rights to her body.

The next morning, Rad carefully dressed for his meeting with Charles. It was not often, he mused, that a man was called upon to be this civilized.

As he walked downstairs to breakfast, Browne was already in the dining room.

"How was your revival meeting last night, Browne?"

"Got a little out of hand, sir."

"Why? What happened?"

"Well, Crete got to speaking in tongues and fainted dead away. Then, when she didn't come to, Bessie got upset and threw the holy water on her to revive her. That caused Crete to jump up sudden-like, and her arm whopped Deacon Jones on the side of the head."

Rad chuckled. "Is Crete all right this morning?"

"Yes, sir. She's in the kitchen cooking your eggs, but Deacon Jones, he's in the hospital with twenty stitches and a concussion from falling against the church pew. We're all going to have to chip in to help pay the doctor bill."

"Maybe Deacon Jones can claim disability from the war, like all the others are doing."

"What's that, sir?"

"I was only making a joke, Browne. A very poor one. I'm sorry about the deacon. How much will it cost?"

"Close to fifty dollars. And Crete and me are s'posed to come up with half of it. That was an expensive revival meeting, for sure."

"Don't worry about it, Browne. I'll give you a check to cover your part."

"I sure am grateful to you. But I didn't mention it just to get a contribution. . . ."

"I know you didn't. But you see, Mrs. Meadors and I couldn't do without you and Crete for the rest of the summer."

"I guess not. What with Mr. Jonathan's wedding coming up and all."

With Crete's entry into the dining room, there was no necessity for making further comment.

"Good morning, Major," Crete said, holding her head down in a penitent pose as she poured the coffee from the silver pot.

"Good morning. Oh, Crete, I let Mrs. Meadors sleep late this morning. Could you send up some tea in a little while?"

Relieved that he'd made no comment on her bandaged face, she replied, "Yes, sir. And I'll fix one of those new grapefruits that Miss Morrow sent from Chicago, too. She ought to enjoy that."

Halfway across town, Stanley Quail was also at breakfast. He was tall and erect, with thin lips partially hidden by his bushy mustache. His side-whiskers were equally fierce— to make up for his bald pate, which shone like a polished apple.

Seated at the other end of the table, Cassie tried to ignore the two nauseous-looking eggs staring up at her from her wedding china.

The summer sun had already begun its relentless morning ritual, soaking up any hint of dew or moisture from the air and causing the minute lines in the fine furniture that Cassie constantly fought against. She used beeswax and turpentine on her furniture as rigorously as she used buttermilk clabber for her skin.

At the east window, a ray of sun escaped past the heavy draperies and swept toward Cassie, as if deliberately seeking her out. She quickly held up her hand and turned her head. Stanley said nothing about her excessive aversion to the sun. To him, a few more freckles made little difference, but evidently to Cassie, even one more across her nose was anathema.

He had not married Cassie for her beauty, for she had little. And he hadn't married her for love, either. A good lawyer on his way up needed more in a wife than the ability to arouse his passions. His mistress took care of that need quite well.

Cassie had met most of Stanley Quail's requirements for a wife: a good family background, the ability to preside at his table well and to order servants about with confidence. And, of course, to give him a legitimate heir. But there was something else about Cassie that had attracted him. She was just as calculating and ambitious as he was. And with a wife like that behind him, there was no telling how far he could go.

"How are you feeling this morning, my dear?"

"Very well, Stanley. Thank you."

He knew it was a lie, but he let her pretend.

"Will you be coming home for dinner?" she inquired, speaking of the midday meal.

"No. I'm having a bite to eat with Mr. Campbell at his club."

Harriet, the maid, brought in a small silver tray with a card on it. "There's someone at the door waiting to see you, Mr. Stanley. She said it was rather urgent."

Stanley frowned when he read the name on the card. She shouldn't have come to the house.

"Please inform the woman that I do not see clients at home. If it's urgent, I will talk with her at my office in an hour. Here, I'll write down the address for her."

As soon as the maid disappeared from the dining room, Cassie said, "Who was it, Stanley?"

He folded the woman's card and dropped it in his pocket. "Oh, probably some hysterical secretary in trouble. Nothing to bother your brain about this early in the morning."

"Serves her right, for being in the workplace with men," Cassie commented.

"My feelings exactly."

As soon as Stanley left the house, Cassie walked upstairs. She stood at the window, as she usually did, watching her husband stride down the street. With a sense of alarm, she saw a woman suddenly appear and begin talking with Stanley. It must have been the woman at the door.

Cassie bit her lip as she watched the two together. He was smiling and talking with her as if he knew her well. And it didn't seem to matter that it was right under his wife's nose.


"I thought I told you never to come to the house, Maryann."

"But what I have to tell you, Stanley, couldn't wait until tonight."

"All right, then. Out with it."

"I saw Mrs. Meadors in the park yesterday. She wasn't alone. She'd come to meet another man."

Stanley was so pleased that he was almost, but not quite, ready to forgive her for coming to the house. He took her arm and moved on down the street until they were out of Cassie's sight.

•   •   •

Still at the window, Cassie looked down at her burgeoning waist. She felt no maternal love for the baby, only resentment for spoiling her figure and more than likely driving her husband into the arms of another woman, as her mother had warned.

Then she thought of her half sister, Ginna. She took special satisfaction in knowing that the same thing would happen to her, too. The young, handsome Jonathan Meadors would not be one to deny himself while his wife was producing a family for him.

Feeling better about it, Cassie went back to bed. And there she spent the morning, deciding on some subtle way to punish Stanley for his infidelity.

# CHAPTER
## 10

Along the shore of Lake Michigan, where the waters lapped against the seawall, a summer breeze finally took form and swept inland. Coming from the northeast, it held no hint of the stockyard odors that choked the city farther south.

To many, the smell of the Chicago stockyards was the smell of money. But the men who stood to gain the most from this pervasive odor could escape from the business district by late afternoon and enjoy the more sweetly scented air along the lake where their great mansions stood.

Others were not so fortunate. Crowded into multilevel tenements, the poor breathed the unhealthy air twenty-four hours a day. And little thought was given to alleviating their discomfort or to eradicating the disease that resulted from their overcrowded conditions.

But on this July afternoon of 1893, one of the more civic-minded young matrons left her brownstone mansion by the lake and began her weekly visit to the tenements. On her arm was a food basket filled with staples for the Andretti family.

The young woman was Allison's daughter Morrow, the wife of Andrew Lachlan, a talented young architect whose firm had been hired by the Pullman Railway Company. Accompanying her on her journey was her maid, Allie.

For two months, the Columbian Exposition had attracted visitors from all over the country, some even mortgaging their farms or selling their cookstoves to raise enough money to get to Chicago. With an eye to taking some of this money, opportunists had set up shop all the way to the entrance of Jackson Park, located five miles south of the business district. Prostitutes vied with the saloons and the chuck-a-luck gambling halls for their share, and the police merely turned their heads since they could do little about this sorry state of affairs.

It was into this melee of humanity that Morrow and Allie were forced to go, traveling by horse and carriage over rough roads paved with wooden blocks. The closer to the tenements they came, the more rude and boisterous the crowd grew.

"Hello, my lovely," a man's voice called out. "Come join me in a game of chance. I'll make it worth your while."

Morrow ignored the man. She kept her attention on the horse while Allie tightened her hold on the food basket.

A few blocks farther down the street, several brightly painted women lolled on a sidewalk in front of a bordello

while a parrot in the window screeched, "Come in, gentlemen. Come in."

Seeing a few toughs blocking the end of the street, Allie
said, "Miss Morrow, you think we ought to give up and go
back home? That crowd doesn't look any too friendly
today."

Morrow shook her head. "We'll be all right, Allie. I'm
sure they won't harm us. And we're almost there, anyway."

"I hope the Andrettis appreciate what you're doin' for
them. Right now they'd starve to death if it wasn't for you."

As they approached, the hostile men made no effort to
move out of the way until a street urchin's voice suddenly
cried out, "That's Mrs. Lachlan. Let her through. She's
come to see my brother Tony."

As if by magic, the crowd parted. The child climbed onto
the step of the carriage, and acting much like a gripman on
a cable car, he directed the carriage down the street. "I knew
you'd come today. I told Tony you'd get here. What have
you brought us?"

Morrow smiled. "Something to eat. And a toy that you
and your brother can play with."

As they drew up to the shabby tenement building where
the Andrettis lived, sharing their kitchen with four other
families, Allie remained outside with the horse and carriage.
Attention diverted for even a moment could result in the
sudden disappearance of the carriage. Allie was a large,
strapping young woman and could look intimidating when
she needed to. Today was one of those days when she felt
it was necessary.

"I won't stay inside long," Morrow said, stepping down
from the carriage. She held out her arms for the basket and
then followed the small urchin inside the tenement.

In a dark corner of the room, a ten-year-old boy lay on

a cot. He was sallow and thin, with a bandage wrapped around the entire length of his right leg.

Morrow walked over to the cot. "Hello, Tony. How are you feeling today?"

He lifted his head and smiled at Morrow. "All right."

"He's much better, Mrs. Lachlan," his mother assured Morrow as she wiped her hands on her apron. "The doctor says he might be well enough to go back to work in several weeks."

Morrow merely nodded. All of the volunteers at the settlement house knew how she felt about child labor. But the families involved were more difficult to convince, for they needed the money that a child working ten hours a day could bring home to the family.

"I brought some fresh fruit for the children, Mrs. Andretti. Along with an extra supply of staples."

"You're a kind woman, Mrs. Lachlan. And we're grateful to you. With Mario out of work and Tony hurt, it's been a hard month."

As the woman emptied the contents of the basket onto the crude table, Morrow said, "I haven't seen Andrea at the settlement house lately, Mrs. Andretti."

"No, the little *bambina* has been selling flowers at the fair. The man she works for lets her keep a few pennies at the end of each day. She should be coming home by dark."

Morrow thought of her own son, David, the same age as the six-year-old Andrea. But he was safe and secure at home with his Irish nanny, not fighting his way through the crowds with a few pennies clutched tightly in his fist.

Determined not to show her distress at the injustice of life, Morrow took a small book and a miniature wooden wagon with red wheels out of her bag. She leaned over the cot and said, "Share the toy with your brother, Tony. But the book is for you. You haven't forgotten how to read, have you, Tony?"

"No, Mrs. Lachlan. I remember."

Morrow was aware of the long drive back home, so she turned from the child and reclaimed the empty basket from his mother. "I'll be back next week, Mrs. Andretti," she said, and left the dark and dingy tenement.

"Marcello, ride down the street with the *signora*," Mrs. Andretti ordered. The child, who had remained hovering in the doorway, rushed over, picked up an apple from the table, and followed Morrow to her carriage. Again he hopped onto the step.

He became fierce in his protection of the carriage. And when a child a little younger than he attempted to catch a ride, too, he shouted a warning in words that Morrow could not understand.

At the end of the street, as the carriage slowed, he hopped down. *"Buona sera,"* he called out to Morrow.

"Good-bye, Marcello," Morrow responded.

The boy stuck one hand into his ragged pocket and nonchalantly retraced his steps homeward, while finishing off the remainder of his apple.

Immigrants loaded down with bundles of clothing—cut-out trousers and coats—hurried home from the sweatshops. Some of the women would stay up all night, Morrow knew, to have the clothes finished on time and taken back to their bosses. Even Tony's mother would be hard at work until nearly morning. She had one of the more thankless tasks and the poorest paying—that of embroidering the button-holes and sewing on the buttons.

"I wish Mrs. Andretti had better light to sew by," Morrow said.

"Then I guess next week one of Mr. Andrew's lamps will be comin' with us."

"Don't be impudent, Allie."

"No, ma'am."

On the way home, the odor of the city was even worse. No one seemed interested in cleaning the garbage from the streets or in building better housing for the poor. And the people themselves seldom complained about anything. They had seen what had happened to the more vocal ones.

"I didn't realize how late it is, Allie. I'll have to rush to get dressed for supper."

"Well, at least we don't have a house full of guests to feed," Allie commented. "Seems like everybody you've ever known has already come to the fair. And stayed with you and Mr. Andrew."

"All except Mother and Papa. I do want them to come before October."

Allie chuckled. "Too bad Miss Allison wasn't here earlier. She'd have put that uppity Spanish woman in her place, for certain."

Morrow sighed. "I'm sure no one on the committee would have invited the Infanta if they'd realized how embarrassing her behavior would be, especially toward Mrs. Potter Palmer."

Allie, who was a great mimic, suddenly developed a lisp. "No, I will not attend the party. I do not care to socialize with that *innkeeper's* wife."

Morrow laughed in spite of herself and then frowned. "Behave yourself, Allie. It's not nice to mock anyone, especially Spanish royalty."

Allie became silent but did not appear to be penitent. It was Morrow who became sad, remembering the beautiful party that her neighbor had given. The guest of honor didn't make an appearance just because Mr. Palmer owned a few hotels in his real-estate empire. But at least the two direct descendants of Columbus had been more gracious.

After all, it was in celebration of Columbus's discovery of America that the exposition had been conceived.

The carriage finally wheeled into the driveway and headed for the carriage house. Morrow turned the horses over to the stablehand and rushed inside to one of the tack rooms, where she had left a night wrapper. Once she removed her outer garments, she left them for Allie to air in the sun, for Morrow had no wish to bring home from the tenements any germs that might infect her son, David. Dressed in the wrapper, she hurried along the secluded path to the house.

While Morrow bathed and put on a fresh dress for the evening meal at home, her husband Andrew left the model community of Pullman, the city that his firm had designed for George Pullman to house his workers. In contrast to the shabby slums of Chicago, the three-hundred-acre community was a paradise, with yellow brick row houses, grass lawns, and parks. The streets were macadam and the sidewalks were lined with shade trees. A theater, a library, and a lake for boating and swimming made it a pleasant place to live. But by 1893, the people living there were far from happy.

As Andrew sat in the railcar at the end of the day and waited for the train to begin its seven-mile journey back to Chicago, he went over in his mind a worker's words he had overheard that morning.

"We're born in a Pullman house, fed from the Pullman shop, taught in the Pullman school, catechized in the Pullman church, and when we die we'll be buried in the Pullman cemetery and go to the Pullman hell."

Such was the frustration over Pullman's control of their

lives. But the man's complaint was safe with Andrew. He was not an informer, even though Mr. Pullman was said to pay many to let him know everything that went on. Yet trouble was brewing. Andrew could feel it in the air. It was evident throughout the town. And it was evident in the conversation of the grumbling shopworkers now gathered on the platform to go home to other areas, for the town had housing for only half of the employees. And that was why Andrew had come: to investigate expanding the project city.

Through the open window, Andrew could hear snatches of conversation.

"See you at the tavern tonight, Reilly," a young man called out to his friend.

"Hush up, Laddy," the man admonished. "You want to lose me job?"

"What's the harm in a pint o' beer after work?"

"Plenty, if your name's Mr. George Pullman."

"Lars, could you loan me the fare home?" one of the Scandinavians asked a fellow worker. "I'll pay you back tomorrow."

Andrew watched as several of the men scraped together ten cents to loan to the man.

The cut in the workers' wages, the rising rents, the lay-offs, and the charging for the train ride that had once been free were now feeding the smouldering resentment of men whose lives were totally controlled by one man. One day soon, the fire would ignite.

By the time Andrew opened the gate to the mansion by the lake, Morrow was seated near the parlor window. She put down her embroidery and watched him approach the house. Her pleasure in seeing him had not lessened, even after seven years of marriage. Tall and vigorous, he walked with an easy grace. He was handsome by any woman's standards, with his strong, craggy face and merry blue eyes.

But it was his sense of fairness and justice and his vision for the future that had caused Morrow's love for him to grow through the years.

She stood and went to greet her husband in the hall. "Welcome home, Andrew," she said, as he gave his hat and coat to Allie.

His smile was heartwarming. "Hello, my lovely," he said in his lilting Scottish brogue.

Allie giggled in spite of herself, for Andrew's words were identical to the ones spoken by the man outside the chuck-a-luck gambling hall that afternoon.

"Have I said something extremely amusing?" Andrew inquired.

"No, darling," Morrow quickly answered. "Allie is being impudent, as usual. I just may send her back to Mother if she can't behave herself."

"Perhaps it's time for your mother to visit us."

"Yes, that would serve the purpose just as well." Morrow smiled and left the hallway, with Andrew by her side.

With words used through the ages by wives greeting their husbands home from work, Morrow said, "Did you have a nice day?"

Andrew hesitated. "It was an unsettling day," he confessed. "But on the way home from Pullman, I finally came to a decision."

Morrow stopped. With her head inclined in a questioning pose, a mannerism inherited from her father, Coin Forsyth, she looked up at Andrew and waited for him to tell her.

"I'm turning down the Pullman project addition and selling my rail stock. There's trouble brewing. I don't know when it will actually come, but when it does there'll be a regular bloodbath. I'm afraid I won't have much sympathy for the owners—only for the poor working men."

# CHAPTER
## II

Charles stood at one of the windows in the Trask Medical Center complex in Washington and stared out at the quadrangle. Already the morning sun had begun its daily sweep along the paved paths between the buildings and in convoluted patterns had begun to attach itself to the Gothic-gray stone buildings as tightly as the aged ivy that clung to its walls.

A slight breeze through the filtered leaves of a nearby tree played about the open arched window and reached inside to riffle the papers on Charles's desk. But the paperweight was sufficient to keep them in order. The proposed medical budget for another six months was much too important to be scattered by the wind.

The medical center, although affiliated with the university system, was a separate entity, with its own operating budget and a near autonomy for its governing medical staff. Only twice a year was the director called upon to attend the trustees meeting, and that was mainly to get the budget approved, a mere formality if one were careful not to be too specific about the research department. Charles had been warned about that. The idea of exploring tissue for cause of death and disease was a touchy issue, for it had not been too many years since it was against the law.

Charles took out his watch to check the time. Nine o'clock. Any moment now, Allison's husband should be appearing. He left the window and sat down at his desk to review the medical journal that had just arrived from England.

He found solace in the familiar, for how did a man prepare himself to see another man who had taken his wife from him? In his medical practice, Charles had seen the best and the worst of humanity—all the follies, all the jealousies that had eaten away at a man's soul and caused him as much distress as any fatal disease of the body.

Since meeting Allison in the park the previous afternoon, Charles had fought hard not to allow his own emotions to rule him. But he was a man first. And he was aware that a medical degree meant little in matters of the heart. Emotions were primitive and could not be excised with the scalpel.

A knock at the door brought Charles to his feet so abruptly that he jarred the skeleton hanging in the corner. A macabre dancing of bones accompanied Charles's trek across the room to open the door.

"Dr. Forsyte?"

Charles stared at the dark-haired man who was several

inches taller than he. It had been over twenty years since he'd seen him, and then only from a distance. Now he was actually facing the man who had appeared in his nightmares during those early years.

"Major Meadors?"

"Yes."

"Come in, please. I was expecting you."

Charles made no move to shake hands. He had gotten out of the habit long ago, after being admonished by his mentor for doing so.

"Charles, your surgeon's hands are priceless. And you'd be a fool to risk harm to them by some sadistic bonecrusher trying to impress upon you how much character he has."

He motioned Allison's husband to a chair instead. "Have a seat, Major."

The two men sat across from each other. Like two stags, they sized each other up. Neither was in a hurry to begin the conversation. But Charles, as host, finally broke the awkward silence.

"I suppose Allison has already told you of our . . . of the past."

"Yes. And I understand the necessity of keeping it quiet for the moment."

"Especially because of Ginna and your son," Charles added. "I've thought about them for the past week, wondering what path we should take. I'd like to hear your thoughts on the matter."

Rad cleared his throat. The man before him was one he might eventually have sought out for friendship, if things had been different. As it was, he would never feel comfortable around him because of Allison. But his son's happiness was at stake and had to be considered.

"I see that we have problems, regardless of which direction we decide—to speak out or to remain silent, to give them our blessing to marry or not." Rad was cautious in his choice of words. "If we refuse to allow the marriage to take place because of some inadequate excuse, there could be trouble. I don't know about Ginna, but Jonathan would never be satisfied unless he was given the complete truth. Even then he might decide to marry her, with or without our blessing."

"And the other problem you foresee?"

"Our commitment to keeping the secret, if we agree not to tell them. There can be no turning back, no changing of our minds, once it's decided. The four of us will be honor-bound to lifelong silence."

"Then what shall we decide, Major Meadors?"

Rad looked at the man's face. It was difficult to tell what he was thinking, for he had hidden his thoughts behind his impenetrable doctor's mask. But Rad, too, was cautious, especially where Allison was concerned. Revealing the truth of the first marriage was tantamount to placing an advertisement on the front page of the Washington newspaper. He did not wish such notoriety for Allison, or his son, either, for that matter.

"I defer to you, Dr. Forsyte."

So here was the dilemma, skillfully placed back in his hands. Ginna had always received shabby treatment from Araminta. And it was only because of her coming to the States several months before the family moved there that his daughter had been able to escape Araminta's attention long enough to meet Jonathan Meadors. The young man would find someone else to marry if Ginna were lost to him. But Charles was not so sure about Ginna. He only knew he could not be the one to take away her chance for happiness.

"What happened in the past should not be allowed to keep the two young people apart, if they truly love each other," he said.

Rad nodded in agreement. "Then, for their sakes, I'd like to leave this office knowing that we have sworn to keep this former marriage a secret."

"Yes," Charles replied. "I think that would be for the best."

"Well, since it's settled, I'll say good day. I have a busy morning ahead of me and I'm sure you do, too." Rad stood, followed by Charles. And despite himself, Charles held out his hand to Rad.

With his departure, Charles felt at peace. The man was fair and honorable, as somehow he'd known he would be. Or else Allison would not have married him. Then Charles began to think of Araminta. And his sense of peace deserted him.

At Bluegrass Meadors in Kentucky, Jonathan galloped along the white rail fence that separated the pastureland from the house grounds. In the distance to the west, the great tobacco barns rose in the fields where the remaining stubble of leaves waited for burning.

And in the paddocks, the spring's drop of foals kicked up their heels and whinnied from sheer pleasure.

Jonathan laughed aloud, for he understood how the animals felt on this hazy day of summer. The music in the air—of bees and June bugs, of horses' neighs, and of the slight creak of the swing on the porch—was far sweeter to him than any sound of symphony or human voice. The love of the land was in his blood.

He would never be happy living in a crowded city, with its tall buildings blocking the view of the sun as it rose in the east. Yet he did not mind the occasional forays into the bastions of concrete, for it made his return to the land all the sweeter. And, of course, he would be forever grateful for the time spent in Washington this past year. If he had not worked on the special project with the Smithsonian Institution, he would never have met Ginna.

Jonathan pulled up at the barn in a cloud of dust and jumped from his mount. He patted the horse's flank. "You enjoyed the run as much as I did, didn't you, Breakers?" The old horse still remembered his derby days, but was now put out to pasture, serving as stud for future champions.

Jonathan walked the horse to let him cool down, and as he strolled leisurely with the reins in his hand, he thought of the changes he would like to make once he settled down with a wife and family. As much as he loved the thoroughbreds, he realized they were not a big money-making endeavor. Their beauty and the pleasure they gave were their own reasons for being, but as head of his own household Jonathan needed to start bringing in revenue rather than spending it.

"I'll talk with Andrew," he mused aloud, remembering his conversations with Morrow's husband concerning the new refrigerated boxcars that had changed the nation's eating habits. Shipping western cattle to Chicago could be the answer.

"Willie," he called out suddenly.

"Yes, Mr. Jonathan?"

"Finish walking Breakers for me and then give him a good rubdown. I have some business to attend to."

The stablehand took over, while an enthusiastic Jonathan, with plans spinning in his head, rushed inside to a paneled office and began a letter to his brother-in-law in Chicago.

That afternoon in Washington, Araminta undertook her midweek visit to Stanley Quail's house to visit her daughter, Cassie. The girl was unenthusiastic about motherhood. Of course, Araminta couldn't blame her. She had never let anyone suspect how she felt, but to Araminta, too, motherhood was vastly overrated, almost as much as being a wife was. They were merely the two duties that a woman had to endure in this life. And the less said about them, the better.

As Araminta climbed out of the carriage and walked up the steps, she realized that Cassie had done rather well for herself. Or rather, Araminta had done rather well for Cassie. For if it had not been for her seeking out all of the single young Americans in London at the assizes, Cassie would never have met Stanley Quail. Ingenuity had to be foremost when one had an eligible daughter. And it had taken ingenuity to arrange the invitations for Mr. Quail. Although Ginna had been much too young to be considered Cassie's rival, Araminta had also arranged for the girl to be away until Stanley had begun to show interest in Cassie.

Araminta frowned as she rang the doorbell for the second time. Then she heard the sound of footsteps.

"Good afternoon, Mrs. Forsyte."

"Good afternoon, Harriet," Araminta said as she entered the hallway. "Is my daughter resting?"

"I believe she is, Mrs. Forsyte. If you'll take a seat in the parlor, I'll tell her you're here."

"That's not necessary, Harriet. I'll go on upstairs myself."

Araminta brushed past the maid and began to walk up

the steps in the darkened house. Once she reached the top of the steps, she stopped to regain her breath.

With her gloved hand, she reached out and brushed the small mahogany table nestled under the small window. Turning her hand over, she saw the streak of dust that had adhered to the white glove. She quickly brushed it against the other glove and resumed her way to Cassie's bedroom.

"Cassie," she called out as she knocked. "Are you awake? It's your mother. May I come in?"

With a start, Cassie opened her eyes. She quickly sat up in bed and brushed her hair back. "Come in, Mama."

Araminta barely looked toward the bed. She walked past it to the bay windows overlooking the garden area. And there she proceeded to open the draperies and lift the windows for some fresh air.

"Mama, you don't have to do that," Cassie protested.

"Being in this stuffy room isn't good for you or the baby, Cassie. You need fresh air, as I've told you on numerous occasions."

And then, with some light in the room, she turned her full attention to Cassie. "You still have your wrapper on? You haven't even gotten dressed for the day?"

"I've *been* dressed all day, Mama. But I certainly don't want to ruin my clothes when I rest in the afternoons."

"Well, see that you take care of your appearance. It's bad enough to be so out of shape. You don't want to be slovenly, too."

"Do you have any other advice to cheer me up?"

"Don't be sarcastic, Cassie. I only have your good at heart when I tell you these things."

"Just as you had my good at heart the other day when you sent Nathan and Ginna here for the afternoon? Did they tell you what happened?"

"Nathan mentioned something about spilling his lemonade."

"It was much worse than that, Mama. They were in a conspiracy against me. They brought a *frog* inside my house—a live frog that hopped all over the place and gave me such a fright that I had to spend the rest of the afternoon in bed."

A sympathetic Araminta reached over to pat her daughter's hand. "There, there, Cassie. Don't worry about it."

"Aren't you even going to punish them? I can understand about Nathan. He's only a boy. But Ginna should have known better."

Araminta smiled. "I think you should be just a little sympathetic with your sister, considering what she's going through right now."

"You mean with the wedding to Jonathan Meadors?"

"There's not going to be a wedding, Cassie. As far as Charles and I are concerned, the engagement never took place."

Cassie sat up straighter. She could barely conceal her delight. "Why? What happened?"

Araminta hesitated. "It's a long story. And if I tell you, you must promise never to divulge it to a soul."

"Of course, Mama. I've always kept any secrets you told me."

"Cassie, you were probably too little to remember. But when Charles came to Savannah, I was a widow with little money. I had just lost the house that belonged to your father. And Charles's wife was *supposed* to have been dead."

"What do you mean, supposed?"

"Well, she has surfaced, after all these years."

"Oh, Mama, that's terrible. What are you going to do about it?"

"Nothing. You see, she has another husband and a bastard child by this man."

"But what does this have to do with Ginna?" Cassie suddenly put her hand over her mouth as she realized the significance. "Then Ginna is a bastard, too, as well as Nathan. Does she know yet?"

"No."

"When are you going to tell her?"

"We're not. We're just going to call off the wedding."

"That's wise. No man would want to be married to a bastard. Poor Ginna. There goes her chance for marriage." Then Cassie looked at her mother. "But what are *you* going to do, Mama? You can't keep on living in sin with Papa."

Araminta's voice grew sharp. "And what do you think I should do, Cassie? Allow myself to be thrown out onto the street? If I don't stay with Charles, then my only other alternative is to move in with you and Stanley. But how do you think Stanley would feel, learning that his own mother-in-law, even though it wasn't her fault, has two illegitimate children?"

"He wouldn't like it at all. I'm sorry that you told me, Mama. I wish you'd kept this terrible secret to yourself."

Cassie's delight at the initial news dwindled when she realized that she would also be tainted in Stanley's eyes, if he were to find out about her family's disgrace.

"But that's not all—"

"I don't want to hear any more, Mama. I have a headache. Please shut the draperies and leave me alone. You know it's not good for me to be upset. I have the baby to think about."

Cassie closed her eyes and rolled over onto her side.

Sometimes Araminta didn't understand Cassie at all. She glared at her elder daughter and then left the room, without closing the draperies.

"Oh, Mrs. Forsyte, I was just coming upstairs to see if you'd like some refreshments," Harriet said, as she met Araminta at the foot of the stairs.

"I really can't stay, Harriet. I just popped in to make sure my daughter was all right. I'll be going now."

Harriet rushed to get Araminta's parasol for her. And she merely shook her head as she watched the plump woman climb into the carriage and disappear down the street. Then she picked up the tray and headed upstairs for Cassie's bedroom.

To Araminta, her short visit with Cassie was unfulfilling. She had meant to tell her about Allison. And Jonathan, too. But Cassie had cut her off.

The heat of the afternoon was almost unbearable. Araminta took her handkerchief from her purse and wiped the tiny beads of perspiration from her upper lip. And in the safety of the carriage, she tugged at her corset stays, much too tight and uncomfortable. Then she again reached into her purse, this time for a small tin of sweets.

The candy had partially melted, but Araminta was now adept at savoring all of the chocolate, even the tiny traces caught in the ridges of the tinfoil.

After the first piece was gone, she chose a second piece and immediately began to feel better.

# CHAPTER
## 12

"It's settled, Ginna. Mr. Wells has recommended me for a position in a law firm. I'm to go for an interview this afternoon."

"That's wonderful, Martha," Ginna whispered, glancing at the art teacher on the other side of the room. "And I have good news, too."

"What is it?"

"Papa has given his consent."

"For your marriage to Jonathan?"

Ginna nodded.

"Oh, Ginna, I'm so happy for you."

"Well, he actually hasn't gotten Mummy's okay, but he will. He promised."

The two suddenly became absorbed in their work as the teacher began to walk in their direction. "Is there a problem?" she inquired.

Martha smiled. "Ginna was just giving me some pointers. I think I've been a little too liberal with the gold. What do you think?"

Miss Radnick put her pince-nez to her eyes and stared at Martha's work: a coffeepot that matched the teapot of the previous day. "Yes, Martha. You've had a rather heavy hand, I must admit. You mustn't be too extravagant. Just enough decoration without any undue ostentation. That's by far the best."

"Yes, Miss Radnick."

Once the woman's attention was diverted to another group working on the far side, Martha again began to whisper to Ginna. "The law firm is Motley, Anderson and Laird. Have you heard of it?"

Ginna's face did not reveal her surprise. So Martha might be working for the same firm in which Stanley was a junior partner. She prayed for Martha's sake that he would not be the one to interview her. If Stanley had anything to do with it, Ginna knew that Martha would not get the job.

"Yes, I know the firm," Ginna finally admitted. "Which one of them will you be seeing?"

"Mr. Wells talked with Mr. Motley, so I expect he'll be the one interviewing me. He owes Mr. Wells a favor, so the prospects are good."

"Oh, Martha, I do wish you well, if that's what you really want to do."

"I have my heart set on it, Ginna. And I'll be so disappointed if I don't get the job. I've been a financial drain on my mother long enough. It's time I started bringing in some money to help her."

Ginna hurriedly changed the subject. "Martha, if everything works out, will you be one of my bridesmaids?"

The young woman's face lit up. "Of course. I'd love to,
Ginna."

"Jonathan is supposed to get back to Washington day
after tomorrow. We'll start making our plans then."

Ginna made no further pretense of working. She was
worried about Martha. And she debated whether to tell her
that Stanley Quail, her brother-in-law, was a member of
the firm of Motley, Anderson and Laird. But no. Martha
might become too nervous if she were warned ahead of time
about Stanley's feelings on women in the work force.

Heaven knows, Ginna had gotten an overdose of his
thoughts and feelings every morning at breakfast during
those three months she'd been a guest in his house. To him,
studying art was all right, a genteel thing for a young
woman to do, like baking cookies or taking long walks—
chaperoned, of course.

But then, when Miss Radnick had seen her horse draw-
ings and consequently recommended her as one of the art-
ists to work on the special Smithsonian display of The
Horse in American Culture, Stanley had clearly showed his
disapproval. But Miss Radnick had won in the end.

She would always be grateful to Miss Radnick. If it had
not been for her, Ginna never would have worked with
Jonathan on the special project.

"You're a thousand miles away, Ginna," Martha said.

She smiled. "I know. I can't stop thinking about Jonathan
and how lucky I am."

And yet there were so many things that were unresolved.
For a brief time, Ginna had blossomed and felt a certain
independence. After all, it was nearly the twentieth century. But then, with her return to her mother's rigid care,

the new independence had vanished. Yet, with her father's blessing, that independence of spirit was finally emerging again. And her love for Jonathan now overshadowed her fear of Araminta.

When the china-painting class was over, Ginna put on her large straw hat with a wide brim. At the entrance to the building, she turned to Martha. "Good luck in your interview," she said as they parted company. And Martha responded by smiling and holding up two locked fingers in a gesture of hope.

Ginna looked across the street. The family carriage was not in sight, and rather than hire a hack to take her home, she hoisted her canvas artist's bag over her shoulder and, despite the heat, began to walk briskly.

She had walked only two blocks when she heard the sound of a carriage approaching and then an all-too-familiar voice. "Stop the carriage, Barge."

Ginna looked up into her mother's face and her shoulders immediately slumped. "Hello, Mummy," she said.

"Ginna, I'm surprised at you. Get into this carriage immediately before someone sees you."

All trace of independence vanished. Ginna obeyed, climbing into the carriage and taking her place beside her mother.

"Let Barge have that smelly bag up front with him," Araminta continued. "I don't want anything to spill out and ruin my new dress."

Ginna noticed the small chocolate stain already on her mother's bosom but said nothing.

"Here, Miss Ginna. I'll take the bag," Barge offered, turning around.

"Thank you, Barge."

As the wheels began to roll again, Araminta's voice took

up its petulant soliloquy. "I declare, I don't know what to do with you, Ginna. It's bad enough for you to be wasting your time in an art class. You have your father to thank for that. But I will not have you parading around Washington like a hoyden. People will get the wrong impression seeing you walk the streets alone like some modern Gibson girl. You have your family's reputation to uphold."

The refrain, "I only have your best interests at heart," was a familiar one to both Cassie and Ginna. Now it was set to the rhythm of the carriage wheels, with Araminta's occasional shortness of breath punctuating her sentences.

"Well, don't you have something to say for yourself, Ginna? Some word of explanation for your behavior?"

"I'm sorry. It's such a beautiful afternoon—"

"It's a hot, humid day," Araminta broke in. "No one in her right mind would be risking her complexion in this kind of weather."

"But I have my sun hat on—"

"Don't be sassy with me, miss."

"No, Mummy."

"No, *Mama*," she corrected.

"No, Mama."

Araminta's wrath was due partly to the way Ginna looked—like a blossoming rose, so in contrast to her beloved Cassie. And although Cassie had not been the meekest of daughters that afternoon, Araminta had already forgiven her. But she could never forgive Ginna for usurping the beauty that rightfully should have belonged to Cassie, her firstborn.

"Another thing, Ginna. With all of this frivolous art business, you've sadly neglected Clara's supervision. As soon as we get home, I want you to go to the kitchen and help her. Then, after supper, you can shine the pots and pans. They're quite dull-looking."

"But I thought we were all going to the theater tonight. Papa told me this morning that he bought tickets for the whole family."

"The play is not appropriate for either you or Nathan to see. You'll both be staying home."

By the time they reached the brownstone, a sad-eyed Ginna reclaimed her artist's bag from Barge and went upstairs to change into a suitable dress for helping in the kitchen.

Twilight hovered over the Potomac basin a long time before complete darkness set in. The day had been a long one for Charles. His conversation with Rad Meadors that morning now seemed as distant as the evening star appearing in the heavens. But the memory had lingered with him, giving his day a serenity despite the two long, delicate operations he had performed. And he was anxious to speak to Ginna. But first he would have to talk with Araminta and make her understand about the agreement.

Spotting the carriage some distance down the street, Nathan, who had been playing with his friend Pinky, said, "I've got to go now, Pinky. I see my papa coming home for supper."

"Remember what I told you. And don't be late tomorrow morning. Eight o'clock."

Nathan began to run down the street to his house. He arrived at the front door at the same time the carriage drew up in the alleyway. He opened the screen door, raced up the stairs, and hurriedly washed his face and hands. His blue shirt had a stain on it, but he didn't take the time to change. He brushed his hair instead and then raced back downstairs, arriving in the dining room as the supper bell rang.

"Hello, Papa."

"Hello, Nathan. Did you have a good day today?"

"Sure did. Me and Pinky—"

"Pinky and I, Nathan," Araminta corrected, taking her seat at one end of the table. "Your English is atrocious."

"Well, Pinky and I collected tadpoles at the creek, Papa. They're in a bucket at Pinky's house, and you can already see them turning into frogs. Their legs—"

"That will do, Nathan," Araminta interceded again. "Tadpoles and their limbs are not a suitable subject for the supper table."

"But, Mama—"

"That will do, Nathan."

"Yes, Nathan," Charles said gently. "We'll talk about them after supper, if you'd like."

"Papa, if one of them lost a leg, do you think it would ever grow back?"

"Nathan, another word about tadpoles and you'll go to your room." Araminta's face reddened in anger.

Charles quickly said, "Where is Ginna?"

"I'm here, Papa," she answered, taking her seat opposite Nathan.

Charles smiled and said, "Now that we're all together, shall we have the blessing?"

The supper went as well as usual, no better, no worse, until Charles mentioned the play that night. Shortly before Clara brought in the dessert—fresh strawberries with cream—Charles glanced at his watch.

"I told Barge we'd be ready to leave for the theater at quarter to eight."

Ginna looked from her father to her mother without saying a word.

With a quizzical expression, Charles examined his daughter's face. "Well, you certainly are enthusiastic, Ginna. Yesterday, you said you could hardly wait to see Mrs. Pelligrew. Have you changed your mind so suddenly?"

"Papa—"

Araminta cut in. "Ginna will be staying at home, Charles. And Nathan, too. I don't know what you could have been thinking, to buy tickets for the children. I've already told Ginna that she has sadly neglected her duties here. Tonight she'll be helping Clara shine the pots and pans."

Charles's jaw tightened. "If you want Nathan to stay at home, that's fine. But I see no reason for a young woman who's engaged to be married to be treated like a child."

His attention turned from Araminta to his daughter. "Ginna, go get dressed in your new pink organza. The pots can certainly wait another day. And Araminta, I'd like to see you in the parlor. Immediately."

Nathan's mouth dropped open at the fierceness in his father's voice. He looked from his mother to his sister and back again at his father as he left the table.

With a decided pout on her face, Araminta carefully laid down her linen napkin and followed slowly. As soon as she was out of the dining room, Nathan whispered, "You'd better hurry, Ginna. Before Mama has a sick spell and *nobody* gets to go."

"You don't mind, Nathan, staying home tonight with Clara?"

"Naw. I got to get up early tomorrow morning, anyway. Me and Pinky . . ." He stopped. "Pinky and I are starting a new project."

As soon as Ginna left the dining room, Nathan looked

at the open door. Seeing no one to observe him, he wrapped the leftover bread and half-filled jam jar in his napkin and carefully stashed them in a wooden box near the rear entrance.

He and Pinky would be gone a long time and he couldn't risk taking too much from the table at breakfast, especially with his mother looking on.

# CHAPTER 13

Charles closed the double doors to the parlor to ensure privacy. "I saw Rad Meadors today. Allison's husband," he added.

Araminta was still angry about his behavior at the supper table. "You mean, the man she's been *living* with all these years."

"No, Araminta. Her husband." His voice was firm. "And we came to a decision. I want you to understand that there is now no turning back. Ginna and Jonathan will be married, as planned, and the secret of what happened in the past will remain a secret. It will go with us to our graves."

"And what if I decide differently?"

"Then you will be turned out into the street."

A shocked Araminta looked at Charles. Tears sprang to her eyes. "What a cruel thing to say to your wife, Charles."

"You can't have it both ways, Araminta. If Rad is not Allison's husband, then you cannot claim to be my wife."

"But that's different. *I'm* the injured party. I was a widow; I agreed to marry you only because I thought you were free to marry again."

"I seem to remember, Araminta, that you were the one to petition *me*. And I felt a sense of responsibility toward you and Cassie because of my friendship with your husband in earlier days. But that is neither here nor there. It's in the past. In the eyes of the world, you and I are still husband and wife, even though we haven't shared a bed for quite a few years."

"You know my condition, Charles. I never really regained my strength after Nathan was born. I thought you understood, being a doctor, that it wasn't good for me to have another child."

"Your childbearing days are over, Araminta. But don't worry. I have no desire to force you into being a true wife again."

To Araminta, it was extremely humiliating for Charles to talk in such a vulgar way to her. "I don't think I want to hear any more, Charles."

She stood up to leave, but Charles detained her. "We're going to finish this conversation, Araminta. Sit down."

Once again, a startled Araminta looked at the gentle Charles whom she had been able to manipulate through the years. She didn't know what had caused him to behave this way toward her. Well, yes, she did. It was Ginna, of course. But the two of them wouldn't get away with it. They'd both be punished. Beginning tonight.

Araminta sat down again and searched for her handkerchief. She said nothing as Charles continued. "From now on, you will behave yourself. You will be an exemplary mother of the bride until Ginna has left Washington. And you will remain quiet about the past. I've given my word to Meadors, and I expect you to abide by our decision. If you choose to do otherwise, then you'll be sorry, Araminta. That, I can guarantee."

"You needn't threaten me, Charles."

"Just so you understand the seriousness of the matter. Now, go on upstairs and get ready. We leave for the theater in twenty minutes."

Araminta stood. "I won't be going, Charles. You've completely devastated me with your tirade. I feel so weak I shall have to take to my bed."

"Then, by all means, do so. Since Nathan will be staying at home, I'm sure you won't mind if Ginna and I go on. It would be a pity to waste *all* of the tickets."

A furious Araminta, panting hard, swept from the room and fled up the stairs. For the first time, she had been completely thwarted by Charles. She couldn't bear the thought of Ginna's enjoyment at her expense. All afternoon the girl had pretended to be a meek and dutiful daughter. Well, let them go to the theater together. By the time Ginna returned, she'd be sorry she'd ever left home that night.

Right at quarter to eight, Ginna appeared at the top of the stairs. Her father was waiting for her in the hallway. He watched as she made her way down each step, the sound of the pink organza swishing as she walked. She had put her hair up and encircled it with pink organza roses, matching the ones on her dress. And on her arm she carried a small white cape. When she saw him looking up at her, she smiled, her face lighting up. "I didn't keep you waiting, did I?"

"No," Charles assured her. "But come. If you're ready, we'll go out the front."

As they started toward the door, Ginna said, "Where is . . . Mama?"

"She's decided not to go with us, Ginna."

"Is she feeling ill?"

"She'll be all right. I've talked with Nathan and told him to watch after her, to see if she needs anything while we're gone."

Still Ginna hesitated. "Perhaps I should run up and tell her good-bye."

"If you wish."

He watched her rush up the steps and disappear. And then he heard the gentle knock on a door. "Mama, may I come in?"

"No, Ginna. Go away. I'm resting and don't want to be disturbed."

"I'm sorry you don't feel well enough to go with us tonight."

There was no reply. Reluctantly, Ginna turned from the closed door and made her way once again down the stairs. "I'm ready now, Papa."

"Brighten up, Ginna. Don't let your mother spoil your evening. I know how you've looked forward to this play."

"Yes, Papa."

Upstairs, Araminta waited behind the curtains of her bedroom window until the carriage disappeared beyond the streetlight. Then she tiptoed down the hall to the narrow staircase leading upward to the attic studio set aside for Ginna.

The stairs creaked under Araminta's weight. Halfway up, she stopped to listen. She didn't want to alert Nathan. But then she heard his excited voice floating up from the kitchen. Clara would keep him occupied for a while. She needn't worry.

Through the studio skylight the new moon cast a glow, its gossamer streaks of yellow touching the easel and the chair directly beneath. Hanging on the peg near the closed dormer window was Ginna's artist's bag; various shapes of paint pots were arranged along the shelves. And on a small table an old brown earthenware jug held an assortment of brushes jutting in all directions, like some futuristic, leafless flower arrangement.

The air was stifling hot, causing Araminta discomfort. She walked to the window and flung it open for some fresh air before pursuing her evening's work. Then, without turning on a light, she began to open the paint pots and dribble their contents on Ginna's works.

The large canvas of horse and rider rested on the easel— Ginna's secret oil painting that was to be her wedding present to Jonathan. With particular satisfaction, Araminta chose a paintbrush from the earthenware jug. And taking the small jar of India ink, she plunged the brush into the indelible black liquid and set to work on the oil canvas, completely obliterating the painting.

Araminta smiled as she finally left the studio. The slight summer breeze coming through the window deliberately left open was the only witness to the carnage done that night.

As Araminta made ready for bed, she frowned at the black stain on her thumb. Despite her scrubbing vigorously with soap, the mark remained.

Finally giving up, she brushed her hair and then climbed into bed. For Araminta, bedtime had an unvarying nightly ritual. Propped up by pillows, she took the latest fashion book from her bedside table, opened the tin of chocolates, and then settled down for a pleasant hour before drifting off to sleep.

Ford's Theatre held a powerful fascination for Ginna. Lincoln's assassination in the president's box was every bit as dramatic as anything that had ever happened onstage.

Sitting only two boxes away from the presidential box, she glanced quickly to see if Mr. Cleveland or any of his family was present that night. But the box was empty.

There was a certain noisiness in the theater. The bustling and chattering of the people taking their seats in the audience vied with the backstage sounds as props were put into place. *The Lady of the Camellias* was to be given that night. It had been made famous by Sarah Bernhardt, the great French actress. But Washington would have to be satisfied with the American actress, Mrs. Pelligrew, instead. Ginna decided that she would be more than content to see Mrs. Pelligrew in the title role, for she had been fearful that she might miss seeing the play altogether.

Shortly before the houselights grew dim, Ginna saw Rad Meadors and a beautiful woman take their places in the private box to the right of theirs.

"Papa," Ginna whispered, "is that Mrs. Meadors with the senator?"

Charles looked up from his program. "Yes, it is."

He and Rad nodded to each other while a shy Ginna tried to get a good look at Jonathan's mother without being too obvious. Their eyes met, and when Allison smiled, Ginna brightened and returned the smile.

Already, Mrs. Pelligrew's performance took second place in Ginna's mind. But once the curtain opened, her attention turned to the play being enacted onstage.

It was all she had hoped for and more. Caught up in the

tragic love story taking shape before her eyes, Ginna was visibly moved. But then she bit her lip to keep back the tears. It was only a play, after all, she reminded herself. And she shouldn't risk being thought too maudlin, especially in front of Mrs. Meadors. She reached into her purse for a linen handkerchief at the moment that the first act ended and the houselights came on, signaling intermission.

"I needn't ask you how you liked it, Ginna," Charles teased. "I see from the tear on your cheek that Mrs. Pelligrew has woven her spell over you."

"Oh, Papa, I didn't mean to embarrass you."

"It's all right, Ginna. There's no need to be ashamed of tears shed over the human condition. Would you like to get up and walk around a bit? The next act is quite long."

The red curtain at the back of the box opened. "Dr. Forsyte?"

Charles stood. "Senator Meadors. Mrs. Meadors. May I present my daughter, Ginna."

"I'm happy to see you again, Ginna," Rad said. "But I don't believe you've met your future mother-in-law. This is my wife, Allison."

"How do you do, Mrs. Meadors."

Allison's face was kind. "You're even lovelier than Jonathan led me to believe."

"Thank you, Mrs. Meadors. And I think *you're* beautiful."

Again Allison smiled. She turned to Rad. "Do you mind if I stay to get acquainted with our new daughter, Rad?"

"Not if I can interest Dr. Forsyte in joining me for a brandy."

"I'd be delighted."

The two men left Ginna and Allison together. The older

woman quickly asked, "Would you like to stroll along the mezzanine?"

"Not unless you wish to do so."

"Then we'll stay here in the box."

Ginna waited for Allison to take a seat and then she sat down also.

"I feel as if I already know you, Ginna. Jonathan has done nothing but talk about you since I arrived back in Washington. I was sorry to miss you the other day when I called on your mother."

"I'm sorry, too, Mrs. Meadors. I was at my sister's house."

"But now that we've met at last, I can tell Jonathan that I agree completely with him. You're a charming young woman. Welcome to the Meadors family, my dear."

Allison leaned over and brushed her cheek against Ginna's in an expression of acceptance. Ginna was overwhelmed by her graciousness.

"Have you heard from Jonathan?" Ginna suddenly asked. "When is he coming back to Washington?"

"His letter stated that he would be arriving some time late this evening. But didn't you get his letter to you? He said he was writing to you at the same time."

"No, I haven't heard from him."

Allison frowned. "That's strange. Something must have happened to delay it." Her frown suddenly vanished. "You'll probably get it after he returns. He was so enthusiastic in his letter to us about a proposed project. He wants to go into some new venture with Andrew, Morrow's husband. They live in Chicago, but they'll be coming to Washington for the wedding."

"I just want you to know, Mrs. Meadors, how much I

love Jonathan. And I'm going to try to be the best wife that anyone could ever be."

Allison's amethyst eyes became moist. "I can see how much you love him, Ginna. That's all that really matters." She reached for her lace handkerchief. "Heavens, how emotional we are." She dabbed at her eyes. "We'll never hear the end of it from the men in the family if we're caught shedding tears this early. We'll have to save them for the wedding."

"I wasn't sure that you would approve of me, Mrs. Meadors. As a suitable wife for Jonathan . . . because of the way we met."

"The way you met was perfectly respectable for a modern young woman. And with my best friend, Peggy Drake, chaperoning you both, no one could fault the courtship. My only regret is that I wasn't in Washington at the time so that I could have met you before Peggy did. She'll never let me forget that it was she who brought you two together. But we can make up for that. Are you free to come for a visit tomorrow afternoon?"

Ginna hesitated. "I'll be at the art institute until two o'clock."

"Then Jonathan can call for you there."

"Yes, that would be lovely."

"Then it's settled."

By the time the men returned and the lights were lowered, Ginna's heart was singing. At last she felt as if a bright future with Jonathan was now in store for her, and not even the tragic ending of *The Lady of the Camellias* could touch her that night.

# CHAPTER 14

Later, Ginna lay in bed, listening to the night sounds—the creaks and groans that all old houses seem to have when its occupants are quiet enough to hear them.

And then the wind began to whistle and moan, as if engaging in midnight conversation with the old brownstone. Somewhere a loose shutter banged back and forth, but Ginna was much too tired to find it and secure the latch. And so, with its steady rhythm, it merely served as a hypnotic pendulum lulling her to sleep.

When, toward morning, the summer rain finally arrived, with flashes of lightning punctuating the sky, she was oblivious to all except the sweet dreams that were hers.

Far too early, Clara was bending over to wake her. "Miss

Ginna, if you don't get up now, you're gonna be late for class."

"What time is it, Clara?"

"Almost nine o'clock. Your papa's been gone for two hours. He said if you weren't up by now, to come in and wake you since you have an important day today."

Ginna sat up and quickly brushed her hair from her eyes. Clara was right. She had so much to do. She leaped out of bed and started to run for the bath.

"You want your coffee first, Miss Ginna?"

"No, Clara. I don't have time. Jonathan's back, and I'm going to have such a marvelous day. Absolutely nothing can spoil it. Please, could you help me? Find my light blue dress and petticoat and lay them on the bed for me?"

"You're not afraid of ruining that pretty new dress? Wearing it to class?"

"I'll just have to be extra careful, that's all. I'm going straight from the institute to Mrs. Meadors's house, and I don't have time to come home and change. Is Mummy up yet?"

"No, ma'am. She's still asleep. But Nathan's up. Had his breakfast a long time ago and he's already gone, too. Pinky was waitin' on the steps for him."

Ginna shut the door and turned on the shower. Clara found the dress and laid out Ginna's underwear. All the time Ginna was in the shower, Clara continued talking. It didn't seem to matter that no one was close enough to hear her. And when Ginna returned to the bedroom, Clara was still talking.

". . . Minnie's my friend, you know. Works at the same hotel where that Mrs. Pelligrew is stayin'."

Ginna smiled and responded as if she had been in the room the entire time. "I saw her last night onstage, Clara. Has Minnie seen her up close?"

"That she has. Made up her bed yesterday. She didn't even get up until late afternoon. And then she lounged around until early evenin'. Had a light supper in her room with that Mr. Garling," Clara confided. "Minnie went back to take some extra towels later, and she still had on her negligee. Sittin' across the table from that man as merry as you please, and her with nothin' on underneath that negligee. They's strange folks, those actors, Miss Ginna."

"Well, it might be nice to live as you please for once," Ginna said wistfully, "not having to care what other people say about you."

"Menfolks have always lived that way. I got me a cousin, Obadiah. Been married four times and only buried one wife, his last one. Now all the widows in the church are chasin' him like he's a saint. One'll get him, too. Mark my words. And then someday one of his other wives will finally catch up with him. And then what's he gonna do?"

Ginna laughed. "He'll have to become a sea captain."

"How's that, Miss Ginna?"

"One of our neighbors in England was a sea captain's wife with six children. Her husband sailed back and forth to China. He was gone at least six months at the time. And it turned out that he had a Chinese wife and eight Chinese children, as well as the English family."

Ginna slipped on her dress. "Close your mouth, Clara, and button me, please. And promise me you won't let Mummy know I told you."

"Is it all right if I tell my friend Minnie?"

"Just so you don't tell her where you heard it."

Once Ginna was completely dressed, she went downstairs to the dining room where the breakfast toast was hidden under a napkin. Quickly, she filled her coffee cup from the silver urn and took several sips. It was tepid.

"I'll get some hot coffee for you from the kitchen, Miss Ginna."

"Never mind. This will do fine. Barge is already waiting with the carriage."

Ginna took one last bite of toast, another sip of coffee, and then rushed to the mahogany clothes tree for her hat and parasol.

"You need me to do anything else for you?" Clara inquired.

"Oh, I almost forgot. My artist's bag. Could you get it for me, Clara, while I write a quick note to Mummy? She needs to know I won't be coming home until late this afternoon."

While Ginna sat down at the desk, Clara trudged up the two flights of stairs to Ginna's attic studio. But when she opened the door she lost all thought of her errand.

As if demons had flown into the open window that night to do their mischief, the once neat studio was in shambles. Clara stood just inside the door and her hand reached up to her throat. "Lordy, Lordy, sweet Jesus," she moaned.

Everywhere, ugly paint had been dribbled over the paintings. The little watercolors thumbtacked to the wall were no longer of delicate wildflowers, but strips and ribbons of dissonant color that didn't stop at the edges of the paper but continued down the walls to form dried pools at the baseboard. It was not a matter of one jar accidentally spilling over. Like a whirling dervish of mischief that twirled about the room, wreaking havoc, someone had come into the room, deliberately removed all the tops, upset every paint pot, and poured the contents onto every example of Ginna's work.

Clara shuddered. She was afraid to look about the rest of the room, especially at the oil painting directly under the skylight.

"Clara, did you find it?" Ginna's voice called out from the landing below.

"I'm comin', Miss Ginna," she replied, and hurried to take the bag from the peg. What was she going to do? The girl had awakened so happy that morning, and telling her now would only spoil her entire day. Maybe she should wait. It wasn't as if the mess was going to go anywhere before she came home.

Carefully, Clara closed the door and began to retrace her steps. "Here it is, Miss Ginna. Now you run on and have a real good day."

"You'll see that Mummy gets the note? I left it on the table in the dining room."

"I'll be sure to put it on her breakfast tray when I take it up in a little while."

With a quizzical expression, Ginna looked into Clara's face. "Are you feeling all right, Clara?"

"Just a little touch of rheumatism, Miss Ginna. It'll pass."

"I'm sorry. I didn't realize. I should have gone after my bag myself."

"Now run along and stop apologizin'. That's what I'm here for."

Ginna hoisted the bag onto her shoulder, stuck on her hat, and hurried toward the back door, while a shaken Clara went back to the kitchen and sat down.

A half hour later, she heard Araminta's bell. Carefully, she poured the hot chocolate into a cream pot, took the sweet rolls out of the warming oven, and set them on the bed tray. With Ginna's note carefully laid beside the plate, Clara climbed the stairs again.

"Good mornin', Miss Araminta."

"Yes, it *is* a good morning," Araminta agreed. She plumped up her pillows and waited for Clara to set the tray across her lap. "Did Ginna get off to school all right this morning?"

"Yes, ma'am. She was in a big hurry, though. Overslept because of last night. But that's her note to you on the tray."

Clara watched Araminta. She made no attempt to read the note. Instead, she picked up the cup of chocolate and daintily sipped it. The telltale smear of black India ink was still on her thumb. Clara saw it and she knew then who had been in Ginna's studio.

"You need anything else for the moment, Miss Araminta?" Clara asked.

"No, Clara. That will be all."

"Then I'd better get back to the pots and pans."

"Well, stop staring at me and go."

"Yes, ma'am."

Araminta frowned and set down the chocolate. She began to butter a sweet roll and then she became aware of the stain on her hand. Quickly, she dropped the knife and hid her hand under the counterpane. She did not resume eating until Clara left the room, closing the door behind her.

She would have to do something about the stain before Ginna came home. It didn't matter that Clara had seen it. The woman was far too stupid to connect her to the devastation in the attic. Or so Araminta thought.

Midmorning at the institute, Ginna stared down at her own hands, dirty with the telltale residue of her charcoal pencil. Absentmindedly, she took out an old white cloth from her bag and wiped them clean. In front of the drawing class, the lush still life of fruits and flowers caught the light as the class continued to capture it in studies of black and gray. But Ginna had lost interest. Of far more importance to her was Martha's empty chair.

She had waited impatiently for her friend to arrive at

school. Ginna had so much to tell her. She was used to keeping disappointments to herself, but happiness was a different matter. It had to be shared for a person to savor its full measure.

The bell finally rang, indicating the end of class. Ginna gathered up her things and slowly walked outside to the small courtyard of trees and grassy lawn. Finding a bench in the shade, she pulled out the sandwich that Clara had prepared for her and began to eat it.

"Oh, there you are, Ginna. I was afraid I wouldn't find you."

"Well, you certainly are a ten o'clock scholar, Martha. I thought maybe you weren't even coming today."

"I know I'm late. But I just had to come to school, even for one class. I got the job, Ginna."

Martha sat down on the bench beside Ginna and unwrapped her own sandwich. "I start on Monday. Isn't that the most exciting thing you've ever heard?"

"I think it's wonderful. Have you told your mother yet?"

"No. I wasn't actually hired until this morning, at the second interview. I'll tell Mama tonight, after all the boarders have left the parlor."

"I have some good news, too."

"What?"

"Jonathan is back from Kentucky. He's coming for me after class, and I'm joining his mother for tea."

"Then you'll probably be deciding on your wedding date this afternoon."

"Probably. Subject, of course, to Mummy's approval."

"Just think. Here we are, all grown up. I'm going into the world of commerce, and you're getting married." Martha took out the other half of her sandwich. As she removed the piece of cheese that she didn't care for and began to feed it to the gathering pigeons, she said, "Why didn't you tell me that Mr. Quail works in the same law firm with Mr. Motley?"

"I just . . . Well . . ." Ginna was seldom at a loss for words, but somehow she couldn't think of an adequate excuse.

"Oh, don't worry. I don't think he really recognized me as your school chum. But I will be typing for him from time to time. At least that's what Mr. Motley said."

"I didn't want you to worry, Martha. About the interview. But now that you actually have the job, it really doesn't matter what Stanley thinks."

"Oh, I get it. He probably doesn't like the idea of women out of the kitchen."

Ginna laughed. "You see, I didn't have to tell you, after all."

"Well, I'll have to tell Miss Radnick this afternoon that I won't be coming back to class after today." Martha stood. "It will more than likely be a relief to her."

"Miss Radnick likes you, Martha. We'll both miss you. But what are you going to do about your china?"

Martha smiled. "I think I can finish some of the saucers today. But since I have such a talented partner in the class, I thought maybe *she* might finish the set for me."

"Why don't we go in and ask her?"

"But that's what I thought I was doing. You don't mind, do you, Ginna?"

"Of course not."

Students in small groups began to stroll toward the classroom building. Ginna and Martha joined them, and they worked steadily in the studio for the remainder of the day.

Then, when it was quitting time, Martha stayed behind to talk with Miss Radnick, while Ginna nervously smoothed her lustrous dark hair, bit her lips for color, and ran down the steps to meet Jonathan.

# CHAPTER
## 15

Jonathan swept down the deserted street in a dead heat with the clock. The carriage careened to the right at the curve and then righted itself on the full stretch as the road widened and became arrow straight and sure.

"Whoa, Angel," Jonathan called out to the lead horse, the big gray with the star set into her forehead. He watched with admiration as she broke pace and caused the big black, Daemon, beside her, to do the same, slowing up and then coming to a stop amid the fury of snorting nostrils and tosses of the head to show Jonathan her displeasure at being stopped just when she was in full stride.

"We made it, Browne," Jonathan said, glancing at the clock in the tower. He thrust the reins into Browne's hands.

"Here, take over for me. I'll be back with Miss Forsyte in a few minutes."

For the last quarter of a mile, the servant seated on the box with Jonathan had kept his eyes closed. The sting of the wind against his face had told him how fast the horses were flying, and he'd clung to the seat with all his might. When Jonathan and his horses got together, it was like being dragged into the Kentucky Derby holding on to the horse's tail.

"One of these days, Mr. Jonathan, there ain't gonna be nothin' left of us except a wet spot on the road."

An amused Jonathan turned his head and looked back. "You can go as slow as you want on the way back. In fact, the slower the better."

He walked on, past the courtyard and toward the side door of the ugly redbrick building.

"Ginna!"

As she stood on the steps, her large-brimmed hat shading her face from the afternoon sun, she looked in the direction of the voice. And when she saw its owner, her heart gave a sudden little jolt. Jonathan's dark hair was ruffled by the wind, giving him a carefree look despite his immaculate attire. It was this that had attracted her to him the first time she ever saw him, that freedom she envied—an exuberance for life, so in contrast to her own staid existence.

"Jonathan."

Her face lit up, bringing love to her eyes, as she followed his progress toward her. He was tall and handsome in a disconcerting, masculine way, with an open, unguarded face that spoke of assurance and an innate trust in mankind. How different he was from Cassie's husband, with his thin lips set in almost constant disapproval.

"Here, let me carry your art supplies," Jonathan said.

Their hands touched as she relinquished the satchel to him, and he was in no hurry to break contact.

"I've missed you this past week, Ginna."

"I'm glad. Because I missed you, too, Jonathan."

They stood, staring into each other's eyes, unaware of the other students walking past. Then Ginna suddenly realized where they were, and she removed her hand.

As he began to direct her toward the waiting carriage, an impatient Jonathan said, "Well, what did you think of the plans?"

She looked up at him. "I'm not quite sure what you're talking about, Jonathan. The wedding plans?"

"The ones I wrote about in my letter. Have you had a chance to think about them?"

"I'm not sure . . ." She stopped as they reached the carriage. She nodded to the driver and waited for Jonathan to help her up. When she was seated, he climbed in beside her.

"Browne, take a turn around the square before you start back to the house. We're in no hurry."

"Yes, Mr. Jonathan."

As the horses began a steady trot down the tree-lined street, Jonathan returned his attention to Ginna. "You were saying?"

"At the theater last night, your mother asked me about a letter. But, Jonathan, I haven't received anything from you since you left. So I have no idea what you're talking about."

"That's strange. I posted both letters at the same time—one to my mother and one to you. I felt sure that you would have gotten it by now."

"But I haven't. So you'll just have to tell me what it contained."

"Oh, no. I think I'll wait until the letter arrives."

"Jonathan, stop teasing me."

He laughed. "We can discuss it later this afternoon. Somehow, just being with you seems more important right now." He reached over to take her hand. "Do you remember that afternoon in the park when we first met?"

His question brought a smile to her lips. "Yes. But I've never told a living soul about it. And you must promise not to do so, either. My family thinks Mrs. Drake was the one who introduced us."

"When it was really my horse."

Ginna sighed and relaxed. As they drove around the square with her hand hidden in Jonathan's, she thought of that April day when she'd taken her watercolors to the park to capture the cherry blossoms and ended up making a portrait of a beautiful horse instead.

"Angel sat quite well for her portrait that day," Ginna said. "Almost as if she knew I was drawing her."

Jonathan smiled, remembering his first glimpse of Ginna in the park. She'd had the look of timelessness about her that all great beauties enjoy. And because of it he had realized that she might seem out of place to some prone to judge beauty merely by the current fashion of the day.

Her auburn hair had framed her face in a manner all its own. She'd appeared unconcerned with its look and oblivious also to her young, budding figure hidden beneath a plain blue dress and artist's pinafore, a figure free from the corsets that others wore in the name of conformity.

There'd been a sweet shyness about her that day that could easily have been misunderstood and taken for aloofness.

"I'll never forget watching you as you sat on the grassy slope with your sketchbook," he said. "You were aware of

Angel and nothing else. And I was afraid to claim her until you were finished, even though I was already late for an appointment."

"Oh, Jonathan, I didn't know that. I'm sorry."

Jonathan tightened his hold on her hand. "I think I was trying to decide whether you were a mirage. You see, you looked as if you had just stepped out of a French painting, with your long hair half hidden under that ridiculous straw hat."

"So you think it's ridiculous, do you? Well, thank you very much."

"You're welcome."

He glanced at Browne sitting on the box and then leaned over to whisper in Ginna's ear. "I adore you, Ginna. Can't you tell? And I don't want to wait much longer before marrying you. When I was at Bluegrass Meadors this time, I wanted you beside me, to see everything that I was seeing, to share my days and my nights, and all my dreams for the future. . . ."

"And I want to be with you, too, Jonathan. Papa has given us his blessing, so we can go ahead and make our plans. I'll have to consult Mummy, of course, about the details."

"Browne, stop dawdling," Jonathan suddenly called out. "Let's head for home."

"Yes, Mr. Jonathan."

Browne grinned as he turned the horses around and traveled east. He'd pretended not to pay any attention to the whisperings in the carriage, but, in truth, he'd listened unashamedly to everything the two had said.

The horses picked up speed, and by the time the carriage finally reached the curved driveway of the turreted, white clapboard house, with its weathervane catching the glint of the afternoon sun, a still impatient Jonathan said, "Let us off at the garden entrance. I want to show Miss Forsyte something before we go into the house."

Browne brought the carriage to a stop, and Jonathan jumped down. He held out his arms for Ginna, swept her to the ground, and led her past the rosebushes to the small white gazebo partially obscured by the crepe myrtle trees.

A questioning Ginna looked at him as he lifted the seat cushion and pulled out a small box from underneath it.

"I have a surprise for you, Ginna. Sit down and hold out your hand."

She did as she was told, while he leaned on one knee beside her and held the small, red velvet box.

"Right after the war, my Uncle Glenn absconded with all the family jewels. But about ten years ago, my grand-mother's ring turned up at an auction in Kansas City. My father recognized it and bought it back, for me to give to my bride one day. I got it out of the bank vault, Ginna, when I was in Lexington three days ago. I want you to have it as my engagement present to you."

He took her hand and slipped the emerald and diamond ring onto her finger. "Wear it in love and happiness, darling."

"Oh, Jonathan. What can I say? It's so beautiful. Thank you."

He stood, slowly removed her wide-brimmed hat, and, with the filtered sun catching the sheen of her hair, pulled her to her feet. Gently, he looked into her moist, azure-blue eyes.

The reality of the kiss was far greater than anything she'd ever imagined. In his arms, Ginna felt his lips on hers, searing his claim to her with the intensity of fire against flesh. He took his time, drawing from some hidden, un-known wellspring in her inner being an emotion that had lain dormant, waiting for its awakening at the appropriate season. And when he finally lifted his head to gaze into her eyes again, she began to tremble, so devastated was she at her response to him.

"My sweet, little, innocent Ginna," he said, holding her close. "There can never be any turning back for us now. You have unleashed a passion that will never be content again with a mere kiss."

"I never knew . . ."

"The sooner we marry, the better. Come now, let me look at you and see whether I've compromised you totally."

"Jonathan, I don't think I can go inside just yet. Your mother will be able to tell . . ."

He laughed. "Yes. You look as if you've been thoroughly kissed. But is that so bad? She was young once. She'll understand."

Allison had heard the sound of the carriage and was waiting for them in the summer room adjoining the more formal parlor. The white wicker furniture with cool aqua chintz cushions gave the room an informality and a serenity, and it was this ambiance that Ginna felt immediately as she and Jonathan entered.

"Welcome to our home, my dear," Allison said, coming to meet Ginna.

"Thank you, Mrs. Meadors. It's a pleasure to be here."

Allison noticed Ginna's hand. "I see that Jonathan has already given you his present."

"Yes. The ring is so beautiful. And I'll always treasure it." Ginna glanced shyly at Jonathan before she continued. "I have a gift for Jonathan, too. When he takes me home later this afternoon, I'll give it to him then."

"Come and have a seat. Would you like a glass of lemonade? Or do you prefer hot tea?"

Ginna hesitated. "Whatever you're going to have is fine with me."

"Lemonade," Jonathan decided. "A nice, big glass of iced lemonade. And some of those petits fours that Crete made this morning."

Seeing the way the two looked at each other, Allison was glad that she and Rad had chosen not to object to the marriage. And if she'd thought that Ginna would stir up unpleasant memories of the past for her, she realized now that it would not be so. The child was endearing, a person in her own right, apart from Coin and Araminta and the emotional vestiges of the past. Or perhaps it was because she *was* Coin's child that Allison could love Ginna already. No, she was *Charles's* child. And she must remember to think of him by that name. Coin had been buried in the Virginia wilderness along with his name.

"I think I'll go and see about the refreshments," a considerate Jonathan suggested, leaving the room so that his mother could have some time alone with Ginna.

As he walked into the kitchen, Crete was arranging the little sandwiches and petits fours on a tray.

"Well, it's iced lemonade, Crete, for the three of us. Don't bother with the tea."

"I'll have things ready in a jiffy, Mr. Jonathan."

"Take your time. We're in no hurry." He reached over and filched a sandwich from the tray.

"Mind your manners, Mr. Jonathan. You're ruinin' my arrangement."

"That's the general idea. We need to stay in the kitchen long enough to give my favorite girls a chance to get to know each other."

"Well, if you eat more than three sandwiches off my tray, I'm goin' on in, acquainted or not."

"Then I'll start on the petits fours instead."

"Maybe you could get the ice pick and chink us off some ice for the lemonade."

A few minutes later, with that job completed, Jonathan walked back from the kitchen to the summer room. "Crete's on her way," he announced.

"We were just talking about the family bridal veil, Jonathan," Allison said. "Ginna would like to use it with her own dress, for the wedding."

"It would mean a lot to me, Jonathan," Ginna said, smiling, "knowing that it had been worn by your mother and your grandmother."

"It would please me, too, Ginna." Then Jonathan suddenly smiled at Allison. "But that's the only family heirloom that will be allowed. I have no intention of wearing my father's wedding clothes. It might start the war all over again."

Ginna laughed. "Jonathan told me that Senator Meadors served in the Union army. And although I was born in England, my mother was from Savannah originally. She was there when the city was captured."

"That's a coincidence, Ginna. My mother came from Savannah, too." He turned to Allison. "Do you think you might have known Mrs. Forsyte's family at one time?"

Allison's hands suddenly became busy, adjusting the ruffled chintz pillow. "I . . . I left Savannah so many years ago. . . ." She looked up and saw Crete coming in with the silver tray. With relief, she said, "Oh, here're the refreshments now. Just set the tray on the table, Crete. We'll help ourselves."

The awkward moment passed. But Allison was now aware of a new danger that no one had foreseen. Once Jonathan and Ginna began comparing family stories, then it was only a matter of time before they would come to the certain conclusion that part of the past had been deliberately kept from them.

# CHAPTER
## 16

By the time Ginna arrived back at the family brownstone, it was late afternoon. Never knowing what her mother's mood would be, she was always a bit uneasy whenever she returned home. But the pleasantness of that particular afternoon spent with Jonathan had dulled her natural caution. And, too, she was anxious to give him his engagement gift.

"I hope you'll like it," Ginna said as she stepped down from the carriage and began to walk with Jonathan past the wrought-iron gate. "I've been working on it steadily for the past three months."

Jonathan's right eyebrow went up in a quizzical, teasing manner. "*Three* months?"

Ginna's face turned pink. "Actually, at the time I began

working on it, I had no idea that you would ever ask me to marry you."

Ginna held up her hand to admire the brilliance of the ring she now wore. "And it's nothing so dear as this beautiful ring, so I hope you won't be too disappointed."

"I'll never be disappointed in anything you do, Ginna."

"You say that now. But wait a few years and then tell me that."

She eagerly walked into the entrance hall, with Jonathan beside her. "Mummy," she called out. "We're back."

But it was Clara who came to greet them. "Miss Araminta isn't home yet. She's gone to look for Nathan. He disappeared early this morning and didn't even show up for his midday meal."

"Do you think we should help look for him, Ginna?" a worried Jonathan asked.

Ginna shook her head. "My little brother's stayed away this long before. He's probably with Pinky. Catching tadpoles again down at the creek. I expect he'll be home in time for supper. But thank you, Jonathan, for offering."

She turned to Clara. "Mr. Meadors and I are going upstairs to the studio, Clara. Please let me know when Mummy is back."

She had taken only a few steps when Clara said, "Miss Ginna?"

"Yes?"

"I think you'd better wait downstairs."

Ginna laughed. "Clara, Mr. Meadors and I are going to be married soon. Besides, you're in the house to chaperone us. That should take care of any likely gossip."

"It's not that, Miss Ginna."

"Then don't be a spoilsport, Clara."

"No, ma'am."

143

Jonathan looked from the servant to Ginna. Then he followed an eager Ginna up the stairs to the attic studio.

"It's hot up here this time of the day," Ginna explained, "so we won't be able to stay long."

They passed the landing of the first flight of steps, walked down the second-story hall to the end, where the narrow staircase to the attic was concealed. The once bare plaster walls of the attic entrance had been painted in a trompe l'oeil effect, giving it a feeling of outdoors, so different from the dark woodwork and walls downstairs.

Noticing the light, frescoed walls, Jonathan said, "Did you paint all of this?"

"Except for the frog in the pond. Nathan did that. He's partial to frogs and tadpoles. That's why I'm not worried about him this afternoon. He'll more than likely come home with another frog for his real pond in the garden."

Ginna stopped in front of the studio door. "Here we are." She turned the handle, pushed the door open, and hurried inside.

Nothing had changed in the studio since early that morning when Clara had come upstairs. Standing in the middle of the room, an incredulous Ginna looked at the disarray, the destruction of all the work she had done for the past months, and a chilling realization took form.

"No!"

Her hands went up to her face. Somehow, she'd always known this might happen. But she couldn't bear it, with Jonathan looking on. She had to protect him. "We shouldn't have come," she said. "Oh, Jonathan, don't look. Let's go back downstairs."

She began to rush for the door, but a frowning Jonathan reached out to stop her. "What's happened, Ginna? Who has done this to you?"

Frantically, Ginna looked at the window. "I must have left the window open. Perhaps a bird flew in during the night—"

"No, Ginna. You and I both know this isn't the work of some poor, trapped bird. This was done deliberately—to hurt you."

"Please, Jonathan. I don't want to stay. I want to go back downstairs."

But Jonathan was in no hurry to leave the studio. Slowly, he walked over to the easel, where he stood and stared at the ruined oil painting. Studying it, he vaguely recognized the portrait of his horse, Angel. And in the saddle sat a man whose face and form had been mutilated by black India ink.

"This was your present for me."

"Yes."

"It was a masterpiece, Ginna. I can tell that despite what someone did to deface it."

A fierce, protective feeling spread through Jonathan, causing a darkness to come to his face that Ginna had never seen before.

"I'm so sorry you had to see this. I don't know who could have—"

"No, Ginna. You don't have to pretend with me. I'm sure you know who did it, but I won't pry. I'll just make doubly certain that you're out of this house as soon as possible. You don't belong here."

His comforting arms drew her close to him. He leaned over and brushed a tender kiss against her forehead. "Clara wanted to protect you, too, didn't she? That's why she didn't want us to come upstairs."

"I suppose so."

"All right. We've seen more than enough. I'm sorry, especially for the loss of the painting. But once we're at Bluegrass, we'll fix up another studio for you—not in an attic but downstairs, near my office, where the breeze comes in. And you can paint to your heart's content."

With his arm around her, he led her to the door. "You're not to come back in here, Ginna, ever again. When we close the door, you'll be putting an end to your life in this house. Don't mention to anyone—not even to Clara—what you've seen today. It's not important. Think only of the life that's ahead of you—the one you and I are going to share."

Clara waited and listened in the hallway. But when Ginna appeared, she merely said, "Mr. Meadors won't be staying any longer, Clara. When Mummy comes home, I'll be in my room."

With a composure she didn't know she had, Ginna walked with Jonathan to the front door.

"I'll call for you tomorrow, Ginna. At the institute." He smiled and added, "I'm proud of you, darling. Hold your head high and don't deign to acknowledge this morbid little charade. It's only important if you decide to make it so."

"I love you, Jonathan."

"And I love you. I'd like to show you how much. But I'm afraid Clara would be quite shocked to witness it."

Ginna smiled. "Then you'd better go, Jonathan. Now."

He took her hand and kissed it. "Tomorrow," he whispered, and hurried out the door.

"Move over, Browne," he said. "I don't know about the horses, but *I* certainly need another run to clear my head."

"Mr. Jonathan, the sooner you get back to Kentucky with that little gal, the safer it'll be for everybody in Washington."

Jonathan did not follow his advice to Ginna. Far from ignoring the travesty done to her, he was furious. Angel sensed his unrest, breaking into a fast stride before the carriage had disappeared down the street.

Like the wind they traveled, leaving the more sedate carriages behind in a trail of dust, while Browne once again held on to the box and wondered if he would live to see his wife, Crete, again.

"Nathan, one more time of staying away all day without letting me know where you are, and I vow I'll pack you off even before the school term begins."

Araminta's day had not been a good one. By midmorning, she had given up trying to remove the stain from her thumb. She had been forced to wrap it in a bandage. But that was not a good idea, either. Especially if Charles demanded to look at the bogus wound. She had even contemplated cutting her finger, but in the end she couldn't bring herself to do it. And then to be faced with a runaway eleven-year-old . . .

Nathan hugged the jam jar, now filled with tadpoles instead of jam. He glanced sideways at his mother. And he knew he'd better keep quiet.

"Well, do you have anything to say for yourself?"

"I lost track of the time. Pinky and I—"

"I don't want to hear that boy's name. He's a bad influence on you, Nathan. And you're not to see him again. Ever. Is that understood?"

"But, Mama—"

"There'll be no arguing with me, young man. I'm going to see that your father gives you a good hiding when he gets home."

A miserable Nathan hugged the jar even closer to his chest as he edged toward the side of the carriage. His mother's bulk had taken up his share of the seat, too. It wasn't that she was that large. She just seemed so when she was angry. And during those times, Nathan had a feeling that he might smother if the carriage happened to lean too far in his direction.

"Stop fidgeting, Nathan. You're going to spill that creek water all over me if you're not careful."

"I'll be careful, Mama."

Barge whistled to the horses, slowing them down as they pulled into the alleyway. He finally drew up at the rear entrance of the brownstone and hopped down to help his mistress from the carriage.

"You'd better start out for the clinic immediately, Barge. Dr. Forsyte will be waiting."

"Yes, ma'am."

"Mama, may I ride with Barge?"

"No, Nathan. You're to come inside and clean up."

A sympathetic Barge glanced at the boy and then quickly became absorbed in adjusting the horse's bridle until Araminta turned her back to go inside.

"You better put those tads in the pond right away, Nathan," Barge whispered. "They had a rough trip home."

"I know. I think one's already dead. He's floating at the top."

"Nathan!"

"I'm coming, Mama. Just as soon as I find my wet stockings."

Nathan ran around to the side yard, hurriedly emptied the contents of the jam jar into the small garden pool, and was back by the time Barge pulled out of the alleyway again.

An hour later, a quiet Forsyte family sat down to supper. Charles looked at Araminta and then at his two children.

"I trust everyone had a pleasant day," he said.

"Yes, Papa."

"Yes, Papa."

"Not everyone, Charles. I certainly didn't. But I'll wait until after the meal to discuss it. I don't believe in airing problems at the table, as you well know."

"Yes, I'm aware of that, Araminta." Charles was also aware that it was Araminta's way of spoiling the family meal—the promise of some insignificant problem, blown out of all proportion, hanging over their heads like a sword—a sure deterrent to good digestion.

Ginna began to eat in the English manner, with the fork in her left hand. As she lifted the fork to her mouth, the light caught the sparkle of the ring.

Charles said, "What's this, Ginna, that I see on your finger?"

"My engagement ring, Papa. Jonathan gave it to me this afternoon."

Charles laughed. "So that's why you've been sitting there as quiet as a little mouse. Just waiting for someone to notice it."

"The ring belonged to Jonathan's grandmother," Ginna explained. She held her hand out for her mother to see. "It's beautiful, isn't it, Mummy?"

Araminta frowned. "Personally, I've never cared for emeralds."

Before Charles had a chance, Nathan defended the ring. "Green is my favorite color, Ginna. Golly, your ring is almost as pretty as Green Boy."

Ginna laughed. "Thank you, Nathan. To be compared with your favorite frog, that's quite a compliment."

"Well, it might be even prettier," Nathan conceded grudgingly. "Green Boy isn't studded with diamonds."

Charles smiled at his two children, while Araminta

looked decidedly sour. Her opinion had been completely ignored. It was almost as if she were not even at the table.

Her mild twinge of guilt about her behavior in the attic studio vanished, and her eyes narrowed as she watched Charles with his children. Even Nathan was growing away from her.

Cassie was right. The only way Araminta could ever hurt Charles would be through Nathan or Ginna.

# CHAPTER
## 17

A pall of heat, heavy and stifling, lay across Washington, with no sign of rain to bring relief. Along the avenues, even the trees with their parched leaves curled tight seemed to have given up all hope for respite from the summer heat.

In the White House, on that early August afternoon, the ceiling fan droned overhead in the presidential bedroom as a recovered President Cleveland sat up on the edge of the Lincoln bed and began putting on his shirt.

"You're progressing quite nicely, Mr. President," Charles Forsyte said. "The sutures have healed well and your heart sounds good. But I might remind you: You've been through a traumatic operation. And even though you might feel almost as good as new, it will still take time to get your full strength back."

Charles folded his stethoscope to return it to his medical bag. "That's why you musn't allow this special session of Congress to overwhelm you. Take plenty of time out to rest."

"I appreciate your concern, Forsyte. And I'll heed your advice as well as I can. But we both know that politics demand more than a modicum of work."

"Yes, I'm aware of that, Mr. President. Only don't allow the *politicians* the same measure of your time."

Cleveland laughed. "That's like telling me to repudiate the sin while still loving the sinner. It will take a far wiser head than mine to separate the two."

A patter of feet down the hallway and a childish voice claimed the president's attention. "And a wiser man than I might not have waited so long to marry and have children."

"How is Mrs. Cleveland feeling?" Charles inquired.

"A bit peckish in this hot weather. But she's the loveliest woman alive. I don't know how I could have gotten so lucky. Sounds strange, doesn't it, Doctor? For a man my age to be so in love with his wife. And to be filling up this creaky old mansion with children."

"This world would be a sadder place if love were reserved only for the young."

"I understand your daughter will be marrying Senator Meadors's son at the end of the summer."

"Yes. But I try to stay away from the house as much as possible these days, with all the activity going on." Charles became serious again. "If your personal physician thinks I should see you again, Mr. President, I'll be at the clinic for the rest of the summer."

The aide opened the door and escorted Charles down the hallway and into the hidden recesses of the basement, where he walked through a servants' door that led outside. He climbed into the nondescript carriage and began the short journey back to the medical center.

On the other side of town in Stanley Quail's house, a swollen Cassie, her baby due any moment, watched while the seamstress fitted Ginna's wedding dress. The material was a cream peau de soie, more elegant and flattering than stark white, which Araminta had chosen for Ginna at first. But the arrival of the mellowed lace veil had precipitated a change of material.

As the seamstress gave Ginna the signal to turn slowly so that she could check the hem, Cassie caught a brief glimpse of her own image in the pier mirror across the bedroom.

She did not like what she saw. Even the shapeless gray dress could not hide her bulk. She bore an inescapable resemblance to the Buddha with his fat stomach that she had seen in the London museum when she was thirteen.

And her mother, sitting in the other chair and watching the proceedings, didn't look much thinner. The only shapely and slender one in the room was Ginna. And although Cassie knew that she, unlike her mother, would be slender again once the baby arrived, she couldn't help but feel resentful toward her prettier half sister.

"Are you nearly finished, Miss Holcomb?" an impatient Araminta inquired. "If I'm to give you a ride home, we need to leave in the next few minutes."

"Yes, ma'am. Just one more adjustment and then your daughter can take off the dress. But it's shaping up beautifully, don't you think?"

"Very nicely," Araminta granted. She stood and walked over to Cassie. "I'll say good-bye now, Cassie, dear. You just rest for this next week and let Ginna run the house. She's used to it."

"Yes, Mama."

Araminta looked in Ginna's direction. "I'm depending on you, Ginna. Send word to me the very moment Cassie's pains start."

"Yes, Mum—Mama. I will."

The seamstress carefully placed the wedding gown in its protective muslin bag. "I'll fix the hem tonight, Miss Ginna, and sew on the little seed pearls. One more fitting and then it will be finished."

"You've done a wonderful job, Miss Holcomb. Thank you so much."

The door closed and Ginna was left alone with Cassie. Hurriedly, she put on her blue dress and began to repair her hair while Cassie watched.

"I think Papa must have bats in his attic to spend so much money on one dress," Cassie complained. "French silk for—"

"But, Cassie, I'm economizing on everything else. And it's not as if it will be a large wedding—just family and a few friends. But I do want to look especially nice for Jonathan's sake."

"Well, it's a good thing that Stanley and I have an excellent excuse not to come. We wouldn't feel welcome around the Meadors family. This was awfully poor timing, if you ask me, for Senator Meadors to pick on Stanley the way he has."

"Cassie, I'm sorry, too. It's most embarrassing, I know. But Stanley brought it on himself. Jonathan's father didn't have any choice. He was only doing his duty as head of the committee."

"Duty? To disgrace my Stanley before all of Washington?"

Cassie's anger overrode her natural caution. She wanted to hurt Ginna, to bring pain to her because of Stanley's censure.

"Well, Stanley might have the last laugh at that. With this wedding, the Meadorses will certainly be getting their comeuppance."

"What do you mean, Cassie?"

"When they find out who their son has married, then they won't be so haughty."

"Cassie, are you feeling all right? You're not making any sense."

"Of course I'm making sense. Didn't Mama ever tell you the deep, dark secret concerning you and Nathan? If she didn't, it's past time for you to know about it."

Ginna stared at Cassie. She had the same expression of anticipation on her face that Ginna remembered from her childhood when her older sister was waiting to squash a toad in the garden, causing the soft-hearted Nathan to cry. And Ginna could no more do anything now about the feeling of impending doom than she had on that day so long ago.

"What are you trying to tell me, Cassie?"

"Papa's first wife is still alive. Do you know what that means, Ginna? It means that he and Mama were never really married. And if they weren't married, you see where that puts you and Nathan."

"I don't believe you, Cassie. You're making this up, the way you used to make up stories just to scare Nathan and me."

"Ask Mama. Or better yet, ask Papa. You see, the joke will finally be on the Meadorses—with their family heir marrying *you*. You were born on the wrong side of the blanket, Ginna. And you don't even have the right to a last name."

Ginna sat down in the chair recently vacated by Araminta. Cassie's story was too horrible *not* to be true. Always, in the back of her mind, Ginna had known that something would come between her and Jonathan. She had been waiting for it to happen. But never anything so disgraceful as this. What was she to do? The only thing she could do was to confront her father. But what if he corroborated Cassie's story that she was illegitimate?

"So what are you going to do, Ginna?"

She nervously twisted the emerald and diamond ring back and forth. "I won't believe you until I talk with Papa."

"And after he confesses the truth to you, what then?"

Ginna hesitated. "If he tells me that he and Mummy were never legally married, as you avow, then there's only one thing I can do. Return Jonathan's ring and then leave Washington."

"Yes. That's probably best. You wouldn't be comfortable living in this city after that. Poor Ginna. You came so close to happiness."

Ginna's eyes were moist. "Oh, Cassie, why did you have to tell me such a terrible thing? Especially today. Is it that you can't ever stand to see me happy?"

"Which would be worse? Going ahead and marrying Jonathan and then finding out later? Or learning about it now while there's still time to do something about it?"

Ginna didn't answer. Instead, she crouched down in the chair as if it could protect her from Cassie's venomous voice. But the damage had been done.

156

Seeing her look so miserable, Cassie lost patience. Nothing more would be gained by prolonging the conversation. "Don't you think you should go on to the kitchen to help Harriet with the supper? Stanley will be here promptly at six o'clock. And he doesn't like to be kept waiting."

A disheartened Ginna rose and left the bedroom. And when she was gone, Cassie smiled. For a brief moment, she felt a glow spreading over her skin, a vivacity that she had not known for some months. Yes, she did thrive on seeing Ginna's smiles turn into tears. And this afternoon was no different.

She stood up and a sudden pain jabbed her. She put her hand on her belly as the child moved. Strange that she still felt no love for the being that she'd carried for nine months now. The baby had only succeeded in making her more uncomfortable with each succeeding month, sapping her energy. Holding her side, she walked to the mirror and opened her mouth wide. She'd been told that with each baby, a woman lost at least one tooth, as well as her husband's interest. But from the day since that other woman had come to the house, she had found subtle ways to punish Stanley.

Each night for supper, she'd seen to it that Harriet had fixed the vegetables he couldn't abide. But he hadn't been able to complain since he'd been told the physician had recommended them for the baby's sake. He wanted a son badly enough to endure the unpleasant change in diet.

With a decided heaviness, Cassie walked downstairs and lowered herself into the chaise longue on the screened porch. She picked up her fan and began to move her wrist back and forth in a lethargic motion, while Ginna saw to the supper in the hot, stifling kitchen.

•  •  •

At the law firm of Motley, Anderson and Laird, Stanley sat at his desk and stared out the window. Methodically, he took out his white linen handkerchief, blew his nose, and then carefully refolded the linen as if his life were dependent on getting the edges squared exactly before he returned it to his pocket.

The noise of the typewriter in the outer office reminded him of the letter he needed to send out before the day was over.

He opened the door and called out, "Miss Gregory, will you please come to my office? I want to dictate a letter."

"Yes, Mr. Quail."

Martha gazed down at the half-finished brief she was working on for Mr. Laird, who'd already gone home. Then she looked up at the clock. It was a mere five minutes before she was to leave for the day. But she didn't complain. If she had to stay late, then she would just have to stay.

After gathering up her pencil and dictating tablet, she walked into Stanley's office. He was standing, looking out the window, with his back to her. He made no acknowledgment of her entrance until she cleared her throat. Then he turned around, walked back to his desk, and sat down. For a moment, he continued to stare at her. Finally, he indicated a chair with his hand. "Sit down, Miss Gregory."

She did as she was told, poised her pencil to begin writing, and then waited.

"To the Honorable Rad Meadors, U.S. Senate. Dear Mr. Meadors: A matter of grave concern has come to me through a colleague concerning your wife. I feel that I am in a unique position to show that I harbor no ill feelings for the unfortunate turn of events on Thursday last, before the congressional committee, of which you are chairman. I shall be pleased to set up an appointment at your convenience to discuss this delicate matter with you."

Martha dropped her pencil on the floor and an impatient Stanley frowned as he waited for her to retrieve it.

"Finish the letter in the usual way, Miss Gregory. Date it for today, and when you've typed it, return it to my office."

"Yes, sir."

Stanley hesitated. "Why don't you read it back to me so that I can hear how it sounds? I don't want it to seem too threatening, of course."

Martha nervously held the tablet up to the light, and with a slightly shaky voice, she repeated what he had dictated.

"Very good, Miss Gregory. And when you type the envelope, make sure you mark it personal."

"Yes, Mr. Quail. Will there be anything else?"

"No. That will be all." Again he hesitated. "I need not remind you, Miss Gregory, that all correspondence going out of this office is confidential."

"I understand, Mr. Quail."

"Then you may get back to your typewriter. I'll be waiting here in my office to sign the letter, once you're finished."

"Yes, sir."

Martha left Stanley's office. As she sat down, she glanced at the unfinished brief still in the carriage of the machine. Regretfully, she removed it, knowing that she would have to start over and retype the page once she'd finished with the letter Mr. Quail had just dictated.

Consulting her tablet, she began the letter to Mr. Meadors. Although the language used was cautious, the letter sounded strange and troubling, almost like blackmail. But, of course, no attorney would be threatening Senator Meadors.

All of a sudden, Martha wished that she could confide in Ginna. But that was impossible. If she were to do that and Mr. Quail found out, she would lose her much-needed job. No, it would be best if she said nothing at all. Just type the letter and forget it.

Within a few minutes, the letter was finished. Again she rose and knocked on Quail's door. "I have the letter ready for your signature, Mr. Quail."

He opened the door only wide enough to take it from her. Then she went back to her typewriter, put a fresh sheet in the carriage, and returned her attention to the brief. She was still typing when she heard his voice beside her.

"I'm leaving now, Miss Gregory. When you finish your work for the day, please lock the door behind you."

"Yes, Mr. Quail. Good evening."

Stanley disappeared with the letter in his hand. At the entrance to the office building, he engaged a runner to deliver it to the government building. With that done, he headed for a quick rendezvous with Maryann before going home to supper.

He was grateful to Maryann for giving him the information that might lessen the large fine imposed on him by Meadors's committee. Keeping up two houses in Washington was expensive, but he was compelled to do it, especially with Maryann's becoming pregnant and producing a child. He would have to take care of them from now on.

From the time he found out she was going to have the baby, he'd had nightmares, worrying that it might turn out to be a monster. It happened sometimes, he heard, with brother and sister. But they'd been lucky. The child was normal.

Well, he'd have to admit that it was probably because

they weren't full-blooded brother and sister. After all, they'd had different mothers.

He would never forget when it had first started, his sleeping with her. He had come home early from school for the holidays when he was sixteen and she was twelve. After that, his passion for her had grown into a full-fledged obsession with each vacation. Throughout those three years, he had taught her well. Too well. He should have known that they would finally get caught and he'd be sent away to England in disgrace—with his father putting an ocean between them. But now his father was dead. And there was no one to stop them—not even Cassie—from taking up where they had left off.

As he walked along to the small house beyond the Mall, he stepped back in time to that day when his world had changed.

He had left school a day earlier than planned, coming halfway home with Robert Landen. Then he'd gotten a ride with a peddler as far as the crossroads. And he had walked the rest of the way.

"Hello, everybody. I'm home."

The house seemed empty at first, with no sign even of Hagar, the black servant. As a disappointed Stanley stood in the entrance hall of the rambling old country house, he heard footsteps. And then he saw his twelve-year-old sister, Maryann, rushing to greet him.

She threw herself into his arms. "You weren't supposed to come home until tomorrow," she said. "Mama and Papa aren't even here."

"Where are they?"

"At the Marsdens's. There's a big Christmas party and they're staying overnight."

"Well, then, maybe I'd better go away and come back tomorrow."

"No, silly. You're already here."

"And where are the servants?"

"Elbert fell in the creek and took pneumonia. So there's just Hagar left, to fix supper and spend the night with me."

Stanley stepped back and began to examine Maryann. She was no longer a little girl. Her body had changed in the past four months.

"What are you staring at?"

"You. When I left, you were a little girl. Now I see you're growing up."

He suddenly shook his head as if to clear his vision. "I brought you a present."

"May I have it then? Right now?"

"I can't give it to you yet. It's in one of my bags. And I left them at the overseer's cottage."

"Why did you leave them there in that deserted old building?" she asked.

"They were too heavy to carry. Want to ride with me to get them?"

"Yes."

"Then let's go to the stable and saddle up a horse."

The two disappeared before Hagar, busy in the kitchen, knew he had returned home.

Thinking of that ride, with Maryann clinging tightly behind him, Stanley brushed his bald pate. His hair had not yet thinned at the time. It had still been brown and thick, and his youthful nose had not yet taken on the thin, aquiline shape of his uncle's.

He remembered helping her down from the horse and seeing her dress slide upward, revealing her thighs before she nonchalantly smoothed her skirt.

They walked into the deserted cottage, and Stanley took a great deal of time to unbuckle the leather luggage. As soon as he brought out the elegant yellow hair ribbons, Maryann squealed in delight.

"Tie them in my hair, Stanley. They're beautiful."

"Well, then, stand still."

He took his time, removing the others and patiently braiding the ribbons into the long brown hair, which felt like silk to his trembling fingers.

"You're clumsy, Stanley. Here, let me finish."

He watched her walk into the bedroom where the dusty old mirror hung on the wall, opposite the small cot. And then he came to stand behind her.

"You like them?" he had asked.

"Of course. I love them."

"Well, then, don't I get a kiss?"

She put her arms around him. But when she'd kissed him, he continued to hold her. "Kiss me, Maryann, like your mama kisses my father."

"But that's for married folks."

"Have you ever wondered what it's like to be married, Maryann? Beside the kisses?"

"Of course."

"Would you like for me to show you?"

"I'm not sure. Mama said that's for my husband to show me when the proper time comes."

Stanley smiled. "We can pretend that I'm your husband, Maryann. And that this is our cottage. We can stay here until suppertime, just pretending."

"You don't think Mama and Papa will be mad if they find out?"

Stanley shook his head. "It will be a secret between us. I can even spend the night here, if you slip some food to me. Then they won't have to know that I came home early."

Maryann smiled. "We can have a tea party, the way we used to in the maze when I was little."

"That's right."

"But I'm a little bit afraid, Stanley."

"You don't have to be. I wouldn't ever do anything to hurt you. Am I not your brother?"

"No, silly. You're my husband," she said, getting into the spirit of pretending.

He was almost sorry that she trusted him. For it made it too easy for him, lulling her with his words while finding her small budding breasts and kneading them.

"You're beautiful, my wife," he whispered. "I love you."

"You're hurting me, Stanley."

"Do you like the yellow ribbons, Maryann?"

"Yes."

"And you want to keep them?"

"Yes."

"Then pretend with me, and I promise to bring you a better present each time I come home."

She was still while he moved on top of her, searching for entrance . . .

Stanley took out his handkerchief and wiped his brow. He had aroused himself with his memories. And he hurried to reach the house where Maryann waited, before he disgraced himself in public.

# CHAPTER
## 18

"Rad, have you heard the latest *bon mot* making the rounds?"

"No. What is it, Miles?"

"They say that a certain oil company—you know the one I mean—has done everything to the Pennsylvania legislature except *refine* it."

Rad Meadors barely smiled, for he was tired after the final day of committee hearings. But he knew the words spoken had more than a grain of truth in them.

"We've been had in Washington, too, Miles. For too many years."

"As long as there's extra money lying around, someone is going to claim it, Rad, whether they deserve it or not."

"But the pension battle seems to have been won. Now if we can only repeal the Silver Purchase Act."

"Depends on the price of senators these days."

"Another *bon mot* making the rounds?"

"I wish it were," Miles replied. "Well, we'll know for sure on the fifth of August, won't we?"

"That we will."

"I'm going home now, Mr. Chairman," Miles said, taking his coat from the back of the chair and switching his cigar from one side of his mouth to the other. "You'd better do the same. It's been a mighty long day."

Rad nodded, but he remained at the large curved desk where various papers still had to be gathered up and returned to the files.

Oblivious to the opening and shutting of doors in the corridors, Rad remained where he was, staring down at the reams of paper before him. Carefully, he piled one on top of the other, while his mind filled with old images and residues of problems that never seemed to change with the legislative seasons.

For seventeen years he'd come back and forth to Washington, always with the expectation that that particular session would be different. But after so many years, he'd finally grown cynical and disillusioned, no longer hoping against hope that the abuses could be stamped out completely. It was like a forest fire. As soon as one firebreak was established, the fire popped out somewhere else.

Senators were still bought and traded as commonly as shares on the stock exchange. Power and money still purchased favoritism for the few—railway magnates, bankers, oil and coal companies—causing private fortunes to quadruple, while some of the politicians grew rich, too, and the poor laborers grew poorer.

The stench in Washington that afternoon could just as easily have been coming from the government buildings, Rad thought, as from the trash bins in the alleys behind them.

For two weeks, he'd watched the men and their lawyers walk in, unrepentant for taking the pensions that had never been rightfully theirs. And then they'd barked like a bunch of mongrels when the stolen bone was wrested from them. The animosity had been so thick that it had hung ominously over the hearing room the entire time.

But the committee had persevered. And now the only thing left to do was to write his report for the president, with recommendations for censure.

"Are you ready for me to help you, sir?"

Rad looked up and saw his aide. "Awbrey, I thought you'd gone home long ago."

"No, sir. I was waiting in your office to lock up the files at the end of the day."

"Then you might as well carry half the papers."

As the aide walked around the curved desk, he said, "A courier has just delivered a letter for you."

"Whatever is in it will have to wait until tomorrow."

"I thought you might want to take it home with you. It's marked personal."

A few minutes later, with the papers relegated to the locked files, Rad picked up the unopened letter from his private desk, stuck it in his coat pocket, and headed for the livery stable where his horse, Sumi, waited.

On the way home, Rad passed a small one-seater carriage. He smiled and touched his hat as he recognized his son's fiancée, Ginna, but she did not see him. Her eyes were on the road and she was going inordinately fast. Too fast, Rad thought, for safety. Just like Jonathan. Uneasily, he rode on, glancing back only once. But she had already disappeared in a swirl of gray dust.

Half of Ginna's life had been spent waiting. Waiting for her mother to notice her. Waiting for Cassie to become the loving sister she so desperately desired. And when she had despaired of either one, waiting to grow up so that she would no longer have any need for their attention, their approval.

But the old life had not been shed. She was still bound to them, even at that moment. Once again, she would have to wait—to approach her father for the truth. Cassie's baby was coming and its birth took precedence over Ginna's grief.

In her mind, she had already given up Jonathan. But in doing so, Ginna knew she could never continue in her present role as a dependent daughter. Hadn't Jonathan already warned her? "Your place is no longer in this house," he'd said.

Yes, she accepted that. But just where was her place in this world? Not as a wife and mother. Never that, because of the disgrace. But she was good with children. She could teach. Or, like Martha, she could work in an office. But not in Washington. It would have to be in another city.

The brownstone at the end of the street had a forbidding appearance to it in the late-afternoon haze as Ginna stopped short. She hurriedly tied the carriage reins to the hitching post and ran to the front door.

In the hallway, she breathlessly called out, "Mummy, where are you?"

In the shadows at the foot of the stairs, Nathan sat, with a cat's cradle of string between his fingers. "She's not here yet. Just me and Clara."

"Do you know where she could be?"

"She's gone over to speak to Pinky's mother."

"Oh, no. Are you two in trouble again?"

"Maybe. Pinky finally came to get some of his tadpoles out of the pool. Mama said he wasn't supposed to come here, ever again."

"Has she been gone long?"

"Depends on what you mean by long. Long as it takes ice to melt? Or long as it takes for her to get mad at me?"

Ginna looked at her little brother's face. She sat down on the step beside him. "Oh, Nathan, you've been by yourself for three whole days, haven't you? And not allowed to go anywhere."

"The bad part is, I didn't even get to see Pinky. Not even for a minute. He came into the garden about the same time she got home from Cassie's."

At the mention of her sister, Ginna remembered why she'd been in such a hurry. "Well, Cassie's baby is coming and Mummy asked me to let her know the minute—" She looked at her brother and hesitated.

"You don't have to stop on account of me, Ginna. I know how babies get here. Papa let me watch when the puppies were born."

"Of course. I forgot."

"Is Cassie yowling like Perserpina did?"

Ginna smiled in spite of herself. "Not at the moment."

She stood and walked to the door, to peer down the street. "Did Barge take Mummy in the carriage?"

"Yes."

"Then let's go to meet her, Nathan."

"She might get mad at me for leaving the house."

"I'll take the blame, Nathan, if it comes to that. You need some fresh air. But I have a feeling that when I tell her the news, she'll forget about both of us."

Nathan removed the cat's cradle from his fingers and stood, pushing the string into his pocket. Ginna knew that he would return it later on to one of the paper bags stashed along the ledge of his bedroom window. In each bag, he kept small treasures, important only to Nathan—bits of string in one; acorns to feed the squirrels in the park in another; agate marbles that he'd traded with schoolmates; and smooth, round pebbles from the creek bed. She suspected that he'd even saved a little dirt from their garden in England, too.

Ginna glanced at the horse harnessed to the one-seater in front of the house. Then she turned to Nathan. "Do you want to ride or walk?"

"Let's walk. It's not that far."

The two started down the street, with Nathan taking a hop, skip, and jump, lagging one moment and then rushing ahead, like a small, eager puppy finally breaking free of its leash.

But when he saw the family carriage returning up the street, he immediately stopped and waited for Ginna to catch up with him. "I see Mama," he said, sliding his hand into hers.

"Yes." Ginna waved to get Barge's attention. She and Nathan crossed the street, and when Barge brought the carriage to a stop, Ginna and Nathan climbed in.

Ginna did not give her mother time to scold Nathan. "Cassie's baby is coming," she announced. "Stanley has already gone for Papa. Harriet is with her right now."

"Hurry home, Barge," Araminta said. "I'll need to get my packed valise."

Then Araminta began to give Ginna instructions. "You're to stay at home with Nathan, do you understand? And you're to let no one into the house while I'm away. I don't think Pinky will be a problem from now on. But you never can tell."

"Will Papa be coming home tonight, do you think?"

"It depends, I'm sure, on what time the baby arrives. But I'll stay overnight, of course. And Nathan?"

"Yes, Mama?"

"We've had word from the school. They're going to take you early. You'll be leaving with Mr. Graves, one of the teachers, tomorrow afternoon. He'll stop at the house for you on his way to the train station promptly at ten o'clock."

She ignored the betrayed look on Nathan's face as she turned again to Ginna. "And I'm relying on you to pack and make sure he gets off on time."

"Yes, Mummy."

"And Ginna, when Maudie comes in the morning to do the ironing, send her on over to Cassie's."

"Before or after she does the ironing?"

"Why, before. You'll be able to manage quite nicely, I'm sure, without her."

When they reached the brownstone, Ginna said, "Nathan, would you like to take the one-seater to the carriage house and unhitch Twoopy after Barge leaves the driveway?"

"I sure would, Ginna."

As soon as the larger carriage came to a stop, Nathan was the first one down. "I'll stay outside to watch," he said, and ran toward the one-seater, which was still at the hitching post.

Araminta stepped down and Ginna came next, following her mother into the house while Nathan climbed into the one-seater out front and thought about taking it and running away with Pinky.

Two hours later, Nathan and Ginna were alone in the kitchen. A few minutes before, Clara had finished the dishes and gone to her lodgings over the carriage house. Now Ginna watched while Nathan dealt the cards on the table for a game of Go Fish.

For Nathan's sake, Ginna tried to keep her mind on the game. But she was not successful. At the end of the fourth hand, Nathan spread out his cards and announced, "I won again."

"So I see."

"But you're not even *trying* to win, Ginna. The game's no fun if you don't try."

"Well, I guess my mind's on other things. Like your leaving tomorrow. I'm going to miss you, Nathan."

He didn't want to think about it. "Oh, I'm used to going away, Ginna. No big deal. Barge promised he'd watch Green Boy for me. He's going to see that he gets enough bugs and flies to eat."

"That's nice."

Nathan took a quick swipe across his eyes with his hand. And then he quickly changed the subject. "You think Cassie's baby has come yet?"

"Probably not."

"Some babies die when they're born, don't they?"

"Yes. But Papa is there with Cassie. So we shouldn't worry about that."

"I'm going to stay up until he gets home."

"Then you might be up all night, Nathan."

"I don't care. Do you think it will be a boy or a girl?"

"I'll say a girl."

"Then I'll say a boy," Nathan replied.

"What do you want to bet?" Ginna's eyes held a teasing look as she waited for her brother to decide.

"A trip to the fair."

Ginna laughed. "In Chicago?"

"Yes. If I'm right, you have to take me. And if you're right, I'll have to take you."

"Do you realize how far away Chicago is, Nathan? I think whoever wins will have to take the other to someplace closer—like the zoo."

"But Chicago isn't really that far away, Ginna. We could go on the train. And it only costs fifty cents to get in."

"How do you know?"

"Pinky's father wrote for information. He's got the train schedule and everything. Pinky showed it to me."

"Is Pinky going? Is that why you want to go, too?"

"Maybe."

"I'd love to go to the fair, too, Nathan. Only . . ."

Ginna was sad as she looked at her little brother. He had his dreams, the same as she. With little possibility that they would ever come true, either. "But it's really time for bed. You're so sleepy, you can hardly hold your eyes open."

"I want to stay up, Ginna. Until I know about the baby."

"Whenever Papa comes home, I'll wake you."

Nathan yawned again. "You promise?"

She nodded.

Nathan slowly gathered his cards together. "What if you don't hear him come in?"

"I've latched all the doors. He'll have to knock. Now let's go on upstairs. You have a long trip ahead of you tomorrow."

Ginna switched off the kitchen light. And together, the two climbed the back steps to the landing. When they reached his bedroom door, Ginna leaned over and kissed her brother. "Good night, Nathan."

"Good night, Ginna."

After he'd closed his door, Ginna walked on to her own bedroom down the hall. She had no plans to go to sleep. Unlike Nathan, she would remain awake, all night if she had to. For it was imperative that she speak with her father—not only about Cassie's baby, but about her own birth as well. Please, God, she said. Please let Cassie be wrong.

Once again, the house began its ghostly conversation in the silence of the night: creaks and noises, with the scamper of something in the attic. A squirrel, perhaps, running along the length of the roof. And a few minutes later, the eerie hoot of an owl caused her to go to the window and look out. But in the darkness she could see nothing.

She sat up in bed, still fully clothed, and stared at the small clock. Its hands had barely moved. In desperation, she rose, opened the bedroom door, and started downstairs to find a book to read. But before she reached the landing, she passed her mother's door. On sudden impulse, she decided to borrow her mother's latest fashion magazine instead.

She groped for the light inside the bedroom door. Her mother had left hurriedly, for the bedroom was in a state of disarray. Seeing the new blue dress draped carelessly across the slipper chair, Ginna started toward it, to hang it up before it became too wrinkled. Then she thought better of it. Feeling a little guilty, as if she were an interloper, she left the dress on the chair and went instead to the nightstand where her mother always kept her tin of chocolates and her fashion magazine.

As Ginna opened the drawer and took out the magazine, an envelope dropped out of it onto the floor. Quickly, she stooped to retrieve it. As she turned it over, she saw that the letter was addressed to her in Jonathan's handwriting. And the seal had been broken. It was the missing letter.

# CHAPTER 19

"Cassie, dear, you'll have to try harder," Charles admonished. "The baby can't be born without your help."

"But it hurts," she wailed. She glared at her mother in accusation. "You didn't tell me there'd be so much pain. I wish I'd never listened to you."

"Hush, Cassie," Araminta scolded. "Stanley is right outside the door. You don't want him to hear you, do you?"

"I don't care."

"Charles, can't you give her something to cut the pain?"

"Not yet. Any drug would have an adverse effect on the baby's breathing. But later, Cassie. I promise I'll give you something as soon as the baby is born. Now, will you cooperate?"

"That's right, Cassie. After you have the baby, precious, then Papa will give you something to soothe your nerves."

"Mama!" Cassie wailed.

Stanley could not bear to sit in the hallway a moment longer. He rose from his chair and rushed headlong down the stairs to the dark-paneled library. Once inside, he closed the door to shut out any sound emanating from the upstairs bedroom.

The clock in the hall struck two doleful, reverberating clangs as he hurriedly pulled out a leather-bound book and reached behind it for the hidden bottle.

He stood with his back to the door and took a large swig of liquid, feeling the mellow brandy trickling down his dry throat. God knew, he needed a little Dutch courage for the rest of the night, with Cassie shrieking like a banshee and his head splitting with a headache. He'd been lucky with Maryann's baby. But what if God decided to punish him by making his legitimate child the malformed one?

With the first draught of liquor offering him a little relief, he took the bottle and sat down in his easy chair. He took another large swig and then finally set the bottle on the nearby table, within easy reach. Allowing himself a drink as each quarter hour struck, he nursed the bottle with long, intermittent swallows until the clock finally struck three and Araminta's voice outside the door called to him.

"Stanley, the baby has arrived," she announced. "Stanley, are you in there?"

Quickly, Stanley pushed the empty bottle under the chair. And none too steady on his feet, he rushed to open up the door. "You say the baby is finally here?"

"Yes, Stanley. You have a son. Come and see."

"Is he all right?"

"Yes. And Cassie, too."

He missed the first step and barely caught himself. But Araminta didn't notice. She was already halfway up the stairs, leading the way.

Charles glanced up as the two entered the room. He gave a warning sign for them to be quiet, for Cassie was settling down to sleep after being given the promised sedative.

And so the two tiptoed over to the cradle, where Araminta leaned over and picked up the child for Stanley to see.

As Stanley examined his son, he saw that the baby was bald, with the same shape head as Stanley. He was small and scrawny, like a wizened little man who only needed muttonchop whiskers to complete the family portrait. Seeing him, Stanley felt a profusion of pride and relief.

He reached out and touched the baby's long fingers. "He looks like me," he announced.

"Yes," Charles agreed. "He has your physical attributes."

"He's all right?" he asked again.

"A bit underweight," Charles said. "But healthy otherwise."

"It won't take him long to fatten up," Araminta said. The baby began to squirm, and reluctantly, she placed him back in the cradle before he awoke.

Stanley's attention turned to his wife. "Cassie had a hard time, didn't she?"

"No more so than any other mother having her first child," Charles said.

"But she needs plenty of rest," Araminta said. "I'll sleep on the couch in here while you two go on to bed."

Stanley nodded. "Will you be staying the rest of the night, Dr. Forsyte?"

"No. Since Cassie and the baby are fine, I'll go on home. Ginna and Nathan are by themselves."

"Then I'll help you hitch up the horse."

Charles looked at Stanley's bleary eyes. He'd already noticed that his speech was slightly slurred and his gait unsteady. "That's not necessary, Stanley. It will only take a minute. And I know you're tired from the long night of waiting. Better for you to go on to bed."

Stanley took out his handkerchief and wiped his brow. "Yes, that's true. It's not every night that a man has a son. It's an exhausting business."

The slight creak of the carriage drawing into the driveway at four o'clock in the morning caused a sleepy Ginna to sit up with a start. She rubbed her eyes and reached her foot out to find her slippers. She had come downstairs to wait, and there she'd remained for almost the entire night with Jonathan's letter clasped to her breast.

Ginna rushed to the back door and waited for her father to come in from the carriage house. When she heard his steps, she opened the door wide. "Papa?"

"Ginna! What are you doing awake at this time of night? Or morning, rather?"

"I was waiting for you, Papa."

"Cassie has a healthy little boy. And she's fine, too. I guess you were waiting up for the news."

"Yes." So Nathan had won the bet. "Do you want anything to drink or to eat?" she asked.

"No, Ginna. I just want to get to bed."

Her father looked exhausted. And once again she knew she'd have to wait. She could not ask him to stay up any longer to answer her questions.

"Make sure I'm up by nine tomorrow. I want to have breakfast with Nathan before he leaves."

"Yes, Papa." Ginna stayed behind, and after he was gone, she turned off the lights. As she'd promised earlier, she went upstairs and opened the door to Nathan's room.

The small brown bags were no longer on the window ledge. He had already packed them in his suitcase, she knew. She walked to the bed and stared down at her little brother, so peacefully asleep, with the tiny stream of light touching his pillow.

"Nathan?" she called gently.

He moved slightly, his hand dropping to the side of the bed.

"Nathan," she called again. "Can you hear me? Cassie has a little boy."

"Ginna?"

"Cassie has a little boy," she repeated. "I promised I'd let you know as soon as Papa came home."

"I won, didn't I?" the sleepy voice murmured.

"Yes, Nathan. Now go on back to sleep."

Ginna tiptoed out of the room and walked along the hallway to her own room.

The persistent ringing of the doorbell awoke Ginna. The sunlight flooded her room as she sat up, completely disoriented. She hopped out of bed and grabbed her robe, struggling with one of the sleeves as she raced to the landing window to see who could be calling at such an ungodly hour.

"Clara," she said, hanging her head out the window. "What are you doing out there?"

"All the doors are latched, Miss Ginna. I can't get into

the kitchen to cook breakfast. And Maudie's waiting out back to start on the ironing."

"Well, stay there and I'll come downstairs to let you in."

A few minutes later, with Maudie sent on her way, Ginna went back upstairs to get dressed, while Clara started breakfast. But Ginna tuned out the stirrings in the kitchen, with Clara talking to herself as usual. Her ears were alerted for the first sign that Nathan and her father might be waking up on their own. As the minutes went by without any indication of either, she finally knocked on their doors.

"Time to get up, Nathan.

"Time to get up, Papa."

And so, by half-past nine, the three were seated together at the breakfast table.

"You have everything packed, son?" Charles inquired.

"Ginna packed almost everything for me last night."

"Well, there's something she couldn't have packed since she didn't know about it." Charles smiled as his eyes took in the small, hunched figure, trying so bravely not to embarrass himself with a display of tears.

"What, Papa?"

"There's something for you on my office desk. A going-away present."

"May I get it now?"

"Yes, but you mustn't open it until you're on the train with Mr. Graves."

Nathan quickly disappeared and then returned to the breakfast table. He held the small package up to his ear and shook it vigorously. "What is it?"

Ginna laughed. "I hope it isn't breakable, Papa."

"It might be, Nathan. So, if I were you, I wouldn't shake it so hard. Just put it in one of your pockets."

"What color is it, Papa? You can tell me that, can't you?"

"Green."

The doorbell rang and Charles took out his watch to check the time. "That must be Mr. Graves now."

"I'll answer the door," Ginna said. "And I'll get Barge to put your suitcase in the carriage, Nathan."

"Let's go upstairs, son. For one last check, to make sure you're not leaving anything you need."

Ginna rushed down the hallway to the front door. The man on the steps was young: in his mid-twenties, with glasses magnifying his robin's-egg-blue eyes, and his immaculate lightweight suit a little too large for his thin frame.

"Mr. Graves?"

"Yes."

"Please come in. I'm Nathan's sister, and he'll be downstairs in a moment."

"I'm a few minutes early, Miss Forsyte."

"We were just finishing breakfast. May I offer you something to drink? A cup of coffee or tea, perhaps?"

"No, thank you. If you'll excuse me, I'll just wait outside with the carriage."

Everything became convoluted, with Barge seeing to the luggage while Clara ran out with the packed lunch. Then Nathan appeared with his father. A hug, a kiss, a wave were part of the family vignette as the two servants, a father, and a sister watched one small boy leave his home with a stranger. Toward the end of the street, Nathan looked back with sad, doleful eyes as Charles and Ginna waved one last time.

For Ginna, the morning had built to a fever pitch. Nathan's departure was the final straw, coming so soon after the arrival of Cassie's baby and the bombshell that her half sister had so expertly left at her feet.

Turning quickly to her father, Ginna said, "Papa, may I ride with you to the clinic this morning? I really must talk with you and I can't wait any longer."

"It's that important?"

"Yes."

"All right."

The entire length of the street was made up of identical three-story brownstones. Despite the steady *clop* of the horse, the carriage appeared to be going nowhere until one noticed the changing colors of the front doors—blue or red, mustard or black.

For Ginna, the doors were a blur and she barely saw them. She automatically smiled and waved to people at the gates without really seeing them, either. And even the morning air seemed alien, fusty and gray, with no promise but scalding heat.

"All right, Ginna, out with it. You've remained silent long enough. What's bothering you? Besides Nathan's departure."

"You must promise to tell me the truth. No matter how much it hurts."

Charles took his eyes from the road and stared at his daughter. Somehow he had a premonition as to what she was going to say even before she said it.

"Papa, Cassie told me that you and Mummy were never legally married because you already had a wife. And that Nathan and I have no right to your name. Is that true, Papa?"

Charles swore and stopped the carriage at the nearest hitching post. What a devilish thing to happen. He should have known that spite and jealousy would not allow the family secret to be kept. Damn Araminta.

In his mind he searched for the appropriate words. What could he say to make his daughter understand? How much should he tell her?

"Ginna, your mother and I were married in good faith,"

182

he began. "And you and Nathan have every right to my name. What Cassie said is only partially true—that my first wife is still alive."

"But I don't understand. . . ."

"Ginna, during the war, many tragedies occurred: soldiers were killed, whole families disappeared and were never heard from again. That's what happened to us. Except that the news of my death was erroneous. I was merely wounded. But when I finally returned home, my wife and child were gone. I spent two whole years searching for them, Ginna. Then I gave up.

"Araminta was my best friend's widow. We had both lost our loved ones. And rather than spend the rest of my life alone, I married her and took her to England."

"But when did you find out? I mean, that your first wife was still alive?"

"Several weeks ago."

"But how? Where is she, Papa? Here in Washington?"

"Yes."

"Who is she?"

"Cassie didn't tell you?"

"No."

"Well, perhaps she doesn't know. I can't imagine Cassie telling you only part of the story if she knew all of it."

"Who is she, Papa?"

Charles hesitated. "I can't tell you without her permission, Ginna. You see, she married again also."

"Then what are you two going to do?"

"Nothing, Ginna. There's nothing to do except remain silent for everyone's protection—your mother's, hers, yours, and Nathan's."

"Because if the truth becomes known, we'll be in disgrace, like Cassie said? That Nathan and I *are* considered illegitimate?"

"Ginna, I don't really know. But I do know that you both had a right to be born, a right to a bountiful life filled with love. And the legal right to a name you're going to shed soon is a moot point. You're going to be Jonathan Meadors's wife."

"No, Papa. I won't be marrying Jonathan."

"And why not?"

"I . . . I couldn't. Not with this stigma hanging over my head."

"Don't be ridiculous, Ginna."

"I'm not being ridiculous. I'll return his ring immediately."

"Ginna . . ."

"Thank you for telling me, Papa. And now, if you don't mind, I think I'll walk back home instead of riding the rest of the way with you."

"You don't need the carriage today?"

"No, I have the one-seater. But I doubt I'll be going anywhere today."

"Don't do anything rash, Ginna." Charles glanced at his watch. "I have a scheduled operation that I can't put off. But promise me you won't do anything until we've had a chance to talk again after supper."

"I suppose a few more hours won't make that much difference, Papa."

A heartsick Charles watched his daughter walk slowly in the opposite direction. What could he do to keep her from making a tragic mistake?

Glancing at his watch again, Charles realized that if he hurried, he would have enough time to seek Allison out before signing in at the clinic. He desperately needed to talk with her, to warn her, before Ginna did something that they would all regret.

# CHAPTER
## 20

"Miss Ginna, Mrs. Meadors is in the parlor downstairs. I told her your mama is away, but she says she came to see you."

Clara's voice penetrated through the closed door to the darkened bedroom where Ginna lay. In a panic, she removed the wet cloth from her forehead and sat up.

"I can't see her, Clara. Please tell her that I'm indisposed."

"Your headache isn't any better?"

"No. If anything, it's worse. Oh, Clara, please. I can't see her looking the way I do."

"Then I'll ask her to come back another time."

"Yes. Tomorrow afternoon. Ask her to come back tomorrow, Clara. I should be well by then."

Ginna listened as the front door finally closed and the creak of the carriage wheels dwindled into silence.

Alone in the bedroom, Ginna finally arose. She could not afford a long, languishing mourning period for what she had lost. And she had to stop depending on others and make plans for her own life. Society's customs and manners, which had constricted her as tightly as the stays of any corset for as long as she could remember, now no longer bound her. Ideals had to be rethought, reforged, in the light of her disgrace.

Yet in losing her status as a lady, she was gaining a certain freedom to be herself. But for one who had never stepped outside the bounds of society before, it was an awesome challenge.

She remembered poor Sarah Trevalyne, forced from school by a hateful letter sent to the headmistress. "Mr. Eastminster and I shall be forced to remove our three daughters from your care if you continue to keep Miss Trevalyne as a student. Her mother has absconded to Italy with a man who is not her husband. And we feel that our daughters might suffer through an association with her daughter."

And so the headmistress had gotten rid of Sarah. Ginna wasn't sure whether it was a matter of moral principle or the fact that it would be better financially to lose one student rather than three. Would Nathan also be forced from school if the truth as to his parentage got out? Sweet, kind Nathan, whose only sin had been to label Stanley's muttonchop whiskers "Piccadilly weepers."

Ginna knew that she would gain nothing by running

away, unannounced. So she carefully packed her valise and then sat down to write her father a note.

Papa—

Because of the circumstances, I cannot remain in this house a moment longer. Since I have enough money to see me through the next month, I have decided to go to Mrs. Gregory's boardinghouse on Pennsylvania Avenue and room with Martha. So that no disgrace will accrue to you, I will not use your name but will be known as Ginna Biggs, taking my mother's name.

Please do not attempt to make me come home. I am grown now and have decided that this is the best course to take. I love you and appreciate all you have done for me in the past. Please take care of Nathan until I am able to send for him.

Ginna.

When she had finished the letter to her father, Ginna wrote a note to Jonathan, breaking off their engagement. She would send the note and the ring by Barge in the carriage and then hire a hack to take her to the boardinghouse, which was half empty at this time of the year.

The boardinghouse on Pennsylvania Avenue was a gray-shingled affair, with cupolas and gingerbread trim and a porch that wrapped around two sides of the multistoried house. Set back from the street, it seemed to sprawl over the grassy acreage with the grace of an aging behemoth.

But its looks from the outside belied its reputation as one of the finest residences of bachelor lawmakers and married men whose wives chose to remain at home with children while Congress was in session. Its proprietor, Maggie Gregory, was genteel, but she ran the house with an iron determination: always giving her boarders impeccable service and excellent meals and, in return, demanding impeccable behavior from them. Being elected by one's constituents did not automatically allow an entrée to her establishment. For she had other full-time boarders: widows and career women, whose sensibilities had to be protected from the cruder type of man.

It was to this boardinghouse that Ginna went, with the hack driver waiting with her luggage while she walked up the steps to ring the bell.

Seeing her daughter's friend on her porch, Maggie Gregory opened the door. "Ginna, my dear, what a pleasant surprise. Do come in. But I'm afraid Martha hasn't gotten home yet."

"Mrs. Gregory, I'm seeking asylum," she said with a frankness that startled the woman. "I would like to rent a room from you, if you have one available."

"Oh, my dear. What has happened? You haven't been turned out of your own home, have you?"

"No. Nothing so disgraceful as that. But I have chosen to leave."

"Then come in, child. Don't stand here in the afternoon heat."

Now assured that she would not be turned away, Ginna motioned for the driver to bring in her luggage. And within a few minutes, he had driven away.

"I'm afraid you will have to share a room with Martha for the time being, Ginna. With the congressmen due back in town any moment, I don't have a spare room that I can give you."

"I don't mind, Mrs. Gregory. That is, if Martha won't mind."

"I'm sure she will love having you here, Ginna. Now come into my office and tell me what's going on."

Later, as she sat across the desk from Maggie, Ginna was hesitant. "I have decided to follow in Martha's footsteps and go out on my own. Tomorrow, I plan to register for a secretarial course."

"But what about your engagement to Mr. Meadors?"

"There will be no marriage taking place, Mrs. Gregory."

Maggie's face was bland, showing neither surprise nor censure. From talking with Martha, she had realized there were difficulties at home for Ginna, especially concerning her engagement. Maggie couldn't understand it. If her daughter Martha had been the lucky one to attract Jonathan Meadors, she would be jumping up and down with joy.

"I'd appreciate it if you would call me Ginna Biggs instead of Forsyte. With the alienation between my family and me, it will be better not to call attention to it with strangers."

"I understand, Ginna. That way, if you reconcile with your family, there'll be no chance for outside gossip."

Ginna reached into her purse. "I'd like to pay you for the first week's board and lodging. Will you please tell me how much?"

"That won't be necessary," Maggie said, ignoring her rigid rules for the first time in years. "We'll wait until the end of the week. And then you can pay me for what you owe."

The girl clearly needed a haven. But Maggie was certain that the difficulty with her family would be resolved long before the week was out.

"Mama, I'm home," a voice suddenly called from the hallway.

"Good. That's Martha now." Maggie stood and walked to the door. "I'm in the office, Martha."

"What a hard day. I had to stay late as usual. Mr. . . ." Martha stopped short when she saw her friend. "Ginna, what are you doing here? Not that I'm sorry to see you, of course . . ."

"Ginna is going to be boarding with us for a while, Martha. Why don't you two go on upstairs and visit, while I see how far along Ethel is to getting ready for supper?"

"I hope you don't mind, Martha. My barging in this way."

"Why, Ginna Forsyte, why should I mind, except that I know something must be drastically wrong if you've left home."

Ginna followed Martha up the stairs. And as soon as she closed the bedroom door, Martha turned to Ginna. "All right, you can tell me. What's happened?"

"First, you must call me Ginna *Biggs*. Not Forsyte."

As Martha's mouth dropped open, she continued. "I've left home for good. And I won't be getting married. I plan to enroll at the secretarial school tomorrow."

"But why? Can't you at least tell me that?"

"No, Martha. Even though you're my best friend here in Washington, I can't even tell you."

"All right, Ginna. If that's the way you want it. But before supper, we'll have to sit down and decide on some story for you. Mrs. Beauchamp is a nosy old biddy, and we'll have to be ready for her—with some plausible excuse for your English accent and your being here alone."

"Well, let's stay as close to the truth as possible. We can say that my parents moved to England after the war. That much is true, at least. That I traveled to the States with a kind older couple. And now I'm in your mother's care until my guardian arrives from California to claim me."

Martha giggled. "That sounds like something Louisa May Alcott would make up. Did you ever read *Little Women* in school?"

"Yes. Sally Belvedere brought it from home one Christmas and we all read it on my floor, despite the headmistress. I can hear her disapproving voice now.

"'My dears, Miss Alcott's father is a vegetarian and a communist. I do hope she has not been influenced unduly by the man.'

"'Oh, it's a perfectly respectable book, Miss Cavanagh. Otherwise, Mummy would never have given it to me for Christmas.'"

Ginna smiled as she recalled the conversation. "That stopped Miss Cavanagh in her tracks. You see, Lady Belvedere was a patron of the school and, of course, the headmistress couldn't say anything against her without risking her patronage."

Ginna's eyes became moist despite her effort to be strong. Seeing this, Martha quickly said, "Let's unpack your valise now that we have a suitable background for you."

She walked over to the large armoire and pulled open the doors. "There's not a great deal of room in here, I'm afraid."

"That's all right," Ginna responded. "Because I didn't bring very much."

That evening, with her mother alerted to Ginna's new history, Martha walked downstairs with her friend. Mrs. Beauchamp was already in the parlor with Miss Alma Counts.

"Mrs. Beauchamp, Miss Counts, may I present another boarder, Miss Biggs."

Mrs. Beauchamp looked Ginna up and down. "And where did you come from, my dear?"

"From England, madam."

Martha hurriedly filled in her brief résumé. "Ginna is staying here with Mama until her guardian can come for her."

"I had a guardian once," Miss Counts remembered. "Treated me abominably he did, taking all my money. I would have had a comfortable married life, but the man left me with no dowry. So, of course, I've had to work for every penny since then. Don't let your guardian treat you the same way, my dear."

Mrs. Beauchamp sniffed. "We're well aware of your reduced circumstances, Miss Counts." The gnarled little woman's attention returned to Ginna. "So when do you expect your guardian to arrive?"

"Not for several weeks, Mrs. Beauchamp."

"He must be awfully far away."

"San Francisco," Martha said hurriedly. "But he has business interests in . . . in Hawaii."

"Oh, my dear," Miss Counts said. "Is he one of those American businessmen who dethroned Queen Liliuokalani? That was such a shame. So few women monarchs left in the world now besides Queen Victoria and the empress of China."

Mrs. Beauchamp sniffed again. "Miss Counts is an avowed suffragist," she said to Ginna. "She doesn't intentionally mean to insult your guardian."

"I quite understand," Ginna said, frowning at Martha for being a little too inventive with her biography.

"I see that you have already met Miss Biggs," Maggie

said, coming into the parlor. She smiled at both women as they nodded. "Mr. Wells is on his way from the Capitol, with Mr. Hathaway. So as soon as they arrive, we'll have supper—just the seven of us tonight. Ethel has prepared an excellent beef fillet, with peach ice cream for dessert."

With the announcement of the menu, both women forgot Ginna. "I do hope Ethel doesn't make the beef too rare," Mrs. Beauchamp suggested.

"Or the ice cream too soupy," Miss Counts added.

"She's well aware of your specifications," Maggie said pleasantly. Then, in a low voice, she remarked, "Since Ethel wasn't sure just when the men would arrive, she cooked the meal to please us women. And if the beef is a little too well done to suit them, I'm afraid they'll just have to bear with it."

Both women beamed while Ginna looked on in amazement. Martha's mother had absolutely charmed the two boarders and brought happiness to them with a few well-chosen words.

There was an element of anticipation as the delicious cooking odors from the kitchen drifted through the house. The ceiling fan in the dining room hummed steadily like the contented purr of a jungle cat. And Ginna listened to make sure another purr wasn't coming from the two women in the parlor chairs.

How different from her own home, Ginna thought, with everyone treading on eggs so as not to make her mother upset. And with that sudden insight, Ginna realized that her education in a totally new world had begun.

# CHAPTER
## 21

Within two days, the town of Washington took on its usual hustle and bustle with the arrival of the power brokers, legislators, and lobbyists for the special session that would pit Silverites against the rest of the country.

The boardinghouse on Pennsylvania Avenue suddenly swelled with full occupancy, and Ginna became a mere decoration at the evening table, as the men, totally wedded to power, acknowledged another face—however, a pretty one—and then promptly returned their attention to the business of politics.

For Ginna, meeting Martha's Mr. Wells was a disappointment. He was far older than she'd imagined. And she could understand why Maggie Gregory had finally given up trying to interest him in Martha. Why would he want a wife when he was so totally occupied with an exciting, capricious mistress, politics, which could stir a man as no woman was capable of doing?

"I think your Mr. Wells is a confirmed bachelor, Martha," Ginna said as she got ready for bed that second night. "But have you noticed how Mr. Hathaway seems to create opportunities to speak with you?"

"I hadn't noticed particularly."

"I think you should start cultivating his friendship, Martha. He seems much more susceptible to your charms."

"He's certainly younger. And nicer-looking, too, don't you think?"

Ginna laughed. "Don't tell me you haven't felt his interest. I think you've known all the time."

"But there probably isn't any future to the friendship, Ginna. He's lobbying for the mine owners. And you know he won't win. He'll lose his job at the end of this session. And Mama will probably lose him as a boarder as well."

"But he can't be blamed if he's fighting for a lost cause. And that's what it is. If he's a good lobbyist though, then someone else will more than likely hire him."

"That's true. I hadn't thought of that." Martha was silent for a few minutes. Then she said, "Did you hear from anybody in your family today?"

"No. I doubt that Papa has told Mummy yet that I've gone. She's so occupied with Cassie and the baby. And as for Papa, he would respect my wish not to be contacted just yet."

"But what about Jonathan?"

"I told you he had to go back to Kentucky. He'll be busy for the next several weeks seeing to the tobacco. So that gives me time to go to secretarial school and then leave town before he returns to Washington."

"I wish things had worked out differently. It's such a shame that—"

"Martha, I don't want to talk about Jonathan."

"All right, Ginna. And I guess we'd better go to sleep since we have to get up so early."

"Yes. Tomorrow will be a busy day at secretarial school."

"And at the law firm. Ginna?"

"What is it, Martha?"

Martha was still wrestling with the letter that Stanley Quail had sent to Senator Meadors. And it was on the tip of her tongue to tell Ginna about it. But then she thought better of it.

"Oh, it was nothing important. Good night."

"Good night, Martha."


By late afternoon of the next day, a tired Ginna walked out of the secretarial school. She had pinned her hair up severely that morning, and with her white blouse, dark skirt, and sad countenance, she hardly resembled the vibrant young woman Jonathan had taken home for tea.

But Allison, seated across the street in her carriage, recognized her nevertheless. "Ginna!" she called out. "Over here!"

Panic swept through Ginna at the sound of her name. She didn't want to face anyone, least of all Allison Meadors. Shifting the books to her other arm, she began to walk slowly down the street as if she hadn't heard her name. But Allison was determined.

"Ginna, you can't run away, my dear. I must talk with you."

She looked at the woman who had hurried to catch up

with her. "Mrs. Meadors, please. I can't talk with anyone. There's absolutely nothing to say. Not now."

"You don't have to talk. Just listen to what I have to say."

"Is it about Jonathan?"

"Only indirectly. It's more about your father and me."

"I don't understand."

"Cassie told you only part of the story. Don't you want to hear the rest?"

"You mean *you* know? Papa told you? And you still want to speak to me?"

"He didn't have to tell me, Ginna. You see, I'm part of the story, too. But it's much too hot to keep on walking. So won't you climb into the carriage and ride awhile so that we can get this terrible misunderstanding ironed out?"

Allison's face was pink from her rushing to catch up with Ginna in the heat. Seeing her discomfort, Ginna said, "I'm sorry. I didn't mean to be so thoughtless. Of course I'll ride with you."

"Good."

Allison turned to retrace her steps to the carriage and Ginna followed. Once they'd climbed into the victoria and Allison had sorted out the reins that had been carelessly tossed aside, the older woman signaled the horses to resume their travel down the road.

Allison headed for home. Ginna recognized the route that she and Jonathan had taken on the day they had become engaged. On the way, she held her books to her breast as if they were a shield against the hurt she now felt.

And the hurt widened in a fuller circle as they approached the driveway and then stopped at the entrance to the rose garden. "Let's go to the gazebo. We'll have more privacy to talk there," Allison said.

Ginna was at a disadvantage, for the gazebo held memories of exquisite happiness and, now, exquisite pain.

"I had a little gazebo like this years ago, at Rose Mallow," Allison began. "And it was under the flooring that I hid a picture of my beautiful dead husband who had been killed in the Battle of the Wilderness."

"My father fought in the same battle," Ginna said.

"I know. I was his wife."

Allison waited for the words to find recognition and understanding. And as she waited, the air was once again filled with the buzz of bees lighting on the last roses of the summer.

But for Ginna, Allison's words brought a sudden chill, striking her like a mountain wind that sweeps off the meltwater and blows through the desolate valleys. She shivered and crossed her arms as if to ward off the devastation.

"No. That's impossible. You're Jonathan's mother. . . ."

"By my second marriage. Just as you are Charles's daughter by *his* second marriage."

"But then that makes Jonathan and me . . ."

"Unrelated. No, Ginna. Don't leave. You must hear the rest of the story. Because to know the entire truth means that Cassie will lose her power to hurt you again."

"Does Jonathan know?"

"Not yet. But I plan to tell him when he returns to Washington."

"But I can't be here. I have to get away. I couldn't face him when he finds out . . ."

Allison's voice was soothing. "I know. And I know what a shock it is for you. But your father and I have discussed it. And we both feel that you do need to get away, to sort things out, to come to terms with your love for Jonathan.

"And that's why I sought you out today before you did

anything rash. To suggest that you go for a long visit to Morrow's house in Chicago."

"Jonathan's sister?"

"Half sister. But she's your relative as well—the bridge between you and Jonathan. She's the daughter that your father never saw, Ginna. *Our* daughter."

"Then she's my half sister, too."

"Yes. And she would welcome you with loving arms."

"I don't know. I don't know what to do."

"You can't stay at Mrs. Gregory's boardinghouse forever. Someone is bound to recognize you and ask entirely too many questions that will lead to embarrassment for everyone. No, it will look much better for you to be visiting relatives out of town."

"I never wanted to do anything that might embarrass Jonathan."

"Then it's settled. I'll wire Morrow in the morning, and you can travel on the train in the afternoon with my friends, the Montgomerys. They'll be visiting the Columbian Exposition. Morrow and her husband Andrew can call for you at the Richlieu Hotel, where they'll be staying."

Allison stood. "Let's go into the house for something cool to drink. Then I'll have Browne drive you back to the boardinghouse to pick up your things and take you home."

Ginna did not protest. She had thought that she was the only one in the world to feel sorrow. But looking at Allison's face, she realized that she was wrong. Both Allison and her own father had suffered. She knew now that sorrow chose its victims at random—not according to merit or just punishment.

As Browne waited outside the boardinghouse for Ginna to pack her valise, Mrs. Beauchamp and Miss Counts came downstairs and seated themselves in the parlor.

From the window, they watched the flurry of Ginna's leavetaking, her good-byes to Maggie Gregory and her daughter Martha.

"I wonder where her guardian is," Mrs. Beauchamp remarked later. "He didn't seem to be in the carriage."

"Oh, he's in Chicago," Martha said, appearing at the threshold. "She's meeting him there."

"Just like a guardian," Miss Counts said. "Probably stopped off to spend all the poor girl's money at the exposition. Or at the gambling halls nearby. She'll be lucky to have any money left by the time she gets there."

Mrs. Beauchamp ignored her as usual. "Martha, do I smell leg of lamb cooking?"

"Yes, ma'am. And that reminds me. Mama asked me to go upstairs to the attic and bring down some of her good mint jelly."

"Good evening, Mrs. Beauchamp, Miss Counts," Maggie said, coming into the parlor. "I trust you both had a pleasant day."

"Tolerable," Mrs. Beauchamp admitted. "Just tolerable."

"We spent the afternoon at the bookstore," Miss Counts said, trying hard to disguise the excitement in her voice. "Mr. Innis located a copy of Hawaiian history for us. We thought it might be educational to read it after meeting Miss Biggs."

"Yes. That should make for interesting reading," Maggie agreed, knowing full well what their dinner conversation for the next few weeks would be.

At the Forsyte house that evening, a shy Ginna sat at the dining table with her father.

He smiled at her and said, "I'm glad that you've agreed

to visit Morrow. An hour ago, I wasn't even sure that you would be here for supper."

"I might be making a mistake, Papa, by visiting her. But I think maybe my curiosity helped me to decide. I thought Cassie was the only sister I would ever have. It comes as a shock to learn I have another one. And I'm sure that Morrow will be just as shocked over me."

"You must write me, Ginna. Tell me what she's like."

"Oh, Papa. How sad for you, never to have seen her. Allison—Mrs. Meadors, that is—told me about the gazebo at Rose Mallow. And how she buried your picture in the silver frame under the floor so that the Yankees wouldn't steal it. She wanted Morrow to have it. But I guess it's still buried there."

Charles quickly looked away and Ginna realized what she had done. "I'm sorry, Papa. I didn't mean to say anything to hurt you." She reached out her hand to him. "I'm still mixed up. Allison is so beautiful and kind that I sort of wish that you and she could have found each other years ago, before you married Mummy. But then, if that had happened, Nathan and I wouldn't be here."

Charles made a supreme effort to smile again. "And I can't imagine my life without you and Nathan. You've both brought me so much pleasure. No, the past is buried, just as surely as the picture."

"Not quite, Papa. But life doesn't seem nearly so black to me as it did three days ago."

"I'll go with you to the station tomorrow, Ginna. To see you off. But I'd like to ask a favor of you."

"Yes, Papa?"

"For Allison's sake, wear Jonathan's engagement ring. The Montgomerys won't question your going to visit your prospective sister-in-law."

"But I don't have it."

"Allison returned the package. It's on my desk in the office."

"But even if I agree, I can't ever marry Jonathan. That's more apparent now than ever. I'll have to give the ring back to him later."

"Whatever you decide, Ginna," he assured her. "But for now, wear the ring."

"Does Allison still have the letter?"

"Yes. We felt it would be best for her to talk with Jonathan first. Then she'll give him your letter."

That night, as Ginna slept in her own bed, she cradled her left hand. Her finger had felt so bare without Jonathan's ring. Now that she was wearing it again, she knew she could not afford to become too attached to it, for it was not hers to keep.

# CHAPTER
## 22

The next afternoon became a whirlwind of activity—hatboxes, trunk and valise packed full of clothes, all brought downstairs at intervals, with Barge placing them in the carriage. He lashed the trunk to the rear with strong ropes so that it would not fall on the way to the station and then placed the other luggage carefully inside the carriage, managing to save barely enough space for his single passenger.

It had been arranged that Allison would meet Ginna at the rail station to introduce her to the Montgomerys at the last minute. And so Charles had said good-bye at breakfast that morning, for in the end it would have been too awkward for both Charles and Allison to be present at the same time to see her off.

"Clara, take good care of Papa while I'm gone," Ginna said as she climbed into the carriage.

"I sure will, Miss Ginna. Now don't worry for one minute. You just have yourself a good time in Chicago. And if you can find a little something to bring me back from the fair, I sure would admire to have it—so's I can show my friend, Winnie."

"I won't forget," she assured Clara, and then waved goodbye.

As the carriage traveled along the route to Union Station, Ginna began to think about Nathan. She had written him, but so far had received nothing from him. The only communiqué had been the letter her father had received from Mr. Graves, telling him that Nathan had arrived safely at Braxton and was settling in with the other young boys who had also been sent to school early for one reason or another. But Ginna knew Nathan well enough to understand what his silence meant. He was either awfully happy or dreadfully sad. Ginna prayed it was the former.

Only a short distance away from Maggie Gregory's boardinghouse, a regretful Ginna remembered her promise to Martha, to finish painting her china at the institute. Somehow, Ginna had lost all desire to paint anything at all. She had not touched a brush ever since that day she'd discovered the devastation in her attic studio. But perhaps she would feel differently by the time she'd had some time to herself, to think and decide what she wanted to do with her life.

"Barge, I can't believe how crowded Washington is," Ginna said, adjusting her lace-trimmed parasol against the sun. "So many people."

He didn't turn around but kept his eyes on the crowded roadway as he replied, "It's always that way when Congress is in session. But we got enough time to get to the station, Miss Ginna. So don't you worry."

"I forgot to tell Clara that I left a note for Mummy on her bedside table. Be sure to remind her, Barge, when you get back."

"I'll do that."

"Of course, I'm not sure just when she'll be home. Probably next week if Cassie and the baby are all right by then."

"What'd they finally name the little fellow?"

"Stanley—for his father."

"That's a mighty big name for a little boy to be saddled with."

"He'll probably wind up with some nickname instead. Like Pinky, Nathan's friend. Did you know his real name is Quincy Talliferro Boswell III?"

Barge chuckled. "Bet that's why he had a black eye the last time I saw 'im."

Ginna settled back in the carriage and rode the rest of the way in silence. She mentally catalogued the contents of her purse: the instructions her father had given her about the letter of credit at the bank and any additional money she might need. Morrow's husband could introduce her at the bank, if necessary. But Ginna was determined not to be any more trouble than she could help.

The station rose up from the landscape, a mammoth stone building slightly blackened with the residue of smoke from the engines that puffed in and out of Washington daily. All train stations were busier than ever now, for people could cross the entire continent from east to west, using sleeping cars, parlor cars, and dining cars to make the trip more comfortable.

Ginna had never slept on an American Pullman before. This would be her first experience. And she looked forward to seeing the cars that Mr. Bok at *Ladies' Home Journal* had called ostentatious. If that meant more comfort, then she much preferred it to a crick in the neck.

When they reached the terminal, Barge drew up to the front doors and stopped. Ginna hurriedly climbed down. "Wait here, Barge, while I find Mrs. Meadors. Then we can get someone to help us with the luggage."

Allison was already waiting on a bench inside the door. Seeing Ginna approach, Allison stood and began to walk in her direction at the same time that Ginna rushed toward Allison.

"I'm glad to see you, Ginna," Allison said. "The train has already arrived in the station. Where is your luggage?"

"Outside in the carriage. But I have to pick up my ticket from the agent first. Papa came by this morning and purchased it. But he left it here for me."

"Good. Then we won't have to stand in the long line."

Allison took over, directing Ginna to the proper window. But it was Allison who asked for the ticket. Then she nodded to a redcap waiting nearby, and the rush to unload Ginna's luggage began as train numbers were called over the loudspeaker. The hiss of steam and the clank of brakes added to the noise of arrivals and departures.

By the time Ginna and Allison returned to the carriage, Barge had already untied the trunk and placed it on one of the long-tongued wagons with oversized red wheels. "I didn't know how many bags you wanted to carry on the train with you, Miss Ginna."

"Just the one, and the one hatbox," she said, indicating the items. Between Barge and the redcap, her luggage was sorted out, with the trunk sent to the far baggage car for storage, to be retrieved once she arrived in Chicago.

"You're traveling quite lightly, Ginna," Allison said.

"Lila Montgomery has six trunks and twelve hatboxes with her. And she's brought along her personal maid just to attend to her clothes."

"I wasn't certain how long I'd be visiting," Ginna replied. But it would not have made any difference. She had nothing else to pack. And it would have been ludicrous for Maudie or Clara to travel with her.

"If you haven't brought along enough clothes, I'm sure that Morrow will be happy to loan you some of hers."

With the redcap pulling the wagon to the dock to load the luggage, Barge returned to the carriage. Ginna stopped, turned around, and waved to him. Then she hurried to catch up with Allison.

"Lila Montgomery and her husband, Richard, are old friends of mine, Ginna. They'll be pleasant company for you on the trip."

"I appreciate everything you've done for me, Mrs. Meadors."

"Just remember, Ginna. I already love you as a daughter. But I'm doing this for Jonathan, too. I don't want your lives ruined by something that happened years ago. Perhaps this will give you an opportunity to sort things out and come to terms with your own feelings."

Before Ginna had a chance to reply, a voice called out, "Allison."

The two looked in the direction of the voice.

"There's Lila now. We're just in time to board."

"Lila, Richard, may I present Jonathan's fiancée, Miss Ginna Forsyte. Ginna, Mr. and Mrs. Montgomery."

"How do you do?"

"What a beautiful young lady, Allison. No wonder Jonathan has finally decided to take the plunge. Now don't worry about her at all. We'll take good care of her on the train, won't we, Richard, dear?"

"Of course we will. No need to worry at all."

The woman was lovely, with her luxurious brown hair swept up into a Parisian roll, a large summer hat dripping with roses—ash pink, to match her traveling costume— a slender crepe dress with an embroidered-sleeve jacket. And the man at her side was equally elegant, with his healthy mustache matching the dark iron-gray of his hair. His Panama hat was the color of light straw bleached in the sun, only a shade lighter than his summer suit.

Seeing them together, Ginna felt an ache in her side. It was almost as if she were looking at a replica of what she and Jonathan might be, twenty years from now, if plans for their marriage had worked out.

"I'll try not to be any trouble, Mrs. Montgomery," Ginna said.

"What a delightful accent. English?"

Ginna hesitated. She looked at Allison first and then replied, "Yes."

"And how long have you been in the States?" Lila inquired.

"A little over six months."

Richard glanced toward the train. "We'd better board. Plenty of time to become acquainted later on. But we don't want to miss the train, do we?"

"All aboard!" the voice called out for the second time.

Up and down the train track a flurry of good-byes took place. And then a most unusual procession began to march down the platform. Mouths fell open; good-byes were stopped midway as twelve women with painted faces and gaudy costumes of every color in the rainbow rushed toward one of the cars farther down.

The older woman in the group frowned and called out, "Come along, Souci. Stop flirting with the man. This trip is supposed to be educational."

The young coquette looked with languishing eyes at the handsome young man. She blew him a kiss and said, "*Au revoir, mon chéri,*" and then rushed to catch up with the others.

"Oh, my dear. Just look. They're getting on *our* train." Lila's voice was indignant. "It's a good thing that Ginna isn't traveling alone if that's the kind of passenger allowed on this trip."

The people on the platform returned to life. Allison hugged Ginna and Lila, then watched them disappear. She waited to catch a glimpse of them once they'd taken their seats inside.

Richard, lingering behind, was the last to board. He stepped up into the vestibule of the car as the conductor removed the portable steps and brought them inside.

"Who were those women passing by a moment ago?" he inquired.

The conductor grinned. "That's a New Orleans madam and her girls. She's taking them to the fair to broaden their minds, I heard. Stopped off in Washington for a few days to see the sights here first."

Richard laughed. "The madam's probably taking them to earn a little extra money instead."

"Oh, no, sir. That's what I thought, too. But evidently it's not the case. And I hear the madam's paying for the entire trip herself."

"Then she must have some awfully rich customers in New Orleans."

"Reckon so."

The train started moving. And as Allison stood on the

platform waving good-bye, Richard walked down the aisle to join his wife and Ginna.

The train was subtly divided for different classes of people regardless of the price paid for the ticket. The less desirable cars were the ones downwind from the kitchen-dining cars, with the cooking odors drifting into them at all hours.

But Nelly Rose and her girls were not aware of this. They were too busy looking at the lavish draperies and the velvet tufted seats that could be adjusted into beds, with suitable curtains to block off the view from the aisles.

The only unhappy ones in the car were Souci, one of the madam's girls, and the frightened Meara McClellan, Lila Montgomery's personal maid.

This was Meara's first trip away from home. She sat with her hands crossed in her lap and a frown marring her well-scrubbed face.

The other girls were cross with Souci for being late, so she was ostracized for the moment. "*Alors*, it matters not a picayune. You're all so boring, anyway."

And with that pronouncement, Souci flounced down the aisle and plopped herself into the empty seat beside Meara. "Do you mind, *chérie*, if I sit here for a little while? The others are being so impossible. I have no wish to talk with any of them."

Meara could only nod and stare at the young woman whose eyes were a strange shade of green. She was beautiful, like a forbidden flame. Meara wanted to reach out and touch her, knowing full well that she could be burned if she did.

"I'm called Souci. What is your name?"

"M-Meara."

"And you are traveling alone?"

"My mistress is in another car." Despite herself, Meara said, "You're very beautiful."

Souci smiled. "Would you like to be beautiful, too?"

"Oh, no. I'm much too plain. I could never change."

"No, you could become *très chic*, with a little artifice. Would you like me to show you?"

Meara nodded.

"Then I'll be back." Souci stood and went to retrieve her makeup case. The idea of transforming this plain girl into one of them would give her something interesting to do, Souci decided. It would certainly help to relieve the tedium of the trip, with all of the others snubbing her.

In the luxurious car ahead, Lila made herself comfortable. With Richard engrossed in his newspaper, Lila leaned over to Ginna. "I do hope my maid is getting along all right by herself. This is her first trip away from home. And I expect she's quite frightened."

"I remember my first trip away from home," Ginna commented. "My school chums and I crossed the Channel to France. And even though we could see the coast for most of the time, we were all quite frightened that the boat would sink."

"At least that's one thing that Meara won't have to cope with. We'll be on land the entire way."

Richard put down his paper and took a good look at Ginna. "Did you learn French in school, Miss Forsyte?"

"Yes. A little Italian also. My father felt at the time that one should know other languages as well as one's own."

"Very commendable. Then you'll be able to converse with some of the foreigners at the exposition."

"Really, Richard. Don't put such thoughts in her head.

Morrow will be much more careful with Jonathan's fiancée than that."

Richard's laugh was uninhibited. "You've forgotten, Lila. Morrow works regularly at one of the settlement houses. She already knows that foreigners don't have two heads."

"But they're so different from . . . from us."

Richard told Ginna, "If you thought your visit was going to be all parties and gaiety, then you're bound to be disappointed. Morrow is a 'do-gooder.' "

Ginna's eyes came alive. "My father has a friend, a doctor who works at Cook County Hospital in Chicago. I understand he does charity work, too, when he has the time. Wouldn't it be wonderful if he and Morrow knew each other?"

Lila was not to be outdone. "My dear, if I were you, I'd stick to shopping, parties, and sightseeing. Charity work is for plain women who never intend to get married, like that Miss Addams I've read about at Hull House. Besides, there're too many infectious diseases one can pick up at a place like that, with all those poor immigrants. But let's find something more pleasant to talk about. Tell me, when are you and Jonathan to be married? And have you selected the material for your wedding dress?"

For Ginna, it was difficult to maintain a casual conversation. Talking about her wedding dress only brought back painful memories of the day Cassie had divulged the news of her birth.

When the call came that the dining car was open, Ginna was relieved. The conversation ceased abruptly as Lila left her seat to tidy up before the evening meal.

Ginna, too, left her seat to wash her hands. But she soon returned. And while she waited for the other woman, she gazed out the window, watching the landscape that flashed

by in lights and shadows. The chandeliers overhead had
not yet been lit, for another hour would pass before the sun
went down.

"Ready, Ginna?"

"Yes, Mrs. Montgomery."

"Then let's go in and see the table Richard has selected
for us."

# CHAPTER
## 23

After three monotonous days and nights of winding its way past corn and wheat fields and vast expanses of prairie interspersed with small villages, the train bringing Ginna west finally pulled into the Chicago rail terminal at five o'clock in the afternoon.

Lila Montgomery's patience had ended several hundred miles before their arrival. "I don't care what they say about the luxury of this train," she complained. "I'm absolutely exhausted from the trip."

Richard gazed at his beautiful wife with a sympathetic eye. He should have taken A.C. up on the private railcar. "We'll soon be at the hotel, my dear. A nice warm bath and a good mattress will work wonders for all of us."

As others left the train, Ginna began to gather up her belongings, returning a book to the valise beside her. The trip had been long and tiring, and she would be glad to leave the train, too.

Although she was grateful for the Montgomerys' generosity in allowing her to travel with them, she had paid for it in a dozen little ways. With her maid in another car, Lila Montgomery was helpless and Ginna had become the maid, without Lila's conscious recognition of that fact.

Whatever she decided to do with her life, Ginna realized that her spirit would never allow herself to be at the beck and call of any demanding relative. To be totally dependent on others for her food and her self-esteem had been damaging enough as a child. Her struggle to emerge as an individual out from under the shadow of her mother and older sister had been a constant one, and if she capitulated now, the battle had been for nothing.

But she had to learn not to react so impetuously. She had signed up for secretarial school when she wasn't sure it was the direction she wanted to take. But because of Allison, she was now being handed another chance—to plan at leisure, to weigh her alternatives—while at the same time, getting to know the sister she never knew she had.

Yet she was reticent. What had Allison written Morrow in the letter she was carrying? Merely that she was Jonathan's fiancée? Or that she was her half sister? How was she to react when she met Morrow for the first time?

Quickly, Ginna finished packing, put on her hat, and waited for Lila to give the signal that she was ready to leave the train.

"I do hope Meara isn't too tired," Lila remarked, fastening her rose-bedecked hat with a long, jeweled hatpin. "All my gowns will be so wrinkled from the journey. It will take her forever to get them looking halfway decent again.

"Well, Ginna, are you ready to get your first glimpse of this heathenish city?"

Ginna smiled. "I'm ready to leave the train, Mrs. Montgomery, if that's what you mean."

"Richard, dear, could you please carry this small case for me?"

The patient Richard took the case, slung it over his shoulder, and then led the way so that he might help his wife and Ginna down the steps.

Once again the platform was filled: a mingling of people going back and forth, looking for loved ones. "I'll take those bags for you, sir," a redcap offered, in the hope of getting a good tip. "You got other luggage?"

Richard turned around and acknowledged the man following him. "An assortment of trunks as well. We'll need a carriage for us and a dray for all of the luggage."

"Yes, sir. And where will you be going?"

"Hotel Richlieu."

Farther down the platform, a ripple of laughter floated through the air as Nelly Rose and her girls also stepped off the train.

There was nothing unobtrusive in their arrival. As in Washington, all eyes turned toward the exuberant, light-hearted group. But this time there was an extra girl, carefully made up, with a lime-green silk dress trimmed in black lace and matching black lace stockings.

Richard, who had been watching for Meara, leaned over and whispered in Lila's ear, "One of those girls bears a remarkable resemblance to your maid, don't you think?"

"Really, Richard. It would seem you might have better things to do than to stand here and stare at those little tarts."

Lila moved closer to Ginna, as if she were protecting her from contamination. "Look the other way, my dear. They'll be out of sight soon."

Once they had gone by, Lila once again began to look for Meara. Her impatience was readily discernible to both Ginna and her husband.

"If you don't mind, my dear, I'll go ahead and see to the baggage."

"Yes. Do that, Richard. And Ginna and I will wait for that straggling little piece to get off the train."

Fifteen minutes later, Richard returned to a nearly deserted platform. "Hasn't Meara shown up yet?"

"No, she hasn't. And I'm quite furious with her, keeping us waiting like this. I really feel we should go on. Let her get her own conveyance to the hotel."

In the end, that was the decision made. Meara had vanished. She was not on the train; she was not in the terminal.

"She's probably already at the hotel, Lila. Don't fret about her," Richard assured his wife.

From the slow-moving carriage, Ginna was content to watch the bustling landscape of a vibrant, sprawling city: the towering buildings, the horse-drawn trolleys and cable cars, the tall cathedral spire. There was a rawness about the city, a loudness that spoke of new wealth and impossible poverty, side by side. Excitement combined with apathy; sights and sounds and smells bombarded the eyes and ears and nose until the senses were satiated.

"What is that awful odor?" Lila inquired, holding her handkerchief daintily to her nose.

"Probably a whiff of the stockyards," Richard answered.

"What have we gotten into, Richard?"

"No worse than Paris, my dear. Is that not right, Ginna?"

"London, too," Ginna agreed, wrinkling her nose. "But

all large cities are guilty. That's why I love to be in the country at this time of year."

Richard laughed. "So Jonathan has found his soul mate, I see. I presume you like horses also?"

"Very much."

"But won't you miss the gaiety of a city, Ginna? I don't think I could bury myself in the country," Lila said.

Ginna gazed down at the ring on her hand. With difficulty, she tried to keep her voice steady. "I met Jonathan in Washington, Mrs. Montgomery," she replied, smiling, "at a party. So I presume we might venture out occasionally."

It was Lila's turn to laugh. "Of course. At Peggy Drake's house, wasn't it? At least she's taking the credit all over Washington for being the matchmaker."

Ginna attempted to change the subject. "Have you met Jonathan's sister?"

"Several times. But that was before her marriage."

"I was just wondering how we would recognize her. . . ."

"At the hotel, you mean? Well, that won't be a problem at all. Unless she's changed drastically. She looks exactly like her mother."

Lila's attention was diverted by the noise behind them. She turned around to make sure the dray with all of her trunks was keeping within sight of the carriage. But she completely ignored the dirty little urchin running alongside the carriage.

The boy was thin and his shirt was ragged. "A dime," he begged. "Lady, could I have a dime to buy some bread?"

Out of pity, Ginna reached into her purse. "Can you catch it?" she called out.

"Ginna, dear, you shouldn't do that. We'll never have another moment's peace if you do."

But it was too late. Ginna had already thrown the coin

toward the little boy. He caught it before it dropped to the ground. "Thank you, lady," he said, and then quickly disappeared down the street.

Several blocks more, and then the carriage drew up before a palatial building with red awnings embroidered with an *R*. Beech and oak trees lined the avenue, giving it the appearance of an extravagant resort, an oasis in the heart of a city.

The doorman, dressed in a smart red uniform decorated with gold braid, blew his whistle, bringing a score of only a little less lavishly dressed helpers. The sight of the carriage, followed by a dray of trunks, indicated that important guests had arrived.

To Lila Montgomery's way of thinking, she was being quite conservative in traveling so lightly. She came from a family of great wealth—a beauty who could have acquired a European husband as easily as a dozen of her contemporaries whose fathers had traded their daughters' American dowries for slightly tarnished European titles. But she had elected to marry her true love. She lived like royalty most of the time, anyway. So she felt that she really had the better of two worlds.

She swept into the hotel with all the panache of a queen, followed by Ginna, hugging her small valise. The manager rushed to greet Lila, bowing and scraping, but she gave him little encouragement.

"My wife is quite exhausted," Richard said. "Please have someone show us to our suite. I'll be down later to sign the register."

"Of course, Mr. Montgomery."

In the space of twenty minutes, the hotel staff had swung into action, catering to the excessively wealthy New York couple who had unwittingly traveled the same route as

Nelly Rose and her girls—stopping off in Washington to visit friends and then continuing the journey to Chicago to attend the exposition.

But that was where the similarity ended. The Richlieu was in a class by itself, providing amenities that the Hotel Moffat was unable to emulate.

Already a special maid was at work unpacking Lila's trunks, while Ginna, feeling slightly out of place, sat on one of the sofas facing the extended bay windows—a hallmark of the sandstone edifices of Chicago.

Looking out the window, she did not hear the footsteps behind her, disguised as they were by the plush peach-colored carpet.

"Ginna," Richard called out. "Look who I found downstairs."

Quickly, she stood and turned around. Ginna recognized the woman immediately, as she'd been promised. For Morrow was a younger replica of Allison, with her striking blond hair and amethyst eyes that sparkled with vivacity.

Morrow didn't wait for Richard to introduce them. "Ginna," she said, walking quickly to meet her with hands outstretched. "I'm Morrow Lachlan, Jonathan's sister. Welcome to Chicago."

"Thank you, Mrs. Lachlan. It's good to be here."

Morrow laughed and, still holding on to Ginna's hands, said, "My name is Morrow. Please call me that."

Lila, hearing voices, came into the living room from one of the bedrooms. "I thought I heard your voice, Morrow."

"How are you, Lila?" she inquired. "Was it an exhausting trip for you?"

"Quite. But this dear child helped to relieve the boredom of the long train ride."

"Thank you for looking after her," Morrow said. "My mother and I both appreciate it very much."

Morrow then turned to Richard. "Andrew will probably have claimed Ginna's trunks by now."

"I'll walk back downstairs with you," Richard suggested.

Amid the flurry of good-byes, Lila held her check for Ginna to kiss. "Have a wonderful visit, my dear."

"Thank you, Mrs. Montgomery. For everything."

"Lila, I'll ring you up tomorrow. There's a wonderfully delicious champagne breakfast at the Union League Club on Sunday morning, given by Julia Atwilder. She's sending around an invitation for you and Richard. I do hope you will be rested well enough by then to attend. Everyone's looking forward to seeing you."

Lila brightened. She loved parties and didn't examine the excuses for them. She was vastly different from her friend, Ward McAllister, the social maven of New York, who saw no reason for honoring Columbus. "In a social way, Lila," he had confided, "Columbus was an *ordinary* man."

"I don't care, Ward, since *he* won't be at the exposition."

Remembering that exchange, she smiled. "A good night's sleep will work wonders, Morrow, as Richard has pointed out. We'll look forward to the breakfast. But, tell me, what is this champagne watermelon that the club has started serving?"

Morrow laughed. "Oh, it's all the rage right now, Lila. A watermelon is plugged, the center is scooped out, and an entire bottle of champagne is poured into it. Then it's put on ice to chill. Quite delicious in this hot weather, if you're careful not to partake too much.

"We really must go. Andrew is probably champing at the bit just like his horses. Ready, Ginna?"

She nodded. The bellman, waiting discreetly at the door, took her valise. And as she followed Morrow out of the suite, Ginna already loved her as a sister.

# CHAPTER
## 24

Andrew Lachlan had been an apprentice architect under Louis Sullivan at the same time as Frank Lloyd Wright. But now the two were out on their own, having chosen to go separate ways, each in a slightly different direction.

The Lachlan house along the shore had been designed and built by Andrew to reflect his own style, one not quite so horizontal as Wright's, but equally open to the sunlight with a spacious quality.

"What an unusual house," Ginna exclaimed, seeing the burnt-clay two-and-a-half-story structure, with its curved arches reflecting the curve of the shoreline.

"Andrew designed it," Morrow said with pride.

"I've never seen anything like it before. It's magnificent."

"It's a welding of the Scottish moors and the western prairies," Andrew explained in his rich voice with the slight Scottish burr. "Built with strong stone to stand against wind and rain."

They stopped in the driveway, the setting sun behind them. Andrew climbed down to help his passengers out of the carriage.

"Come, Ginna. We'll go inside while Andrew attends to the luggage. I'm anxious for you to see the interior of the house as well."

Ginna followed Morrow as the carriage disappeared behind another curved archway. Even the landscaping was wedded to the house, as if the land and house were one. The white gingerbread trim and the green ivy that had enveloped the various country houses she had seen across the miles, from the window of the train, would never be at home here.

"This is Allie," Morrow said, seeing her servant standing at the open door. "Allie, this is Mr. Jonathan's fiancée, Miss Forsyte."

"Good evenin', ma'am. Welcome to Eagleroch."

"Mommy, did you bring me anything?" David asked, rushing to greet his mother.

"I brought a beautiful visitor, son. She's going to be your Aunt Ginna."

The small boy resembled Nathan so much that, for a brief moment, Ginna was speechless. Recognizing the same frown of disappointment, she quickly said, "If you're David, I have two presents for you—one from your grandmother Allison and one from me."

"I'm David," he assured her, brightening at the prospect of two presents. "Where are they?"

"David, let Aunt Ginna catch her breath first."

Ginna laughed. "Just as soon as my bags are brought into the house, David, we'll find your presents."

There was a golden glow to the spacious living room that opened from the entrance hall. A row of windows, unusual in shape, provided a breathtaking view of the sparkling lake beyond. Like coastal houses along the seaboard, the living level was really the second floor, to allow for rise of storm tides or waves. The openness seemed to go on forever, with furniture grouped to delineate where walls might have been. One end of the room possessed an arched fireplace, filled with greenery, and to its side a large potted palm reaching toward the skylight.

"Would you like me to show you to your room now, Ginna? Supper won't be long."

"Yes, please."

David followed them up the steps, as if afraid the bearer of gifts might vanish for good. He stood in the doorway watching Morrow walk into the guest bedroom. It, too, faced the lake, with a wonderful view from the same elongated windows flanked by blue-green draperies the color of the water beyond.

A breeze swept through the open windows and flapped the draperies with its force. Morrow immediately walked to one of the windows and half closed it. "If it gets too cool during the night," she said, "the windows are quite easy to adjust."

With her hand, she indicated the room to the right. "Your bath is on the other side. If you need anything, just ask Allie."

"You're so kind, Mrs. Lachlan—"

"Morrow," she corrected again. "Remember, if we're to be relatives, then we mustn't be so formal."

So Morrow had no inkling. Perhaps it was just as well.

"I want you to feel right at home here, Ginna. To see Chicago as *I* see it. It's such a growing, exciting city. Yet there's so much poverty here that it sometimes breaks my heart."

"Mrs. Montgomery said that you work at a settlement house sometimes."

"Yes, I do. And tomorrow is one of my days to work." Impulsively, she said, "Would you like to go with me tomorrow? I really would like to show you what we're doing—especially with the children."

"Yes, I would like that."

"Of course, if you'd rather stay here . . ."

"No. I really want to go, Morrow."

"Good. Then that's settled."

There was a noise on the stairway, as Ginna's trunk, valise, and hatbox were brought up. And David, hearing the commotion, ran to the top of the stairs to direct the carrier. "In here," he said. "Hurry, Mateo. I have *two* presents to open."

Morrow shook her head as David watched Ginna open the valise and remove a package from it.

"Here's the one from your grandmother," Ginna said. "You can be opening it while I find the key to my trunk. Your other present is in it."

David immediately sat on the floor and tore off the wrapping paper. A small carved rocking horse appeared. As soon as he placed it on the floor to rock it back and forth, music began to play.

"Mother always adds to his collection of wooden horses if she can," Morrow said.

Ginna removed the top tray to the trunk and searched for a box nestled amid her dresses. "I'm glad you love horses, David. So do I." And she handed him the box.

Very politely, he looked up at her. "Thank you, Aunt Ginna."

She waited as his excited hands removed the lid and carefully took out each piece, wrapped in tissue paper. He sucked in his breath as they became visible: a toy calèche made of tin, painted brown and white; two white horses to draw the carriage; and a coachman and a lady, dressed in the French fashion.

"Oh, Ginna, how exquisite," Morrow said.

"It was my own. But I've outgrown it now, and I wanted David to have it."

"Thank you, Ginna." She turned to her son. "Well, David, let's take your presents and go find Nanny. I'm sure Ginna is ready to rest." With that, the two left the bedroom and Ginna suddenly found herself alone for the first time in days.

She slowly walked to the window and looked out. She had not told Morrow that her father had given her the French calèche the Christmas she was nine, and that it had been one of her favorite toys. Passing it on to David now was her way of making her father's presence in the house real. He had missed so much.

At the sound of a knock on the door, she turned from the window.

"I've come to tell you that supper will be ready in fifteen minutes, Miss Ginna. And right after supper I'll help you unpack your trunk. So don't bother with it now."

"Thank you, Allie."

She took her comb and brush from the valise and hurried toward the bath. She had just enough time to wash her face and comb the tangles out of her hair. A time for introspection would come later that night, when she was alone. For the next few hours, she would have to force herself to be congenial company, not a small task with her problems threatening to overwhelm her. She had not left them behind in Washington. She had brought them with her as surely as the clothes that waited to be unpacked.

Once she was ready, she walked downstairs.

The evening spent with Morrow and Andrew was a decidedly pleasant one, containing no stilted words or awkward silences. They accepted her readily, and for that one evening, Ginna pretended that she and Jonathan were still engaged. She was part of a warm, loving family—feeling safe and secure, the way she had that day in Jonathan's arms when he had given her the ring.

And later that night, when she was finally alone, Ginna had no wish to disturb the dream. She drifted off to sleep almost as soon as her head felt the soft pillow. Harsh reality could wait another day.

By the next morning, the sounds and breakfast smells of a house awakening slowly spiraled upward and teased Ginna, causing her to wrinkle her nose and finally open her eyes. From the foot of her bed, Morrow's son was watching her.

"Good morning, David."

He climbed up on the side of the bed. "Mommy said not to wake you until Nanny told me I could."

"Then it's time to get up?"

"Yes." He immediately slid off the bed and ran out of the room, leaving Ginna alone.

Once she was up and dressed, Ginna followed her nose to the breakfast room, where Morrow was already waiting. "Good morning, Ginna. I trust you slept well?"

"Oh, yes. I didn't realize how tired I actually was. One minute I was awake and the next minute David was telling me it was time to get up."

As Ginna and Morrow sat down at the table, Morrow said, "Andrew left early this morning, so we'll have breakfast to ourselves. And after breakfast we'll start out. This is the day I usually take a basket of food staples to a poor family in the tenements—the Andrettis. We'll go there first, if you don't mind. And then we'll be at the settlement house by ten o'clock."

She glanced at Ginna's dress. "But if I were you, I'd wear something that I don't care about. Sometimes we get down on the floor with the children."

"I have my artist's pinafore with me. Perhaps I can take it to put on over my dress."

"Perfect."

As the carriage traveled from the more elegant section along the lake toward the slums, Morrow said, "You'll have to ignore some of the language you hear in the streets, Ginna. And Sunday morning, when we attend the champagne breakfast at the club, please don't tell Lila Montgomery that I brought you along today. She would be absolutely appalled."

"I understand."

They passed through the carnivallike atmosphere, the same route that Allie and Morrow had taken the previous week. And though the men gathered in the streets presented no obstacle, the noise as they approached the bordellos was considerable, with the parrot screeching his raucous cry. Ginna's eyes widened at the sight of a half-dressed woman leaning out of one of the windows.

"I'm sorry, Ginna. This must be a little shocking to you. But it's part of life. And nothing will be gained by merely turning one's head and pretending it doesn't exist. The sad part about many of these women is that they didn't start out this way. And each attempt to get them back into working for a living doesn't last long."

"I heard about the sweatshops and how little money the people make."

Morrow nodded. "The woman we're going to see works for just a few pennies a day. She and her children are nearly starving. It doesn't seem right, Ginna, when a man like Mr. Field spends seventy-five thousand dollars on a birthday party for his son and then pays women so little to make the clothes he carries in his store.

"But that's enough from me. Andrew says I preach too much and that the people who really need to hear are the very ones who won't listen."

When they reached the tenement, Morrow gathered up the food basket. "Do you mind waiting with the carriage, Ginna? I won't be but a minute."

The morning that had been planned so carefully by Morrow was completely disrupted within a few minutes, for as Morrow hurriedly left the Andretti tenement, a bloodcurdling scream in the next tenement spooked the horses, and it was all Ginna could do to calm them down.

"Heavens, what was that?" Morrow asked, turning to Mrs. Andretti in the doorway.

From the reaction of the other women standing in the street, no one seemed to have heard it except for Morrow and Ginna and the horses.

"Mrs. Andretti, what's wrong? Why is no one going to see about that terrible cry?"

Mrs. Andretti looked cautiously at the group of women. Then she whispered, "It's Tasha Slavonsky having her baby, poor thing. But no one will help her."

"In heaven's name, why not?"

"The girl isn't married."

"Well, if no one wants to help her, why hasn't a doctor been called?"

"Everybody's afraid they'll have to pay the doctor bill."

Morrow's face showed her fury. "Then *I'll* pay the bill. Marcello, do you know where there's a doctor near here?"

"*Sì*. Dr. Scaglia. He lives three blocks from here."

"Then go and fetch him."

He looked at his mother and then at the women down the street. As he hesitated, Morrow said, "Oh, never mind, Marcello. I'll go myself. What does the building look like?"

"It's painted green, *signora*. And his sign hangs over the door."

Morrow climbed into the carriage beside Ginna and took over the reins. As the carriage hurried down the street, the group of women parted to allow it through.

"I suppose you heard?" Morrow said.

"Yes."

"One day, Ginna, women are going to be kinder to other women regardless of their sins. And one day women will only have to work eight hours a day, and children will go to school instead of to the factories and the stockyards."

Ginna looked at Morrow's face. The dream was in her eyes, and watching her, Ginna felt an excitement that she had never felt before. Morrow was strong, with a sense of right and wrong that did not depend on what others thought.

And at that moment, Ginna wanted to reach out to her as a sister and tell her the truth.

# CHAPTER
## 25

By Sunday morning, Ginna was in another world, far from the squalor of the ward surrounding the settlement house where Morrow had taken her two days previously.

It was the private club of business leaders and corporate executives, two hundred of whom were self-made millionaires. They were the power brokers of Chicago, whose influence was more subtle than the "gray wolves" that controlled the political precincts. Yet, in the East, they were all considered upstarts, which bothered them not at all. They were far too busy building and trading and forming western empires of their own.

"Good morning, Andrew," R. T. Atwilder said, extending his hand.

At the same time, Julia, his wife, smiled at Morrow. "I'm so glad you could come and bring your houseguest."

"Julia, this is my brother's fiancée, Ginna Forsyte, from Washington. Mrs. Atwilder, our hostess."

"How do you do."

The woman stared frankly at Ginna and said to Morrow, "What a pity that she's already spoken for. There're so many eligible young men here this morning. I could have been a matchmaker six times over."

They quickly moved on as other people got into the receiving line. Andrew looked on in consternation as he was separated from Morrow and subsequently buttonholed by a group of men.

"Morrow, hello."

Lila was a vision in her morning dress—blue, this time, with lace and pearls swathing her throat and bosom. "Do come over and settle a dispute," Lila said, "between Richard and me."

Ginna hung back, entranced with the room that might have been in Buckingham Palace, it was so grand. Except for the overdone drapery cornices that were not quite *de rigueur*, in her opinion. But the oil paintings were magnificent, and, with Morrow occupied, she quietly walked over and stood before a still life with fish and cat.

"It's Flemish probably," said a male voice behind her. "Seventeenth century?"

"No, sixteenth century," she answered without thinking. Then, in surprise, she turned to face the voice.

The young man was tall—almost as tall as Jonathan, but any resemblance ended there. He had a more effeminate build, and there was a blasé look about him, as if he were already tired of the morning. But his face changed immediately as Ginna turned around.

His eyes came alive. "Hello." He drew the word out, as if he'd suddenly made a great discovery. "I don't believe I've seen you before."

Ginna did not care for his manner. "Probably because I've never been here before." She took a step away as if to return to Morrow's side.

The young man said, "Please. I didn't mean to sound impertinent. I'm Peter Atwilder. My mother and father are giving this party. So, in a way, I suppose I'm one of the hosts."

"Oh. Then, how do you do? I'm Ginna Forsyte."

"Who are you with?"

"I'm with the Lachlans. I'm their houseguest," she added.

Peter smiled at the information. "Do you already have a breakfast partner?"

A puzzled look flitted across her face. "I thought I was to be seated with the Lachlans and the Montgomerys."

"So you probably are. But you'll be bored to tears. Let me see what I can do."

"Please," Ginna called out. "I'll be perfectly happy. . . ." Her voice trailed off. Peter Atwilder had already gone.

In consternation, Ginna walked across the room to where Morrow was still standing with Lila and her husband.

"How lovely you look this morning, Ginna. Pink is such a wonderful color for you. She looks delicious, don't you think, Richard? Like a Watteau."

"Absolutely."

No, she wanted to cry out. If anything, I want to be a Fragonard. That's how Jonathan had pictured her that day in the park. Instead, she merely said, "Thank you, Mrs. Montgomery."

The signal that it was time to be seated was given. Some of the people went immediately to find their seats, while others lingered in small groups. Andrew struggled through the crowd to reach Morrow's side. "I'm sorry, darling. I was waylaid and I couldn't seem to break away." He shook Richard's hand and nodded to Lila. "Good morning. I trust you've gotten over your long trip?"

"Yes. We went to the exposition yesterday for the first time. Quite an experience, wasn't it, Richard?"

He laughed and winked at Andrew. "It could have been an even more interesting experience, but Lila wouldn't let me go into the sideshows."

"Well, good for her, old boy."

"Andrew, you're supposed to take up for me. Not agree with her."

Ginna stood, enjoying the easy camaraderie, content just to listen.

"Andrew, at which table are we sitting?" Morrow asked.

"Three, I believe."

"So are we." Richard spoke up.

"Then let's go and find our seats. I expect Ginna is quite hungry," Morrow said. "She took David for a long walk by the shore this morning, and she's only had a cup of tea."

"Which she won't find here," Andrew finished. "More like Chateau Leoville, sherry, Malaga, cognac, or Pommery sec. Or coffee," he added.

"Or champagne," Lila said. "After all, it's supposed to be a champagne breakfast."

"You mean we'll have that many spirits for breakfast?" Ginna asked, surprised, remembering the disapproval of Miss Counts and Mrs. Beauchamp over Mr. Wells's Madeira and waffles.

"You don't have to take them all, darling," Morrow said. "Or really any of them. Except that a mild beverage will probably be safer than the water served."

As Andrew found the table and Ginna was ready to be seated, Peter came up to claim her. "I'm sorry, Mr. Lachlan, but there's been a change in seating at the last minute. Miss Forsyte is to come with me."

"Oh, how lovely," Lila said. "She deserves to be with young people her own age. How kind of you."

Ginna glared at Peter. He was not kind at all. Merely impertinent, as she had surmised the moment she laid eyes on him. Only to make a scene would embarrass everyone. So she allowed Peter to take her arm and guide her.

"I did some place-card switching," he confided in her ear. "I've put us at an interesting table, away from all of the old fogies."

Ginna said nothing. But Peter didn't seem to notice. Or if he did, he ignored her silence and continued to guide her to the table ahead, where a group of young men and women was already assembled.

"Well, here we are," Peter said to the group. "I told you I would bring the prettiest girl in the room with me—Miss Ginna Forsyte, a visitor in our fair white city. So everyone be nice to her."

"Hello," Ginna said, looking at the silent, hostile faces of the young women. They did not respond. Instead, they became preoccupied with taking their places, the young men holding out their gilt chairs.

Peter did not seem surprised at their behavior. "The whole bunch doesn't have any manners, Ginna. Their fathers can't afford to hire anybody to teach them."

"Stop being so snide, Peter," one of the young women complained. "*My* father can buy a whole school if he wants."

"Whereas Margaret's poor father has only made enough money to buy *one* chair," another young man commented.

"The medical chair at Northwestern," he added, to the laughter of everyone.

"And where did you go to school, Miss Forsyte?" Henry Blakesley inquired.

"In London and Paris," she answered.

"Oh, pardon me," Margaret retaliated. "I should have known by your accent. They did a good job of changing it."

"Not at all. I was born in England."

"And where do you think this oyster was born?" Peter inquired, spearing it with his fork and letting it slide down his throat.

"Nantucket."

"High Hampton."

"No, Newport."

Peter was the pied piper, lulling them all into laughter. Where he led, they followed. Except for Ginna. She felt completely out of place and wished she were at the table with Morrow instead.

But with the food being served, the hostility toward the outsider waned. And Ginna became fascinated with the menu—food that, except for the eggs served with rice, she had never equated with breakfast. Her plate was laden with woodchuck, cooked tomatoes with onion, veal chops in sauce, olives, and peppers. There was strawberry shortcake laced with kirsch awaiting as the final course.

And as to the spirits, Andrew was right. Every beverage he'd mentioned was there, with several others Ginna didn't recognize.

"You're not drinking your Chateau," Peter chided.

"I think I'll just have coffee," Ginna said.

"But that would be an insult to the host," Peter countered.

She took him seriously. "I really don't mean it as such," she said. "It's only that I might not be able to walk across the room afterwards."

"Well, my head is already buzzing like a saw," Edward, seated across from her, said.

She smiled. "Then you would be no good at all helping me to navigate back to the Lachlans."

"Is that who you're visiting?" Margaret asked. "My mama said that, between Mrs. Lachlan and Mrs. Palmer going back and forth with all their charity work, they could easily start an epidemic in our own social group, with all the germs they bring home."

Ginna grew angry with the slur against Morrow. But perhaps she would have remained silent if it had not been for the Chateau that Peter had urged on her.

"Oh, I disagree. An epidemic might be much more likely to come from one of your large department stores. I understand one of them was finally made to destroy a group of women's clothes that had been sewn in a smallpox-infested tenement."

For a moment, there was complete silence. Peter sat back in his chair and looked with relish from Ginna to Margaret.

It was Edward who calmed the situation. "Wasn't that how the Spanish got rid of nearly half the Indian population?"

"With women's clothes?"

"No, silly. With blankets from some of their sick."

"How did we ever get off on such a terrible subject?" Henry asked.

"Margaret brought it up," Peter answered.

"Well, she'd better be quiet. Or I'll have trouble keeping my breakfast *down*," Edward said.

They were an irreverent group, close-knit and sure of

themselves. Ginna didn't fit in any more than Nathan would have fitted in, with his talk of tadpoles and frogs. She toyed with the strawberries on her shortcake, and with her back to the double doors into the large dining room, she did not see the latecomer as he stood in the doorway surveying the people in the room.

"Look at that beautiful young man standing in the doorway," Elizabeth said, nudging Hannah. "I wonder who he is."

"I don't know. But I think he's headed this way. Peter, who is he? If you know him, promise me you'll introduce me," Hannah begged.

"No, Hannah. Remember, I always have first choice," Margaret reminded her.

"Not this time, Margaret. You owe me a favor. And I'm calling in my marker right now. Peter, introduce him to me first."

As the man approached the table, Ginna turned around to look, while Margaret and Hannah leaned forward in eager expectation.

"Ginna."

"Jonathan."

What was he doing in Chicago? He was supposed to be in Washington. Or even at one of the derbys. But never here in the Union League Club.

Jonathan towered over the table. In a voice filled with confidence, he said, "Please excuse me, but I've come to claim my fiancée."

His hands reached toward the chair to help Ginna up just as Peter stood.

"May I present Jonathan Meadors. Peter Atwilder, my host."

"Weren't you at Saratoga in May? One of your horses, if I remember, came in second."

"First," Jonathan corrected, shaking hands with Peter. He didn't bother to acknowledge anyone else at the table. "I've just arrived from Washington, so I know you'll understand if I spirit Ginna away from you."

Peter gazed ruefully at the young woman beside him. "I understand. But I still don't like it."

"Good-bye, Peter. Please thank your mother and father for a delightful breakfast."

And with that, Ginna began to walk across the expansive floor, Jonathan's hand at her elbow. She was almost afraid to leave the Union League Club with him. For she had already seen the look of battle in his eyes.

# CHAPTER
## 26

"Just what did you think you would gain by running away like this?"

Ginna glanced at the doorman as they passed by. His eyes looked straight ahead and he politely gave no indication that he had heard Jonathan's question.

"I didn't run away. My family knows perfectly well where I am."

Jonathan still kept his hand at her elbow, guiding her down the steps and to the curbing where the phaeton waited. Ginna recognized the Lachlan crest, but the small carriage was unattended except for a street urchin standing nearby. Jonathan tossed the boy a coin, and with a sweep, he lifted Ginna into the carriage and climbed in beside her.

"Then what did you think you would gain by trying to break off our engagement?" he countered. "Especially when I was out of town."

"*Trying?*" she repeated. "The engagement is broken. I could never marry you now, Jonathan."

"I see you're still wearing my ring."

"Only for appearances. I sent it back with the letter, but your mother returned it to me."

Jonathan laughed, but it was a harsh sound, not intended to show pleasure.

"As soon as we reach Morrow's house, I'll give it back to you. Unless you want me to take it off now."

"You're not going to take it off ever again, Ginna. We're going to be married, and that's final."

"No, Jonathan. I could never marry you now."

Jonathan pulled out into the street traffic, his anger at Ginna showing in his face. But he was careful with the horse, for the surface on the macadam street was slippery.

Once he was into the steady flow of traffic, he said, "My mother told me the whole story, Ginna. But the fact that my mother and your father were once married to each other has little to do with *us*."

"Oh, Jonathan, can't you see? It has *everything* to do with us. When you asked me to marry you, I was a different person, with a suitable background—a family name. Now I'm an imposter, with nothing to offer."

"My God, it must be that damned Victorian influence that makes you talk like that. We're different in America, Ginna. Here, any man can rise above his name or lack of one, or the society in which he was born."

"A man, yes. But not a woman, Jonathan. The other day when I went with Morrow, a woman was dying in a tenement room because no one would help her. And do you

241

know why? Because she didn't have a name for the baby that was trying to be born."

"And you equate yourself with some poor immigrant here in Chicago?"

"Yes."

"Then the sooner we marry, the sooner we can leave this place."

"I don't understand your logic, Jonathan."

"You and I are going back on the train to Washington together. You'll have no Lila Montgomery to chaperone you. If you think your reputation is compromised now, then think how you will look to the gossips when they find out you traveled alone with a man."

"But—"

"I don't want to hear any more from you, Ginna. We'll talk with Morrow when she gets home and then make our plans."

"She couldn't possibly go along with such a harebrained scheme."

"She just might see that what I propose is an obvious solution to the whole problem." Jonathan smiled. "Now tell me how much you've missed me."

"Jonathan, you're incorrigible."

"But lovable, don't you think?"

Ginna didn't answer. The effects of the Chateau Leoville still had her brain operating at half capacity. And she couldn't seem to win an argument with Jonathan even at the best of times.

"It's a good thing I got here when I did," he said, breaking the silence. "Otherwise, you would have been fair game for Peter Atwilder."

"That's where you're wrong. Peter was just trying to be kind to a stranger."

"From the stories at Saratoga, Atwilder is *never* kind. He selects his victims carefully. And then walks away from the scene of the crime with nary a thought for the young woman he's ruined."

"Now who's sounding Victorian?"

He didn't bother to answer her. Instead, he let the horse have its head as they reached the stretch along the shoreline near Andrew's house. They raced by the huge Palmer mansion with its glass porte cochere, and within five minutes, the phaeton was home.

Jonathan drove straight to the carriage house, where he turned the phaeton over to the stablehand. "Better check the horseshoe on the right front hoof," he said, and then guided Ginna down the concrete path, through the garden, and on to the deserted house.

He took her in through the side door from the garden. And once they were inside, he turned and drew her into his arms. "Darling, I've missed you," he said.

Before she had a chance to protest, his mouth claimed hers, forcing from her the same unbidden feelings that had so unnerved her that day in the gazebo.

"Jonathan," she finally protested, pushing away from him. "We can't."

"There's no one else in the house, Ginna. Until Andrew brings Morrow home, we're completely alone. No David, no nanny, no Allie. Just you and me. Promise me you'll marry me as soon as I can arrange the ceremony, or I swear I'll take you upstairs and make love to you right now. And then you'll be begging *me* to marry *you*."

Ginna laughed.

"So you think I don't mean it?"

He swept her into his arms and began to carry her past

the fireplace, past the elongated windows that looked out on the shimmering gray water and onto the stairs.

"Stop being such an idiot," she said, still laughing, "and put me down."

"I can't do that until I get all the way upstairs."

She didn't take him seriously, for his eyes were teasing and merry. He seemed to know which bedroom she'd been assigned, for he went directly to it, pushing the door open with one hand and then closing it behind him.

"This has gone far enough, Jonathan. Put me down. Please."

"All right, Ginna." With that, he dropped her onto the bed. But before she could get up or even straighten her skirts, he was beside her, pressing her hands against the lace coverlet and staring down into her eyes.

The teasing look was gone, replaced with a serious mien. "I adore you, Ginna," he whispered. "Tell me that you love me, too."

Her head still had not cleared from the Chateau. She felt too lethargic to struggle. "Yes, Jonathan, I love you."

"Darling."

He brushed her face with kisses, lingering at the corner of her mouth, still teasing her, taunting her, driving her almost to despair. And then his lips were no longer teasing but demanding, full upon her mouth, drawing a sweet ecstasy from her that she wanted to last forever.

"Promise me you'll marry me, Ginna."

She wrapped her arms around him, feeling his body against hers. "Yes, Jonathan. Yes."

Then they heard a child's voice downstairs. "You think Mommy has come back, Nanny?"

They parted as if a knife had severed them, sharp, clean.

Ginna sat up and brushed her hair out of her face. "Quick, Jonathan," she said, "leave before David comes upstairs."

"But we're to be married," he said. "I see no reason for behaving as if we've done something sinful."

"Please, Jonathan. Go. Now."

He smiled. "Have I compromised you so totally?"

"Yes."

"Good. Then you won't be able to back out now, will you?" He turned around and walked nonchalantly past the door and down the stairs.

"Hello, David. How's my boy?"

Ginna heard a squeal of delight. "Uncle Jonathan," David said. "Did you bring me anything?"

Jonathan sounded so normal, as if absolutely nothing had happened upstairs. But Ginna was a wreck. The mirror reflected her flushed face, her disheveled hair, and her twisted bodice. She quickly smoothed her dress, took up her brush, and began to put herself together again. She shuddered to think what else might have happened if the child had not come home in time.

But perhaps nothing else would have occurred. Ginna examined her face again. Yes, Jonathan was right. She *had* run away from him. Only now he had taken her past all propriety. Marriage was the only way to set things right, as Jonathan must have known all the time.

Feeling the way she did, Ginna knew that she was still bound by society's rules. She was still a fledgling. But perhaps one day she could be like Morrow, soaring with assurance and freedom. But that freedom to do good would only come with wealth and power. She had learned that much during her few days in Chicago.

The women in the tenements had no power, no control over their lives. It took someone like Mrs. Palmer or Morrow to point the way—to make the men listen and then do something about the terrible conditions of the slums.

But perhaps it had taken the shame of her own illegitimacy to make her sensitive to the needs of others.

With the approach of the second carriage, Ginna put down her brush and walked to the stairs. By the time Morrow came inside, she was leisurely reading a book in the living room, while Jonathan and David sat on the floor nearby playing with the calèche that Ginna had brought her nephew.

Morrow smiled at Ginna and immediately walked over to Jonathan. "I got the message you left at the club. But I suppose I'm not really surprised to see you here."

Jonathan was serious. "We've got to talk, Morrow. The four of us. Is Andrew coming in?"

"No. He merely brought me home. Unfortunately, he has an appointment with Gladney Shelburne. It was something he couldn't get out of."

"Maybe it's just as well, since it really involves the three of us—you, Ginna, and me."

Morrow stood, smoothing David's blond hair as he leaned against her. "Darling, run and find Nanny," she said.

"Do I have to?"

"Yes, David. But don't go far. I'll call you when we've finished talking and perhaps we can go for a walk by the lake."

The child obeyed, picking up his toy and taking it with him.

"All right. What is it, Jonathan?"

Ginna sat in the curve of the beige sofa and listened as Jonathan began to talk. The story from his lips was gentle, loving, not at all like Cassie's. Yet the facts were the same.

And when he had finished, Morrow said, "Poor Mother."

"It's a complicated, awkward situation," Jonathan added. "But it's in the past. Nothing can be undone. But it needn't bring any more heartbreak than it already has."

He looked over at Ginna. "I've already told Ginna that she had no business running away from me. It still doesn't change the fact that I love her and want to marry her."

Morrow walked over to the sofa and sat down. "And how do you feel about it, Ginna? Do you love Jonathan enough to marry him?"

"He's my life," she said simply.

Morrow smiled and reached out to take Ginna's hand. "And you're really my sister, aren't you? You'll have to tell me about our father. I want to know everything about him. But that can wait until later, when we're alone."

Ginna nodded, but it was Jonathan who spoke again. "Ginna has suffered from her mother's abuse. And if she goes back to Washington without marrying me, Araminta will find some way of keeping us apart. That's why I want us to be married here."

Morrow hesitated. "Has your . . . our father given his blessing for this marriage?"

"Yes. We were to be married at home in three weeks. I already had my dress fitted and I was going to wear the Meadors family veil. . . ."

"Perhaps the solution would be to have a private cere- mony here. That way, if something happens once you get home, then you would already be married. But I under- stand how a mother would feel wronged, especially if the daughter eloped and turned her back on the plans already made. If you didn't go through with it again, that might cause a schism between you and your mother that could never be mended."

"You mean, have *two* weddings?" Ginna inquired.

"It's done all the time here, among our Catholic friends. A civil ceremony first, followed by a church wedding."

Jonathan smiled. "I'll go to see Dr. Brunson tomorrow, as soon as the church doors open."

"He's not in his office on Mondays, Jonathan. You'll have to wait until Tuesday."

"Then we'll all go to the exposition tomorrow," Jonathan commented. "There won't be much time for that later on."

"Well, I'll leave you two to make your plans," Morrow said. She reached out and hugged Ginna. "Welcome to our family, sweet Ginna." Then she walked out of the room, calling to her son. "David, it's time to take our walk."

When she was gone, Ginna whispered, "You don't think we'll get into any trouble doing this, Jonathan?"

"I'm determined not to lose you, Ginna. No one need know unless it's absolutely necessary. It will be our secret."

# CHAPTER
## 27

Another secret was taking shape several hundred miles away in a dormitory room at Braxton School, where Nathan Forsyte lay in the dark and listened. For almost an hour, he had waited for the sound of a gentle snore that would indicate Mr. Graves in the next room had finally gone to sleep.

Most of the dorm beds were still empty, for the school session had not yet started. But the younger boys would be arriving with their parents the next day, a full week ahead of the older students.

He and Pinky had already hidden their few belongings in the woods, just over the hill, with the railroad timetable and the map. They didn't dare leave from the Braxton depot, for they would be sure to run into some of the school officials. Instead, they planned to walk the three miles to Holborne and buy their tickets there.

Nathan had written only one letter home and that was just a few lines. He was afraid he might let the cat out of the bag—that Pinky had been sent to the same school. If his mother ever got wind of that, there'd be trouble. But he guessed it didn't matter much, anyway. He'd be in trouble as it was, going off to the exposition. But it wasn't as if he'd be missing any classes. He and Pinky would be back by then.

He felt under his pillow for the note he would leave on Mr. Graves's desk downstairs. He and Pinky had worked long and hard wording it just right, a little different from the one Pinky was going to leave with Mr. Riley. But the handwriting was the same—in Spencerian script, which Nathan had copied from his old penmanship book, and each had the signature of his respective father.

The sound he was waiting for drifted past the partially closed door: breath in, breath out, with a rattle at the end. Hearing it, the fully clothed Nathan crawled out of bed, reached underneath the cot for the food satchel, and, with the letter in his hand, stole down the hallway.

The stairs creaked badly and, midway down, Nathan stopped. Then, not hearing anyone stirring, he slowly walked the rest of the way, checking each tread as if he might have been walking on eggs or balancing himself on the rail track.

The moon seeped through the transom glass with barely enough light for him to see the outline of the desk. And there he placed the letter, anchored to the desk by the brown tortoiseshell Toby jug that Mr. Graves used to hold his pencils.

Back in the hallway, Nathan groped for the front door, slid the iron bar out of its catch, and opened it only wide enough for him to slip out. And then he began to run, straight for the woods.

In the dark, an owl hooted and a hound bayed, sending shivers along his body. But he kept running, never looking back, even when he reached the blackness of the woods.

Then he heard another sound, this time in front of him. And he wasn't sure whether it might be from man or beast. "Pinky," he called, trying not to sound scared. "Are you in there?"

"Yes. What took you so long?"

"It was Mr. Graves. He wouldn't go to sleep."

"Well, I've got the satchels. Here's yours. You better put your food in it quick before some animal smells it and comes after us."

Nathan knelt down, unfastened the larger satchel, and stuffed the food bag inside. Then the two walked out to the edge of the road and began their night journey to Holborne.

Each carried a big stick to ward off any night creature that might attack. Nathan didn't say anything, but he wasn't too sure how much protection the stick would be against a cougar or a bobcat. But he and Pinky were best friends. They'd already exchanged crosses in blood. A cat would have to carry both of them off, if it attacked, for the two had sworn to protect each other to the death, through thick or thin, forever and a day, so help them God.

"What's that, Nathan?" Pinky whispered.

Nathan saw the shining eyes, like luminous phosphorus, glaring at them from the middle of the road. Then it began to move away from them, and Nathan saw what it was.

"Just a possum, Pinky. Probably has babies clinging to its back."

"Oh."

They started up again, a little faster this time.

While Nathan was slender, with long legs, Pinky was plumper. Nathan could hear his breathing and the legs of his knickers rubbing against each other. "I think we'd better stop to rest, Pinky," he said.

"You tired, Nathan?"

"Yes," Nathan lied.

"Me, too."

A few minutes later, they started out again, digging into the sandy road with their long sticks, while the straps of their satchels dug into their shoulders.

"Uh-oh. I hear a horse. You think they might have already found out we're gone?" Pinky said.

"I doubt it. But let's hide, anyway, until whoever it is goes by. I wouldn't want anybody to see us on the road this time of night by ourselves. They'd be bound to ask questions."

Nathan and Pinky climbed over a rickety wooden fence, and they waited behind a briar bush for the horse to go by.

"Whoa, Jennie," a man's voice said, almost directly opposite them.

Nathan and Pinky put their heads down even more as the man dismounted and allowed his horse to wander close to the fence, while he went off to the other side of the road.

The horse whinnied and lowered its head, parting the large bush hiding the two boys.

"He smells the apples in my satchel," Nathan whispered.

"Shoo. Go away," Pinky croaked, taking off his cap and attempting to discourage the horse from further exploration without its owner seeing.

The man whistled through his teeth and the horse reluctantly moved away from the fence. While the boys watched, the man remounted and the horse trotted away.

"Let's eat the apples now," Pinky suggested. "I'm already a little hungry."

So Nathan brought out the apples and they sat there behind the fence eating them. Finally tossing the cores over their shoulders, they crawled out from under the fence and started another mile toward their destination of Holborne.

When they arrived, red and green lanterns were hanging on the side of the depot. And a tarpaulin mail bag was suspended like a side of meat on a hook beside the tracks, waiting to be snatched by the next train that passed.

Inside the gray wood depot, Nathan could hear the telegraph keys working their magic, sending messages up and down the line for anyone who could read their code.

"I'm sleepy," Pinky said.

"But we can't go to sleep until we're on the train. We might miss it. And we've come too far to do that."

So Pinky and Nathan kept each other awake. When one saw the other nodding, he reached out and pinched him. At the puffing sound of a steam engine and the strident whistle, they both sat up, alert. They watched as the train passed by. If they had blinked twice, they would have missed seeing a man in the mail car reach out and snag the mail pouch from its hook.

"Did you see that?" Pinky said.

"Yes. Just like a polar bear swiping a fish with his paw."

From their vantage point beyond the porch, they saw the old man through the window. He was getting ready for the morning shift to relieve him. And that's when Nathan and Pinky made their move.

"Good morning," Nathan said politely, standing at the wire-screened window.

"Good morning, young fellow. What can I do for you so early in the day?"

"We need two children's tickets to Chicago on the seven-forty," Nathan said.

"You two wouldn't be runnin' away, would you?" he asked suspiciously.

"Oh, no, sir." Pinky spoke up. "We want to get tickets for *tomorrow*, not today. Our papas have decided to let us go, too. And they said we could come ahead today and buy our own."

The man smiled. "You going to the fair?"

"Yes, sir. We sold our mules to get enough money." The two plunked the correct amount down at the window and waited for the man to write the tickets. "Day coach," Pinky added.

"One man was in here last week," the station agent commented. "Sold his burial insurance policy to get there. Said the exposition wouldn't wait. But if the Lord was good to him, *He* would."

When the tickets were filled out, the two boys left the depot and walked around to the side where the baggage wagon stood. They climbed up on it and stared down the tracks.

"What are we going to do now, Pinky?" a distressed Nathan asked. "We can't wait until tomorrow. They might start looking for us before then."

"It's all right. We'll just wait until the night stationmaster goes home. And when the day one comes on duty, we'll walk in and exchange our tickets for today's train."

• • •

An hour later, with the tickets exchanged, Nathan and Pinky climbed aboard and left Holborne behind.

"I'm hungry again," Pinky said.

"Just drink some water," Nathan suggested. "We don't have that much food left. And we have to make it last for the next three days."

Pinky leaned over and took from his satchel a Mason jar filled with water. "This is my tadpole jar," he said. "But I washed it real clean before I left."

At Braxton School, Hansel Graves was awakened by a loud knock at the front door. He hurriedly got up and glanced out his window. There stood a man with his son, two hours before anyone was to arrive.

Disgruntled, he put his academic gown on over his night-shirt and rushed downstairs. But Annie had already let them in.

"I'm sorry to be so early," the man apologized. "But it was either now or not at all. I'm Rupert Bragg and this is my son, Treadway."

"Quite all right, Mr. Bragg. Hello, young Treadway. I'm Mr. Graves. We'll be seeing quite a lot of each other this term."

Treadway turned and hid his face in his father's morning coat. "I want to go home," he wailed.

Rupert pulled at his muttonchop whiskers in embarrassment.

"Have to make a man of him. You understand, Graves? This is the first time he's been away from his mama."

"Quite all right. I understand, Mr. Bragg. Annie," he called to the motherly-looking woman still lingering in the hall. "Can you take young Treadway here with you to the kitchen? I already smell the sweet buns ready to come out of the oven."

From the door, Annie smiled and held out her arms. "Come, Master Treadway. It's into the kitchen for a nice glass of milk and a sweet bun with honey."

He went with her immediately, to Rupert Bragg's relief. "Annie looks a lot like our Nelle at home."

"That's why we have her here, Mr. Bragg. To mother the boys a bit when they get a little homesick."

Within a few minutes, Rupert Bragg left and Mr. Graves hurried back upstairs to get dressed before anyone else arrived. He barely had enough time to wash and eat his breakfast. The arrival of the new boys was always a pain. Hectic, too, with all of the parents vying for private interviews to tell each dorm master what made the boys ill or scared or to give suggestions for their diets.

The day progressed, with no time for Hansel to relax. But as the last carriage drove away and the last boy had been settled in, he finally sat down at his desk to arrange the papers that had accumulated all day. As he began to sort them in alphabetical order, he came across the note from Nathan's father.

With a frown, he stood and walked back to the small tea pantry, where Annie was busy, getting ready for the boys' afternoon snack.

"Annie, did you see Dr. Forsyte when he came for Nathan today?"

"No, Mr. Graves."

"That's strange. Neither did I. But I found a note on my desk saying he's taken him away for a few days, but assuring us he would have him back by the beginning of school."

"Well, it's not so strange, Mr. Graves. He could have come at a dozen or more times today and I wouldn't have seen him. What with Treadway throwing up, and the two Roberts boys getting into a fight . . ."

"Well, I suppose no harm's done. But tonight, after the boys are asleep, I'll report it to the headmaster. We can't be too careful, you know, where these boys are concerned."

Hansel Graves had been a member of the Braxton staff for three years. He'd come at the same time the old school had been completely renovated. That night, with the proctor keeping tabs on the boys, Hansel set out for the headmaster's house.

On the grounds plot, it was located to the left, with the various dorm cottages clustered around it in a spokelike fashion. The living plan for the students was unique. In a reproduction of a real home, the boys were grouped according to various ages and grades, with each dorm cottage a separate working unit: kitchen, dining room, housemother, and a dorm master, who was also one of the teachers.

For a moment, Hansel was content to stand on the steps of his own dorm cottage and gaze toward the lighted clock tower of the new administration building, shining like a beacon in the darkness. Situated in the center of the complex, the building was flanked by two ells containing the classrooms and chapel.

Far to the right were the playgrounds and ballfields. Beyond those were the vegetable gardens, stables, and dairy barn. And still farther away, completely covered by the darkness, was Braxton Woods.

With a feeling of pride, Hansel breathed in the healthy air and continued his journey down the walkway.

By the time he arrived with the note in his hand, another

teacher, Hammond Riley, was already in the parlor with the headmaster.

"Come in, Graves," the headmaster greeted him. "We've got a small problem here. Quincy Tallifero Boswell has vanished, leaving behind this note from his father. But Riley never saw the man, only the note left on his desk."

"I have a note, too, Dr. Pemberton. And a missing boy, Nathan Forsyte."

"Those two boys are good friends, are they not?" Pemberton asked.

"Inseparable," Riley responded.

With a sinking feeling, Hansel laid his note beside Riley's. The paper was identical. The Spencerian script was identical. And the signatures of the two names were of the same configuration.

Pemberton held up his pince-nez and gazed at the letters. "Gentlemen, I'm afraid we've got a problem."

"The boys have run away," Hansel said.

"Yes, I'm afraid so. A very clever maneuver. If you two hadn't come at the same time, we might not have suspected until next week."

Riley leaned over and looked at the notes again. "But evidently they plan to get back to school before the term begins. What do you think we should do, Dr. Pemberton?"

"We'll send out a search party first thing in the morning. But if we don't find them, there's nothing left to do but contact their parents."

In the middle of the night, the steady clack of wheels produced a monotonous, metallic rhythm as the train sped west. While first-class passengers slept in luxurious berths, two small boys, curled up on a seat in one of the day coaches, were oblivious to the sound.

# CHAPTER
## 28

With the Columbian Exposition in full force, the former mud flats of Jackson Park possessed a fairy-tale quality, with islands, lagoons, and wide sweeps of lawn amid a white and gold city. Frederick Olmstead, who had landscaped the parks of New York and Washington, had worked his magic again.

The Columbian Guard, dressed in old-world clothes, resembled the Vatican Swiss Guard with their hose and doublets and swords, as Ginna and Jonathan walked past the statues and fountains on the way to the Transportation Building, which Andrew's mentor, Louis Sullivan, had designed.

"The exposition is supposed to point to a new age," Morrow said, joining them. "But Andrew says the architecture has only looked backward to antiquity—all except for Louis. He's the only one with a vision."

"But the landscaping is certainly a work of art," Ginna said.

"Yes. And I suppose we should just enjoy the hoopla like all the other tourists and forget the architecture."

Jonathan laughed. "That's a little hard to do with all the turrets, pagodas, and Parthenons—all painted white and gold."

Trimmed with stucco, the twelve main buildings designed to hold exhibits took up twenty acres each, and interspersed among them were over two hundred smaller buildings of diverse architectural styles. And along the Midway were a Ferris wheel and a merry-go-round, dime museums and freak shows, booths selling cotton candy and iced champagne, and birds on a stick and snake charmers.

After they had spent nearly an hour in the Transportation Building casually viewing the displays of horse-drawn carriages, railcars, steamboats, gondola balloons, cable cars, and the brand-new horseless carriages, Morrow said, "What else would you like to see, Ginna?"

"The artistic exhibit, especially the collection of Gobelin tapestries and porcelains."

"And you, Jonathan?"

"The map of the United States made out of pickles."

Ginna nudged him. "Be serious, Jonathan. That sounds like something David would say."

"Oh, no. David doesn't like pickles. He would choose the bearded lady, more than likely," he countered.

"And I might have to choose some headache powders," Morrow said, "if that cannibal drum on the Midway doesn't let up."

"I'm sorry, Morrow," Ginna said. "Do you really have a headache?"

"No, dear. I was only making a joke, too."

Ginna gazed in the direction of the Midway tents. "Do you think Siamese twins get headaches at the same time?"

"I don't know. Let's go and ask them," Jonathan said, taking Ginna by the hand.

"Morrow?"

"You two go ahead. Why don't I check on Nanny and David, then meet you at the pavilion in an hour? We'll all be ready for something cool to drink by then, I'm sure."

They parted company, and Ginna and Jonathan went on alone. They held hands so that they would not be separated by the crowd. As they approached the Midway, Ginna stopped suddenly.

"Look, Jonathan. Do you see those women over there?"

"It would be hard to miss them, Ginna."

She giggled. "The Montgomerys didn't know I overheard. But all twelve of them came up on the same train from Washington. The older woman, Nelly Rose, brought her girls all the way from New Orleans to see the sights."

"They seem to be attracting almost as much attention as the sideshows."

"Which reminds me, where are the Siamese twins?"

"You really are serious about wanting to see them?" Jonathan asked.

"Yes. My father operated on Siamese twins several years ago. Only they were from England, not Siam. But they were lucky, he said, because most can't be separated. I want to tell him about these."

The barkers along the Midway vied for the crowd's attention. As show times neared, people gathered at the ticket boxes and paid their money to see the sights they had never seen and probably would never see again.

Music was everywhere—from the cannibal drumbeat to Sousa's band—played by small, dark-skinned natives in scant clothing made of leopard hide juxtaposed against tall, fair-skinned men in bright red uniforms with brass buttons and plumed hats.

From one attraction to another Ginna and Jonathan went, sampling the flavor of the exposition like wine tasters who are careful not to imbibe too much on a single bouquet. And when the hour was up, they had seen only a small portion of the exposition's offerings.

"I wonder if anyone has been to every exhibit and every show?" Ginna asked as she and Jonathan began to walk toward the pavillion.

"I doubt it. Although some act as if they're trying. It would more than likely take several months of constant attendance. And who has the time to do that?"

"Certainly not us."

Jonathan took Ginna's hand again. He leaned over and whispered, "No, we have other things much more important to do."

Ginna smiled, thinking of the upcoming wedding and the honeymoon later. Suddenly remembering the letter she'd found in her mother's nightstand, she said, "I finally found your missing letter, Jonathan."

"Oh? Where?"

Ginna became uncomfortable. "Don't ask me. But I love the idea of our honeymoon being out west. Are you and Andrew really going to go into the cattle business?"

"We're discussing it, Ginna. Of course, if we do, he'll put up some of the money, but I'll be the one running it. That's why it would be nice to take a western tour—to look over land and possibly buy some. That is, if you don't distract me *too* much, darling."

"I'll be quiet as a mouse. No, as quiet as a little dogie."

Jonathan laughed. "You don't know much about cattle, do you?"

"Why?"

"A motherless calf is about the noisiest creature in an entire herd."

"Ginna, Jonathan. Over here."

Morrow waved at them to get their attention. She was seated at a large, round umbrella table with Nanny and David, who was already sipping a large lemonade.

The two wove their way past other tables to the one in the shade. David immediately set down his glass and looked at Jonathan. "Did you see the bearded lady, Uncle Jonathan?"

He laughed. "Yes. And the world's strongest man. But what you see before you right now is the world's *thirstiest* couple."

"Then we'll certainly have to do something about that," Morrow said, and signaled for their waiter.

A short while later, they left the pavilion. They had almost reached the exit gate when Morrow stopped. A short distance away, a small child sat by a flower stand. Like the flowers, the child looked as if she'd remained too long in the sun.

"Oh, Jonathan, there's the little Andretti girl. Do go over and buy some of her flowers. She looks so unhappy and tired."

Ginna and Morrow watched as Jonathan walked toward the stand. They saw the child come to life at the approach of a potential customer. Jonathan pointed to one bunch, then another. But a large group of tourists passed by, blocking their view. By the time Jonathan came into sight again, he was heading back to Ginna and Morrow with his arms full.

"Oh, no," Morrow said. "I didn't intend for him to buy all of them."

"Uncle Jonathan, you look like a flower man," David said.

"And so I am. For you, Ginna," he said, bowing as he presented her with the roses. "And for you, Morrow. A bunch for you, Nanny. And two bunches for David."

"I didn't mean for you to be so extravagant, Jonathan," Morrow chided..

Jonathan smiled. "Then why did you send me over to the little charlatan? She plainly told me that if I bought all of them, she would give me a good price and then she could go home for the day."

When Morrow looked back at the flower stand, she saw that the child had already vanished.

That night, as the breeze along the lakeshore provided respite from the hot summer day, Morrow and Andrew lay in bed and recounted the day's events to each other, as all married couples do once their children and houseguests are sound asleep.

"I wish you could have gone with us today, Andrew," Morrow said.

"If you remember, my lovely, I met you in a stampede, and it seems that there's been a crowd of people around you ever since. I'd much rather have you to myself, like now."

He reached out and took her hand in the dark. "Come closer to me."

Morrow smiled and moved over into his arms. She lay

there, contented, while her mind drifted back to Charleston and the nightmare that had brought them together—two strangers, caught up in a panicked mob, fleeing from the earthquake that had set the city on fire. . . .

Maum Lena's happy song in the kitchen drifted through the open windows, answered by the lilt of a Gullah street vender hawking her wares a block away.

To Morrow, standing on the upstairs piazza of the grand old house facing the Battery, it seemed a peaceful aubade to the morning, an affirmation that all was well with the world.

She held the flower basket while Preston's mother snipped the heavy wisteria blossoms and placed them carefully in the woven reed container. The tortuous-shaped vine threatened to take over the entire top balustrade if not dealt with immediately.

"This has been such a lovely time together, Morrow," the white-haired woman said. "Do you have to leave tomorrow? Couldn't you possibly stay another week?"

Morrow smiled. "I've already stayed much longer this time than I intended. I really must get back home."

The woman's faded blue eyes showed her sadness. "This would have been your home if Preston had lived. And I still look on you as my daughter."

Morrow's voice was gentle. "We've mourned together, Mrs. Legare, for two years. And somehow I think my being here doesn't help either of us."

"I'm a selfish woman," Juliette admitted. "It's time for you to make another life for yourself. But somehow, when you're here, I can still pretend that your wedding is next week. That Preston isn't really dead."

Morrow set down the basket and reached out to Juliette

in sympathy. The woman smiled, brushed the tear away with her cotton work glove, and then went back to snipping another purple cluster of wisteria.

Down below in the garden, Rook, the small black and white spaniel, began barking. But it was more like a howl than his usual yapping at squirrels.

"I declare, that's the second time Rook's howled this morning. He sounds so unhappy. You think there might be something wrong with him? A briar in his paw, maybe?"

"I'll go down and check if you'd like me to, Mrs. Legare."

"Yes, that might be the thing to do, Morrow. I'd hate for the little fellow to be in pain and for us just to ignore him."

Morrow left the piazza, walked downstairs and out through the garden door at the side. She saw the small dog half concealed under the steps. He appeared frightened at something and she immediately became sympathetic. "What's wrong, Rook? Come out and let me see," she said as she sat down on the steps.

At first, the trembling dog remained where he was. But when Morrow called to him again, he whined in answer and slowly crawled toward her.

She lifted him into her lap, and he reached up to lick her face. "There's nothing to be scared of," she assured him, examining one paw and then another. The pads were smooth and there was no sign of injury.

A shadow fell over the sundial in the garden and a small tremor caused a flowerpot to rattle. Morrow looked up at the sky, but no cloud marred the cerulean still life.

Within a few minutes, all that had changed. The sky began to turn a strange shade of gray and an uneasiness entered the garden, while on the Battery a sudden wave lashed against the seawall.

As Rook cowered in her arms, Morrow remembered what Rad had told her when she was a child—that animals could sense something even before humans could, an eclipse of the sun, a hurricane, or a tornado. Was that why Rook was behaving so strangely? But Morrow was not aware of any prediction in the almanac.

She stood, set Rook free, and then started up the steps. But then the earth shuddered, causing the steps to shift. She lost her balance and fell to the ground. Before she could pick herself up, she saw the sundial slowly sink into the lawn, while behind her there was an awful creaking noise. She looked back just in time to see the disintegration of the house, as it split in two, with the heavy slate roof hurling its broken tiles toward her.

"Mrs. Legare! Maum Lena!" she screamed.

Another tile grazed her temple as Morrow crawled toward the wrought-iron gate that miraculously stayed attached to a post, even though the fence was gone.

"Someone, help!" she called out to anyone who might hear her. But no one answered. And no one came to help. Like a drunken sailor attempting to stand on deck in a storm, Morrow swayed, took one step and then another, trying to reach the area where the piazza had once stood.

At her feet lay the reed basket, with clusters of wisteria unbruised, as if someone had gently placed it on the ground. A cotton-gloved hand was barely visible under the debris. And seeing it, Morrow started to cry. She pushed a broken baluster aside and began to dig with her hands. But then she realized that she was too late. Juliette Legare was dead.

Then she became aware of the smoke rising from a hole that had once been the kitchen. "Maum Lena!" she cried out.

In horror, she watched the flames take shape, hissing and

popping against the dry wood of the old house, with the crack in the earth widening and separating her from further exploration. The flames quickly spread, reaching the wisteria vine and climbing like a tightrope dancer to the top, the air pungent as a funeral pyre laden with flowers.

A dazed Morrow finally reached the sidewalk. And in her arms she held Rook, the small black and white spaniel, the only other survivor from the house facing the Battery.

All around her, people were running. The city was on fire; the sky was no longer visible beyond the great layers of smoke. She continued to walk slowly, being pushed aside by others in a hurry.

And then she felt a hand on her arm. "Are you alone?" the voice asked.

"Yes. They're dead. All dead."

Her blond hair had come down, hiding a portion of her smoke-stained face. Only the amethyst eyes were visible, staring straight ahead, not seeing the man who had spoken.

And then she was separated from the man by a horde of people struggling to reach safety. She walked on, caught up in the swelling tide, buffeted about, shoved, then pushed back by the stampede, until the voice once again spoke to her.

"Here, let me carry the dog. You hold on to my arm, and I'll take you to safety."

She did as she was told, giving up Rook to the stranger and clinging to his arm.

"There's a ship in the harbor," he said. "If we can reach it, then we can ride out the earthquake on the water."

He didn't speak to her again for another half hour, for the crowds were becoming more panicked, everyone racing for the wharf at the same time. And it was all he could do to keep his balance and see that she was not separated from him again.

Where he led, she followed, trying to dodge a particularly vicious jab from someone's elbow. And yet she barely felt the blow. She was only aware of the blood trickling down her face as the wound at her temple began bleeding again. Then she was put in a boat, headed out for the ship. But the stranger remained on the wharf, with Rook still in his arms, for there was no room for a dog in the boat.

Several hours later, the ship was full and riding out to sea. By that time, Morrow had washed the blood and soot from her face and pinned up her hair. Not nearly so dazed now, she sat quietly in a deck chair and watched the bonfire that had once been Charleston.

"Excuse me," a familiar voice said. "But isn't this your dog?"

Morrow looked up. "Rook," she said, holding out her arms for the little spaniel. "Thank you," she added, "for everything. You've been so kind, Mr. . . ." She hesitated, waiting for him to supply the name of her benefactor.

"Andrew Lachlan."

"And I'm Morrow Forsyth."

In the house along Lake Michigan, Morrow snuggled closer to her husband.

"What are you thinking about, Morrow?" he asked.

"The earthquake. The day we met."

"Luckiest day of my life," he said.

Morrow smiled a bittersweet smile. "Mine, too."

# CHAPTER
## 29

Three days later, Jonathan and Ginna stood in the walled lakeshore garden, with Andrew and Morrow the only witnesses to the secret marriage ceremony performed by the Reverend Brunson.

Morrow had sent David away with Nanny for the afternoon, for she believed that small boys should never be entrusted with family secrets. It was against their very nature to keep them, no matter how hard they tried. Only Allie had been taken into their confidence. But, after all, she was family, too, just as her mother, Rebecca, had been.

That afternoon, Morrow was at peace with herself. Ginna and Jonathan were so right for each other, and she felt no trepidation in being a party to their decision to marry, es-

pecially with her mother's blessing on the union. But sometimes relatives could be cruel to young lovers, needlessly
putting obstacles in their way and ultimately parting them
forever. And she didn't want that to happen to Jonathan
and Ginna. They deserved their happiness.

But it was a pity that they would only have one night
together as husband and wife. Morrow knew that Jonathan
had discussed it with Andrew, who had pointed out that
the marriage would have to be consummated so that it could
not be annulled later on. But to share a bed for longer than
one night would be too risky for Ginna. If the ceremony
were to remain secret for a time, then Ginna could not
afford to become pregnant.

Morrow moved closer to Andrew as the minister began
to intone the words of the ceremony.

Standing before the small altar of flowers, Ginna held on
to the nosegay that Allie had made up for her with the pink
roses in the garden and bits of white baby's breath tied with
long, white satin streamers. Morrow's white lawn dress had
been taken in slightly to fit Ginna, and even her shoes had
been borrowed from Morrow's closet.

"Do you take this woman . . ."

"I do."

"And you, Ginna Forsyte, do you take this man to be
your lawfully wedded husband . . ."

"I do."

"By the powers invested in me through the covenant of
God and the state of Illinois, I now pronounce you husband
and wife."

Ginna looked up at Jonathan. His dark eyes held the same
loving expression as they had on that day when he'd first
given her the ring of emeralds and diamonds. Now the same
ring was once again placed on her finger, for she could not

yet wear a wedding band for all the world to see. That would come later, when she put on the creamy peau de soie dress and the family veil and was given away by her father in the parlor of the brownstone, in the presence of Martha, her bridesmaid, Araminta, her mother, and Jonathan's parents, Allison and Rad, and perhaps Cassie and Stanley. That is, if Cassie was well enough to come.

Jonathan's kiss was gentle, tender, as the minister looked on in approval. And then the ceremony was over, with Morrow and Andrew hugging her and welcoming her into the family.

Now she was a part of them, twice over—related by birth to Morrow and by marriage to Jonathan.

"Come into the dining room," Morrow urged. "Allie has made a wedding cake and we have iced champagne."

For Ginna, that afternoon was made up of small vignettes and impressions. She was like an onlooker in a dream, knowing that what was happening involved her. *She* was the bride who had said "I do" in the garden. And in the dining room, *she* was the one who cut the first slice of cake with Jonathan's strong hand guiding hers. The two drank from the same goblet. And she politely answered Morrow and Andrew, and even thanked the minister before he left.

But now, three hours later, with the wedding supper over and the house returning to near normal, she waited for Jonathan to slip into her bedroom. She sat up in bed, her brown hair loosened against the embroidered linen of the pillow-slip, and gazed toward the open windows and the stars that had begun their nightly journey in the heavens.

And then she heard the handle of her door and Jonathan's voice whispering, "Ginna."

"Yes, Jonathan."

The door closed quietly, and in the shadowed room, she watched as he made his way to her side.

"I have just spent the longest hour of my life," he whispered, "waiting for everyone to go to bed. In the hallway, I felt like some philandering fool in a farce, waiting to be caught out."

Ginna giggled. "I read a play once where the hero wound up in the wrong bedroom. I must say, I wouldn't like it much if you had stumbled into Nanny's room tonight."

"And I would have liked it even less, I assure you, darling."

With the endearment, the playful tone vanished from Jonathan's voice. He was now the impatient bridegroom come to spend the night with his bride.

He came to her in the darkness, and his slow, sensual caress was part of the eloquent language of love, a prelude to deeds that would bring new meaning to utterances of the heart: I love you. I want you.

He spoke them all—the phrases that Ginna had longed to hear from his lips, the same truths, the same ageless desires that lie so tenderly under the surface of every young girl's mind as she dreams of her prince.

But this was no dream. Ginna was in Jonathan's arms. She felt his bare flesh against hers, muscles and sinews straining, arms entwined, and mouth against mouth, drawing a sweetness inexorable. Pain and pleasure became one and then the other, while giving and taking became the same, too. And the world outside no longer existed. Only two lovers entwined, while the stars shone and the waves lapped against the shore in perfect rhythm to the pulse of love.

"My darling, Ginna," he cried.

"Jonathan. My dear, sweet husband."

With the gentle breeze finding its way into the room through the open windows, Ginna and Jonathan lay awake, determined not to waste their one night together in sleep.

"I feel sorry for the world outside," Jonathan said. "For people who've never known love like this."

"I think Morrow and Andrew must know," Ginna said.

"You may be right. But it's rare in this world."

"I want to be such a wonderful wife to you, Jonathan. I'll always love you for what you are and what you've done. I was in such despair ten days ago when I left home. Now I'm almost afraid, I'm so happy."

"There's no need to be afraid, Ginna. Ever again. I'll always cherish you and protect you."

Ginna sighed. "I don't think I can stay awake much longer, Jonathan. I'm so sleepy."

"Then go to sleep, my darling."

As the sun made its morning round from east to west and warmed the lake waters with its golden light, Ginna awoke. The pillow beside her was still curved with the shape of Jonathan's head. But he was gone, and she was alone.

She felt lethargic, as if she had been on a long voyage of discovery and now was content to rest. But how much more pleasant it would have been to wake up with Jonathan, her husband, beside her.

She stretched and yawned, then looked at the clock. And she knew that she could not put off getting dressed any longer. She would have to appear at breakfast as if nothing momentous had happened during the night. But could she do that? Seeing Jonathan and acting as if she remembered nothing of the night, when the imprint of his love was still so strong, a physical reminder that she now belonged to him, heart and soul?

By the time Ginna heard the breakfast bell, she was dressed. And with a particularly vulnerable look on her face, she walked down the steps.

He was standing in the hallway when she descended. "Good morning, Ginna. I trust you slept well?"

"Oh, yes, Jonathan. Quite well, thank you. And you?"

"A wonderful night."

"Well, *I* had a nightmare," David commented, watching the two standing there together.

"Probably the aftereffects of all that cotton candy you ate," Jonathan said.

"How did you know that, Uncle Jonathan?"

"Because you still had a pink mustache when you and Nanny finally returned home."

The three walked into the breakfast room together as if nothing had changed from the previous morning. Even Morrow's face was bland when she greeted them. Only Allie threatened to give away their secret with her knowing smile as she poured the morning coffee.

"I'm having tea this afternoon with Lila Montgomery," Morrow commented, "after I return from the settlement house. Would you like to come with me, Ginna?"

Jonathan quickly spoke up. "I promised I'd take Ginna back to the exposition today. She missed seeing the Gobelin tapestries."

"Then will you be back in time for supper?"

"No. We'll eat at one of the restaurants at the fair."

"I suppose the Montgomerys are going to be leaving in a few days, if they've kept to their schedule," Ginna mentioned. "Will you please ask Mrs. Montgomery if it's still convenient for me to travel back to Washington with them?"

Morrow ignored Jonathan's frown. "Of course. But I'll

certainly hate to see you leave. It's been wonderful having you here with us."

"Don't go, Ginna," David said. "I want you to stay. Tell her to stay, Uncle Jonathan."

"We both have to leave, David. You'll just have to come and visit us once we're settled on the plantation in Kentucky."

"Yes, I could do that," he answered, very seriously.

At Braxton School, other little boys were also at breakfast that morning. But a pall lay over the entire school, for two of the students, Nathan Forsyte and Pinky Boswell, were still missing.

The headmaster, Dr. Pemberton, had exhausted all leads. And as he looked at the two anxious fathers, Charles Forsyte and Quincy Boswell, both seated in his front parlor, he was concerned not only for the welfare of the boys entrusted to his care but for his own position as well. The trustees would not look kindly upon a man who could not even keep track of his students.

"And you don't have any inkling where they might have gone, Dr. Forsyte?"

"No. Mr. Boswell and I discussed it coming up on the train yesterday. The boys are good friends, so we know that wherever one is, the other is bound to be there, too."

"Only we don't know where that might be," Quincy offered, rubbing his hand over his full, ruddy face. "But I wouldn't have been surprised if you'd told me that Pinky had taken off for the exposition in Chicago."

"We checked at the train station. They didn't leave from Braxton on the train," Dr. Pemberton said.

"How far away is the next train depot?" Charles asked.

"Let me see. That would probably be Holborne, over

three miles from here. Or Woodbine, five miles in the other direction."

"Have you inquired at either station?" Quincy asked.

"Why, no. I don't believe anyone thought of that."

Charles and Quincy looked at each other, and as Charles stood, do did Quincy. "We'll go to both and then check back with you later in the day," Charles said.

Getting the directions from the headmaster, Charles and Quincy walked out of the cottage.

As they climbed into the carriage and left the school grounds, Quincy said, "My wife is beside herself with grief. We thought we were doing the right thing sending Pinky away to school. But if something happens to him, we'll never forgive ourselves."

"In England, it's the standard procedure. Nathan is used to it, being away at school. But he's never pulled this kind of stunt before, running off."

"Your wife blames Pinky for being a bad influence on Nathan. And with this thing happening, maybe she's right."

"No, Mr. Boswell. I know Nathan. And he's quite capable of getting into mischief on his own."

"I appreciate your saying that, Dr. Forsyte." Quincy pulled out his handkerchief and mopped his brow. The morning was already extremely hot and would get hotter before their journey ended.

When they reached the Holborne station, a passenger train had just deposited its passengers and left in a trail of white smoke. Under the shade of a nearby elm tree sat an empty wagon with a pair of mules harnessed to the wagon tongue.

Tying up their own carriage and horses, they witnessed the reunion taking place on the platform.

"Was it worth it, Pa?" asked a strapping youth dressed in overalls. He reached out to take the shabby luggage from a middle-aged man and his young wife.

"You bet it was, son. Me and Prudie here saw the most gol-durned sights—even a cannibal cooking pot." He winked at the boy. "There was even a naked lady dancin' behind a fan. But when she dropped one of her fans, Prudie grabbed my arm and pulled me out of that tent so fast I didn't even have time to say 'Spit in the bucket' before I was on the outside."

"Is that any way to talk to Ethan?" Prudie complained. "There was lots of educational things, too, Ethan. I'll tell you about them when we get home. And I brung you a special present, too. It's in the suitcase."

Charles and Quincy walked past the family and on into the depot.

"Yes, sir. Can I help you gentlemen?" the young station agent inquired, impressed with the way they were dressed.

"We're looking for two eleven-year-old boys," Charles said, "who're missing from Braxton School. Did they happen to buy train tickets from you about five or six days ago?"

"I just started work here yesterday, so it wouldn't have been from me." The young man turned his back and called out, "Mr. Anthony, did you happen to sell tickets last week to two little boys who were by themselves?"

"I seem to remember two young fellows coming in. But they were traveling with their papas the next day. Sold their mules to get enough money for the tickets."

A disappointed Charles said, "And you didn't see a rather slender little boy with blond hair?"

"Or a chubby little fellow with sandy-brown hair?" Quincy added.

Mr. Anthony said, "Sorry, but all little boys look pretty much alike to me. Wish I could help you. Have you inquired over at Woodbine?"

"Not yet."

"Well, they might have left from there. Good luck to you. Sorry I couldn't be more help."

"Thank you, anyway."

"Hope you find them," the younger man called after them.

When Charles and Quincy left the station to return to the carriage, Mr. Anthony looked at his new man. "You think you'll be all right for the rest of the day, Stoddy?"

"Yes, sir."

"Then I'll get on home. It was a long night."

"I appreciate it, Mr. Anthony. Staying with me till I got the hang of it."

"You're a good lad. You'll do fine."

At the same time that Charles and Quincy made their way toward Woodbine, their sons, Nathan and Pinky, were just waking up in a secluded shelter behind the bandstand in Jackson Park.

"I'm hungry," Pinky complained.

"So am I," Nathan said. "But I guess we'll just have to go hungry today unless we find a job."

"I didn't even *feel* the pickpocket," Pinky said.

"It wasn't your fault, Pinky. So don't beat yourself about it."

"But now I don't even have my train ticket home. And school starts in two days. You'll have to go on without me."

"Do you think I'd do that, Pinky? Go off and leave you here? That would be reneging on our vow. And I'd never do that to you."

279

"Then what are we going to do?"

"Let's go to that white and gold pagoda where they serve the Chinese stuff. We can ask to sweep the floors or wash the dishes—just for something to eat."

"That's a good idea, Nathan."

The two boys set out with high hopes. But although they were very polite, their offer was turned down. They kept walking, from one café, one food stand, one restaurant to another. At each place they got the same answer. No.

Thoroughly discouraged, they finally sat down on the steps of the pavilion where they watched Nelly Rose and her girls enjoying a wonderful breakfast.

"Look," Pinky whispered. "Waffles and syrup and sausages. You think they might leave a little bit on their plates?"

They watched as the women stood and began to depart two by two, until finally only two remained, still deep in conversation. But then they saw the waiter coming to take away the plates.

"Oh, no," Nathan said. "We can't let him take away the food."

"Then let's go. I'm not too proud to beg."

The two boys rushed to the table where the two women sat. "Excuse me, please," Pinky said, using his best manners. "But my friend and I are awfully hungry. Do you think it would be all right if we sat down and finished the food on the plates?"

Nathan backed him up. "You see, our money was stolen yesterday, and we even had to sleep in the park. . . ."

Souci's heart was touched at the sight of the two hungry little boys. "Of course, *mes petits*. Sit down with us, and we will treat you to a lovely breakfast, won't we, Meara?" She didn't wait for Meara to answer. Instead, as Nathan and Pinky sat down, Souci smiled at the waiter. "Leave the plates, *monsieur*. And we'll have two glasses of milk and some fresh rolls, please.

"My name is Souci. And this is my protégée, Meara."

"You're very kind, Miss Souci," Nathan said. "I'm Nathan Forsyte."

"And I'm Quincy Tallifero Boswell III."

"But everybody calls him Pinky."

"*Enchanté*," Souci replied.

"*Et moi aussi, mam'selle*," Nathan responded.

"*Petit*, you speak French."

"Only a little. It isn't my best subject in school," Nathan confessed.

"And I don't speak it at all," Pinky said, popping a stray sausage into his mouth.

Pinky and Nathan sat in the pavilion, eating their breakfast and enjoying their conversation with the beautiful Souci. Already they thought of her as a wonderful lady, treating them to jam and bread and milk when they didn't have a single penny to repay her.

And when they had finally stuffed themselves, taking the rest of the rolls to eat later, Souci waved to the waiter to settle the bill.

"Thank you very much, Miss Souci," Nathan said. "You've been very kind to us."

She smiled her usual dazzling smile. Surely Nelly Rose could not complain if she and Meara had two such youthful escorts for the remainder of the day. "Would you like to come with us, *petits*?" she inquired. "And be our protectors for today?"

Pinky, already thinking of lunch, nodded his head.

"Then come. The others will be wondering what has happened to us."

As Nathan and Pinky left the pavilion with Souci and Meara, his sister Ginna climbed out of the carriage with her husband Jonathan and entered Jackson Park.

# CHAPTER
## 30

The terse telegraph communication from Charles to Ginna,
telling her that Nathan was missing, caused Ginna to
change her plans about going home.

"Jonathan, I think I know where Nathan might be."

"Where?"

"Here in Chicago, at the exposition. He was talking about
it the night Cassie's baby was born. Pinky had a railroad
timetable for the Baltimore and Ohio and information on
the fair. So I know they're here. Only I don't have any idea
where two little boys could be staying by themselves."

"If you're that certain, I'll wire your father, Ginna, and
we'll start combing the exposition grounds. But it will be
like looking for the needle in the haystack."

"I realize that. But we'll have to try."

"Of course, darling."

The morning was cloudy, with a threatening chance of rain. But the weather did not deter Ginna from leaving as early as possible for Jackson Park. And on the way she and Jonathan discussed the exhibits that might capture a young boy's fascination.

"The freak shows," Jonathan suggested. "You heard David asking about the bearded lady."

"Yes. And Nathan likes anything having to do with water and frogs."

"Then we'll watch the aquarium, too."

"And Pinky is always hungry."

Jonathan nodded. "Why don't we keep to the Midway today? The Ferris wheel, the merry-go-round. In fact, it would be a good idea for us to ride the Ferris wheel the first thing since we can get a good view of the grounds from the top."

For the entire morning, Ginna and Jonathan were as thorough as Pinkerton detectives, scouring the grounds for any sign of Nathan and Pinky. But they were not successful.

Unaware that anyone was looking for them, Nathan and Pinky had joined Nelly Rose's troupe and were now enjoying their good fortune after being penniless. So while Souci showed the two boys how to eat Chinese food with chopsticks in the expensive restaurant, Ginna and Jonathan were watching the cotton-candy stand and the peanut vendor along the Midway.

At one point in the afternoon, their paths almost crossed. Nathan and Pinky disappeared through the exit of a tent show as Ginna and Jonathan approached and watched the people standing in line to purchase tickets for the very next show.

By late afternoon, a dejected Ginna turned to Jonathan. "I didn't know it was going to be so hard to look for somebody in the crowds."

A sympathetic Jonathan said, "Darling, you really have no proof that the boys are even here. But we'll take one more ride on the Ferris wheel, to look over the grounds, and then I'm taking you home. You're exhausted."

"All right, Jonathan."

Soaring high above the crowds milling about, the wheel suddenly stopped with Ginna and Jonathan in the topmost cage. "Looks as if we might be here for a while," Jonathan commented, putting his arm around her. "Something seems to have happened to the motor."

"I guess being at the top has its disadvantages, too."

"Don't worry. We won't have to climb down. The mechanic will have it fixed soon."

"Jonathan, look over there, where those women in the bright dresses are standing. The boy beside them looks like Nathan."

"Aren't those the pretties from New Orleans?"

"And that looks like Pinky. Over there. Oh, Jonathan, we've found them. They're here, just as I knew they would be."

"You're sure?"

"Well, almost. Oh, why doesn't this wheel start up again?"

An impatient Ginna leaned over, trying to keep the two boys in her sight. But then Jonathan reached out to restrain her. "Sit back, Ginna. You're tipping the cage. I don't want to lose you, too."

"But they're getting away. It looks as if they're leaving the park."

The music started up and the wheel began to move. Jonathan signaled that they wanted to get out, but the wheel continued its path, up and around, giving its occupants an extra ride to make up for the delay. By the time the wheel finally stopped and a frustrated Ginna touched ground again, the boys had completely disappeared.

"But if you recognized them, then we know they're here, Ginna. That's the important thing."

"Tomorrow, Jonathan, I want to get to the park before it opens. And we can watch the gates as the people enter."

"I was thinking we could check the places where those New Orleans women might be staying, too. If Nathan and Pinky confided in them, then we might be able to find them even before tomorrow."

"But we don't know the women's names. And there're so many hotels and boardinghouses."

Jonathan laughed. "But very few of them cater to clientele of that sort. Let's face it. How many New Orleans madams with a bevy of her girls can there be?"

That evening, from the corridor of the Hotel Moffatt, Souci tiptoed into the room she shared with Meara. And in the corner, where a pallet had been made for them, Nathan and Pinky were sound asleep.

"What's going to happen to them tomorrow, Souci," Meara whispered, "when we leave?"

"Why, they will go with us. One still has his ticket. So it will be easy to smuggle the other one past the conductor."

"How?"

"Oh, Meara, you have so much to learn. There is an art to turning men's heads. And conductors are particularly susceptible, especially if a skirt is lifted a little more than necessary. But leave it to me."

A knock on the door startled Souci. "Yes? Who is it?"

"Me, Nelly Rose. Can I talk to you, Souci?"

Frantically, Souci signaled for Meara to camouflage the area where the two boys were sleeping. Meara quickly sat down on the edge of the pallet and became busy, spreading out the petticoats and crimping the ruffled lace on one of Souci's dresses.

Souci opened the door. "Yes, madame?"

"There's a fellow downstairs asking about those two little boys. Do you have any idea where they went after they left us?"

"Why, no, madame."

"Maybe you'd better come downstairs and talk to him. But I'm warning you, Souci. If you made a date with this man behind my back, you're going to be in trouble."

"*Mon Dieu,* I take pity on two hungry little boys and then you accuse me of an assignation. I am innocent," she averred.

"You weren't so innocent in Washington, Souci."

"That was different."

Souci closed the door and followed Nelly Rose down the steps to the small, dark lobby. As if she were suspicious of both Souci and the man, the woman stood within hearing range.

"I understand, monsieur, that you are looking for two small boys," Souci said.

"Yes, the ones leaving the exposition with you late this afternoon. Do you happen to know their names and where they might be staying?"

Souci turned her head slightly before answering. Nelly Rose was still eavesdropping. "No, monsieur. But if you would like to leave your name and where you can be reached, I might bump into them tomorrow."

Jonathan nodded and walked to the lobby desk where the custodian was half asleep.

As he took a pencil and began to write, Souci said, "These are your sons, monsieur?"

"No. My wife's little brother and his friend. They've run away from school. And the families are quite worried."

"When you're finished, Souci, come on back upstairs." Satisfied that Souci had not made an evening assignation, Nelly Rose began to climb the steps.

As Souci took the slip of paper with Jonathan's name and address, she quickly whispered, "What did you say their names are?"

"Nathan and Quincy, or Pinky."

"They're asleep in my room—one oh three. But you understand, Madame must not find out I'm sheltering them. Wait at the back entrance and I will bring them out to you."

Jonathan nodded. "Well, thank you very much," he said, loud enough for Nelly Rose to hear. "Miss . . ."

"I'm called Souci, Monsieur Jonathan."

As he walked past the shabby red carpeting to the front door, Souci rushed to catch up with Nelly Rose. She put her hand over her mouth as she yawned. "Such a long day, madame. And I am so tired."

"Yes, we'd all better get to sleep early. Our vacation is over and tomorrow's a long traveling day."

When Souci reached her room, Meara was waiting for her. "What happened?" she asked.

"The family has come for Nathan and Pinky."

"How did they know they were here?"

"The man saw us together at the exposition, and he traced us here."

"Are we going to get into trouble because of it?"

"Only with Madame, if she catches us. We will have to wake the boys and take them down the back stairs. The man will be waiting in the alleyway."

Souci went over and knelt by the pallet. "*Petit*, you must wake up," she said. "Someone has come for you."

Nathan was sound asleep and it took him a long time to wake sufficiently to understand what Souci was saying.

"You must get up, Nathan. Your family has come for you."

"Papa?"

"No. Monsieur Jonathan."

"Is Ginna with him?"

"I do not know. Perhaps so."

"Pinky, wake up," Nathan said. "We're going home."

In the alleyway, Andrew and Jonathan waited in the carriage. The section was not a good one to be in after dark, and Andrew was wary. He kept his hand on the small pistol he'd brought with him, for cutthroats and murderers could easily be lurking around the corner.

A large rat came out of the trash and shuffled down the alleyway, causing the horse to snort.

"Easy, boy," Jonathan said, soothing the nervous animal.

"What's keeping them?" Andrew said. "We should have walked in and gotten them."

"No. If we had done that, the woman would be in trouble with the madam. From her manner, I could tell she was afraid of her."

Down the alleyway, a man leaned against the side of the old building and waited, while the slow rain dripped from the sharp-angled eaves. His knife was stuck into his belt where he could retrieve it at a moment's notice. And beside him, he slowly positioned the barrel so that he could roll it in the path of the carriage as it started out of the alleyway. He was quite adept at working alone in the mean streets at night. But it wasn't often that a carriage so fine wandered into the neighborhood. Already he was calculating how much money the men's wallets held.

"Quick, Nathan. Down these steps, *petit*," Souci whispered, guiding the boy while Meara followed with Pinky.

Nathan suddenly balked. "Why are we going this way, Souci?"

"I told you, little one. Madame would throw me out in the streets if she discovered I had you in my room."

"Then we don't want you to get into trouble on account of us. Do we, Pinky?"

"No."

And so the two boys hurried on, with Souci leading the way. Quickly, she slid the iron bar back and opened the door. In the carriage, Jonathan heard the squeak. "I'll go to the door, Andrew," he said, and jumped down from the carriage.

Clandestinely, Souci put her hand over Nathan's mouth to keep him from speaking. Without saying a word, Jonathan lifted Nathan into the carriage and then came back for Pinky.

He stood there for a moment in the faint glow of the old gaslight hanging inside the dingy hallway. "Thank you," Jonathan said, and pressed a large bill into Souci's hands.

"*Merci*," she whispered, stuck the bill into the bosom of her dress, and then quickly closed the door, leaving the alleyway in almost total darkness.

"Jonathan, I'm so glad—" Nathan began.

"Hush, Nathan," he whispered. "Don't speak until we're out of this dark place."

The horse's hooves made a metallic sound against the slippery cobblestones. And then the racket of the barrel rolling directly in front of the carriage caused the horse to rear in fright.

The shadow moved and jumped onto the carriage. "Your wallets, gentlemen," the man said, pressing the knife against Jonathan's throat.

Before he knew what had happened, the robber was on the ground with his knife wrenched from his hand and his elbow in terrible pain. In surprise, he watched the carriage disappear down the alleyway.

"That was an expert maneuver," Andrew complimented Jonathan. "I thought I was going to have to use my pistol."

In the back of the carriage, two small boys held tightly to each other as the carriage careened around a curve and the horse galloped toward the light ahead. But once the carriage slowed, they realized they were safe.

"Boy, I can hardly wait to tell Ginna. This was really an adventure, wasn't it, Pinky?"

"You won't be telling Ginna or *anybody* about this, Nathan," Jonathan said. "This is a secret the four of us men will have to keep always. Do you both understand?"

"Yes," the two replied in unison. Nathan and Pinky held their arms together where the blood crosses had been scratched. And in low voices they intoned, "To the death, through thick or thin, forever and a day, so help us God."

# CHAPTER
## 31

Araminta left Cassie's house to go home. The past two weeks had been worrisome, with the colicky baby and then Nathan's disappearance from school. But she had left Maudie to be a nursemaid to little Stanley, and Nathan had been found. So perhaps life would get back to normal.

And yet Araminta knew that when she arrived home, the reception from Charles would more than likely be a cool one. But *she* certainly was not to blame for Ginna's finding out the truth. Didn't a mother have a right to confide in her elder daughter in times of trouble? Charles shouldn't be upset with Cassie, either, even though it probably would have been better if she hadn't blurted out the truth to Ginna just when she did.

But Araminta, riding along in the carriage to the brownstone, was rather glad that Ginna knew. Maybe now she would realize how impossible it would be to marry Jonathan Meadors in the circumstances.

She was still furious with Ginna for traipsing off to Chicago when she should have been at home taking care of the house and overseeing Clara and Barge.

Araminta narrowed her eyes as she thought about her wayward daughter and her equally wayward husband, Charles. They were two of a kind, meek on the outside but with an inner stubborness that was finally getting out of hand. And Nathan was becoming exactly like them. But at least she wouldn't have to worry about him for a while now that Dr. Pemberton was willing to accept him back at Braxton School.

But both Charles and Ginna needed to be taken in hand immediately. "Barge, do hurry on," she said. "I want to get home before dark."

"Yes, Miss Araminta."

The horses quickened their pace, passing several other carriages. Araminta nodded her head to their occupants as the carriages drew level with each other, then passed on by.

"First thing tomorrow, Barge, I want you to rid the pool in the garden of all the frogs and tadpoles that Nathan put in."

"But, Miss Araminta, I promised Nathan I'd look after them while he's gone."

"Then you can tell him they all died, Barge. He won't be home until the Christmas holidays, and he won't know the difference."

"Yes, ma'am." Barge muttered under his breath, "But *I'll* know the difference."

"What did you say, Barge?"

"I said, there're not any tadpoles left. They're all frogs now."

He drew into the driveway and stopped. "I'll bring your valise inside soon as I put the horse up, if that's all right with you."

"Yes, that will be fine."

As Araminta walked up the back steps into the house, she heard Clara singing in the kitchen. For a moment, she stood at the kitchen door and watched the servant kneading bread. "Hush that caterwauling, Clara," Araminta finally said. "I don't want you to disturb the neighbors."

Clara stopped in midsong and looked up. "But I'm happy, Miss Araminta. Miss Ginna's back home."

"Where is she?"

"Setting the dining-room table for supper."

Araminta walked through the butler's pantry to the dining room. "Ginna?"

Ginna looked up and, seeing her mother, smiled. "Hello, Mummy. It's good to see you." She walked over to give her mother a kiss, which Araminta grudgingly accepted.

"You seem to be awfully satisfied with yourself, miss."

"Well, I had a wonderful time in Chicago visiting my sister, Morrow, and her family."

"She is *not* your sister, Ginna," Araminta corrected.

"Oh, but she is, Mummy. Just as much as Cassie is. And it's the strangest thing. Her son, David, looks exactly like Nathan did when he was six. It's incredible." Ignoring the apoplectic look on her mother's face, she quickly said, "How are Cassie and the baby?"

Her mother's look softened at the mention of Cassie. "Doing quite well. The baby is gaining weight, even if he is a little colicky. And Cassie is slowly regaining her strength."

"That's good."

Ginna turned back to the silverware. But Araminta said, "Turn around again, Ginna."

"Yes, Mummy?"

"There's something different about you. I don't know what it is, but I don't like it."

"I'm sorry."

"No, you're not. You're standing there as if you don't give a tuppence for my opinion. If that's Morrow's influence on you, then it's a good thing you're not marrying into that family."

Ginna was hesitant. She was not prepared for a head-on clash with her mother. She so longed to tell her that it was a fait accompli, but she did not. Instead, she said, "May I finish setting the table for supper, Mummy?"

"By all means. It's high time you were back where you belong, seeing to things in your own home. I really didn't appreciate your running off, when I was depending on you."

"But Clara said she took care to have good meals on the table for Papa. And as for the house—"

"That will do, Ginna. I'm tired, and I didn't come home to have an argument with you."

"Yes, Mummy."

With Barge bringing her valise inside, Araminta's attention was diverted from Ginna. But as she walked up the stairs, she could hear Ginna singing. First Clara. And now Ginna. Well, in a few days, neither one would have anything to sing about. Araminta would see to that.

At Union Station, the train eased into the terminal with a

puff of smoke and a squeal of brakes. Charles wasted no time in debarking, followed by Quincy Boswell.

"My carriage will be waiting, Charles. Let me give you a ride home," he said.

"Thank you, Quincy."

Sharing the problem of their two runaway boys, the men had finally gotten to a first-name basis. They had spent a large part of the trip from Braxton in the smoking car, discussing not only their children, whom they had delivered back to the school, but a wide range of subjects as well.

"I'll never be able to thank you enough, Charles, for finding Pinky."

"We both have Ginna to thank for that, Quincy. I doubt I would ever have thought to look for them in Chicago."

"Well, they're safe now. And I think Pinky has learned his lesson about running away. He seemed quite contrite."

Charles laughed. "But you really have to admire the little fellows and their ingenuity in getting to the fair."

"Yes. I guess that's the reason I can't be too hard on my boy, even if he did scare ten years' growth out of his mother and me. It was something I might have done at Pinky's age."

From the platform, the two men claimed their luggage, found the Boswell carriage driver waiting at the front of the terminal, and within a half hour they were home.

"We'll have to meet for dinner at my club sometime soon," Quincy said, as Charles stepped down from the carriage in front of his house.

He nodded. "Good night, Quincy."

"Charles."

Hearing her father, Ginna rushed to open the door for him. "Did you get Nathan back to school all right, Papa?"

"Yes. But I'm afraid he and Pinky are going to be little

celebrities among their classmates. Only two of the teachers and Dr. Pemberton know they actually ran away. The official records state that Mr. Boswell and I took them to the fair and got them back two days late for classes, which they will have to make up."

"I'm glad Nathan's not going to get into any more trouble."

Following Charles down the hall, Ginna said, "Mummy and I waited supper for you, Papa. So while you wash up, I'll help Clara put it on the table."

"When did your mother get home?"

"An hour or so ago. She said Cassie and the baby are doing fine."

Fifteen minutes later, Araminta, Charles, and Ginna were seated at the round dining table covered with embroidered white linen. In the center of the table, Ginna had placed a hurricane candle globe with a garland of fresh flowers from the garden.

And Clara had outdone herself, with freshly baked bread, broiled chicken, fruit salad, and fresh green beans, with blackberry preserves and iced tea.

As a hungry Charles finished several bites, he turned to Ginna. "It looks as if we might be celebrating something special tonight, Ginna," Charles said, for the care she had taken with the place settings and the menu was obvious.

"We have a lot to be thankful for," she answered, smiling at her father and then at her mother. "Cassie's baby. Nathan's safety."

"And don't forget your upcoming marriage to Jonathan," Charles added.

Araminta looked at Charles. "No, Charles. The marriage is off. Ginna will remain in this house."

With a determined set to his jaw, Charles said, "The wedding is still scheduled in three weeks, Araminta."

The warning signs of one of Araminta's classic temper tantrums were taking shape. Her face turned beet red, her eyes blazed, and her lips became rigid against her teeth.

"Over my dead body, Charles. Cassie and I both know it's no good aligning ourselves with Allison again. We never liked her. And we don't like her son, Jonathan, either."

"It really doesn't matter what you and Cassie have decided, Araminta," Charles retaliated. "It's Ginna who will be marrying him, and she has my blessing to do so."

Like an embarrassed bystander, Ginna listened to the heated exchange between her parents. The conversation would have devastated her earlier. But now she knew there was nothing her mother could do except cause a little extra unpleasantness. For she and Jonathan were already husband and wife. That was what Araminta had seen in her—the happiness that she was trying so hard to keep to herself.

"I think we need more bread," Ginna said. "I'll take the tray to the kitchen."

By the time she returned from the kitchen, her father had left the table. "Where's Papa?" she asked.

"He's gone to the clinic. Men are like that, you know. They always leave rather than face any unpleasantness."

"Do you think he'll be back soon? Clara and I made his favorite dessert."

"I don't know or care, Ginna, whether he comes home tonight at all. So don't keep asking me about him."

"I'm sorry, Mummy."

Ginna sat down at her own place, but she had lost her appetite. She watched as her mother continued to eat.

"And why are you staring at me like that, Ginna? Haven't you ever seen anyone eat before?"

Ginna did not respond. She sat in silence, trying not to do anything that would upset her mother even more.

"I'll tell you one thing, miss. You act as if you have your father wrapped around your little finger. But, in the end, I'll get my own way. I'll see to it for sure that you and Jonathan Meadors never get together again. And you might as well remove his ring right now."

As if her mother had never spoken, a disheartened Ginna said, "I think I'll go and see how the dessert is coming along. You would like some, wouldn't you?"

Araminta nodded. "And tell Clara not to be so stingy with the whipped cream this time."

When Ginna returned to the dining room, she took her place again. "Clara is whipping the cream now. She'll bring in the dessert just as soon as she finishes."

There was no response from Araminta except for a strange wheezing sound.

"Are you all right, Mummy?"

Araminta's eyes widened and she tried to speak even as she reached out toward Ginna. But no other sound came except the terrible wheezing.

"Mummy?" Ginna jumped up from the table to go to her mother just as Araminta slumped over with her head in her plate.

"Clara!" Ginna screamed. "Come quick! Something's happened to Mummy."

"What's wrong, Miss Ginna?"

"I don't know. She might be choking on something or maybe having a seizure."

Clara wrung her hands and cried, "Lordy, sweet Jesus."

"Come and help me get her on the carpet," Ginna said, "and we'll loosen her corset so that she can breathe better."

"She don't appear to be breathing at all, Miss Ginna."

"Did Barge take Papa to the clinic?"

"No, ma'am. He drove himself."

"Then tell Barge to run down the street to get Mr. Boswell and then go on to the clinic to fetch Papa."

Ginna had already begun the artificial respiration that her father had taught her. And within a few minutes, the ruddy-faced Mr. Boswell was kneeling beside her.

"Ginna, what can I do to help?"

"Take over the artificial respiration while I breathe into her mouth."

She kept it up for twenty minutes, with the two of them working in a steady rhythm. Sweat poured down Quincy's face from his efforts. Then, seeing Charles appear and rush to Araminta's side, Quincy stopped.

"Charles, she's dead," Quincy said. "I think she was dead even before I got here."

But that did not deter Charles. "She might have choked on something; it might be blocking her air passage. I'll have to do a tracheotomy."

While Ginna stood in the doorway, with Clara's arms around her, she saw the scapel poised in the air as Charles made an incision to Araminta's windpipe.

"Here, Quincy, hold the napkin to stanch the blood while I take up the artificial respiration."

"Charles, she's already dead."

"No, Quincy, we'll keep working."

He was both surgeon and husband at the same time, with emotion governing his actions. As a surgeon, he had to try to do everything possible to restore the life of the woman who had brought him so much pain through the years. Perhaps this was the reason that kept him going far beyond all normal procedure. The supreme effort was not only for her but for himself.

In the end, he knew it was useless. Araminta was dead. But, of course, he had known that the moment he'd knelt beside her.

# CHAPTER
## 32

"Darling, I came as soon as I heard."

A subdued Ginna sat in the darkened parlor to receive guests offering their condolences. They were mainly her father's colleagues at the medical center and a few neighbors. But now she was alone except for Jonathan.

"Oh, Jonathan, it was terrible."

"I know, Ginna. I'm so sorry. What can I do to help?"

"Papa's taking care of the funeral arrangements, so there's little to do beyond that." She looked toward the door. Then she whispered, "But I'm glad you're here with me now."

He took her hand. "How I wish I could be beside you the entire time. You're my wife, and it's driving me mad not to be able to acknowledge it."

"I know. Sometimes I think Chicago was just a dream. That it never really happened."

"But it did, Ginna. And we'll be together soon."

"Not really. Now that Mummy has died, the wedding will have to be postponed for a long time. We both know that."

"So even in death, Araminta has had her way. To keep us apart."

"That's what's so tragic, Jonathan. The last conversation she and Papa had together they were fussing over me. And when Papa told her our marriage would take place as planned, she actually said 'Over my dead body.' How can I live with that, Jonathan? Always remembering that it might have been my fault?"

"Don't be ridiculous, Ginna. It was the chicken bone stuck in her throat. It would make more sense to blame Clara for cooking the chicken for supper."

A tapping at the door indicated other visitors, and Clara immediately went to the front door. "Good morning, Clara. I'm Mrs. Drake. Is Ginna at home?"

"Yes, ma'am. She's in the parlor with Mr. Jonathan. Do come in."

Peggy Drake swept into the parlor, and Ginna stood to receive her. "Poor Ginna," she said, holding out her hands to her. "What a sad time for you. But I know what a comfort Jonathan is to you now." And then after a few words of sympathy shared, the three took their seats.

For a moment, Peggy looked at Ginna and Jonathan, seated beside each other on the small sofa. "I'm glad I found you two alone this morning because I wanted to talk with you both."

She nodded in Jonathan's direction. "I've just spoken with Allison, so she knows what I'm going to suggest. And if the plan meets with your approval, then it has her blessing, too."

"What plan, Mrs. Drake?" Ginna asked.

"It might seem much too early, Ginna, dear, to be discussing it. But at the risk of seeming hard-hearted at your recent loss, I'm going ahead, anyway. It's something that will have to be dealt with sooner or later: your wedding."

"We were just talking about it, Peggy," Jonathan said. "Under the circumstances, Ginna tells me we'll be forced to postpone the ceremony indefinitely."

"Only about six to eight weeks, really, if the wedding is a small, private one with just the immediate family. That's why I want to have the wedding at my house, Ginna. I feel I brought you two together, and it's the least I can do, especially now that your . . . your mother won't be able to fulfill her duties."

"That's most kind of you, Mrs. Drake, but—"

"Now, Ginna, don't decline before you take time to think about it. I understand your half sister has just had a baby, so she won't be able to help. And you can't have the wedding here, with a funeral wreath so recently on the door. I suppose you *could* have the wedding at Jonathan's house, but it would *look* so much better if you would allow me my little pleasure."

Her smile was endearing. "You know how much I enjoy entertaining. Now just consider it settled, and once this awful week is behind us, then we'll get together and discuss it at length."

"I don't know what to say."

"Well, discuss it with Jonathan, dear, and we'll talk another time." She stood, with both Ginna and Jonathan following suit. "I really must go. But know, Ginna, dear, you both have my deepest sympathy in your sorrow."

"Thank you, Mrs. Drake."

"I'll see you to the door, Peggy," Jonathan said, accompanying her out of the parlor.

For the rest of the day, Allison was strangely absent. Instead, she sent Crete over to help Clara in the kitchen and to receive the food offerings from the various neighbors.

That day passed. The night came and then morning. And when the private interment, with only a graveside service, took place in the afternoon, Allison stood apart with Rad at her side, while Jonathan took his place with Charles and Ginna. Nathan, who had been sent for from school, held his father's hand. And Stanley Quail was a part of the family group, too, representing Cassie, who was still in bed after childbirth.

The cemetery was a peaceful one, in a green meadow with wildflowers visible before the forest of trees beyond. But as the minister began the service for the dead, few of his words were heard. Each was thinking his or her own thoughts—of praise, of blame, of guilt and sorrow combined with tears, of loss and relief at Araminta's demise.

Charles was aware of Allison. He had seen her as he'd stepped out of the carriage with Nathan. He tried not to be bitter at life, not to continue the dreadful thought when he'd first seen Araminta's inert body—that he was free now. That if something happened to Rad, too, then . . . But no. He must put that out of his mind. Only think of Ginna and Jonathan. Their happiness, which Araminta had sought to destroy. And little Nathan, so baffled at the death of his mother.

While Charles was struggling to put Allison out of his mind, she was retracing the distant past—the happy times at Cypress Manor with her brother Jonathan, her son's namesake, before he'd brought Araminta home as his bride. Araminta had been *chic*-looking then, with her coquettish demeanor hiding a certain pettiness that had eventually caused such heartache in the family. Poor Jonathan—to be disillusioned so soon. And her poor invalid father, with his last days spoiled by Araminta. But now Araminta was gone, too. And Allison prayed for forgiveness for remembering the petty things about her former sister-in-law.

Standing in the background with Allison, Rad was one of the few who truly grieved at Araminta's death—not because of the woman herself, but because of her husband. For if he were in Charles's shoes, Rad knew exactly what he would be thinking. With Araminta's death, he was one step closer to getting Allison back.

Yet he was the one who had defended Allison's meeting with Charles in the park. He'd acted as if it were with his urging that the two had met. His manner had surprised Stanley that afternoon, summoned as he was to Rad's office to discuss the so-called delicate matter he'd referred to in his letter.

And he'd felt almost sorry for Stanley when he'd casually brought up the subject of the woman and child he was keeping in the townhouse. Stanley's face had turned a sickening shade of green, almost as if he were ill. That had been the end of any threats on Stanley's part. And he'd paid the large fine, too, without objecting. But it was Awbrey, his aide, who'd discovered the incongruity in Stanley's righteous pose. He had Awbrey to thank for deflecting Stanley's gossip about Allison.

". . . And bestow thy blessing upon these dear children . . ." The minister continued the eulogy, the prayers, as the bereft continued their private thoughts.

Stanley Quail exhibited an unrequited sadness etched

across his face. To those present, he seemed the epitome of a grieving son-in-law. But the truth of the matter was that he couldn't have cared less about Araminta.

It was Maryann who occupied his thoughts that afternoon. Because of Rad Meadors, their alliance was ending. And all he could think about was his last conversation with Maryann.

"It's a sickness, Stanley—between you and me," Maryann had said finally. "Heaven knows, I've tried to stop it before it caused any more anguish for us both. But now I have a chance to be free—to marry someone and have a reasonably normal life."

"And who is this man who would take another man's mistress for his wife?"

"He thinks I'm a penniless widow with a child. He knows you're my half brother and that you have been supporting me."

"But I can't do without you, Maryann. You're the only one who's ever been able to satisfy me or to match my need."

"But you have a wife now, Stanley. You'll have to look to her for comfort from now on."

"But she can't be my wife again for a number of weeks. Surely you won't deny me comfort while she's still recovering from little Stanley's birth."

"No, Stanley, I won't be that cruel. But once she recovers, then it's all over between us. It's for your good as well. I know how strapped you are for money, having to pay the fine. It will be a relief for you not to have to support me anymore."

"But I can't bear the thought of another man touching you."

"You've already spoken of denial, Stanley. Please don't deny *me* my one chance for happiness and self-respect."

"Then come into the bedroom, Maryann. I need to hold you."

A few minutes later, with the curtains drawn, he lay beside her and caressed her lustrous, beautiful hair. "Do you remember the yellow ribbons I gave you that afternoon in the deserted cottage?"

"Yes. So many years ago. They're still packed away in my small trunk. When you were in England, I'd take them out occasionally and look at them."

"Get them out, Maryann. Now. I want to remember that afternoon—the first time I ever made love to you."

He watched her as she walked to the foot of the bed and opened the curved lid of the hobnailed metal trunk. Her naked body was still firm, but with a ripeness that had not been visible when she was twelve. He continued to watch while she brought the faded ribbons back to bed and stood.

Like an ancient ritual, he took the ribbons and bound her hair. "We'll always be one body, Maryann. Remember this when you're being loved by your husband. . . ."

"Please, Stanley. You're hurting me. . . ."

"Stanley?"

The voice was a man's and he gave a start. "Yes?"

"The service is over," Charles said. "It's time to go."

"Yes. It's over," he repeated, and followed Charles, Ginna, and Jonathan out of the cemetery.

# CHAPTER
## 33

In that August of 1893, the personal problems that divided families and caused such uncertainty ran parallel to the economic distress felt by the majority of working-class Americans.

"It's that damned eastern moneyed group," Tug Birmbaugh complained to Rad and Tripp Drake. "The poor western farmer and the city laborer don't have a chance in hell against them."

"You Silverites in the West haven't helped, Tug," Tripp responded. "Forcing the government to buy silver to be redeemed in gold has just made *all* money scarce."

"The whole situation is a lot more complicated than that,"

Rad responded. "We've overspent and overproduced ever since the Civil War, and it's finally catching up with us."

"Maybe we need another war," Tug said in a joking manner. "That always helps in time of economic depression."

Rad frowned. "You didn't fight in the last war, did you, Tug?"

"Not between North and South. I was too busy trying to keep my scalp from the Indians."

"Then you should know what devastation war wreaks on a nation. So I assume you said that in jest."

"Maybe. But I think the people are beginning to spoil for another fight."

"Preferably with some poor island dictator or monarchy," Tripp said.

Tug became slightly belligerent with his two colleagues, for he knew that Congress would more than likely defeat the Silver Purchase Act, which would do harm to his own silver mines. So the words spoken in jest began to take on a more serious, argumentative note.

"Well, the British are sending troops into Nicaragua to protect their interests. I don't see why Cleveland doesn't do the same for American interests," he said.

"I would have thought that deposing Queen Liliuokalani and annexing Hawaii would have sufficed the expansionists' urge, at least for a while," Tripp replied.

"I think the real war is going to come from within," Rad cautioned. "It's going to be a class war, between the haves and have-nots—the owners versus the workers. Just look at what's happening in Chicago. George Pullman has laid off any number of workers and cut the wages of those still employed by twenty-five percent. Yet he hasn't reduced the high rents for the houses his workers live in. My daughter writes that the mobs are becoming unruly because they're so desperate for food."

Their conversation continued, bringing into the open the division that separated the people as well as members of Congress.

The hot days of August passed into September and October. While the debate over the money situation raged in Congress, the white and gold fantasy of Chicago's Columbian Exposition quietly vanished, leaving in its stead an inherited legacy of riffraff to roam the city and get into mischief.

Morrow returned to her work at the settlement house. But she still made her weekly visits to the Andretti family, who were more destitute now than ever. But because of the mobs, Mateo rode with them.

"It's just a losing battle, Miss Morrow," Allie said, as they traveled through the littered streets toward the tenement. "How can one basket of food make any difference in this sea of starving faces?"

"It makes a difference to *me*, Allie. If it hadn't been for some stranger here and there with a meager offering of food years ago during the war, my mother and your mother surely would have starved to death."

"I guess you're right, Miss Morrow. My papa, Big Caesar, used to tease my mama about being beholden to him since he let her take his fishing hole from him. That used to rile her 'cause she was so proud. Proud till the day she died."

"Have you heard from him lately?"

"Yes, ma'am. Last week. And he's proud, too. Said Mr. Jonathan told him he didn't know what he'd do without him running the farm and taking care of the horses while he's gone."

"Well, it's been hard on everybody. Jonathan and Ginna, I'm sure, had no idea they would be apart for so long."

"I never understood why they just didn't come out with it and tell everybody they were already married."

"Once Mrs. Forsyte died, it was too late. It would have seemed such a hole-in-the-wall affair. But it won't be long now. The three months are nearly up."

A worried Mateo, looking at the sky, saw a cloud of black smoke beginning to spiral above the buildings. And in the distance a clang of firebells indicated that a fire had broken out.

"Mrs. Lachlan," he said, "I'm afraid there's a fire ahead."

"Keep going, Mateo," she said. "Maybe it's not that close."

But a short distance away, a policeman waved them back. "I'm sorry," he said. "This street's blocked. Carriages won't be able to get through."

"Is a tenement building on fire?" Morrow asked.

"Yes. And you know how dry wood burns. The whole street is likely to be covered in flames in a few minutes."

"Wait here, Mateo."

With the policeman occupied elsewhere, Morrow stepped down from the carriage. "Come on, Allie. We'll travel by foot."

Holding the basket, Allie trailed behind Morrow. Drawn by the smoke, a large crowd had begun to assemble. And with each step, a few more people joined the throng on their way toward the fire.

But then the smoke turned into flames, angry and red against the sky. Tongues of fire began to lap at the roofs of other buildings, and soon the heat swept toward the crowd, forcing them back.

"There're people still trapped in the buildings," someone shouted.

"Can't you get them out?"

"It's too late."

Morrow and Allic stood in the crowd, watching the flimsy tenement buildings crash down like matchstick playhouses. And all around the cries of relatives matched the screams of those trapped inside.

"Get back! Get back. There's nothing you can do."

"Please. My wife and baby are on the fourth floor."

"I'm sorry. They're dead by now. No need for you to die, too. Stay back."

But then a figure appeared at a window as flames encircled the opening.

"There she is! There's my wife."

"Catch my baby," the woman screamed, and without waiting for anyone to get into position, she threw the child from the window. Within seconds, flames had obscured the figure at the window.

The crowd looked on in horror at the drama unfolding. Yet there was a certain excitement that gripped them, akin to watching a fight to the death between gladiators in a Roman arena.

But in Chicago that day, the fight was not between equals matched in size and strength, with an emperor deciding on the outcome at the end. Poverty was the all-powerful adversary, with no regard for human lives.

The fire had been quick, complete. Now only smouldering ashes covered the ground, a sad reminder of immigrant dreams of a better life in a new land.

"We'd better be getting on home, Miss Morrow."

"Yes. We'd never find the Andrettis now."

Carefully, the two began to fight their way through the crowd. But suddenly Morrow stopped.

A small, dirty child sat on a door stoop. Her brown curls were tangled; her tears had stained her dirty little face. And her dress was ragged, with one of the sleeves torn from its stitching.

"Andrea?"

She looked up as her name was called.

"Where is your mother, Andrea?"

She pointed toward the burned-out tenement building.

"You mean she was caught in the fire?"

The child nodded.

"But Tony and Marcello. Where are they?"

Again the child pointed in the same direction.

"Oh, Andrea, I'm so sorry."

Morrow stood, looking at the child as if debating what to do. Allie waited, already knowing what her mistress's decision would be.

"Come with me, Andrea. You can go home with us. And then we'll decide tomorrow what to do with you."

She held out her hand and smiled. And the child, who had worked all summer selling flowers until the exposition had closed, brightened.

Her thin, fragile fingers reached out and took Morrow's hand. She clung tightly to her, with all the strength she could muster.

And Morrow, feeling that strength, knew that Andrea was a true survivor.

In the last days of October, the business in Washington finally ended. After a display of every senator's filibustering oratory, the vote was taken. The silver purchase bill was outlawed, bringing victory to another survivor, President Grover Cleveland.

But the victory left a trail of bitterness that would plague him for his last two years in office. His enemies began to regroup, biding their time for eventual success in other matters.

Though many of the lawmakers went home to await the winter session, Rad and Allison remained in Washington for the private family wedding of their son to Ginna Forsyte.

The wedding gown that had been finished for months now hung in the guest room of the Drakes' Georgian red-brick house situated on a knoll overlooking the Mall.

But one afternoon, two days before her wedding, Ginna paid a visit to her half sister, Cassie.

"I want you and Stanley to come to my wedding, Cassie," she said. "I don't see why we can't all be friends again."

"We'd feel out of place."

"Out of place, with Papa there? And Nathan? Even though Mummy is gone, we're all family, Cassie. And we have to accept each other for what we are. I'm willing to let bygones be bygones, if you are."

"Don't plan on my being there, Ginna. If I feel well enough to come, I will. Otherwise I'll stay home."

"Are you not feeling better these days, Cassie? I would have thought you'd be strong again by now. After all, the baby is three months old."

"Oh, Ginna, you're so naive. Don't you know what's wrong with me?"

"No. You look a little pale, though, I'll admit."

"I'm going to have another baby." Cassie looked decidedly sour as she spoke.

"Already?" Ginna's look was incredulous.

"These men don't even give you time to catch your breath, Ginna. And you might as well learn it, too. Mama didn't prepare me for this part of marriage. She kept talking about how Stanley would soon lose interest in me. My God, I wish he would. Most of the time, he even comes home in the middle of the day, but it's not food that he wants. Today's about the only day this week I've had any peace. But if he keeps up this perverse behavior, I'll be as fat as Mama was, with more than a dozen children."

"Large families aren't so bad, Cassie."

"You sound like such an expert. Tell me that after *you* go through all the pain. I think you'll change your mind."

"But you love little Stanley, don't you?"

"When he isn't crying."

Ginna stood. "Cassie, I need to go. Jonathan is coming for me early. His mother's having a small dinner party at his house tonight. Morrow and Andrew have just gotten here. The only other ones who're not family are the Montgomerys. If you remember, I traveled to Chicago with them."

At the sound of an outside door opening, Cassie looked exasperated. "Don't tell me Stanley's come home early." She looked at Ginna. "Sit down, Ginna. Stay a while longer."

"I can't, Cassie. I just told you I'm already late."

Ginna met Stanley in the hallway. "Good afternoon, Stanley."

"Ginna," he said, nodding. "Are you leaving?"

"Yes. I've been visiting with Cassie and the baby."

He looked relieved that she was on her way out. "Don't let me keep you. I know how busy a bride is two days before her wedding."

"I was telling Cassie that I hope you'll both come to the wedding."

He smiled knowingly. "If Cassie feels up to it. She's been a little peckish within the past week."

He didn't wait to see her out. Stanley rushed on, calling from the hallway, "Cassie, where are you?"

"Hush, Stanley. Don't wake the baby. He's just gone to sleep."

"Good. Then Harriet can watch him for the next hour."

"I'm not feeling well, Stanley. I'm beginning to get a headache."

"Then come up to the bedroom with me, and I'll soothe it away."

Ginna rushed down the steps to the small phaeton. She didn't want to hear any more. Poor Cassie. Who would have thought that Stanley was that kind of demanding husband?

# CHAPTER
34

The leaves on the beeches had turned a glorious yellow, lining the Washington streets in a brilliantly strewn path for the wedding coach to follow.

It was the last week in October and the slight chill in the air indicated that winter was on its way. The absence of the mourning band on Charles's arm also indicated a change of seasons. For it was not appropriate to call attention to family sadness on such a day of joy.

For the occasion, Barge was dressed in formal livery and a top hat. He sat proudly on the box and kept the horses in a steady, slow pace. He had reason to be proud, for the leather carriage had been given a thorough cleaning and polish. The metal on the wheels shone with the reflection of the afternoon sun. And he had seen to it that the horses had been given an immaculate grooming, with their tails braided and their harnesses decorated with flowers. The smaller phaeton, holding Clara and Nathan, followed at a discreet distance. It was no less splendid than the larger carriage in which Charles and his daughter Ginna rode on that brilliant, sun-swept afternoon.

"It's taken a long time, Ginna, but the day is finally here," Charles said. "Are you happy now, pet?"

"Oh, yes, Papa."

He looked at his daughter, sitting so composed, with her cream peau de soie dress set off by the heirloom veil. He knew where it had come from and he tried not to think of the last time it had been worn. Instead, he said, "You're quite a beautiful bride, Ginna."

Ginna smiled. "I *feel* beautiful, Papa. So it really doesn't matter whether I actually am or not. The important thing is that Jonathan loves me and I love him."

"Yes. That's what is important."

Ginna wanted to reach out and touch her father's hand to console him. But there was something that kept her from doing it. She would always love her father and treasure that time in her life when he was the most important being. But now a metamorphosis was taking place. It had begun in the walled garden at Morrow's house. And although she had longed to tell her father of that secret wedding as soon as she had returned from Chicago, she had not. Her allegiance belonged to Jonathan first, not to her father.

But she would not take this special day from him.

They rode in comfortable silence until they reached the driveway of the magnificent Drake mansion on the hill. Then, in a low voice, Charles spoke again. "Ginna, I don't know how much your mother spoke to you about married life. But I assume it was very little. If you have any questions, then now is the time to ask. We probably won't have another opportunity."

What could Ginna say? That she already knew? That Jonathan had been such a wonderful, sweet husband? No, that would not do at all. "I can't seem to think of anything to ask you, Papa."

"Then it's just as well. But remember, Ginna: man and woman were created by God to be together, to love each other in a very special relationship. Love Jonathan with all your heart. And trust him, Ginna. I know he'll be a good, kind husband to you."

Now Ginna could not help but reach out to her father. She laid her hand on his and said, "I'm sorry that you and Mummy didn't have that kind of love. But I understand, Papa. Really I do. And someday, I hope you'll find someone else to share your life."

"Let's not talk about me. Today's *your* day, Ginna. And it looks as if a large crowd has already gathered for the wedding."

"I thought it was only going to be family."

"Mrs. Drake probably considers the entire Congress as an extended family. Allison was afraid she might go overboard, but there's nothing to do about it now but smile and see it through."

Barge brought the carriage past the circular entrance and followed the directions of a white-coated runner, who was motioning the wedding coach and the phaeton on toward the back. It had been decided earlier that Ginna and her maid would not risk coming through the front entrance but would take the back stairs to the guest bedroom where her bridesmaid, Martha, would be waiting.

At the same time, Charles and Nathan would be relegated

to an upstairs sitting room, to wait until it was time to walk down the winding stairs to the conservatory below.

With her usual flair, Allison's best friend, Peggy Drake, had decorated her Washington mansion for the wedding and reception to follow. Baskets of white dahlias and birdcages of white doves filled the conservatory, while an altar of white camellias, flanked by tall, standing candelabra, waited for the exchange of marriage vows.

Later, in the upstairs bedroom, Ginna stood very still as Martha and Clara smoothed the few wrinkles from her gown and adjusted her wedding veil.

"Oh, Ginna, how lucky you are," Martha said, "getting to wear such a beautiful heirloom."

"Mr. Jonathan's the lucky one," Clara countered. "I'll bet no other Meadors bride looked any prettier than Miss Ginna does today."

"Enough about me," Ginna said. "Just look at Martha. Doesn't *she* look beautiful?"

Clara nodded. "Blue is her color, that's for sure. Mr. Wells ought to see her now."

Martha laughed. "Wouldn't do a bit of good. And you know why?"

"Why?" Ginna asked. "Because he's a confirmed bachelor?"

"No. Because I think he yearns for my mother instead."

"What are you saying, Martha?"

"It's true. I took your advice and sat with Mr. Hathaway on the porch the other night. Chaperoned, of course, by Mrs. Beauchamp and Miss Counts. And when I came inside, Mr. Wells and my mother were in a deep discussion. I only overheard a little of what he said, but it was enough. He wants to marry her."

The faint sound of music wafted up the stairs. "I think I hear the music. Must be time to go," Clara said.

"Isn't it wonderful that Mrs. Drake hired a string quartet to play for the wedding and the reception afterwards? Now that's class," Martha said.

Clara paid no more attention to the music. Getting Ginna and Martha downstairs was her priority. "You got your bouquet, Miss Martha?"

"I'll get it."

"And I'll get Miss Ginna's." Clara walked over to the florist's box and lifted the pale cascade of flowers, with its cream-colored streamers, from its resting place and handed it to Ginna.

One last inspection in the pier mirror, one last-minute adjustment of veil and bridesmaid's ruffles, and then Clara gave her consent for the two to leave the bedroom.

"Good luck," Martha whispered.

"Thank you."

Charles waited at the head of the stairs. As soon as Nathan started down the steps, Charles offered his arm to Ginna.

"I should have checked Nathan's pockets," he whispered, "to make sure he didn't bring a frog with him."

"Well, if he has one, I just hope he doesn't get near Cassie."

Downstairs, Peggy nodded for Martha to descend the stairs. And when she was at the last step, Peggy nodded up at Ginna and Charles.

"Ready, Ginna?"

"Yes, Papa."

The gilt chairs were in rows on each side of the aisle. At the entrance to the conservatory, Ginna stopped. Standing in front of the bowered altar, two men stood, one young,

the other more mature. Yet they were of the same mold—
Rad Meadors and his son Jonathan.

The fanfare began in a different key, announcing the arrival of the bride. All eyes turned to the open doors. Charles squeezed Ginna's hand, and then they began the long walk down the aisle toward Jonathan and his father and the robed minister, who was holding the open prayerbook.

"Dearly beloved . . ."

Morrow and Andrew sat beside Allison. And on the other side of the aisle sat Cassie and Stanley, representing Ginna's family. And once Charles's role was over, he took his seat beside Cassie. He had an overwhelming urge to look over to where he knew Morrow was sitting. But his view was blocked. And he supposed it was just as well. His second daughter was being married. And it would not do for him to let his attention stray, even for a moment, from the ceremony.

If Ginna and Jonathan felt like imposters, they gave no outward indication of it as they swore eternal love for the second time. Of the guests, only Morrow and Andrew knew that an earlier ceremony had taken place.

The vows were spoken quietly, with conviction, and a few of the more emotional guests pulled out their lace handkerchiefs and dabbed at their eyes, for the bride and groom looked as if they had been destined for each other. Only the immediate family was aware of the obstacles that had almost separated them for good.

"With this ring, I thee wed. . . ."

Ginna heard Jonathan's deep, rich voice and felt the plain gold band slide onto her finger. She gazed into his eyes, and the two, standing there, seemed almost oblivious of the guests as they were pronounced husband and wife for the second time.

"You may now kiss the bride."

Jonathan slowly pushed back the veil from Ginna's face and claimed her mouth. And a little ripple of satisfaction swept through the conservatory, followed by a louder gasp as two dozen white doves were released from their white and gold cages to soar overhead and finally light on the tall green trees behind the altar.

Martha returned the bridal bouquet to Ginna and straightened her train. As Jonathan and Ginna disappeared down the aisle, Martha then took Nathan's arm and followed.

Nathan had come back for Cassie, then immediately returned to escort Allison, the mother of the groom. And with a nod from the minister, all the guests began to disperse, while the string quartet continued to play.

It was at the reception that Rad came up to Charles. "Charles, I don't believe you've met Jonathan's sister. My daughter, Morrow."

"How do you do, Dr. Forsyte."

For a moment, the intervening years had vanished and a young Allison was standing before him, smiling with those same dramatic amethyst eyes. He took a deep breath and forced himself to speak.

"How do you do," he said. But no. He didn't want to say anything so mundane. He wanted to shout to everyone in the room that the beautiful young woman who was greeting him so formally was not Rad Meadors's child but the one he'd given up when she was only three. Instead, he said, "I understand you live in Chicago."

"Yes. My husband is an architect there. Oh, Andrew, do come and join us. This is Ginna's father, Dr. Forsyte. My husband, Andrew Lachlan. And, of course, you know my mother, Allison."

Lila Montgomery and her husband, Richard, joined the group. Allison, sensing the awkwardness and the potential explosion, turned to Lila as the men began to talk.

"Did you ever find out what happened to your new maid, Lila?" Allison asked. "The one who disappeared on the trip to Chicago?"

"No. I even filed a missing person's report on the little baggage. But Meara McClellan disappeared off the face of the earth. And she hasn't shown up anywhere. Richard suspects foul play."

Nathan, standing at Charles's side, popped another mint into his mouth. "Did you say Meara? I think I know where she is."

"Where, dear heart?" Lila asked, suddenly perking up.

Andrew's attention left the other conversation. Before Nathan could reply, he gave him a severe frown.

And then Nathan remembered. He and Pinky had sworn to keep the Chicago episode a secret for all time. He shrugged his shoulders. "I guess I was thinking of somebody else by that name. She's a friend of Pinky's, my school chum."

Lila suddenly lost interest in Nathan and began to chat again with Morrow and Allison. Forgotten by the grown-ups, Nathan wrapped some of the wedding cake crumbs into a napkin and disappeared into the conservatory to lure the doves from their perches in the small trees.

And Ginna disappeared with Martha to the upstairs bedroom where she changed from her bridal gown to her traveling outfit: a rust-colored coat suit with matching hat, trimmed with bird of paradise feathers.

A few minutes later, she reappeared on the stairs with Jonathan, who had also changed into traveling clothes.

"Everybody, come into the entrance hall," Peggy Drake summoned. "The bride and groom are ready to depart."

The crowd gathered at the base of the stairs, waiting for Ginna to toss her bridal bouquet. With a proud Jonathan at her side, Ginna searched the crowd for Martha and then let go of the bouquet. It almost landed at Allison's feet. But she stepped back in time for Martha to reach out and secure one of the satin streamers.

Through a shower of flower petals, the young couple ran. They paused for a moment on the front portico, waved good-bye, and then dashed down the steps to the waiting carriage.

"I love you, Mrs. Meadors," Jonathan whispered, as the carriage disappeared down the driveway.

"And I love you, Mr. Meadors," Ginna replied.

A few minutes later, the guests began to leave. Peggy and Tripp Drake stood by the door as each couple passed by.

"It was so wonderful of you, Peggy," Allison finally said. "Thank you."

"It was the least I could do," she replied. "After all, I *did* bring them together."

"I think we should ask the Forsytes to stay for supper with us," Tripp said. "Have you mentioned it to them?"

"The Quails declined," Peggy said. "I understand she's in the family way again."

"What about Ginna's father and her little brother?"

"I haven't had a chance to speak to them. I'm not sure where they are at the moment."

"Dr. Forsyte went to look for Nathan," Morrow said. "I think he's in the conservatory. If you'd like, Peggy, I'll go find them and issue the invitation."

"That's lovely, Morrow. The rest of you, come on into

the family parlor. And Lila, I can hardly wait to hear all about your trip to the exposition."

In the conservatory, Charles stood and quietly observed his son. With his cake crumbs, he had already lured a dove from the tree. There was a special quality about the child, with his love of animals and all other living creatures. Oblivious to being watched, Nathan continued his cooing sounds, intermingled with the doves' responses.

"My son David looks like Nathan," Morrow said, coming up quietly to stand by Charles.

"And you look exactly like your mother."

"But she always told me that I had your smile."

A surprised Charles forgot Nathan. "You know?"

"Yes."

"Who told you?"

"Jonathan brought a letter from Mother. And then he and I talked."

"I never intentionally abandoned you and your mother, Morrow. After the war, I looked everywhere for you."

"I had a feeling that you might have done so."

"And even though I married someone else, I never forgot you both."

"That reminds me. I almost forgot the reason I came to find you. The Drakes want you and Nathan to stay for supper, if you can."

The emotional crisis was averted by Morrow's words. Charles regained his distant mien. "I'm afraid that won't be possible. I'm taking Nathan back to Braxton School on the eight o'clock train tonight."

"Then I'll give Peggy your regrets."

"Nathan," Charles called out. "We have to go now."

There was a flutter of wings as the doves sought safety once again in the trees.

"I don't know how Peggy is going to round up all these birds," Morrow said. "I suppose she hadn't thought that far."

"She could open up the doors," Nathan said, joining them. "Then they'd fly out."

"Which is exactly what we're going to have to do, son. It's past time to go."

"Good-bye, Nathan," Morrow said. "I hope to see you again soon."

"I'm going to visit Ginna and Jonathan next summer," he told her. "Maybe we'll be there at the same time."

"Perhaps."

The three walked through to the front hall, where Tripp was still doing his duty as host. And standing with him was Rad.

"Sorry you won't be able to stay, Dr. Forsyte," Tripp said, "but I understand."

"Thank you."

"Good-bye, Charles," Rad said, relieved that Charles was going.

"I like your lily pond, Senator Drake," Nathan offered, as he also shook hands with one man and then the other.

Father and son walked down the steps, where the smaller phaeton was waiting. Charles had long ago sent Barge and Clara home in the wedding coach. Now, within an hour or so, he and Nathan would be on their way to Braxton.

After that, Charles would be entirely alone. But today was not the day to think of that.

# CHAPTER
## 35

In most lives, the passage of time has a way of bringing relief from past sorrows and hope for the future. That was true for the Forsytes and Meadorses after the wedding that united Ginna and Jonathan. During that winter, Charles immersed himself in his work; Rad was involved in the Senate's business. Life once again fell into a familiar, steady pattern.

Only Allison was restless.

When she should have been happy, she was experiencing a poverty of the soul, a feeling that had nothing to do with her own physical wants or needs. Her children were happy in their lives. Jonathan and Andrew had formed a new enterprise; Ginna and Morrow were well settled into married life, with their own independent projects that were so necessary for women of spirit. Why, then, could she not feel perfect peace? She had so much to be thankful for.

One wintry afternoon, when the last vestiges of snow had disappeared under the life-giving sun and the yellow crocuses announced that spring was on its way, Allison sat in her Washington parlor and poured tea for Peggy and Lila.

"I still don't understand why Morrow wants to adopt a little Italian immigrant," Peggy said. "It isn't as if she can't have children of her own."

Allison stopped pouring. She held the porcelain teapot in midair and said, "If you've ever been homeless, Peggy, then you have empathy for other homeless people, especially children."

"But the war was so long ago," Lila said. "Surely Morrow was too little to remember what happened."

"I don't know. She never talked much about it. But I noticed, when she was growing up, that she had a propensity for bringing home any injured bird or orphaned baby animal."

Allison continued pouring, handing the cups to her two friends.

"Well, I know President Cleveland is beginning to get worried about what's happening in Chicago," Peggy confirmed. "The unemployed workers are getting out of hand. Tripp says if we have another war, it will be fought in the streets between law and order and those union people who're threatening to stop the trains."

"The workers have a just cause, Peggy," Allison responded. "Morrow writes that it's been such a dreadful winter. The children have no shoes to wear to school, and the families have no coal to burn to keep warm. There's so much unemployment and distress. And if a man who does have a job complains about the scant pay, then a hired scab is sent in to break his arms."

"Really, Allison," Lila complained. "This is a terrible subject to talk about. Will you please pass me one of those marvelous petits fours?"

Peggy laughed. "You might pretend the problem isn't there, Lila, but Allison's right. And it won't go away merely by looking the other way. Just recall the Haymarket Riot."

"I think we're spoiling Lila's afternoon, Peggy. Perhaps we'd better find another subject to talk about."

But true to Peggy's prediction, the problem did not go away. For the rest of the congressional session, it occupied the thoughts of Cleveland and the lawmakers. And it hadn't ended when the summer of 1894 arrived.

The previous July, Rad had made up his mind. He had decided that he would take Allison on a surprise trip, a tour through Italy and France. But today, as he rode his horse, Sumi, home from his office, he realized that his secret plans would now have to be postponed, even though arrangements had already been made.

Once again, Cleveland had called on him—this time, to go to Chicago to investigate the seriousness of the railroad strike that now threatened the operations of the U.S. mail. But he could take Allison with him. And they would go in comfort—in a private sleeping car. Allison was overdue for a visit with Morrow, anyway. She should like that, seeing her grandson David again and being with her daughter while he was busy consulting with Governor Altgeld, the mayor, and the railroad lawyers—and perhaps some of the unionists also, to hear their side of the story.

As Rad galloped down the avenue, the heat rising from the road was oppressive. But he kept going, and by the time he reached the entrance gates to his house, he and his horse were both winded. He slowed Sumi to a trot and followed the pathway to the stables, where he turned the animal over to the stablehand. Wiping the perspiration from his face, Rad hurried inside to the coolness of the garden room, where the overhead fan droned steadily, circulating the air.

"You're home early," Allison said, coming to greet him. "Would you like something cool to drink?"

"Yes. It's hot as Hades out there," he replied.

A few minutes later, they sat opposite each other in the white wicker chairs. As soon as Rad finished his iced lemonade, he set down the glass and stood. "I have to go to Chicago, Allison. And I want you to go with me. So pack your bags. I'll wire Andrew tomorrow morning to meet us at the station on Thursday."

"Isn't this rather sudden? Why the rush?"

Rad stared at Allison. "Would you rather stay here alone in Washington?"

"Of course not, Rad. But you've taken me by surprise."

"I only found out this morning. Cleveland wants me to go to assess the damage of the strikes for him."

"I see."

"And I thought you would want to visit Morrow at the same time since we never got there for the exposition. You don't have anything else planned, do you?"

"Nothing that can't be canceled. A benefit for the orphan asylum and the boat trip with Lila and Peggy down the Potomac."

"Then let them know that your husband wants you with him. The other things can wait until we get back."

Allison frowned as Rad disappeared from the room. She gathered the empty glasses to take back into the kitchen. It wasn't like Rad to demand her presence. Usually, he was much more accommodating, consulting her before he made final plans. But this time he acted almost as if he were afraid to leave her. As if she would choose to remain in Washington rather than go with him.

She was sorry now that she had allowed Lila to hire Maggie, who was such a wonderful personal maid. Yet, at the time, Allison had felt that she could get along quite well with only Crete and Browne in the house. The main reason she'd kept Maggie so long was her concern that the girl might not be able to find another job. But if she were to get her clothes packed in time to leave, Allison would have to get busy immediately since she had only herself and Crete to rely on.

By the next afternoon, Allison had finished packing her trunk and was now waiting for Browne to bring the carriage around.

She was dressed in the same pale green silk dress with matching hat and umbrella that she had worn the previous season to call on Ginna's mother. She had not worn it since. But it was just as fashionable as on the day the little Parisian seamstress had made it for her. And there was no real reason not to wear it again.

"I don't think I told you, Allison. You're going to be traveling in style. The president has put a private palace car at our disposal."

"That was kind of him."

That afternoon, as they left the white clapboard house with its comfortable Victorian porch and turret, it did not occur to either one of them what danger this decision would place them in.

The Pullman palace car was attached to the end of the train that began its journey west from Union Station on the Baltimore and Ohio line.

Several hours later, as the passenger train passed the small town of Braxton, Allison laid down her needlepoint and gazed out the window.

"I wonder how Jonathan and Ginna are getting along, having Nathan visiting for the summer?" she said.

Rad lowered his newspaper. "What caused you to think of the Forsyte boy just now?"

"We're passing through Braxton, Rad. This is where Nathan goes to school."

"Oh." Rad went back to his newspaper, leaving Allison with her thoughts. Finally, she picked up her needlepoint again and began working. The light was still good and she became occupied in finishing the seat cover for one of the dining chairs at Bluegrass Meadors.

Time passed monotonously for Allison. And yet she was traveling in comfort, with her husband. The elegant dinner was served promptly at seven o'clock. And the beds were turned down by their own special attendant, who catered to their every need. Still, the past haunted Allison. She would never be comfortable on a train. For she associated it with loss and hunger. And tonight was particularly difficult. As the darkness closed in, it didn't matter what her mind told her. Her heart was in the past, reacting to the sound of the clacking wheels and the haunting whistle bleating over the deserted countryside, as four hundred and fifty women were being transported north, away from their loved ones and everything they held dear.

Allison stood. "I think I'll retire, Rad. I'm getting rather sleepy."

"Then good night, Allison. I believe I'll stay up a little longer." He leaned over, kissed her, and watched her disappear from the sitting area.

But that night, as the train passed through the small

towns, stopping for only a few minutes and then going on, Allison lay awake and watched the small railway lanterns appear and disappear: red and green lights that announced arrivals and departures from the gray wooden structures built along the sides of the tracks.

For two days the routine was the same, except for some minor incidents along the way. Not far out of Chicago, the train came to an unscheduled stop.

"What's wrong, Rad? Why are we stopping in the middle of nowhere?"

Rad leaned out the window and stared down the track. "Looks as if something has blocked the railroad track."

"You think it's intentional?"

"I don't know. But the work crew is getting off. They'll have the debris removed soon."

Within minutes, the train had started up again. Allison put on her hat and gathered her belongings in preparation for arrival at their final destination.

The trouble began suddenly. At the entrance to the yards, the smell of smoke was everywhere as dozens of railroad cars were set on fire. Unruly mobs raced in all directions, doing their mischief, pretending to be strikers when only a few actually were. The hooligans had taken over, getting back at the moneyed few.

Rad could hear the uncoupling of their private car as the train was stopped before it even reached the station. In anger, he marched into the vestibule. "Now, see here. Put down that torch. You're destroying private property."

But it was too late. Another torch had been thrown through the open window, barely missing Allison. "Rad," she screamed, brushing the sparks from her dress. The draperies became a solid sheet of flame, sending her running toward the vestibule, where Rad was trying to fend off the mob, determined to do their damage.

"Quick, Allison. We've got to get out of here," Rad said, lifting her down from the private car as clubs swung and people cursed and the mob became caught up in violence. No longer responsible for their own behavior, the mob became one anonymous entity, fighting and clawing and ruining a humane cause of labor by turning it into an opportunity to loot and burn.

Rad fielded the blows as he became a shield for Allison, guiding her through the mob toward safety. But they were surrounded, with no way out.

Morrow, waiting with Andrew in the carriage, prayed that Allison and Rad had missed their train and that they were not caught up in the riot.

But her prayers were in vain. As she watched, she saw a woman dressed in familiar green silk break from the crowd and begin to run, pulled along by a tall, dark man.

"There's Mother. Oh, Andrew, please do something," Morrow cried out.

Andrew pointed the horses in their direction and the carriage raced to reach them before they were swallowed up again in the crowd. But Andrew was too late. A few seconds before he got to them, a runaway carriage bore down.

"Mother, look out," Morrow screamed. "Behind you."

With one last-minute action, Rad knocked Allison out of the way. But, for him, it was too late. He was struck by one of the wheels and was dragged under the carriage as the runaway horses raced onward.

A few minutes later, someone managed to grab the reins and stop the carriage. "Do you think he's dead?" a man asked.

"I expect so," another answered.

"No, he can't be," Allison cried, reaching her fallen husband and kneeling beside him. "Rad, speak to me."

"Mother?"

Allison looked up into her daughter's face. "He's hurt, Morrow. Terribly hurt. We'll have to get him to a hospital."

"Yes, Mother."

Andrew directed the lifting of the large man into the carriage. And as they left the train station, a subdued crowd parted to let them through.

# CHAPTER
## 36

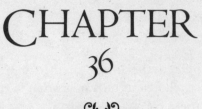

"I'm afraid he's gravely hurt, Mrs. Meadors. The broken leg is the least of our worries. Your husband's spleen has been damaged and he's hemorrhaging internally. It's only a matter of time now."

"But isn't there anything at all that can be done for him?"

A frantic Allison stared at the physician at Cook County Hospital. Her amethyst eyes took him by surprise, prompting him to speak when he had no business to give her any further hope.

"A splenectomy might save his life. But there're only two men who could perform such an operation with success. And they're both in England—old Gaylord Runyard in

Harley Street and the doctor he trained to take his place eventually."

Andrew stood beside Allison and listened. "Isn't that the man Dr. Forsyte studied under?"

"I don't know," Allison answered.

Edward Meeks lifted his head. "You're not speaking of Dr. Charles Forsyte, the London surgeon, are you?"

"Yes," Allison answered. "But he's in Washington now."

"Then that's extremely fortunate for you. That is, if you can persuade him to come immediately."

"Do you think he'd be able to do the necessary surgery?" Allison asked.

"Yes, of course. He's as competent as Dr. Runyard."

"But what about the trains?" Allison inquired. "I wouldn't want to put him in danger, too."

"I understand the president is sending in soldiers to make sure nothing like this happens again, Allison," Andrew assured her. "They should arrive within the next twenty-four hours."

In the end, it was Morrow who wired Charles to come. And Charles knew that he could not refuse. For this was the first time in his life that his elder daughter had ever called on him for anything.

And so, with Nathan spending the month in Kentucky, he was able to cancel his schedule at the clinic and leave for Chicago immediately. As Barge took him to the train station, Charles held on to the medical kit containing the blue steel surgical instruments that had become an extension of himself.

The same sounds on the same track accompanied Charles as he sped toward the lake city, home of extravagant wealth and excruciating poverty, which resided side by side. But it was the medical facility that he was thinking of—that and his acquaintance, Edward Meeks, who had received his medical diploma at the same time as Charles. But instead of remaining in England, Edward had returned home to become a part of the medical complex of the University of Chicago. It would be good to have him at his side for the operation.

By the time Charles arrived in Chicago, the strikers and hooligans were nowhere in sight. Soldiers in army uniforms stood guard, making sure that another tragedy did not occur. So, without incident, Charles left the train and walked into the station, where Andrew was waiting for him.

"Dr. Forsyte, thank you for coming," Andrew said. "Mateo, take charge of his luggage."

As usual, Charles preferred to keep the medical kit in his hand, but he allowed Mateo to take his other baggage to the waiting carriage.

"Would you like to go to the house to rest first, Dr. Forsyte?"

"No. I'd rather see the senator immediately. I presume Dr. Meeks has stopped the bleeding as much as possible?"

"Yes. But Rad needs more blood. It was a disappointment to Dr. Meeks that Morrow's blood didn't match."

An hour later, a well-scrubbed Charles stood over the bed where a weak Rad lay. He had examined his patient and the records that Meeks had kept. Now it was up to him to assure Rad of his chance for recovery. But before he could do so, Rad held up his hand. "I'd like to speak with you privately, Charles, if Dr. Meeks doesn't mind."

Meeks nodded and left the room.

"You've seen Allison?"

"No, I came directly to you. But I understand she's resting in one of the suites down the hall."

"There's something I need to discuss with you, before the operation."

"Save your strength, Rad. We can talk afterward. I've scheduled the surgery for tonight. And I can tell you that you have an excellent chance for recovery."

"No, Charles. I want to talk with you now."

Seeing his agitation, Charles nodded. It would not do to get him upset further. "All right. What is it, Rad?"

"Do you still love Allison?"

"That's hardly an appropriate thing to talk about, right now."

"But it is. Tell me the truth, Charles. Do you still love Allison?"

"I suppose I'll always love her. But she's *your* wife. And I have no intention of making it difficult for either one of you. Once the operation is over, I'll leave. And she'll be at your side for your recuperation."

"But if I don't survive, Charles, you must promise me one thing. Take good care of her. She was mine for a while. But now she belongs to you again."

"That's not true. You'll both grow old and gray together. Now that's enough of this nonsense. I want you to rest. I'll be back to see you shortly before we take you to surgery."

Charles left the room, wrote up orders for the nurses, and then, without seeing any other member of the family, went with Edward Meeks to his apartment and promptly fell asleep in the guest room.

By five o'clock, he was up. After taking a small meal and a cold bath, he was refreshed. And in the cool of the evening, he walked the two blocks to the hospital with Edward.

By the time he arrived, the family was in the waiting room: Allison, Morrow, and Andrew.

"Charles, thank you for coming," Allison said, greeting him with outstretched hands. "Do you think he has even a ghost of a chance?"

"I won't deny that he's gravely ill, Allison. And I would feel better if he hadn't lost so much blood. But he's strong and he stands a good chance of recovering, if the damaged spleen is removed."

"Which you intend to do," Andrew said.

"Yes."

He looked at Morrow. "Thank you for telegraphing me in time."

"You understand how much I love him."

"Yes. He's the only father you've ever known."

Charles looked at Allison. "I'll do my best for him, Allison."

"I know you will, Charles."

He left the three and went to join Meeks.

Within an hour, Charles was in the operating theater where medical students had already gathered in the glass-partitioned gallery to observe the operation.

Once again, the steel scalpel was poised in the air; the anesthetized Rad waited for the initial incision. The operation became one of many that Charles had performed. And the tangled family relationships were forgotten as Charles and Edward Meeks sought to save Rad's life.

Carefully, surely, Charles proceeded, and as the spleen lay exposed, Edward nodded as he saw the irreparable tear in the highly vascular organ.

The operation continued; the spleen was removed. A spurt of blood was quickly stopped with clamps until Charles could suture the gape at the cardiac end of the duodenum. Then sponge and clamps were removed and the outside sutures closed the initial incision. The operation was over.

In the gallery above, the medical students applauded. But Charles did not look up or acknowledge their adulation. His mind was still on his patient.

Charles walked beside the rolling stretcher that took Rad into recovery. And he remained at his side for the next half hour until his patient came out from under the anesthesia.

As the man struggled to open his eyes, Charles smiled at him. "You're going to be fine, Rad. The operation is over."

It was now midnight. Charles scrubbed up again, putting on a fresh surgical gown, for it would not do to greet the family with the bloodstains visible on his operating gown. With the surgical mask still hanging to the side, he walked into the waiting room.

"The operation is over," he announced. "I've done all I can. Now it's up to Rad."

He wanted no thanks, no reward, but the relief showing in Allison's eyes.

"How can we ever repay you?" Morrow asked.

"There's no need even to think of that. I was glad I could help."

"When will I be able to see him?" Allison inquired.

"Give him another twenty minutes or so. Then you can sit with him for a few minutes. He'll more than likely be a little ill, Allison, from the anesthesia. But the nurses can handle that."

Charles slept the rest of the night in Meeks's apartment, only a telephone call away, should anything go wrong with Rad. And early in the morning, as the carriage waited with his luggage, Charles went back to the hospital to check on Rad before he left for the train station.

"How was his night?" Charles asked the special-duty nurse.

"A little rough," she admitted. "But his nausea has subsided now."

"Good. And his temperature?"

"Normal."

Charles walked inside the room. Rad's eyes were still closed, but his color was better than it had been the previous day. "Good morning, Rad. How are you feeling?"

The man opened his eyes and looked up. "I feel as if a herd of Jonathan's steers has just galloped over me."

"You're bound to be sore for the next week at least. And, of course, it's going to take you six months before you can walk without a cane. But you're well on the road to recovery."

"I hope you're right, Charles. But whatever happens, remember that I'm still holding you to your promise."

"You'll outlast me, old chap," Charles said, momentarily reverting to his English speech. "So forget that little scene. You just make sure you take darn good care of Allison from now on."

He laid his hand on Rad's shoulder, smiled at him, and then left the hospital room.

Several hours later, when Allison returned to the hospital, she saw only Edward Meeks. "Has Dr. Forsyte been here this morning?" she asked.

"Yes, he came by to check on your husband before he left for the train station. That was a brilliant operation, Mrs. Meadors, I can assure you."

"Do you mean he's already left to go back to Washington?"

"Yes. But you needn't worry. His job was over last night. We'll be able to care for your husband through his recuperation."

"But I never got to thank him properly. Or even to pay him . . ."

"I understand his daughter is married to your son, so I'm sure he considers it all in the family. And I have a feeling that he would be offended if you offered him money."

"Then we'll have to think of some other way to pay him."

"Why don't you go on in to see your husband? He was asking for you earlier."

A week went by, with Rad growing gradually stronger each day. And none was more surprised than Rad himself. He had assumed that, with the arrival of Jonathan, the entire family had gathered to be with him in his last hours.

At first, he had been too ill to care whether he lived or died. But once the nausea had subsided and the draining tube had been removed from his side, he began to feel human again. And on the eighth day, a regular breakfast—the first since the operation—had done wonders for his morale.

Gingerly propping himself on his elbows, he gazed at Allison, who was sitting quietly in the chair near the hospital bed. She looked up when he cleared his throat.

"Allison, I think we need to talk."

"Yes, Rad?"

"In the last day or so, I've had plenty of time to lie here and think. Some hard decisions concerning our future will have to be faced."

A wary Allison waited for his next words.

"You remember my mentioning that I wasn't planning to run again for the Senate? Well, now that I'm laid up, with a long recovery period facing me, I think it would be better for me to resign immediately. That way, the governor could appoint Edgar to fill my unexpired term, which would make it a heck of a lot easier for him to win the next election."

"Is that what you really want to do, Rad? Resign from the Senate?"

"Yes. But I rather hate to think that it's time for me to be put out to pasture, like Standing Tall and old Bourbon Red. . . ."

At that moment, Morrow and Jonathan entered the room. And Jonathan, overhearing his father's last sentence, came over and patted him on the shoulder.

"You could be in a lot worse shape, Papa. Remember, we had to shoot Silver Dawn when he broke his leg." He nodded toward the heavy cast supported by pulleys.

"Jonathan," Morrow admonished. "That's not funny. Here Papa almost died, and you're making jokes about his condition."

Rad smiled. "Actually, Morrow, it makes me feel better to hear such remarks. It's a lot more encouraging than all those hushed tones and whisperings that went on for the first few days."

Allison stood. With an air of nonchalance, she said, "I'll let Morrow and Jonathan entertain you for a little while, Rad. I'll be back later."

Allison left the hospital room and walked down the corridor to the room that had been reserved for her. Rad's recovery had been miraculous so far, and she had Charles to thank for that. But, according to Dr. Meeks, he was still not out of danger. The break in the leg had been severe, and because of it, there was always the danger of an embolism from blood clots. But she mustn't think of that. Especially now.

Forcing herself to remain calm, she casually glanced about the room—an antiseptic green square, sparsely furnished with bed, nightstand, and chair. One small mirror on the far side and one small, wooden cross over the bed were the only wall hangings to break up the expanse of that ugly shade of green that was so depressing to the spirit.

But from the open window, a scent of new-mown grass drifted through the room, and the neighing of horses from a passing carriage brought relief from the monotonous tranquillity of the afternoon.

The sounds and the smells triggered a memory, so long ago, when she had stood in the meadow with her child, Morrow, and Rad had come galloping toward them on Bourbon Red. . . .

The sound of bells in the corridor brought Allison back to the present. She glanced at her watch. Twenty minutes had now elapsed. Long enough for her to return to Rad's room without appearing overly solicitous. She smoothed her hair and left the room, pausing long enough to allow two nurses rushing down the hallway, with the life-saving machinery, to pass by.

With a sense of alarm, Allison watched as they approached Rad's door. Allison began to rush also. Could something have gone wrong in that short period of time she had been away?

With a sinking feeling, she saw Jonathan and Morrow emerge from Rad's room, as the machinery disappeared inside.

"What's wrong? What happened?"

"I'm sorry. You can't go in, Mrs. Meadors," a nurse said,

barring her entrance. "Dr. Meeks is with your husband now."

"Jonathan? Morrow? Tell me! What happened?"

Seeing the tears in Morrow's eyes, Allison imagined the worst. And when Morrow did not answer, she turned again to her son. "Jonathan?"

"Come, Mother. Let's find a quiet place to sit down." He put his arms around her and led her from the door.

# CHAPTER
## 37

Several weeks later, on a summer afternoon at Bluegrass Meadors when the birds flitted through the trees and the blue haze clothed the pastureland where the young colts romped, Allison stooped down and picked up a clump of rich, tobacco loam. Instinctively, she crumbled the dirt into dust as her eyes swept over the land.

She was surrounded by memories, each playing against the others in a polyphony of sound—voices from the past; years that opened to her like the bluebells and then were gone, replaced with the wind blowing through the trees, with the scent of cured tobacco, fresh mint from the herb garden, and the strong, sweet odor of leather washed down by saddle soap.

In the background, the redbrick house with its white columned porch stood as it had the first time she'd seen it—magnificent and warm, reminding her of her childhood home and a way of life she'd lost because of the war. But through Rad, she had regained her heritage—and more.

His imprint was on the land; his voice, part of the evening sounds. Everywhere she looked, he was there—racing along the whitewashed fence that lined the drive; jumping over the railings. And yes, even urging his horse up the steps of the house itself, marring the winding stairs with the hooves of his horse, as he became the impatient lover with Allison in his arms.

She had come so close to losing Rad on that fearful afternoon, nearly a month ago, when the clot had broken loose and gone to his lungs. But he had survived, and now his recuperation was assured.

But how she missed being with him at that moment. Yet she knew it was best for him to remain at Morrow's house in Chicago, while she came back to attend to business matters and to close the house in Washington.

She hoped he had done the right thing by resigning from the Senate. His injuries would slow him down for a while, but once he was well, he might not take that readily to retirement. And it would not be good for Jonathan to have his father around all the time now that he had taken over the entire running of Bluegrass Meadors.

Even Ginna had brought a newness to the old house, with the family portraits hanging on the walls. Allison smiled as she thought of how busy Ginna had been in her studio. Allison's portrait now hung beside Rad's in the formal parlor, and Jonathan, the equestrian, gazed down from his place in the upstairs hallway.

No, Ginna had no need of another woman in the house

all the time, either. And perhaps it had been a mistake to lease the house in Washington. But it was too late now. They had already promised it to Edgar and his wife.

With her mind sorting out her problems, Allison did not see the carriage driving up until it was nearly beside her. As she looked up, she recognized Royal Freemont from the neighboring plantation. Frail and stoop-shouldered, he wore the same old-fashioned suit that she had sewn for him nearly thirty years before, when she was destitute for money and the war had not yet ended.

"Good afternoon, Royal."

He tipped his hat. "Afternoon, Allison. Saw you from the road and decided to come up and ask you how Rad is getting along."

"Much better, thank you. But it was touch and go for a while."

"When is he coming home from Chicago?"

"Not for at least another month. He's at Morrow's now and will stay there until I close up the house in Washington."

"Edgar's still wet behind the ears. Rad shouldn't have resigned from the Senate."

Realizing that this was Royal's way of complimenting Rad, despite his constant grumbling and complaining to Rad about every bill in Congress, Allison nodded and said, "I was just going back to the house. Would you like to join me in a glass of iced tea on the porch?"

He shook his head. "Can't stay. I'm on my way to Widow Smith's house. She's got a calf I might buy, if the price is right."

"Then I won't delay you. But I'll write Rad that you inquired about him."

An amused Allison watched the carriage disappear down

the long driveway. Royal must have some other purpose, she thought, beyond the purchase of the calf. For he only wore his suit on special occasions.

Allison began to walk back to the house. If she were to leave for Washington early the next morning, then she mustn't linger long over her glass of iced tea. She would have to finish her packing.

When the sun was just beginning to come up over the horizon, an impatient Jonathan stood by the family phaeton and waited for his mother and Ginna to appear. Caesar had already tied Allison's luggage to the back of the carriage for the trip to Louisville, where she would board the train.

"Come on, you two," Jonathan called out, seeing them standing in the doorway. "We've got a long trip this morning."

"We're coming, Jonathan," Ginna replied. "Just as soon as I give Mollie some last-minute instructions for the day."

As the two women walked down the steps, Ginna turned to Allison. "I still wish you'd let me go with you. I might not be a lot of help to you, sorting things out. But I could certainly keep you company at least."

"And I don't doubt that you would be anything but wonderful company, Ginna. But no, darling. You and Jonathan have been apart long enough because of Rad and me. . . . Now, what did I do with my small case?"

"It's already in the carriage," Jonathan said, responding to her last remark.

Several minutes later, with Ginna and Allison seated in the carriage, the horses trotted smartly down the fenced driveway to the main road.

"Once I finish in Washington, I'll go directly to Chicago," Allison said to her son. "And when the doctor feels it's safe for your father to travel, then we'll come back here. But, of course, I'll write you when to expect us."

Jonathan nodded. "And what do you want me to do with the crates shipped from Washington?"

"Don't bother to open them. Just store them in the attic. We'll have plenty of time over the winter to see to them. There shouldn't be that many since we're leaving almost everything in the house for Edgar and MaryBell."

"You're certain that someone will be meeting you at the station?" Ginna asked.

"Yes. Peggy and Tripp. So don't worry about me. I'll be fine."

Once again, Allison was amused. Almost overnight, there had been a subtle shift, as if in Ginna's and Jonathan's eyes she had suddenly become someone to take care of. Their solicitude was an endearing trait, but how glad she would be to see Peggy and Tripp and the Montgomerys—to feel vibrant and scintillating again. Nothing made one feel older than being in the constant presence of the young.

They traveled steadily down the road, with Jonathan stopping at intervals along the way to give the horses a rest. When they finally neared the railroad station, Allison turned to Ginna. "I want to tell you what a fine hostess you've been," she said. "I know how proud Jonathan is of you."

Ginna smiled and gazed lovingly at her husband. "He's made me feel a part of this wonderful family."

"And so you are. Just like Andrew. I thank heaven each night that Jonathan and Morrow found you both."

"According to Andrew," Jonathan said, "he wasn't so sure about Morrow. He might have passed her by if it hadn't been for the dog in her arms." In an exaggerated Scottish burr, Jonathan imitated his brother-in-law. "She was wandering in the streets, she was, like a lost bairn. And she had so much soot on her face that I mistook her for a chimney sweep. . . ."

"Oh, Jonathan," Ginna said, "you know he was only teasing Morrow when he said that. Just like you still tease me about the ridiculous hat I was wearing when we first met in the park."

Ginna quickly put her hand to her mouth, as if she'd said too much.

And Allison, noticing it, said, "But I thought Peggy introduced you."

Jonathan laughed. "Don't ever tell her any differently, Mother dear. But the truth seems to be out. A week before we met formally, Ginna was in the park—with her paint box. That's when I first saw her and spoke to her."

The whistle of the approaching train sounded, ending the conversation. In the next few minutes, Allison's luggage was transferred from carriage to baggage car. And once the good-byes were said, Allison boarded the train and found her place by a window in the parlor car.

As the train began to pull out from the station, Allison waved to the young couple standing on the platform. They looked so happy together, and for that, Allison was grateful.

Down the track the train went, picking up speed, until the Louisville station was left behind and the engine began its journey toward Washington.

By late afternoon, Allison was restless. For her, sitting and waiting had always been extremely difficult, whether in a hospital room or on a long train trip. How she longed to be riding Marquessa at that very minute, rather than to be sitting sedately by the window and watching the familiar landscape as the train sped through the countryside.

She had taken this trip more times than she could re-member, sometimes with Rad, other times alone. That was one of the perquisites of being a senator's wife—being able to travel back and forth at will, on a familiar train, with familiar faces surrounding her. But this trip heralded the vast change taking place in her life. And even as she rec-ognized the lay of the land, she knew that it was different this time. For when she returned, she would no longer be the wife of the senior senator from Kentucky.

As she looked at the line of fences in the distance giving way to small groups of stores and clusters of little houses that faced the tracks, Allison was almost sorry that she had not allowed Ginna to come with her. She would have been pleasant company, helping to pass the time and keeping her mind off the inevitable chore of closing the house and pack-ing a part of her life in crates that were to be relegated to some dark corner in the attic.

With a sense of relief, Allison heard the call for the dining car. From that she knew that the hours were slowly passing into evening.

She deliberately waited for the second call before going into the car for dinner. That way, she could savor a quiet, leisurely dinner, with a second cup of coffee, rather than rushing through it to make way for the next group.

It was almost eight o'clock when the porter from the din-ing car stood before her. "I have your table ready, Mrs. Meadors. Anytime you'd like to come into the dining car, we'll be pleased to have you."

"Thank you, Grayson. I'll be there in a few minutes."

"Yes, ma'am."

The black man in a pristine white coat disappeared as Allison undertook a few repairs to her hair. And then, smoothing her skirts, she walked into the dining car.

As Allison took her place at the reserved table by the window, a man seated at the next table put down his fork and stared openly. He was more or less like most businessmen who traveled by rail, with his gray suit, high-necked collar, and gold watch chain. Only the silver in his hair proclaimed him to be slightly older than the usual traveler.

Continuing to stare, he waited to see if Allison was going to be joined by a companion. But by the time she began to eat her soup, he realized she must be traveling alone. And that fact delighted him, making her seem a little less formidable.

Like all beautiful women who are used to being stared at, Allison paid little attention to the man. But he continued to watch her, for there was something vaguely familiar about her. Had he known her when they were both young?

He ate slowly, pacing himself so as not to finish too soon. And when she ordered coffee, he did the same. The other diners slowly left the dining car until, finally, only the two remained.

He stared down at his empty cup and then, with a nervous gesture, he stood. "Excuse me, please," he said, "but haven't we met before?" Then he silently cursed himself for using such a mundane approach.

"I don't think so," she replied with an unencouraging look.

In a split second, Grayson stood at her side, as if he had come to defend her from a savage onslaught. "Will there be anything else, Mrs. Meadors? You want me to walk with you back to your car?"

"No, Grayson. That won't be necessary."

A belligerent Grayson stood at her side while a totally rebuffed man left the dining car. But the porter had given him his answer. And nothing would be gained from introducing himself to the former Allison Forsyth.

But it was strange, after all these years, to come face-to-face with the woman he had searched for after the war. It had taken him a long time to get her out of his mind, even though she'd married again. For he had been the Union captain responsible for uprooting her and delivering her to her enemies.

"I declare, you never know what this ole world is comin' to, Mrs. Meadors. I thought Mr. Ferrell was a gentleman," Grayson said, still hovering at Allison's table.

She laughed. "I'm sure he is, Grayson. But a very bored one."

The name tugged at her memory. Suddenly she looked up at the porter and said, "Ferrell? I met someone by that name long ago. Do you happen to know his given name?"

"Mars. Mr. Mars Ferrell."

Allison stood. "On second thought, Grayson, I'd appreciate it if you'd walk back to the car with me."

"Of course, Mrs. Meadors. And I'll tell Lump to keep a good lookout tonight to make sure you're not bothered again."

"Thank you, Grayson."

# CHAPTER
## 38

"Surprise! Welcome back to Washington, Allison."

Before her on the platform stood Peggy and Tripp Drake, with Lila and Richard Montgomery.

"Peggy wanted to hire a band to greet you," Lila said, "but the rest of us discouraged her."

Allison laughed, caught up in the homecoming with friends. "Oh, it's so good to see all of you. Thank you for meeting me."

"How's Rad?" Richard inquired.

"Improving every day."

The surge of people along the platform prompted the five to keep moving steadily toward the station itself.

"Give me your baggage ticket, Allison," Tripp said.

"Browne will get your luggage for you and take it to our house."

"But I'm staying at my own house," Allison protested.

"No, you're not," Peggy said. "We've already decided. You'll be with us instead. So hurry up and give Tripp your ticket."

"But how can I sort things out and pack from your house?"

"Easy. You can do that during the day. But you're staying with us."

"Is there anything else I should know? Any other plans you have for me, too?"

Lila took Allison seriously. "Oh, yes. The most marvelous plans for the winter. The four of us have already talked about it. And it only takes an okay from you and Rad."

"Well, let's not overwhelm her," Richard suggested. "Give Allison a chance to breathe first."

Mars Ferrell stood in the distance and watched Allison Meadors disappear with her friends. Then he summoned a porter to see to his own luggage.

That evening, Allison sat at the dinner table and listened to the plans that Lila had hinted at that afternoon. She was glad now that Peggy had insisted on her being their houseguest. For, more than likely, if she were in her own house, she would have had a cold supper and then gone to bed.

"I told you we had it all planned," Lila said, smiling. "We're going to postpone our European trip until Rad is able to travel. And then we'll lease a villa in Italy for the winter."

"And Tripp and I will join the four of you for Christmas in Paris," Peggy added.

"But I have no idea what Rad wants to do," Allison said. "He may not want to go to Italy."

"Well, it's not as if he'll be bogged down with all those hearings," Lila said. "Or the business of the railroads . . ."

Richard cautioned his wife with a glance. "What Lila means is that Rad deserves a nice long vacation. Besides, sitting in the golden Italian sun will put the bloom back in the man's cheeks, after all he's been through."

Richard's words made sense to Allison. "Rad always talked about going back to Europe someday."

"And this is as fine a time as any," Tripp said. "While he's recuperating, it'll give him a few months to think about what he wants to do for the rest of his life."

And give Jonathan and Ginna a few months to be alone, too, Allison thought.

"Would you like to go into the parlor?" Peggy inquired, rising from the table. "We can have our coffee in there while Richard and Tripp stay here and smoke their cigars."

The evening ended early, and a grateful Allison, tired from the trip, went to bed and slept soundly until the next morning.

By nine o'clock, Allison was in her own bedroom, with Crete and Browne helping her to pack the personal things to be shipped back to Kentucky.

Packing at the end of a long journey was somehow different from the initial planning and the excitement of first starting out, Allison decided. Now, after all the time spent in Washington, it was a chore, to be done as quickly as possible.

"Mr. Awbrey came yesterday and brought Mr. Rad's personal papers from the office," Crete said as she took several suits from Rad's closet and placed them on the bed.

"Where did you put them, Crete?"

"On the floor in the library."

"Well, keep on folding the clothes, Crete. And I'll go downstairs and take a look, to see how much space we'll need for them."

"Yes, ma'am."

Allison never intended to read any of the personal correspondence. The letters and papers belonged to Rad and would have to be attended to by him. It would be his decision as to what should be kept and what should be destroyed. But Allison's name leaped from one of the pages, and on seeing the signature of Cassie's husband, Stanley, she was baffled. Why would he be writing to Rad concerning her?

Her frown deepened as she read the letter to the end. She shouldn't be surprised that Stanley had used her visit with Charles in the park for a little leverage—if not outright blackmail—against Rad. After all, things like that happened frequently in Washington.

Seeing Charles after all those years had been traumatic enough without having her reactions monitored by some stranger and then passed on to Rad's political opponents. Even now she felt an uneasiness, as if her privacy had been violated.

An overwhelming urge to talk with Rad sent her to the telephone. "Operator," she said, "I'd like to place a long-distance call to the home of Mr. Andrew Lachlan in Chicago, Illinois. . . ."

Twenty minutes later, the telephone in Washington rang. And the long-distance operator said, "I have your call for you, Mrs. Meadors."

"Rad? How are you?"

"I'm fine. Is anything wrong, Allison?"

"No, everything is fine here, too."

Allison did not want to confess her need to hear his voice. Instead, she said, "Lila and Richard are taking a villa in Italy for the winter and they want us to go with them. How do you feel about that?"

There was a hesitation at the other end of the line. Finally, Rad said, "Do you want to go, Allison?"

"Yes, Rad. Very much."

"You realize, of course, that I won't be able to do much sightseeing for a while."

"That doesn't matter. You'll have a lovely place to rest and relax and really get your strength back. I think it would be good for both of us."

In the end, Rad agreed to the plan. And with a sense of relief, Allison finished packing. She was more than ready to leave Washington and politics behind.

As the days swept by, time became a personal commodity for Allison—to be spent at leisure with Rad or to be squandered unashamedly in a lazy afternoon, doing nothing but strolling with David on the shore and stopping at intervals to watch the birds. Sometimes the hours were used in a modicum of social exchange, given to the poor in her hours of service with Morrow at the settlement house. And then the calendar pronounced a change of seasons, putting an end to the hiatus in Chicago and propelling Allison and Rad toward New York and the planned trip to Italy with Lila and Richard.

"It's such a long time until next July," Allison said, finally kissing her daughter good-bye. "I hope we haven't made a mistake embarking on this extended trip."

Morrow laughed as she hugged her mother. "You and Papa will have so much fun that the time will pass quickly,

I know. And don't worry about us. We'll all get along quite well while you're away."

Andrew helped Rad to his compartment on the train, where the porter took over, elevating his injured leg onto the cushioned stool.

As the train pulled out, Rad turned to Allison. "This trip isn't exactly the way I planned it to be. But promise me you won't let me slow you down. Any time you want to go off with Lila and Richard to see the sights, you must do so."

"You'll be walking without the cane in no time, Rad." Allison smiled. "And then I'll have a hard time trying to keep up with you."

She reached out and took his hand as they began a new journey together.

# CHAPTER
## 39

Ten months later, Allison stood at the gallery window in Florence and looked down toward the Ponte Vecchio. A golden glow washed the yellowed stone walls and red-tiled roofs of the surrounding buildings, while white-clad tourists warded off the glittering sun with their lace-trimmed white umbrellas and strolled along the bridge.

Allison had come one last time to see the Michelangelos and the Raphaels, the Botticellis and the Cellinis—those magnificent paintings and sculptures that caught the spirit that was Italy. And now she drank in the scenic view from the art gallery window while she waited for Lila, who was still standing in the rotunda before the marble statue of David.

The villa in the hills had been closed up; their main luggage sent on to the station. Tonight would be spent in the *pensione* off the square, and then they would be on their way home.

The year had been a good one in a lot of ways. Settling down to a domestic life in the Tuscan countryside, while Rad slowly recovered his strength, had been an idyllic interlude. But it was almost as if the two of them had been cushioned from reality while the world continued with its business. Now it was time to return to America and get on with living their own lives.

"Oh, there you are, Allison." Lila approached her at the window. "Are you enjoying the view?"

"Very much. And did you enjoy your last look at the statue?"

"Yes. It's seldom that a woman gets to admire the beauty of a male torso without having society think of her as . . . well, as perverted."

As Lila whispered the last word, she quickly looked around to make sure she hadn't been overheard.

Allison laughed. "Are you ready to leave now?"

"I suppose so. Richard and Rad are probably tired of waiting for us."

The two women walked down the marble staircase and rejoined their slightly impatient husbands, who were sitting on the portico. Then the four walked out onto the street, and as they passed the cathedral, the bells began to clang.

In the square, the white pigeons scattered. Lila, carefully stepping past them in her expensive shoes, said, "I think the only mistake Peggy ever made in entertaining was to release those awful doves at Jonathan's wedding. Richard's suit was absolutely ruined."

"But it was a spectacular wedding, wasn't it?" Richard replied, laughing.

"Indeed it was," Rad agreed. "Almost as spectacular as this trip to Italy."

"Where shall we go next, you two?" Lila asked. "Spain, perhaps? Or the Greek isles?"

"Hold on, Lila," Rad protested. "It's past time for Allison and me to get home."

"Yes. If you want to change the itinerary, then you and Richard will have to do it without Rad and me."

"Why don't we save those countries for our trip next year, Lila, dear?"

"Only if Allison and Rad promise to go with us."

"No promises, Lila," Allison cautioned. "Rad and I don't even know what the next few months will bring."

That final evening was spent in a late alfresco dinner, with the sound of romantic music all around them. Red-checked tablecloths covered the café tables; the candles sputtered in the slight breeze, and the red wine flowed. One toast followed another until the golden Spanish melons laced with port arrived for the dessert.

"A golden dessert . . ."

". . . to end a golden day."

"And a golden headache to match—from all this wine," Allison responded to the two men.

"If we don't feel like traveling tomorrow, then we'll have to stay another day, won't we?"

"No, Lila," Allison said gently. "Our sabbatical is over. Headache or no headache, we have to leave tomorrow."

As the sun came up over the Tuscany hillsides and traveled past the vineyards to light the square in Florence, the four

Americans left the *pensione* where they'd spent their final night.

"You're not supposed to look back," Lila said sadly as they traveled in the carriage to the station. "Something about being turned into a pillar of salt. But I have to take just one more teeny look at the square."

"Then let's all do it at the same time," Allison suggested. "That way, if something happens, we'll still be together."

The four turned and drank in one last view. They waved to the city of Florence as Allison called out, "*Arrivederci.*"

The trip home by steamer was uneventful. The weather was good, with no storms to churn the mild waves into a tempest. And Rad, completely recovered except for an almost imperceptible limp, was a vastly different passenger en route home, participating in all the activities rather than spending his time in a deck chair, as he had on the way across.

He and Allison played croquet and took long walks on deck. And she was the one who lounged in a deck chair while Rad swam up and down the pool and grew even tanner under the summer sun.

When the ship finally docked in New York harbor, Allison and Rad prepared to leave Lila and Richard, who were traveling to Newport to visit other friends.

"Will you go back to Kentucky now?" Lila asked.

"No," Rad said. "We'll rest a few days here in New York. Then we have one more trip to take."

"Oh? Allison didn't say anything about another trip," Lila replied, feeling slightly out of sorts.

"I didn't tell her. It's still a secret."

The dimple in Lila's cheek showed as she said, "Then I

won't pry. But, Allison, as soon as you know, promise to write me all about it."

"I'll write you, Lila," she promised, still staring at her husband.

Lila and Richard disappeared down the gangplank into the vast rush of passengers disembarking. But Allison and Rad, with no strict schedule to adhere to, took their time and waited for the crowds to thin out before leaving the ship.

And so it was that a voice calling to Allison came as a complete surprise.

"Mother! Papa! Over here!"

She looked up to see Morrow, David, and Andrea, the adopted child, waving to them from the dock.

"Look, Rad! There's Morrow. Did you know she was coming to meet us?"

"No, I didn't."

Quickly, they negotiated the remainder of the gangplank and rushed toward their family. "What a wonderful surprise, darling," Allison said. "We weren't expecting to be met."

Amid the hugs, Morrow said, "I know. But Andrew has a commission to design a skyscraper building for Wagner and Stark and we decided to come along. We're awfully glad to see you. You both look marvelous."

As Rad scooped David up into his arms, the child said, "What did you bring us?"

Rad responded, "A hug for now."

"And wonderful presents when we get to the hotel," Allison added.

"Did you remember to bring Andrea something, too, Nana?" David asked.

"Of course. We couldn't forget the newest member of

the family, could we?" she said, smiling at the little girl who was still hiding behind Morrow's skirts.

"Andrea may not be the newest one for long. Did you get Jonathan's letter telling you their wonderful news? That Ginna is expecting a little one?"

Allison shook her head. "We had a slight problem with the mail. When is the baby due?"

"Two months from now."

That evening after dinner, as Andrew and Rad discussed business in the hotel suite, Morrow and Allison walked across the hall to put the children to bed. Soon, David and Andrea were asleep, with a Parisian doll and an Italian organ-grinder monkey still in their arms.

It was then, in timeless tradition, that mother and daughter sat down, apart from the men, and talked of intimate, family matters.

"I did as you and Papa asked, Mother. I found out from Ginna that Dr. Forsyte had wanted a piece of equipment for the operating room at the institute, but the budget hadn't allowed for it. So we made the donation in Papa's name."

"Thank you, Morrow, for taking care of it."

"And we had a nice thank-you letter from him, as well as from the institute."

Morrow gave a rueful smile. "It's still a little awkward, not knowing what to call him. Dr. Forsyte sounds so formal, especially for a long-lost father."

"Sometimes it's difficult for me, too, Morrow. I suppose I'll always remember your father as Coin, instead of as Charles."

"Mother, are you certain that I never saw him when I was little?"

"Why? What makes you ask such a question?"

"Well, it's not his face. It's his watch—it plays that funny little tune. I heard it at the hospital in Chicago—and it sounded familiar, as if I'd heard it before."

"Where?"

"I've been trying to remember ever since then. I decided it was that first season in Saratoga when Jonathan was a baby. A man came up to Rebecca and they talked for a long time. I was worried because I'd fallen on the green and gotten a grass stain on my dress. But when I went up to Rebecca, she stopped talking. The man just stood there and stared at me with the strangest look on his face. And that's when I heard the watch."

"That's ridiculous, Morrow. It couldn't possibly have been Charles."

"No, I suppose not. It was just a coincidence that the two had the same type of watch."

Morrow quickly changed the subject. "So tell me about your Paris trip at Christmastime. You didn't write much about it."

"There was the usual round of parties. Lila especially enjoyed the one given for the Infanta Eulalia because of all the repercussions. You remember how the Infanta snubbed Mrs. Palmer in Chicago at the exposition? Well, it was Mrs. Palmer's turn to do the snubbing. She refused to come to the soirée, sending her regrets instead: 'I do not choose to spend my time with a bibulous member of a decadent monarchy.' I tell you, the Paris gossips had a field day. And so did Peggy and Lila."

Morrow laughed aloud and then quickly looked toward the children's bedroom. "Don't make me laugh anymore, Mother. We'll wake the children."

"Sorry."

From that time on, they spoke in hushed tones until Rad came looking for Allison.

"I hope you two have finished talking because Andrew and I have completed building the skyscraper."

"Besides, it's after eleven o'clock," Andrew joined in beside him. "Past my bedtime."

Allison and Morrow smiled, hugged each other, and rejoined their husbands.

Across the hall from Andrew and Morrow, Rad and Allison made ready for bed. And within a few minutes, with the lights dimmed in the bedroom, steady breathing indicated that Rad had drifted off to sleep.

Although she was extremely tired, Allison remained awake for a while longer, recalling her conversation with Morrow.

Ever since that day in the Washington park, Allison had carried a vast hurt inside her because Coin Forsyth had evidently not cared enough to look for them after the war.

But suppose Morrow was right? Suppose he had looked for them and finally found them? Too late. What would she have done in his place, realizing that his wife had married another man, and had a baby son by this second husband?

"Oh, Rebecca," she murmured. "Is that the reason you were so upset that day?"

Why couldn't Rebecca still be alive? She was the only one Allison could have asked. It would be impossible now to question Charles.

As Allison, too, drifted off to sleep, two images stood before her—the young Coin and the older Charles, each separate in his own identity, each refusing to become the same man.

# CHAPTER
## 40

Three days later, Rad and Allison left New York, with Allison still in the dark as to their destination.

"Surely you can tell me, Rad, now that we're on our way. Where are you taking me?"

The whistle of the train as they approached a crossing delayed his answer. But Allison, watching him, saw the slight frown appear and then vanish—a gesture far more telling than words. And from that she knew that it was a serious matter.

"Allison, what month is this?" he finally said.

"Why, July, of course. But what does that have to do with the trip?"

He cleared his throat. "We're going on a pilgrimage—to put a ghost to rest, once and for all."

"What are you talking about?"

He reached out and took her hand. "Allison, for as long as I can remember, I've been fighting with that same ghost for your love. And through the years, whenever I felt I'd made some headway, July would roll around again and I could see you withdrawing from me."

"That's not true. . . ."

"I don't think you've even been aware of it. And I never said anything about it. It was a part of you that I had to accept.

"But from the day Charles reappeared in our lives, I knew that we were both in for a rough time. Because you'd never really given up your feelings for him in the past."

He had not finished. Allison could tell that he had more to say and she did not interrupt him.

"It's not just your mental picture of a dashing young husband going off to war that you still carry around in your mind. It has just as much to do with the tragic things that happened to you because of the war."

"I suppose nightmares die hard, Rad."

"Unfulfilled dreams, too, Allison. For when we think we've done with them, we find that they're like weeds cut off level with the ground. They sprout again because their roots are still deep in the soil.

"I'm taking you back to Roswell, Allison. For if you and I are to have any sort of life together from now on, then you must choose what to do about your past life. Either see it as something that has little to do with us in the present or else embrace it totally, now that Charles Forsyte is free to remarry you."

"Do you mean you would actually stand aside and allow that to happen?" An incredulous Allison stared at the husband she had thought she knew so well.

"If that's what you want. It's one or the other, Allison. You can't have both."

The conversation was over. Rad had delivered his ultimatum and he had no more to say. And even though Allison could number a dozen or more retorts to make, none would serve to do anything but widen the breach already between them. And so she, too, remained silent.

A mixture of dread and excitement stayed with her during the ensuing miles. And the hot gusts of air coming through the windows served to remind her that she was traveling south, where the July heat bleached the earth and sapped the strength of plant and animal alike.

Languidly using her lace fan, Allison finally said, "Are we traveling all the way by train?"

"No. Only as far as Marietta. There'll be a carriage waiting to take us the rest of the way to Roswell."

"But that's sixteen miles," Allison protested, "over difficult roads. Do you realize how uncomfortable such a ride is?"

"Not nearly so uncomfortable as an army wagon, I'm told. But we don't have to be that authentic. A carriage will do just as well."

"I can't believe you're going to such lengths. . . ."

It was early morning when the train reached its destination, and with a giant shudder, the engine released its great billow of steam as it settled on the track before the Marietta depot.

Outside, the panorama of the station was far different from the way Allison remembered it. No soldiers swarmed over the yard; no army wagons loaded with military supplies waited for loading. The depot seemed smaller—a little shabbier, perhaps. And the sun was shining, with dazzling light playing upon the rails.

"It was raining hard that day," Allison commented, as Rad helped her down from the train and walked beside her to the waiting carriage. "Lightning struck a wagon and two of the animals were killed."

Allison heard her voice, dredging up the memories of so long ago, when she had been a young mother with a three-month-old baby.

To each comment spoken aloud, Rad merely nodded. He did not intrude. Besides, he could tell that Allison had still not forgiven him for forcing her to take this trip into the past.

They traveled steadily through the town, with two pieces of luggage strapped to the back of the carriage. And when they had gone some distance, the last vestiges of civilization vanished and the land became a wilderness of trees, shrubs, and the ever-present passion-flower vines encircling the ruins of chimneys where houses had once stood.

Up hill and down, the road toward Roswell twisted and turned, with the horses laboring in the heat. And Allison, deep in memory, forgot Rad at her side. It was Rebecca's presence she felt, the black woman who'd been both friend and servant to her in those disastrous times, sharing the nightmare when Allison had been rounded up with the other women and accused of treason by General Sherman because of her sin of seeking a job in the Confederate mills to keep from starving.

Each mile traveled brought back another memory. And Allison struggled to draw out all the pain and indignity that had lain buried in her for all these years.

They stopped and rested, ate their noonday meal in a

shadowed glen, and then continued their journey. By late afternoon, as the carriage reached the square of the little manufacturing town, the pilgrimage was half completed.

Seeing the bandstand in the square and the same white clapboard Presbyterian church beyond, where Coin's memorial service had been held, Allison expected the rush of emotion that had begun to build the moment she'd stepped onto Georgia soil. But she felt no sudden surge of emotion.

She climbed down from the carriage and walked to the empty bandstand. There she stood, surveying the town in all directions: the long row of shed-roof buildings across the street, the wide lane to Bulloch Hall, the meandering dirt road that led into the mill village. She waited, but no great feeling of homesickness welled up within her. Surprised, she realized that she was viewing her surroundings as a detached visitor would, much the same way she had viewed the small towns of Italy. But seeing Rose Mallow would be different. She knew that.

When she returned to the carriage, Rad said, "Where to, now? Shall we drive toward the mills?"

"No. Let's bypass them. I'd rather ride on to Rose Mallow."

Allison directed the driver away from the mill village and the mills, which were once again in operation. Down the Roswell road they traveled, until they reached the wooded entrance to Rose Mallow, the upcountry mansion Allison had shared with Coin. That would be the true test—to see the house again, if it were still standing.

The carriage turned into the long, curving driveway. But before the house came into view, Allison called out, "Driver, stop here."

He did as he was told, bringing the horses to a stop. Rad helped Allison down but made no attempt to follow her as she began to walk along the familiar winding drive, paved with the same smooth gravel she remembered. The wooded areas on each side had changed little over the years. The same tree azaleas, with their flame-colored blossoms, loomed tall in the woods, and the gentle breeze that had suddenly stirred held the same perfumed, delicate scent of the sweet-shrub bush.

Allison quickened her pace. For, just beyond the curve, Rose Mallow would soon come into view.

When the house appeared, she stopped and stared. It was not her house. Instead it was a carpetbagger's house, shining and freshly painted. The summer kitchen was gone; two wings had been added. And, worst of all, the classical Greek Revival lines had been destroyed by the gingerbread trim.

"Is it the way you remembered it?" a voice asked gently at her side.

She turned her head. And for the first time that day, she smiled at her husband, who had come up behind her. "No," she answered. "Not at all the way I remembered it. I wonder if it's just as monstrous inside?"

"Would you like to knock on the door and see if you can go inside?"

"No, there's no need to bother the owners. I've seen enough, Rad. I'm ready to go now."

She began to walk back to the carriage. Then she stopped to take one last look. "At least it doesn't leak. I see they put on a new roof."

She climbed into the carriage again; then she heard Rad say, "Driver, we'll go to the hotel now."

"Hotel?" Allison repeated. "I didn't know there was a hotel here."

"Actually, it's one of the old mansions converted into a hotel. I wired ahead for reservations."

She recognized the house, but the owner had long since sold it to a newcomer, a Mr. Jones from Ohio. Allison was now the stranger, and she gave no indication that she had ever seen it before. As they registered, she allowed Rad to answer the questions that visitors are usually asked. And he gave nothing away that would tie his wife to the town.

Later, as they settled in the large old mansion, with its wide porch holding a long row of rush-bottomed rocking chairs and the bedrooms filled with dark, polished furniture, Allison stood by the open window in their bedroom.

"How long are we to stay here?" Allison asked.

"As long as it takes you to make up your mind."

"Then I hope you haven't paid for more than one night."

"Allison?"

She ignored the wary look in Rad's eyes. "It's difficult to put things into words," she began. "You know I would never have chosen to come back here on my own. But you forced me, and I suppose you'll have to suffer the consequences."

"And exactly what does that mean?"

"Coin Forsyth died years ago. I realize that now. And the man we both know as Charles Forsyte is merely Ginna's father."

He stared at her as if he had misunderstood. But then she smiled and reached out to him. "That means you're stuck with me, Rad, for the rest of our lives."

"You're sure? Absolutely sure?"

"Yes."

He squeezed her hand and said, "Then let's go downstairs for dinner. Suddenly, I'm very hungry."

That evening, as they sat on the porch and listened to the whippoorwills amid the faint rush of water in the distance, Allison was content. For the first time in her life, she had rid herself of the old animosities. And along the pilgrimage, she'd discovered truth as well.

It had not come in viewing wood and stone, but had been found as she looked into her own heart along the way. She'd had her share of joys and sorrows, partings and coming togethers, experiences with birth and death.

Now she could accept them all as part of life, with love as the ultimate hope and love as the ultimate sacrifice. Life went on, flowing as constantly as Vickery Creek toward the millrace gate. It could never turn backward to yesterday. And in that knowledge, Allison had finally found freedom.

## About The Author

Frances Patton Statham lives in Atlanta, Georgia. She has received five national and eight regional awards for her novels, including the prestigious Author of the Year award in fiction from the Dixie Council of Authors and Journalists in 1978, and again in 1984. She has conducted numerous writing seminars throughout the South and has appeared on a number of television shows, including "The Southern Voice," a PBS documentary. A lyric-coloratura soprano with a master's degree in music, Ms. Statham has also made recent guest solo appearances in such cities as Vancouver, Budapest, Madrid, and Singapore. She is listed in the *World Who's Who of Women*, the *Dictionary of International Biography*, the *International Who's Who of Intellectuals*, and *Personalities of the South*.